GW01454517

Countess Lucy
And
The Curse of Coberley Hall

Guy Sheppard

ISBN-13: 978-1537577623

ISBN-10: 153757762X

Cover design © Socciones

Design & formatting by Socciones Editoria Digitale

www.kindle-publishing-service.co.uk

Lucy Countesse of Downe was buried the 8th day of Aprill 1656.

She fasted from eating or drinking before her death ten dayes.

Coberley Parish records in Gloucestershire.

1

This time of year the fog is certainly to be expected – it comes drifting and slithering very low across the fields quite late in the morning. Nothing that inanimate should be able to bind the house in clammy white sheets right up to the chimneys, but it will, it'll envelope me for days.

I can detect the raw touch of its chilling vapour, but few of the things it chills.

I stand here so long in order to peer in the general direction of church and graveyard that I forget I'm not already blinded. Rebecca takes me by surprise, tells me that I'll catch my death if I press my face to the glass any harder. She, not mist, should have my rapt attention, it seems. Why take chances when I have felt so much better recently? The ancient green-tinted panes are draughtier than they appear.

Her advice, of course, I ignore. She would have me confine my hopes to mere tricks of winter.

When a man's cortex begins to peel away from his retina, his first thought will be that there is something wrong with his eyes. Whatever apparition strays across the watery, jelly-like substance that befogs each lens, he expects some medical definition for the spectral, black-edged form that suddenly floats into sight. Because the jelly normally stays so firmly attached to the retina, any separation of one from the other stimulates the light sensitive membrane until his brain begins to interpret signals as flashes in his peripheral vision.

Suddenly something darkens in the filmy fog or swirl of air: the posterior vitreous detachment, in all the bloody spots and cobwebs of my eyes, assumes the shape of someone approaching.

No one, it's no one, I think, but I hope I'm wrong.

How many years has it been? Two? Three? With my sight has gone the time.

April 8th, 2014 will forever be fixed in my mind. Like winning the Lottery, people said. On that day my wife passed away after breathing her last in my presence.

Given the circumstances, not to mention any misconstrued intentions on my part, her body was subjected to a coroner's inquest where a post-mortem testified that her demise was due to perfectly explicable causes. Clearly, in no sense was I to blame. Having a matter-of-fact view of death himself, the pathologist was quick to dismiss the slightest doubt in my mind, which was a great help to me for a while.

He and I had worked closely together for many years and that probably made a difference.

Because Lizzie had stood absolutely no chance of survival, any cold shiver of concern on my part should not have led me to disbelieve the obvious. She died. I saw it happen. Since then there has been so much else I ought to testify, since who can judge me now if I reveal things about this house that once lay hidden? Will anyone listen? Nor can I actually turn to the authorities. No police investigator will understand. I should know, I was one.

Back then, sceptics dismissed me as unprofessional, or blasphemous, or worse. There will be those who will, for a certainty, still call me deranged. Better my critics do as I do now, then, and watch who walks with the mist on the lawn. There's only so long that anyone can defy doubt with denial. They are the blind ones, not me.

They should come here and see for themselves.

2

On a very wet New Year's Eve I quit London in an awful hurry. Even then, I was less concerned with the inheritance than with the condition on which I inherited it.

That day was foggy, too. It took me a moment after I woke up and howled to realise that I was literally no longer moving. Then, in a panic, I banged my hand on my window and gave it a rub.

Pretty frantically.

Beyond my misted porthole a red farm tractor busily scratched stony hieroglyphs across the surface of a nearby field with a row of rattling rotary discs of steel. Between me and my scribe, naked white spears of shorn blackthorn stood slashed and broken where some monstrous blade had done battle with all the hedges. Nobody else showed up so high on the hills. No one much for miles was likely to recognize me despite the ugly gash on my brow that was not yet quite healed.

'What the devil?' I asked and left the view to cloud back over.

At my side, a startled nun goggled at me through her designer glasses. She scowled while I gasped for air in the recycled, soporific atmosphere of our National Express coach.

'Such a vulgar young man!'

I had no idea what other indiscretions, if any, I had just cried out. Looking red in the face, my fashionable grimalkin glared at me over her bag of shopping from Harrods.

Not so holily.

'Sorry,' I said. 'Bad dream.'

*

Once a man decided to dispose of a body then there had to be nothing left to love or hate. If there was nothing left to love or hate he should not have had something to bury or scatter apart from her ashes. Either way he could take heart that she was irrefutably at peace if only he could find somewhere decent to secrete her remains

3

without any nasty after-effects.

On my knees balanced my small black leather case that weighed so little.

'Well, off you get, then.'

It was the coach driver. Eyeing me severely in her mirror, she it was who had already traumatised everyone on board by forbidding us to talk on our smartphones.

'Can you, you know, give me a minute?' I replied.

'This is the right place, isn't it?'

'I'm not entirely sure I know.'

First I had to climb over the nun between me and the gangway in my big brogues.

'Do look where you're going, you clumsy oaf.'

'Don't mind me, Sister, I'm sure,' I said, disengaging my foot from her robes.

'I do believe you reek of whiskey.'

'That's not massively helpful.'

Stumbling from seat to seat, I reeled to the exit, but not before I stopped by the driver to give her what I owed.

'Think me a bloody taxi, do you?' she muttered and drummed her garish pink fingernails hard on the steering-wheel. 'The 444 never calls here. No driver ever would.'

I dealt a second fiver from my wallet.

'I won't tell if you don't.'

The remotely opened door hissed out and back to set me down. Gingerly I lowered one leg at a time into a world grown bitter.

'You all right, sir?'

'Oh no, I'm good, yeah. I'm fine. Definitely.'

'For someone who made such a fuss you don't look too thrilled to be here.'

'It's strictly business.'

'Grin and bear it, sir, that's what I say. Everyone loves a smile, usually.'

'I very much doubt it.'

'Just step away from the coach, will you?'

Too late, the door hissed shut in my face. After the rain, the sinking sun tinted my blue eyes crimson. Two flickering coronas of fire ringed my sunken sockets while my hollow cheeks somehow stayed pale. A red tear trickled down one side of my slightly crooked nose. Not my tear. I was looking at wet reflections only. We're all ghosts next to glass.

I had arrived at my phantom stop.

*

Just to be clear, this was not simply about my total distrust of all things rural. When a far off buzzard screamed 'seeioo', 'seeioo', 'seeioo' at me, I could be forgiven for thinking it somewhat ghoulish? I watched dark wings cross the sun's blind iris, noticed expansive feathers flex my way like fingers. This was about me breaking into a cold sweat because I was still nauseous after so much time spent on that oh-so-slow coach from Victoria.

For a moment I had to wrench free the top three buttons on my coat and snake a hand inside my classic tweed jacket. The shop assistant, a child half my age, called it a single-breasted country essential, impeccably tailored with classy herring-boned lining. Frankly, I didn't give a damn what it was when it was the best I could find at such short notice. What else did a renegade wear to the sticks, anyway?

After the respite, the reckoning. I hadn't nearly begun to realise how icy it would be. Shivering, I raised my cord collar and buttoned the cuffs on my gloves.

Had hell frozen over it would have felt like the Cotswolds.

A moment later, my phone pinged in my pocket.

'Colin, WHERE are you? Maria and I are going out tonight for a meal to celebrate our engagement. You simply must come.'

It was a text message from DS Jan Shriver, my best detective sergeant in the Flying Squad back at New Scotland Yard. After three other texts, two Snapchats and a voicemail she was doing her upmost to breach my radio silence.

Against my better judgement I rang her back.

'Can't talk right now, I'm standing in a puddle up to my ankles at the side of some God forsaken road or other.'

'Doesn't mean you can miss our meal, does it?'

'Okay, it's just that I'm not in London any more.'

'I have to say you're an absolute asshole, Colin.'

'The nun thinks so, too.'

'You with a nun?'

'I can't exactly explain this minute.'

Instead I stood choking on the coach's excruciating exhaust fumes even as my erstwhile fellow passenger flicked two fingers at me in dignified slow motion upon departure. How long did it take, I wondered, to forgive a man whose glottis had wheezed in your ear for three hours like an old kettle? I waved back, as if in glad receipt of her munificent blessing. How long was it before you forgot a stranger in his grey woollen scarf and black coat all alone at the kerbside? More to the point, how much time had to pass before you forgot to miss someone at all?

The voice buzzed again in my ear.

'That all you got for me, Colin? A nun and wet feet?'

'No, I'm looking at two griffins.'

'You off your head?'

'Actually they remind me of the boundary dragons that guard London's Square Mile. Never have I stared so closely into the faces of something quite so horrid, not even in Holborn.'

'You're not exactly making a lot of sense.'

'No, but who does?'

'You drunk, or something?'

I referred hastily to my map. According to its strange hieroglyphic squiggles, the grassy entrance and lost driveway should lead to a place called Coberley Hall.

'I never knew the countryside could be so messy.'

'Never mind that, Colin, what the hell are these griffins?'

'Oh, just a couple of big birds.'

Better suited to a city necropolis, they rose level with my head and were topped with great crowns of untidy ivy. Rusty metal spikes jutted from cracked Cotswold stone blocks on which large metal gates had once opened and closed. I gave one wreath of shiny green leaves a tweak or two only to discover myself nose to beak with a cross looking eagle. The other pillar was the same.

'Really, Colin? And there's me afraid that you were back in hospital. So what are you in a field for, anyway?'

I consulted the birds. Demoted to a bus stop, each funebrial sentry squinted yearningly back down the main road, as did I.

'Legend has it that griffins once followed their instinct to find gold.'

'You've lost me.'

'Er, I'm following mine.'

'Yeah, I mean, should I be worried?'

As I crossed the field I gave a kittenish squeal. Quite frankly, no man worth his salt should have to suffer such awful cowpat on his heels.

'Most definitely you should be worried. I'm ruining my shoes.'

'So tell me, where precisely are you again, Colin?'

I blocked her, then glanced at my fake Rolex. I had to hurry. At this rate, by quarter past four it would be virtually dark.

Frigid, white-topped hills wore wrinkled quilts of snow which were not unbeautiful, I supposed, given that it was that afterwards time of year when most life lay fallow. I sneezed and pulled a handkerchief from my pocket. With it came a letter. Embossed at its top was something bafflingly heraldic. That was silly Gothic birds, too.

The thick, single page could have been vellum and began politely enough: 'Dear Mr Walker, with regard to your sudden, extraordinary good fortune I feel I must warn you....', but the rest I already knew by heart.

3

Somehow I had managed to evade all attempts at encouragement and understanding at the office. Undoubtedly those good Samaritans had been gearing up to help me out over New Year, feel or express sympathy to my face, force-feed me with forgiveness or, God forbid, squeeze my hand, but I had decided before then to be gone.

So what if I was drinking so much that I daren't drive my own car, it was for the good of my soul.

My rank in the police had been Detective Inspector. It still was. Technically. Right up to Christmas I had been sitting at my desk struggling to make the best of crime statistics and flowcharts. I had been allotted the unenviable task of trying to explain why brazenly cocky drug barons and inept jewellery thieves had enjoyed such a good year. I'd tried to be exactingly optimistic in the face of increasingly severe government cutbacks in money and personnel, but even I'd had to admit that some tasks were beyond even God.

I had been allotted the job for my own peace of mind.

Some very self-important people had decided that my behaviour ever since my wife's passing had been beyond the pale. A danger to myself, no less. When his whole world quaked but a man tried to cling to it in the aftershock, he should not have to wear a sign round his neck saying that he was being heroically stoic and not slightly insane.

I scratched my head in earnest. The thickest fell of snow-white hair was bound to feel that bit thinner after such an upheaval. People remarked on it. They noted *so disapprovingly* that I had not taken a single day off work since my bereavement. To these alarmists my stiff upper lip was more obstinacy than fortitude and therefore suspicious. Then, by walking out of hospital, I had done my level best to disregard their sidelong looks and sad estimations of what they privately refused to dismiss as my 'car accident'. To say of a man that he was suicidal due to guilt should never be sufficient.

Such moments were becoming all too frequent. My mind could paint vivid pictures of what happened, yet explain few of the things pictured.

In the mean time there were the midges. Thousands of them, off an ancient fishpond, apparently. 'How many of the insatiable, fluttering things can a man survive?' I wondered aloud as I stumbled over a bridge.

If only I had not left my hat behind, if only everything had not been so last minute.

The devil take those who said I would bring ruin upon myself.

Honestly, this was no time for a change of heart.

*

I scraped muck off my shoes and straightened my hair now grown horribly damp. The building before me resembled a small fortress. There was no doorbell. Instead a large wrought iron ring invited me to give it a bang.

Now that I had come this far it was to be hoped that I could abstain from any further, awful exertion. Since I was still the subject of such intolerable press inquiries, let the hacks think I was still in town.

So it was that I soon became aware of eyes fixed upon me. Mounted on the gatehouse wall was the ugliest head I had ever seen. Bulging pupils had brows of lichen. So ancient and weatherworn was the face that it literally appeared to grow out of the stonework. More streaks of yellow parasitic growth had taken root on run-offs of rainwater and so formed two long waterfalls of dirty blond hair or mane. My first thought was a beast. But because the sculptor had so carefully incised neat, parallel lines into the skull's stony scalp and chin, tight wiggly curls were more suggestive of both hair and beard. Large ears, too, had been artfully chiselled into something surprisingly, recognisably, human.

Really I could not be entirely sure because the upper lip had been blown away by blasts of weather or even gunfire.

Not that any human cranium I knew of was so big and square. This anthropoid smiled obscenely from ear to ear, it challenged me to its silly grimacing-match. Lips parted to reveal two rows of very regular, small and sharp teeth like a bat's. So unconventional was

10

the smile that at first I thought the face would make me laugh. So it did, but its own was either greatly amused or indulgently sceptical.

That's not to say that I did not detect a certain baleful intelligence. Mirthful or devilish, the expression suggested that I was standing below some sort of maniacal bugaboo. Like a Cheshire cat, it smiled at me constantly.

I gave a maniacal grin, too.

*

When the curtain first dropped on my life I went into turmoil. Because it had been my job to view people and places in terms of hard, irrefutable facts that would stand up in a court of law, it did me no good to find myself on the other side of the tracks, so to speak. I'd lost face in the world as I knew it. Crashing my car was almost an irrelevance.

Worse, doctors told me to give up drinking and smoking.

Really?

Every condemned man should get to smoke the equivalent of a last chance.

They promised me I would be fine if I placed all my faith in my police psychiatrist. This was said with the offer of so many pills and such confiding wiles that I had done as I was bidden.

Until now.

*

My phone bleeped again in my pocket. It was Jan texting me as she tried to run me to ground.

This time I ignored her completely. She was not the only one to feel rebuffed. In the last twenty-four hours my pass into the office had been rescinded and nobody important answered my calls. If I declined to take hers without the ghost of a reason it was because I, too, knew what it was to be ghosted.

I stepped up to the twisted iron ring and, banging it, felt it jar and numb my bones. Something rattled above me. I looked up to see a flame light a leaded glass window, watched as the wick of a candle flared into a bold little beacon. Beside the flame appeared other points of illumination. Something was all white lustre and pure radiance. They were pearls.

A moment later the wearer had dissolved back into shadow.

'Hi, there,' I called hopefully. 'Can you, like, open the gate for me?'

Quick to retreat, my bejewelled onlooker chose to double the distance between us.

Stamping my cold feet again on the frozen ground, I waited.

I waited quite a while.

Meantime, the sun in the west set lower and lower.

'I could really do with a hand down here,' I shouted, executing wild semaphores with my bag.

Whoever lit the candle with a smoky spill from her fire simply did not worry whether or not I froze to death in the open. How many other poor people before me had bludgeoned these gates, I wondered. Slashed into both wood and wall were all sorts of crooked irregularities. Each hole and crack looked as if they had been plugged long ago with new mortar to patch old wounds made by firepikes, small shot or, God forbid, swords. Staying back from the glass, someone was behaving as if they were disappointed.

Not that I cared.

That said, what widower did not soon long to be the subject of someone else's ludicrously high hopes?

Then, I did not realise the significance.

*

Mercifully, a bolt slid back from its staple.

By the sound of it, twin interlocking levers slowly freed reinforcing bars top and bottom from their otherwise rigidly fixed positions. Next, some incorporeal hand opened a wicket-door a few inches.

Such a gatekeeper 'fears not God nor regards man', I thought. He called to me without emerging.

'Please state your name, sir.'

'I'm Detective Inspector Walker. Is this, you know, where Lord Hart lives?'

'Today is not a good time. Please try again tomorrow.'

'What makes one day different from another?'

'I really couldn't say, sir.'

From the tone of his voice, my turning up like this was highly irregular. Worse, it totally belied my own self-importance. When a man was in no mood to parley he expected to be let in whatever the excuse, he at least expected his arrival to take priority over petty security.

'Here,' I said, thrusting my letter past the door. 'Let this put a stop to your nonsense.'

A little old man's slate-grey eyes bore into the page. Still he behaved as if I might actually have stolen my missive from the real Colin Walker.

'Forgive me, sir. You appear to be who you say you are.'

'There's no real doubt about it.'

Instead, he went to prise my luggage from my fingers.

'Just the one, is it, sir?'

I snatched it back.

'Leave it! Don't touch it!'

'As you wish, sir, but I take it that you won't be staying long at Coberley Hall?'

'Not if I can help it.'

I had no idea just how empty my threat must have sounded. Shamefaced, I lifted my black bag through the narrow door and dived after it, only to have the heavy oak planks bang shut horribly behind me. It was too soon for me to distrust my lack of welcome, if not the distrust with which I was welcomed.

4

A spooky old manor-house was a trite, even hackneyed notion, but that didn't mean that a man should not be able to share in the joke. Pulling my phone from my pocket, I prepared to take a photograph of weather-worn transoms and imperfectly patched dripstones. I aimed my camera at the fortified walls in my first, minor act of ownership or 'selfie'.

But walk up and down as I might in the cold, echoing courtyard, I failed to capture its pale, rendered stonework as I saw it, could only manage to photograph blank miasma. No matter how much I pressed or aimed my lens at some new angle, the screen showed a void only.

Peeved, I put my phone back in my pocket. I seemed to be standing in the midst of some electronic black hole.

Might I not do what I liked with my own?

My flat-footed guide looked aghast.

'Has sir quite finished?'

'Just thought I would, you know, celebrate my arrival,' I said. 'I thought I'd record the moment in real time but my phone has stopped working.'

'Seeing ye shall see and shall not perceive, sir.'

'How is that different from taking a picture?'

'Seeing is believing, sir.'

'If that were true, ghosts would be real.'

'This way, sir,' replied the gatekeeper and rattled a set of keys on their chains on his belt.

It was both rebuke and a genuine, not to say fretful, desire to get in out of the fog. I should show greater respect, he hinted, before I strutted about with my toys.

*

For a place that had only a moment ago been invisible to the naked eye, its impressive frontage reared up very wide and tall above me

15

with a stubborn resistance. Not all the exigencies of time, war and people had quite destroyed its ability to impress me, so powerfully did it suggest a distinguished, if violent pedigree. 'Many a country retreat is rooted in fears, folly and heroics,' I told myself. 'Why should this be any different?'

Everything about the house looked as dark and sealed as a tomb. Set into the window above the porch was an armorial roundel. From where I was standing the heraldic shield's dull colours would not come to life until I was shut in with them. I assumed it was the same ghastly coat of arms with nine hearts that was embossed beneath the griffins at the top of my letter.

When gloominess quite took a man's breath away like that he had to rid his head of romantic notions of a Palladian home of perfect proportions. Other oriel windows with castellated tops jutted from the walls amid hundreds of tiny leaded panes that gleamed like black mirrors. In fact, no part of the ugly building complemented or balanced the other. Its walls, roofs and chimneys stood side by side in an asymmetrical union that hinted at a certain dissent or dissonance not unlike my own.

Inescapably, such an abode had to have silly dragons for gargoyles but, really, did their teeth have to drip icy rain on my head? Each bloody drop bled red in the last gleams of sun through mist. I was able to shake off the sudden splash of cold but not of unpleasantness.

*

Facing me was a door neatly framed with two crudely carved Doric pilasters. A heavily ribbed weather moulding traced the pointed archway over the entrance in a poor precursor to that classical portico that I had already discounted. Someone, at some time, had altered the door in a sop to fashion, they had tried to tack Greek temple onto something Tudor and Jacobean. Chiselled in stone above the miniature porch were the initials TP and LP next to the date 1638.

Frankly, to suggest the maximum mystery a house as old as this had to be covered in plants that crept along the ground or up the walls. I was disappointed. No untidy tangle of wisteria hung round the entrance or rooted itself in the oddly sized and elaborately shaped stones that were so suggestive of monastic quoins and dressings. When someone lived in a house constructed from all sorts of pilfered but significant pieces they could do more than imagine its history, they could hear the monks take their vows of poverty, celibacy and obedience. They could listen to the stolen stones speak by themselves, if only they knew how to listen.

With his head bowed, my processional guide ushered me indoors and dropped the latch quickly behind us.

'Well I never,' I said, with a groan. 'Who would have thought anywhere so decrepit could last into the twenty-first century? Time could have stood still here. I just hope nobody has already sold off all my furniture and silver.'

My guide turned to me and stared. I saw him disregard my grin with horror. He looked right into my pitiable eyes. The wish was father to the thought, he seemed to say, but then thought better of it.

Suddenly he reverted to butler, valet and general factotum.

'Wait here, sir. I will inform his lordship of your arrival.'

'Please give him my apologies for not phoning.'

'Few come this way to pay their respects, sir. Few choose to make the effort.'

I stamped my feet. Surely something good about this dreadful cliché of a house had to offset the clammy chill that rose from the cellars?

5

Left to myself, I became conscious of an awful noise that marked the silence. This was no pleasing, recurring tick but the grinding mechanical judder of springs, cables and gears. In a corner of the hallway stood a ten-foot high pendulum clock, I noted, all resplendent with oyster veneers and floral marquetry. The front of its case boasted a black bird atop a funeral urn. With its beak turned towards its tail, this was no bird of paradise but rook or crow, whose choice of wood gave it eyes of gold.

Still I was gripped by my very own cardiac arrhythmia. For, dolefully, then, the clock's bells sounded in the rest of the house. Heavy brass weights tapped their trajectories to and fro inside their hollow wooden cases like coffins. Each hypnotic ding-dong shook in the same way my eye sockets ached at their edges, they pulsated and throbbed absurdly loudly as though this was how pain should sound.

Frankly, I thought they'd never stop.

*

Not one to stand too long upon ceremony, I marched along the entrance hall and peered through a round-headed archway with broad stone imposts and heavy keystone which marked the beginning of the screens passage. Four hundred years ago, busy pantlers, butlers and other servants had ferried wine and food through here to the great hall from the kitchens.

Suddenly I became aware of much scratching and fluttering. All that noise from the clocks had sent something into a panic. Almost immediately there was a violent collision. It missed me by a fraction and hit a window. Down it crashed in a cloud of feathers and broke its neck. Another bird was already dead on the floor. I was not entirely sure why a starling had been left to rot at my feet, but whatever the reason it had been there for some time. A dozen maggots had crawled out of the corpse onto the cold black and white diamond tiles after they had feasted on its rotten flesh, then failed to turn into flies.

Trapped birds were commonplace in old houses, they fell down many a chimney or flew in open doors. I refused to accept that they had to signify anything else or possess any analogous occult qualities.

Clearly, though, I needed to have a quiet word with the cleaner.

*

I knew I should not go so far, or forget where I had come from, but immediately found myself face to face with a hideous long-tailed ray-fish carved into the nearest doorjamb. The goggle-eyed, bare-breasted creature greeted me with such alluring lips and broad smile that I could not help but admire her folded arms. I could dismiss her gesture of grim decidedness, if not of my own indecision. Cut into shiny black oak, all sorts of rhombic patterns had been created by bevel and bezel to create waves and clouds in a way that was both decorative and bizarre. Because this was no fish but a mermaid.

The other side of the doorway was similar.

When ignorant men had yet to map every last corner of the globe, many a terrified sailor had claimed to have caught such weird and wonderful creatures on their first far-flung voyages to new worlds. Straight from the ocean, each sinuous and sexy temptress was a fantastic interweaving of fish and human. I smiled. What voyager wouldn't see devilish sirens with not a soul to speak to for miles around?

I was in a great hall that had been panelled with well-seasoned oak that had since turned black with age, as if that were now its natural plain colour.

Advancing to the dais, I deposited my precious black bag on its table's knotted planks and surveyed all before me. Whoever sat up here every evening liked to do so within sight of the fire. All the appalling old furniture and wall hangings reminded me less of a museum than a theatre. The props positively cried out for a film crew to use them as a backdrop to some dreadful costume drama. I felt like an actor with stage fright. Anyone foolish enough to live here, I told myself, was no simple student or collector of stagy antiquities, they literally lived and breathed according to the ridiculous dictates of some anachronistic previous existence.

At first opportunity I'd sell the lot.

On my other feelings it was pointless to ponder. Every burnt child dreaded the fire, but what cold traveller could forgo the chance of a friendly hearth?

No sign yet of my guide.

Crudely split beech logs lit up and roared at the slightest prod of my poker. There had come a strong, hot draught of air. It did not blow down the chimney exactly. Rather the flames flashed and flared because of some movement behind me, they became more than spontaneous combustion, they became the fiery, muscular organs of something glowing and living. They spat, hissed and moaned in their own incomprehensible language.

I jumped at the logs' roar like some vehement emotion. I registered the slither close by me of the thing that rustled, but not the thing that did the rustling. It might have been another bird.

I was five years old again, reliving the kick in the back from my so-called parent.

*

I was alone except for a man's hideous portrait that hung in a silvered pine frame over the fireplace. My heart sank. 'Please, spare me the sinister painting,' I said aloud. Executed in the style of the Old Masters, the large picture had been daubed with massively too much paint for my taste. The thick oils gave his face a translucency that rendered his flesh china-like and fragile. It was not how an ordinary person could have looked in real life.

If I was genuinely perturbed it was not simply by the gaze that addressed me, but by the chilly fixity with which it did so.

My step-father's ice-blue eyes had been that cold, too.

The portrait hung very oddly. Clearly this handsome trophy, all pompous pedigree and important descent had once been one of a pair. Cut into the stone chimney breast and framed by geometric patterns of black and brown marble was space for a second picture.

With that, the cold air crept from each corner of the hall to reclaim and chill me. Stamping my feet, I began to practise a lordly gait up and down the floor when I stopped to inspect a buffet lined with rather fine and expensive silver spoons, cream dishes, a crizzled glass or two and a wine cooler. I mocked the good health of the dragoon in the picture with an empty tankard.

Actually, I was in desperate need of a real drink. I had begun to parody the dream when the butler returned.

'Mr Walker! It is absolutely forbidden to remove anything from its proper place.'

'I haven't, you know, nearly begun to see what's here,' I replied, 'under all the dirt.'

'Just put that back where you found it.'

'Okay, okay, yeah. Will his lordship see me now?'

'Lord Hart is not entirely well, sir.'

'Not well?'

'Your arrival has left him feeling a little out of sorts.'

'I hope this doesn't change anything?'

'If you would like to come this way, sir, I'll show you to your room in the west wing.'

Illness I had reckoned without. No wonder that the tone of his letter had been so irrational and desperate?

*

It was up the most lavishly carved handrail that I slid my fingertips rather squeamishly. I had passed but a few banisters decorated with oak leaves and acorns when the revulsion in my stomach reversed my step a tread or two. A sacred bearded monkey danced astride a newel post. Overseeing the first landing we came to, this sharp-toothed, catarhine mammal was one of several ghastly monstrosities that lined the stairs while a naked boy Pan blew us all a tune.

Such figures were the Devil's imps and familiars from a time when people literally still believed in demons and witches, I decided.

Then again, my host would not have been the first to fake history, not when the Victorians had practically reinvented everything medieval and Gothic. Somebody had placed these monsters on the stairs to help create a dark mood because that was their weird idea of good fun?

*

My worst fears were confirmed when I found myself next to a line of portraits of mounted Cavaliers as I passed along a narrow gallery. All eight anonymous dragoons boasted cool blue eyes and slightly crooked noses and looked resplendent in their large floppy hats and lacy white collars. Like the other Cavalier over the fire in the great hall, they had long curly black hair, little pointed beards and moustaches in a strange familial likeness.

'For heaven's sake,' I thought, 'why *do* the well-to-do always have to immortalise themselves in such preposterous costumes?' I found the whole idea of being a Cavalier rather lame, anyway. How could such popinjays ever fight in battle? There ended my curiosity.

We were about to exit the gallery at the far end of the landing when I noticed the black and gold frame of an altogether different picture. Where the door rested against the wall, whoever hung behind it remained tantalisingly obscured. I stopped dead in my tracks, squinted behind it. To look at an unknown portrait for the first time was not unlike meeting a real person. I had to suspend all feelings of suspicion, embarrassment or even fear, I had to take the new face on trust for a moment.

Pretty much.

Dressed in a gown of greenish-gold silk, my tall, thin-waisted observer adopted a very upright and dignified pose. As I swung the door slightly away from her, her robe's delicately woven fabric gave off a certain lustre while an edge of worsted petticoat showed it to be lined and faced with gimp lace twisted into braid. She wore roses on her green velvet shoes that showed off her ankles. This was no stiff gown whose skirt was spread over a cone-shaped framework of any farthingale but fell full and flowing from a high bust-line. There was no ruff. Instead, soft scalloped bobbin lace edged her soft collar. Since wearing gold and silver lace, cuffs, gartering and fancy shoes had all been a crime immediately after the English Civil War, she had to be wearing clothes from about 1640.

Her ladyship rested her right hand on a fold of red curtain that draped the pillar of a lakeside loggia, I noted. The trees behind her suggested a substantial country estate where sleek thoroughbreds grazed in green paddocks. The painter had set out to portray someone of means, had captured her in exquisitely dressed but urgent pose in her garden.

My boldness only emboldened her. I switched on my otherwise useless phone to shine its light about her neck, breasts and dress. At once her black pupils regarded me with outrage. As her face half turned to me, so that she stared at this world over one smooth, partly bare shoulder, she struck me as distinctly at odds with her years of neglect in her varnished prison. Really, she wanted to jump on her horse and go for a gallop.

'This someone's unloved heirloom?' I asked. 'Or was she bought in a job lot, too, to complete some bizarre Gothic theme park?'

My agitated guide averted his gaze. He refused to look at the woman in the picture in the same way a man might seek to protect his eyes from glare or dust. Instead he ticked his head from side to side like a pendulum.

'She came with the house, sir.'

Which was probably why I had the urge to do something, if only tilt my head in mock chivalric response to the faintest wink of her left eyelid.

I turned to my gloomy usher.

'I'm sorry, who did you say she is?'

'Best you come away now, sir.'

After that, my fingers went instinctively in search for a switch on the wall. Despite all evidence to the contrary, I was sure that I had failed to see some great electric chandelier or other that could shed real light on the way ahead.

'Don't any damned bulbs work anywhere?' I complained.

My guide shot me another puzzled stare.

'You'll find nothing like that in this house, sir.'

'You a victim of the flooding, too? It's busy knocking out power supplies across half the country.'

'Surely his lordship told you about that in his letter?'

'H'm, well, yes. Not exactly.'

*

At long last we entered a musty smelling, sparsely furnished room that contained a cupboard, a table and a settle, the latter placed beneath a three-light window. A painted frieze of ribbon scrolls ran across the top of one wall above its panelling to set off the plaster barrel ceiling. On either side of me, however, the panelling incorporated thick oak posts whose mortise-holes showed where a tie-beam had once been braced in a way that suggested a somewhat clumsy rebuild. I was probably standing in a former solar room where the old house met the new.

'I really could do, you know, with a wash,' I said with alarm.

'I'll have Sara bring you an ewer of hot water from the kitchen, sir.'

'There's not, like, a bathroom anywhere?'

'No, sir.'

'Jug it is, then.'

'That's easier.'

'What about when, h'm, I have to…?'

'You'll find a chamber pot under the bed, sir. Leave it on the

24

landing in the morning. The maid will see to it.'

'So, please, as far as you can tell, when can I eat something?'

'Supper will be served at six in the great hall. Will there be anything else, sir?'

'A cup of tea would be nice. That wretched coach really left me parched.'

'I'm afraid I can only offer you hot chocolate.'

'Honestly? No tea?' I asked, disappointed.

'No such thing has ever been drunk in this house that I know of, sir.'

Since he appeared to refute something not advanced by me, it left me wondering what I should have asked. He did not simply refuse to admit that he possessed any tea, he looked at me with sheer incredulity. He behaved as if tea had not yet been invented.

'Then let it be chocolate,' I replied. 'I'm sorry, but I didn't catch your name.'

'James, sir.'

'Thank you, James, for being so considerate.'

He bowed his head with exemplary indifference. In that moment I detected a flash of dislike in his otherwise pale, emotionless face, a stab of feeling born perhaps of the disappointments that constantly dogged his daily life? Working in such a cold, inhospitable house could not have been easy for a man like him, not with the first signs of a disease such as Parkinson's. He rolled his head and shoulder in perpetual motion as he promised to return with bread on a platter.

'Will that be all, sir?'

The question, I surmised, was purely rhetorical, but something still preyed on my mind.

'Wait. Over the fireplace in the great hall there hangs a portrait.'

'That'll be Joseph Jones, sir. He was Lord Hart's step-father. Thanks to him the estate was saved from ruin in the 1950's.'

My restless attendant rolled his head but it was hardly

affirmative, so I tried again.

'What about the missing picture?'

'Missing picture, sir?'

'Yes, next to Mr Jones there is a matching recess cut into the stone chimney breast ready to take another frame of the same size. That would suggest that someone else should hang next to him.'

'No picture ever hangs there, sir. Will you require a warming-pan to heat your bed when you retire for the night?'

At that point I had the sense that he was hiding something from me, but could sense nothing of the thing hidden.

'Warming-pan? Really?'

'I think it best, sir. The countess's room can be very cold.'

6

Not usually one to believe that a musty old bedroom could have its own special atmosphere, I did sense something of its past life as soon as I entered. A hideous four-poster with its elaborately gilded tester still stood in situ, I feared. Just to turn my face to the canopy's rich red velvets was enough to make me sniff and snuffle when the slightest brush against the curtains shook so much dust from the tassels. Real age receded as soon as I put out my hand to touch and explore the cleverly carved pillars. The instant I withdrew my fingers the sense returned. When I extended them again, it faded. It really did stink of the 1600's, though.

'Already I feel as if I have been in this house for ages,' I thought, 'but I can't have been here half an hour. My sock is still wet.' All over the flooded southern and western parts of England people were having to slum it as though in the Middle Ages, they were having to do their ablutions in buckets due to the power cuts and lack of piped water in their houses. It was because the Thames had broken its banks that my coach had been diverted.

I hugged myself to keep warm. 'I can do nothing until supper, so I might as well try to light a fire,' I told myself. Paper and sticks placed ready in the rusty dog grates lit with reluctance in a flame from my cigarette lighter. Quickly I became aware of how white my fingers were, how bloodless. Their paleness was not exactly unexpected but grew steadily more anaemic. I withdrew my hands from the flames and the colour returned. When I again tried to warm them they paled.

'What the hell!' I said, unamused and went back to walking in circles.

Judging by my clouds of white breath the temperature literally was already on the point of freezing.

It could have been more unbearably inhospitable. No, actually, it couldn't.

After that, I pinched my nostrils between finger and thumb and plucked up the courage to deposit my chamber pot outside my door. Which was when I became steadily more aware of a terrible ache in my head, almost a migraine at first but gradually less and less like real pain. I sat on the bed and listened as I pressed and squeezed my skull like a vice. It was the awful weight of silence. The less I listened the more I heard. I put it down to being in the remote countryside.

The rest of the world could have died.

Yet the house was not entirely as still as the grave. I clamped my hands to my ears and the clamour was one great meaningless storm like surf on a seashore. Remove my fingers and the roar divided into many distinct, individual noises each of equal significance and succinctness. I might never have noticed them in the bustle of my previous life – not before had I felt compelled to pay such attention.

The patter of a rat was different from the claws of a bird.

*

That night, either my travel sickness returned or the wine I had drunk at supper agreed with me too well. From the candle-lit garden below my window came voices.

'Don't worry, your lordship, he'll be gone again tomorrow.'

'He's a fool if he isn't.'

*

The last thing I saw before I climbed into bed was the podgy, bug-eyed cherubs that grinned at me from the ceiling.

Overcome by an unexpected discomfort, I felt the need to close my eyes on my pillow.

Then I dreamed.

Day 10. March 30. 2014.

Where is she? Desk marked enquiries: no one there. Various auxiliaries pushing tea trollies.

DON'T ASK THEM.

Doctor, or someone who exudes air of importance is in a backroom talking earnestly to a nurse. I think they're talking about me.

DON'T ASK THEM, EITHER.

Too many bays sub-divide the ward. All faces look the same, ill in bed.

Now I realise (on my second visit) that a chart on the wall in the corridor details who's lying where.

It's all a waste of time because Lizzie is sleeping.

'You the husband?'

Thanks to the grey-haired old lady in the next bed I have someone to talk to.

'Yes, I'm Colin.'

'They had to sedate your wife because she was raving, poor dear. Ripped her drip out of her hand. Kept shouting that someone was coming to get her.'

'Did she mention my name, at all?'

'No.'

'Are you sure? Did she say anything about me to the doctors?'

'Don't worry, I've seen it all before. It's the painkillers, they can make you see cats run across ceilings. Poor dear! She kept screaming it: Don't let anyone in! Don't let anyone in! Her eyes were rolling. She was so terrified she was choking. What's wrong with her? Is it fatal?'

I sit on a hard plastic chair to gaze at Lizzie's shut eyes, wondering how someone's face can be so white and yet still alive.

7

After such a poor night the day so dazed me that I could shake off neither the dizziness in my head nor confusion of feelings. I knew only that I woke in a great dark house far away from whichever street or city I used to inhabit. Of course my insobriety didn't help, but it was more than that. A hangover was not a tragedy, nor did any man succumb long to it.

Parting my embroidered bed curtains, I observed dirty cobwebs dangle and dance on the ceiling, but drapes alone could not account for the dreadful draught.

'Damn it! Where can it be coming from?' I wondered.

I slid out of bed and wrapped myself in my itchy counterpane.

The room was as cold as the grave.

At which point my eye settled on a long red arras that hung on the wall not far from where I was standing. What I had taken to be mere decoration the previous evening fluttered on its rail this morning. I trod the icy floorboards and hooked aside the mosaic of birds and flowers sewn into the curtain's rich fabric. A perfume called to mind sweet violets. I could have been back in the days when petals were strewn on bedchamber floors every day to mask the smell of damp and sickness. Each time I breathed in, the scent was very apparent then lost again, which I put down to a trick of the iodine.

Because of the cold I was shaking. I was astonished and intrigued, not simply by the other chamber's existence but by the eagerness with which something appeared in it. It was a dog.

To my astonishment, a three-legged, white greyhound with a slender grey muzzle and wall-eye took up position beside me. Where the flea-bitten creature had come from I had no idea. Possibly, it had followed me upstairs from the great hall last night?

With its head inclined to one side, it gave me a quizzical look. Muddy and in need of a good brushing, it would become closely acquainted with all my aims and desires, evidently. Or it couldn't understand where I had come from, either.

'Well, look at you,' I said. 'How did you learn to walk on three legs?'

Its white eye blanked its socket as well as its secret. Clearly the glory days of coursing hares were long gone. Indeed, my companion soon slunk off to the other little room where it lay with its head on its paws to shiver and slaver.

All that drool was fine. No, absolutely, it was not.

*

I fully expected to feel trapped by such looming walls, because although very high the room was also very narrow. I had a sudden stab of misgiving, but that was entirely separate from my morbid dread of closed spaces. The dog gave me confidence. I made the disciplined effort to inhale and exhale very calmly. I steadily replenished my lungs, the emptiness of which took me totally by surprise since I had not been aware that I had ever stopped breathing.

If it had been slightly outrageous of me to sleep in a lady's bedchamber, then it had to be uncivil and rude to invade this other, equally intimate space once called her closet. That's because somebody had sat here on her stool and read her favourite books or penned letters at the desk still littered with ink and quills. Such a woman of rank had owned nothing, not even the dress on her back. She had been forced to rely for everything from her husband who led his own very separate existence. Back then, her duty had been to look after the house as its chatelaine but stay away from the kitchens and outbuildings. Only here, in the tiniest yet richest of places had she been able to relax and be her true self, not merely someone's beautiful appendage.

I drew my counterpane tighter across my chest as I nosed about among a few books on mathematics when my hand alighted on a very old multiplying glass. Except, when I drew the flame-stitch curtain at the window in order to put the primitive looking telescope to the test, I suffered a flash in my eye – a sharp stab, unbearable in intensity at first, then becoming much more like simple agony. I lowered the lens and the pain eased immediately – lifted it again and it blinded.

'What the…?' I asked myself, irritably and stared again out the window with my naked eye.

The dog at my feet let out a whine.

There was a bright spot or secondary image in the telescope's field of vision due to a defect in the curvature of its glass, I decided reassuringly. Not for nothing did astronomers call such defects ghosts.

Whoever had stood here studying the stars had been as interested in their significance as they were in their movements and positions. The stargazer had clearly considered astronomy synonymous with astrology, I realised. Beside a marble fireplace stood a globe depicting the heavens. From these could be judged the stars' occult influence upon the affairs of humans.

I let drop the hangings to block out the window, did it to shield the fragile embroidery and me. I could entertain the notion of second sight but not of blindness. In doing so, I noticed that, scratched on the open wrought iron ventilation panel in the otherwise fixed leaded panes, there was a very bad rhyme:

It is part of Virtue never to abstaine
From what we love tho it shall prove our bane.

*

As I shut out the appalling draught I was drawn to a very small painting that hung over a desk on a new shiny nail. The moment I peered at the oils I felt the claustral room tighten around me, or I shrank in proportion to it. Conversely, my eye enlarged to absorb a whole other world – an intense reversal, scarcely credible at first, but redrawing me to scale. I looked closer and saw my body was gone – withdrew, and it returned.

But bemused was I not, neither did I fail to imagine that I was now the same size as the elegant young lady perched on her red silky cushion. Beside her, a gentlewoman helped fasten to her earlobe an earring from which swung the lock of someone's hair like a keepsake or love token. In addition, gloves and pots of frangipane stood arranged on her desk. She appeared to be asking for an opinion on what jewellery would go best with her full-length green and white gown. Nearby rested her multiplying glass and astrological globe.

If I could peer in, she could peer back telescopically.

I put my eye right up to her strong, lean profile. A set of short chains was attached to her belt from which dangled a large bunch of keys, I noted. Hundreds of years after the event, I had the privilege of treading in the footsteps of the room's noble occupant. My misty breath fogged her mirror.

I was that close.

On her walls were familiar floor-to-floor, fiery red, yellow and blue hangings.

'Well I never!' I exclaimed.

I withdrew my hand and blinked. Around me, my bedchamber expanded back to full size. Obversely, its counterpart in the painting imaged mine in correct dimensions proportional to the actual one. Replicated in both were seven pretty lunettes that depicted the cardinal virtues. I saw how a flint-eyed Patience crushed her flower-press to her naked breast to show how determined she was to endure her heartache. I was staring at a depiction of the very same room in which I was standing.

Seconds later there came a loud knock on my door. I lifted its latch to find myself face to face with a young woman with red hair and very bad skin. In her hand steamed a large copper kettle. The dog left as she entered.

Slightly built and wearing a thin blue dress, she flapped about in her cheap plastic sandals as she went to push past me. She did it as if I hardly existed, but not before I detected several bloody scratches under her right ear which she tried hard to keep from my view.

'You hurt, at all?' I said. 'Let me see.'

'Never mind me, Mr Walker.'

'But how did it happen?'

The open wound bubbled red where somebody or something had

not so much scraped as clawed at her.

'You Sara?'

'Apparently.'

'That it? That's my hot water?'

She flashed her emerald green eyes at me.

'Do you want to shave or don't you?'

Without asking, she filled a basin on the table. Then she folded her dress beneath her bony knees and used the shovel in the fireplace to rake ashes messily into a bucket.

'You really ought to let me look at that wound,' I said.

When a hired help was brazen enough to give someone the look of the devil, he could be forgiven for suspecting that something else had gone wrong before his arrival.

'Excuse me Mr Walker, but as I say, I'm only the skivvy to everyone round here. I have to get on.'

'What about my chamber pot?'

'You'll find a privy at the end of the orchard.'

'But I'm the new owner.'

'Good luck with that.'

*

After my ablutions I began to ferry my slops downstairs when clocks chimed nine o'clock. I looked at my watch disbelievingly. The stupid thing was still stopped at the time of my arrival. Nor would my phone work. My inability to tell the hour except by the house's mechanical monsters was a real hindrance, I felt I was in danger of deferring or delaying matters of urgency too long already.

'Ah, James! Good morning. Not too late am I?' I said, sauntering into the great hall. 'I can't nearly begin to tell you how badly I slept.'

'I'm very sorry to hear it, sir.'

It was hard to see in such a wizened, craggy face what he was really thinking. Yet he appeared relieved when I went where directed. Dressed head-to-toe in black with his lacy collars a fresh starchy white, he guided me to my place at the table on the dais. Slanting shafts of dusty light streamed down from the windows. A warm glow came from the log fire and sent a red stain up the walls where it tinged a row of ancient paintings of the Sibyls and the prophets.

My mouth gaped, my eyes stared as a sweat turned me slightly cold. I stood where I was as if stricken. I had been more or less alone after my mother had passed on when many a long day was spent hiding above my step-father's second-hand bookshop in Brighton. It had seen me read prodigious amounts of stuffy history. Through such neglected annals I had learnt to live and love past heroes. So when my favourite hero Aeneas sought the Abode of the Dead to learn his future, the Sibyl gave him a warning that I could still remember: 'The descent to Avernus is easy. The gate of Pluto stands open night and day. But to retrace one's steps and return to the upper air, that is the toil, that is the difficulty.'

James pointed me towards a hideous, high-backed chair of ornately carved Portuguese mahogany at the head of the table, which suited me very well. Before me stood a small silver drinking cup, gently smoking. Its contents did not smell like tea or coffee.

'This is what, exactly?'

'A drink of posset and syllabub, sir. I thought you might need it after such a cold night.'

'Looks serious.'

I went to raise the rim of the cup to my lips but James coughed gently.

'Suck not sip, sir.'

'Honestly?'

'That's easier.'

On closer examination I discovered that protruding from each side of the strange silver vessel was a spout. By drawing liquid through one or other of the hollow handles I could drink it right down to the bottom. So creamy was it that it stuck to my thin upper lip. Hot milk had been curdled with ale and flavoured with spices to make a very peculiar, heady pick-me-up.

'Nothing wrong, I hope, sir?'

'Oh no, it's fine. Yeah. It's great. Definitely.'

Except it was not in any way a meal fit for a king, more like the first of my prison rations.

*

'I also have eggs,' announced James in his next breath.

'The thing is,' I objected, surveying the vast empty hall before me. 'There appears to be an exceptionally bad smell in the little room adjoining my bedchamber.'

'Bad smell, sir?'

'Of something dead and rotting.'

'Are you certain?'

'Yeah. No. I don't know. Sara has tried to mask it with the smell of dried flowers.'

James placed a sharp knife before me with his shaky fingers. Habitually on the look-out for something or someone, he observed the shadows with disconcerting thoroughness.

'That'll be a dead rat, sir.'

'Did the greyhound catch it, do you think?'

'Greyhound, sir?'

'Yes. You know, the large one-eyed mutt that slept on my bed last night.'

'We don't have a dog, sir.'

'So why, like, shut the dog-gate at the foot of the stairs?'

'That gate is as old as the house, sir.'

'Okay. H'm, I see, but I can assure you I'm not imagining things.'

'A dog like that once belonged to his lordship's brother, sir. It disappeared when he died two years ago.'

'Okay, it's just that it's back now.'

'Then it must have returned when you did, sir.'

'Well, h'm, moving on. I'm not at all sure I like Sara. Her belligerent attitude is rather tiresome. Is she the best you can do?'

James stopped dead suddenly. With his back to me he was about to go into a cool room to fetch a jug of milk, I presumed.

'She's Sullivan O'Leary's daughter, sir. Her mother is dead and she lives with her father in one of the estate's cottages.'

'What is O'Leary to his lordship, in your opinion?'

'He's his former terrier man, sir. He used to dig out foxes every autumn when Lord Hart still went cubbing, but he was dismissed for poaching deer. Now he has too much time to snoop about if you ask me. You'll have to keep an eye out for him in case he filches food from the kitchen.'

'So how does he make a living?'

'He occasionally does odd jobs around the estate.'

'Lord Hart and O'Leary aren't exactly on the best of terms, then?'

'He's a bully not to be trusted, sir.'

'Got it.'

James drew a deep audible breath expressive of sadness but also relief from some inner tension. Naturally, he was glad I had taken his side.

'And James, please go easy on the poor dog. From now on, this will be its home.'

'It always was, sir.'

'That's settled, then.'

Not only did he vehemently dislike the greyhound, there was something distasteful about its return which genuinely repelled him.

37

'Is there anything else I can help you with or will you be leaving us today, sir?'

My butler-cum-waiter sashayed to and fro across the echoing floor.

'It is imperative that I see his lordship right away. He does know that, doesn't he?'

'Lord Hart will receive you in the long gallery at eleven o'clock, sir.'

'Is that the best he can do? Is everything okay?'

My gloomy attendant gave a slight bow.

'Rest assured, sir, it is all arranged.'

'Because I heard loud voices in the garden last night.'

I hadn't travelled all that way to be palmed off with breakfast.

'One egg or two, sir?'

As for my host's no-show I felt ever more annoyed, but short of exploring the house down every corridor, I could do very little. Whatever obscenities this morning might bring would have to wait on his beck and call.

Fact was, I needed to explain myself pretty soon. Otherwise, how could I hope to see beyond tomorrow?

*

Buzzards circled high in the sky the moment I let myself out of the gatehouse. They mewed to each other like petulant sentinels ready to protest every departure. I scurried across the narrow lane to the stile where James had told me to look for a path across the fields. Each irritating bird spread its wings to wheel through the air in bold vulture-like fashion. In no way did their broad, rather stubby wings transform them into fast and fat little dragons. No, really, they did.

But everything was fine because when I glanced at my wristwatch it had restarted where it had left off, as though a whole evening and night had simply vanished. The higher I climbed the grassy slope, the better my recalcitrant phone found its signal as well. Right now, though, I was in no mood to fire off any messages to friends.

When someone was no longer impeded by place or people he could take a much needed deep breath and stride along with bigger paces, he could climb like a free man.

Once at the top of the hill I turned to take a long look back across the valley.

Shrouding everything, the thick ground mist clung to the gatehouse and crenelated walls that kept me a stranger to their secrets. Rather than solid courtyards, roofs and chimneys, my view conjured up a more fluid creation, it signalled new forms and shapes the longer I studied them. It could have been a picture still in the making. I would have delighted in it, except my back ached so much. Never should any man have endured a bed as bone-achingly hard as I had last night. I held my hand before my eye to focus between fingers and thumb like someone suddenly in dire need of dimensions.

Then I saw it. From such a high vantage point my eyes fixed the glittering proportions of a ghostly, white-walled manor-house which had until a few hours ago existed for me in name only, Coberley Hall. At long last, I could feast them on what was now all mine. Of course, what I really needed was a telescope.

8

I was resolved, but truly my next step proved vague. Bounded by high thorny hedges, a five-bar gate was the only exit off the frightfully soggy hilltop which was so overgrown as to be almost impassable to someone of my stature.

Where there had once been a directional finger-post the wooden digit had been torn off as if by some mighty hand. Worse, the gate had long ago been chained shut with an enormous rusty padlock that even the most hardened hiker might have found discouraging, but I was wrong. One person at least had recently vaulted the slippery bars to bulldoze a path through all the briers and dog roses, I discovered.

When a civilised man took to the hills, however unconscionably, he should not have to tip-toe daintily through the wet grass like someone too afraid to step off the beaten track. I was soon following the solid, unhesitating footsteps of some bold pioneer. My alter ego and I were squelching along the edge of a field on the estate's very margins while parallel with us a mischievously energetic river ran along a half hidden gully.

With the chuckling water came the ghastly melody of some unkind and cruel tune for which there was no earthly song. No, really, it was just a stream. A few yards further – it felt more like miles – the footprints in which I trod were spaced left and right quite regularly which suggested a diagonal walk, not the parallel steps of a bound or gallop. Scored in the mud, they showed less structural resemblance to a man's, being all split indentations and long toes. In some places the spoor was yet more slurred and irregular across the ground's muddy surface. I was treading in the footsteps of some lonely forager as he dragged behind him a log or kill. Here one indent overlapped another like a deer. Then again, cloven hooves with claws would have been another way to describe them. Prints like that could play the devil with one's eyes.

Afterwards, I trod large white shells. Such popping, crunching molluscs were no ordinary scavenging gastropods but Roman snails. I stopped to pick up one shell but found it to be translucent and empty. Clearly my hungry epicurean had felt no qualms about sucking each one as clean as a whistle as he strode along.

All this poking about disturbed the birds. Dozens of troublesome fieldfares, those ghostly migrants from faraway Russia who liked to squat for the winter in remote, quiet places, gazed on blood-red hawthorn berries in the hedges. Opening their dripping, crimson beaks at me, the pillagers denounced my passing with their frantic twittering as though I were some sort of revenant come to rob them of their spoils.

Already I was thrilled, nervous and alert. The question of whether someone was living illegally off my land or whether it was some harmless, passing vagrant spurred me on.

*

'You lost at all?'

Spinning round, I met a handsome woman who looked about sixty. Dressed in a pair of gaudy green trousers and jumper, she stood very stiff and upright at the front door of a Cotswold stone house that went by the unusual name of Slack's Cottage. With rather fine gables, it was a miniature version of Coberley Hall but without the gruesome gargoyles and finials.

A pretty hungry tabby cat, wild-eyed and filthy, gnawed the head off a rabbit at the foot of an oil tank in a nearby yard.

'I've just come across the fields,' I replied, fingering my sore eye. 'Do you, like, have any eyewash by any chance? I've come off worst with some burdock.'

My stern interlocutor dusted her long fingers on her white apron.

'Doesn't mean you can wander in here, does it? Can't you read? It says No Cold Callers.'

'Would you be Susan, at all? James gave me your name.'

She looked hot from her kitchen, narrowed her grey eyes at me and screwed her fingers back into her apron's pocket. From the house's half open door came the warm smell of cakes fresh from the oven. Elsewhere a dog gave a howl.

'Do I know you?'

'I'm staying in Coberley Hall.'

The cook became both confused and flustered. Hurriedly poking her very neat, short grey hair with her floury fingers, she had to fight to regain her composure.

'You're that wife killer. Aren't you?'

'I'm Detective Inspector Colin Walker.'

'You're Lizzie's husband....'

Okay, so bad news travelled far.

'A man has the right to tell his side of the story, don't you think?' I replied sternly.

'I don't believe you.'

'Never trust what you read in the press.'

'Not that, the other thing.'

'What thing?'

'You don't mean 'Hall', do you?'

'Seems I do. How many Jacobean fortified manor-houses is it our misfortune to see survive so unaltered anywhere else in England?'

My wide-eyed baker wavered slightly. When she did speak it was calmly but robotically.

'You've …been…*inside*?'

'It's not a good thing. I mean the house is very cold and empty. This morning it's a relief, in a way, to get out and talk to someone. Even you.'

'Adrian and I never go further than the gatehouse. The thing is, Mr Walker, we don't exactly welcome outsiders round here. I just want to say that I'd be careful if I were you, I wouldn't go poking my nose into other people's business. My husband and I have been 'ere over thirty-five years and not even we can explain everything that goes on after dark, that we can't. Honestly, you wouldn't want

42

to get mistaken for some badger or deer one night, would you? You don't want a poacher's bullet in the head, I suppose?'

'People do a lot of that kind of thing, do they?'

'You often meet a man with his long gun.'

Susan threw back her wide shoulders and thrust out her chest to stave off any more impertinent questions. She stumped right up to me. She did it so resolutely that I became a little unnerved myself. Still she didn't shake my hand, not slightly.

'Aren't poachers with guns a bit scary?' I protested. 'Not to say illegal.'

'We all keep guns round here, Mr Walker, because you never know who might come calling.'

'How's that?'

'Do you shoot, at all?'

'Only criminals.'

'Doesn't mean you can't aim straight, do it?'

'I'm a little rusty.'

'Best go to the Shooting School. Just follow them bangs you can hear in Chatcombe Wood. Peter Slater will put you right. We need all the firepower we can get, Mr Walker, that we do.'

So saying, Susan patted the side of her nose and left a neat dab of flour-paste on one nostril.

'If I could maybe speak to your husband?' I pleaded, suffering my eye to weep to no avail.

'You go right ahead, Mr Walker. Adrian's in one of the barns behind you. But maybe the fact that his lordship now has some London lawman to help him says something? Finally, perhaps, he realises what it's going to take to police this place or else why put himself through it all again? But if it's more eggs you want, I can't give you any cos someone got all the chickens last night.'

What followed was an oily path thick with smoke and sawdust to some waste ground at the back of a crew yard, I discovered. There somebody had set light to a stack of timbers so high that it looked like a funeral pyre.

Kicking idly at a sizzling puddle, I picked up a hand-forged nail torn from some ancient beam. I squinted at the fire and the massively solid timbers did look as if they had once formed the labyrinthine eaves of some very old roof or other.

At which point I detected a noise in the barn closest to me. The bleached wooden building was totally open on one side, Dutch-style, although at first I could see very little past its fitful shadows. I had a man's name to go by but had no idea who that man might be.

'You the farm manager? You Adrian?'

'Who the devil wants him?'

I followed the voice to a corner high up on a great pile of bales. Atop it all, a bony man in blue denim jeans and a checked brown and white shirt was sorting hay. His jeans sagged off his skinny buttocks most alarmingly. However, there was no denying how agreeably hard he was working. He kicked at the hay with his burnished steel-capped boot and paused only to mop his closely cropped hair with a swipe of his sleeve.

Below him, I wheezed in the thick haze of spores and mould that flew about my head like flies.

'I'm the new owner, DI Colin Walker,' I cried. 'You may have known my wife. To you, she was Lizzie Dryzek.'

Just in time I heard him gargle a big ball of phlegm, had to leap back before a bale big enough to break my leg rolled my way.

'So it's true, then. Now she's gone you get to have everything?'

*

I rushed to dust frightful wisps of hay off my lapels.

'You moving all these bales by yourself? How come?'

'I am on my own, yes,' replied Adrian. 'Absolutely I am. I've got four years' worth of hay here and only the last two are any good for his lordship's horses. The rest is so mouldy it has to go on the fire. Not that he rides out much any more, anyway.'

'Sounds ambitious. How do you fancy I help you?'

'Make an offer like that round here, Mr Walker and you'll likely get your hand bitten off.'

'Oh, why's that?'

He tipped more bales off the top of the pile while I did, at great inconvenience, quell my disgust and bend down to give him some assistance.

'Ever since his lordship's brother died he has lost interest in farming.'

'So he really is ill?'

Adrian paused in mid-heave.

'Lord Hart has started behaving like a recluse but he didn't always hate it all. Absolutely he didn't.'

I began dragging bales to the fire. The blocks of hay, each four feet long, might have been tightly compacted and bound with two lengths of tough, shiny binder twine that cut into my gloves, but unbalance the load and I was soon in trouble. When I put too much pull on one string and not the other, the whole diabolical construction simply split into slices before I could move a muscle.

'Practice makes perfect,' said Adrian with the same deadpan voice.

Suddenly I could see his face, albeit in profile. It confirmed that it was stretched and almost fleshless. I could have been looking at a skull itself, since he was clearly a man who liked to work himself to the bone.

'You trying to suggest that the shock of losing his brother has, like, triggered some sort of agoraphobia?'

'It's not a permanent thing, Mr Walker. You shouldn't put a label on someone just because you sometimes see them in a wheelchair.'

'More ME than MS, then?'

'Or maybe the fact that he has something on his mind says it all?'

I watched Adrian descend his pyramid so that I no longer had to address any questions to the dreadful miasma.

'So what is it about this estate that makes people so reluctant to work on it?' I asked.

'All I know is that one person doesn't have to be alive for another to love them dearly. Death doesn't always have the final say, it's what comes after.'

'He must be bad if he won't ride his horses?'

'How many of us don't have regrets?'

I declined to ridicule his melodramatic empathy, but not its ridiculousness.

*

'What is that awful stench?' I asked as Adrian led the way back to a tractor. His mug of lukewarm tea rested on its bonnet.

'That's rotten food Mr Walker. Absolutely it. Bacteria breaks down organic matter in little or no oxygen by way of anaerobic digestion. The semi-liquid residue comes to us as fertilizer for the fields from the local authorities.'

'But it smells so putrid and maggoty.'

'Gets everywhere, doesn't it? You can't breathe in bed at night, sometimes.'

'It tastes horribly metallic. Like something decomposing.'

'That'll be the 'digestates'. Everything rots, Mr Walker. Even us.'

Adrian rinsed out his mouth ready to spit at my feet. With that, he climbed into the cab of the enormous red tractor and reached for a shotgun. He broke open its breach and checked it was loaded. Then he placed it close to hand on the seat beside him, I noted.

Meantime, a sparrow-hawk perched on a fence post and clawed

the feathers off a robin. It shed the breast feathers with its talons in a shower of crimson petals while its victim was still living.

Never before had I watched a bird act so cruelly, even if peregrine falcons did daily cruise the skies over London.

'If Lord Hart won't leave his house who decides what to do round here?' I shouted over the noise of the engine.

Adrian passed me his empty mug.

'I do, on account of the fact that I have a degree in agriculture and he doesn't. All he knows is what he learnt from his step-father, Joseph Jones, many years ago. His brother Philip was the same.'

'That's Lizzie's father?'

'So they say.'

'Is it true that he deserted her when she was seven?'

'Deserted? Is that what she told you?'

'For most of her life he was as good as dead to her.'

Dusting down his bare forearms, my belligerent driver was busy studying the screen on the tractor's computer.

'Not dead Mr Walker, disconnected. By then her mother was lying safe in her grave but Lizzie couldn't understand why her father wasn't able to keep her with him. Absolutely she couldn't. Once it was done, it was done, though. She didn't know if it was some sort of punishment. She pleaded and pleaded but that was no good, she was driven away. As you say, she was a child put up for adoption.'

'What else can you tell me?'

'Some things are best forgotten.'

I stared straight ahead into the distance.

'Would it be fair to say that during her few years at Coberley Hall Lizzie was abused or neglected by someone to your knowledge?'

'What I can say is that she had few new clothes and she literally missed meals. Whenever I met her she was looking for bogy men, bugbears and bogles, she said. A special friend had told her all about them. The thing is, she was so thin she looked like a phantom herself.'

'Lizzie was very imaginative like that, was she?'

'Because those weren't good times, Mr Walker. The old man was dead and the estate was in trouble again. Lizzie's mother had been drinking heavily for years right up to the end. Nevertheless, Lizzie didn't seem unhappy, more guarded.'

'Against her father?'

'Against everyone.'

'Sounds chaotic.'

'It's always best to take care, absolutely it is.'

'But care about who or what exactly?'

'Do you believe in good and evil Mr Walker? Do you believe that one or the other can stalk a family in response to a great sorrow?'

'As a detective you stop caring about such things after a while.'

'Your wife didn't. She thought about it a great deal, even as a child. That's how she came to be in a world of her own. Everyone feared that she had become better friends with the dead than the living.'

'You mean she was so traumatised by the loss of her own mother that she conjured another?'

'Never just conjured, though.'

'Did this 'other' have a name, by any chance?'

'She called her the countess.'

*

I felt more than a little inquisitive but could not in any way think how best to inquire. Meanwhile Adrian drove across the yard in order to hitch a high-sided trailer to his tractor, ready to ferry more foul food waste to fertilize the fields. I went to head him off but suddenly thought better of it. One wrong turn of those massive black tyres could crush a man to nothing.

9

'Never thought you'd dare show your face round 'ere, Inspector. Never thought you'd have the nerve after what you've done.'

Susan stood patting gnomes on her patio from where she presided over my advance.

I did not reply. Obviously, she had taken to brooding about me in my absence.

'So what are you gonna, like, do now then,' she continued, 'with this place, *with us*, now your wife's gone?'

Any more questions and I might have to answer.

Whacking a wet rag mercilessly from one pointed hat to another, she prepared to crack it my way should I trespass any closer.

'What's she to you, anyway, Inspector? She's gone for ever.'

I slowed my pace very slightly. One false move could only highlight, all too prematurely, any qualms of my own.

'I never realised how little one person could know about another,' I said. 'After all, this was once her home.'

'Think it's easier to know the dead than the living, do you?'

'Why should I listen to you?'

'You're going to regret it. Honestly.'

'Regret what, exactly?'

That I was somehow the Devil, though the notion filled her with the vilest dilemma, she now had not the slightest doubt. For a moment she glared at me beside the concrete ramp of an abandoned cattle dock where I had stopped to face her.

'I just want you to know Inspector, that there never was a good reason to disown your wife. You hear what I'm saying? It wasn't her they should have abandoned. It was Coberley Hall.'

'I don't understand you.'

'It's like this Inspector. The poor little thing would hang around

Slack's Cottage whenever she smelt my baking. Some teachers at her school said that she wasn't quite right in the head, but I never believed that for one moment.'

Of my own dilemma it was too foolish to dispose.

'Say what you like, I know Lizzie had a very vivid imagination. She could be dark and Gothic. Scary, even. Doesn't mean I didn't take her seriously.'

'It's what she put into her writing and paintings that started the trouble, Inspector. All those fantastic creatures, blood and claws. No teacher would pin them on the classroom wall.'

'What child doesn't like a good monster?'

'These were so lifelike that they scared the adults. The headmistress said that they reminded her of drawings done by traumatised children who had witnessed a war.'

Before I could quell this uninvited intrusion into my wife's history, Susan shot me a dark, cunning smile. She would throw at me things to which, thanks to my studied indifference, I had hitherto been immune.

'Never ask the dead what we can't the living, Inspector.'

In a flash her eyes sought to plumb the depths of my marriage that she had convinced herself must have turned sour.

'Okay, just tell me one thing Lizzie drew that you remember fully?' I demanded.

'She drew the deadliest creatures from the deepest seas.'

'Let me stop you right there.'

'Has no one told you about it properly, not ever, Inspector? They were wondrous things, such as a pair of bearded, three-toed sea-gods whose skinny black chests sprouted pairs of naked breasts. With a man's bulging cheeks and nose, those louring, sharp-toothed Neptunes popped their eyeballs at us as if they stirred in dire discomfort at being so far from their oceans. Their shark-like lips quite literally seemed to squirm and coil, but then I thought, 'How can paint come alive?' When asked where she'd seen them she said that they lived with her in Coberley Hall.'

'All you're saying is that, thanks to a lot of hideous gargoyles and Jacobean wood carvings, she felt haunted.'

'Not haunted, just guarded.'

'That's funny. Adrian used that word, too.'

'It was always the same, Inspector. Whenever she was asked why she surrounded herself with such ugly creatures she said that she had to take care.'

'Take care? Are you sure that those were the words she used?'

'Yes, why? Did she say them to you, too?'

'Never you mind. I'm sure that whatever happened back then that his lordship had Lizzie's best interests at heart.'

'His lordship indeed!'

'Did I say something funny?'

'No proper titled family has owned this land for hundreds of years, Inspector. Him over there is no different from you or me, despite all his airs and graces. You ask Peter Slater. He and the brothers played together on the estate when they were children. Peter knows the family history better than anyone. Joseph Jones began it all, he dreamed up the whole idea of some grand family going back generations to suit himself.'

'You mean it's all a lie?'

Susan placed both hands on her hips and tossed her chin.

'Don't get me wrong, Joseph Jones was a clever man. He made a lot of money designing underground pipes to heat airfields during the Second World War. Only he could keep them ice-free in a time of national crisis. It's also true that his family once owned a farm in East Anglia and it was certainly his ambition to recreate his childhood dream, so to speak, which is why he bought what remained of Coberley Court as it was called by then, in the 1950's. You would have thought that he had discovered some great ancestral link going back centuries, but a rabbit-run other people called it, which sold at auction for a song.'

For a moment I was dizzy with doubt.

'Not a real nobleman, then, more a fantasist?'

'What man doesn't like to invest himself with another man's trappings, Inspector, especially if he can pretend to be grander, richer and more powerful than he really is? What better way to fool some silly young girl who'd fall for a lineage going back centuries?' Susan added meaningfully. 'Who doesn't want to be addressed as his lordship in his own Hall?'

'Don't look at me.'

'No? I wonder?'

'Well, h'm, okay, but it's a nasty bit of tittle-tattle. And I don't understand where the name Hart comes from?'

Susan uttered a hollow laugh.

'Hart is simply another name for deer and it was in nearby Hartley Wood that rich Norman lords liked to go hunting, but it changes nothing. Many a man has chosen to call himself Lord of Coberley Hall but none ever lived long to enjoy it.'

'Sorry, but I'm not the superstitious type.'

With that, Susan went back to scrubbing her wet gnomes even harder. She banged a few heads together with considerable anger as though the very air we breathed was corrupted. Of course, it was only that awful recycled food being spread on the fields. No, frankly, it wasn't. I could stomach the stinking 'digestates' but not the air of sour disappointment. I hurried on before she came up with any more of her ridiculous tales.

*

It was but a dozen paces downhill from Slack's Cottage back to the busy main road. There, an endless succession of cars and lorries rushed at me round a sharp bend.

Quickly, the absence of gaps in the traffic saw me overtaken by a terrible urge – a silly imperative, easily overridden in the beginning but sounding louder and louder in my head. I took a step forward and the command to cross ceased – stepped back and it doubled in volume.

'To hell with it!' I thought carelessly. 'No man should have to stand here kicking his heels.'

Several times I went to step out the end of the lane only to feel the full force of a car's slipstream strike my face.

Several minutes passed before I chanced it.

Which was when I heard them.

Those words.

Before I made it across.

So piercing.

Not normal words at all. Not like any voice I'd ever known.

Not that I should *not* have listened…

Distracted, I spun round and saw a coach heading straight for me. Its great white front and claw-like mirrors looked set to run me down with a deafening blare of its horn. In the middle of the road I was whirled about by a vertiginous storm – no longer felt my feet touch the tarmac. Light flared at the edge of my right eye. Being a sudden but transitory blaze, the white flash repeated itself like a signal. To see lightning burst into view took me completely by surprise, because what I was seeing did not appear to be anything external. Like bolts from the blue the dazzling gleams threw into silhouette black lines between retina and lens. Slowly but surely, flotsam and jetsam began to coalesce to form one material person in detail. It might have been a woman.

I heard the saxophonic horn and the agonizing squeal of locked brakes, saw passengers tossed forwards in their seats as the coach skidded round me. In a split second I was picked up and flung at one side of the highway – the far side – then onto the grassy bank which kept me from the coach's rear axle.

The abrupt somersault, the knock on my head, dazed me but I let out a scream with relief. I clawed at the grass, hauled myself higher up the bank and retched at the smell of hot rubber in my nostrils. It smelt like barbecued bones, hair, flesh. There was nothing more hellish with which to compare it. I could have died in a rash move fraught with disaster.

Instead the National Express driver expertly steered her vehicle out of its violent manoeuvre. She straightened her vehicle a short distance down the road. It was the 444 bound for London.

I had just had a very close shave with the same coach on which I had travelled yesterday.

I sat there shaking and blinking. Lying out of reach and mangled amid the traffic was one of my green Wellingtons. What were the odds that I should have been killed? Yet dead I was not and surely did I still breathe.

Born of blank hurt, the figure on the opposite side of the road studied me closely. It was as if sheer force of vision were somehow enough to remind me of the terribleness of something.

Then I *heard* Susan.

'Are you all right, Inspector? This is a most treacherous corner. A muntjak was hit here only the other day. Adrian and I were going to cook and eat it but someone else dragged it away in the night. You wouldn't want your brains dashed out like some poor deer, I suppose?'

Next second, time caught up with me again. My legs worked under me now that I no longer felt literally limbless. I had been blown clear of the coach in a way I still could not fathom. I managed to stand up and wave, someone wanly. Since I had come to little harm I said nothing. Instead I chose to limp away blithely. I kept to the verge in order to look for my path back to Coberley.

And there, pinned to a post at the roadside was a cocky little arrow marked 'diversion'. Instead of being directed over the stile, all walkers were now to stay on the narrow, grassy bank despite the dangerous proximity to the traffic. Unbeknown to me, my path had been rerouted.

My chin was bloody and putting my fingers to my chest I felt it rasp with each frantic breath I could manage. A moment ago, I had not cared nearly enough if I had consigned myself to oblivion, but for now I had to marvel at an escape that felt like a miraculous stay of execution.

Whatever misplaced hints of spring there might have been in the yellow hazel catkins in the leafless hedges or scattered daisies that spotted the banks, a chill entered my bones. It was not only the prospect of frequenting Coberley Hall's gloomy walls that alarmed me when I passed under the leering looks of its unfriendly gargoyles, it was that ugly shout that had caught me so dangerously off guard in the middle of the road.

I should have demanded from Susan why she had so brazenly barracked me, but I was already late for my appointment. As for my 'earful' it was soon distant to my ears:

That poor dead girl. Will she ever rest?

10

My heart ticked furiously, my lungs panted and there was a dryness on my tongue. Deliberately I straightened my shoulders and strode forwards into a long narrow room where the lightest touch of my toes caused ancient floorboards to groan.

The heavy oak door clicked shut behind me.

I could stand the tension in my head but not in my bowels.

'Is anyone, like, there, at all?' I asked, swallowing hard.

With the best will in the world, I was a fool if I counted on a friendly reception.

'Damn it man, come closer where I can see you. What the devil kept you? I was all set to send out a search party.'

Someone formed a misshapen huddle in front of a far off window, I realised. A man appeared in black profile on a white background like somebody cut out of darkness and dazzle. Suddenly he rode straight at me in his wheelchair. Dressed in an immaculate white suit and dark tinted glasses, he gathered speed on the dirty boards, then squealed to a halt by the fire. He looked me up and down.

Although instructed, I was intruding.

'Walker? Is it really you?'

Either I had changed a great deal or he could not tolerate the sight of a face that it was not in his best interest to remember.

I still felt a queasiness of my own.

'It's been a while, George.'

'So sorry I wasn't there to welcome you yesterday,' he said darkly. 'I was feeling a little indisposed.'

'Honestly, some things can't be avoided.'

'I trust James took good care of you?'

'I'm staying in the countess's room, apparently.'

'You cold, at all?'

'Pretty much, yeah.'

'Pull up a chair by the fire.'

'Don't mind if I do.'

'Not that one!'

With a lunge, my host described a savage arc in the air, he drove his dragon-headed cane into my thigh before I knew what was happening. I forgot the person I had met briefly years ago. Instead I saw someone dreadfully agitated – staringly, thrillingly, passionately so. Anticipation and prospect marked every crease of his face. Worry was no less a feature. His white suit was stained with spit, his long hair he wound tightly round his fingers in a way which was both nervous and child-like. If he appeared physically wild so was he also sufficiently mentally agitated for some to have said that he belonged in a madhouse.

'Excuse me, old chap, I didn't mean to startle you but don't sit in that chair. Please, use the other one.'

'That's in the house rules, is it?'

'Now see here, Walker…'

Whereupon he used his cane as a prop in order to infer something – in a house as old as this and according to ancient courtly manners, was it not *uncomely* to approach a fire nearer than others?

'Forgive my lateness, sir, I shouldn't have gone to see the farm manager.'

The rumbling rubber treads of his chair circled me on the uneven, disjointed boards.

'Damn it, Colin, drop the niceties. You're only here for one reason. The house. You've come to kick me out.'

'Is this place even worth saving?'

*

'Now then, old chap,' said Lord Hart, picking his large red nose, 'don't act so unimpressed. Not only did an earl and countess once parade up and down these very boards for their daily winter exercise but so did King Charles I. Twice during the English Civil War, he stayed under our roof.'

'He probably thought he'd get arthritis and rheumatism, too.'

He gave a quick laugh. Diamond rings flashed on his fingers as his face set in a scowl.

'Well, now that you've had the brass neck to show up here, you skinny bastard, tell me, how is it you've lost so much friggin' weight since I last saw you? Have you been ill?'

'In a way, yeah.'

'Been in the wars, have we?'

I felt my hand rise involuntarily to my freshly grazed face.

'Not that. Your brow. Looks awful.'

'I wrecked my 1978 MGB Roadster, but I'm all right now.'

'Devil take you, old chap, how long has it been? Ten years? Last time we met I was walking my niece down the aisle at your wedding. What were you, then? Twenty stone?'

'Sixteen. It's only these last few months…'

'By the look of you, you haven't had a decent meal for ages.'

'Food isn't always a friend.'

'Remind me. How old are you now?'

'Forty-five.'

'Must be the strain, you look so anaemic. Such a rotten business. The whole thing stinks. And so bad for you! I read about it in the Daily Telegraph. I must say you made a very strong case for yourself. De mortuis nil nisi bonum. Tell me, where does a man like you go from here? What's his future? How can he bear to wake up and look himself in the mirror each morning after everything that has happened and been said?'

'As someone mentioned to me on my way here, a smile works wonders, usually.'

'If only we could move on and be sure to leave our troubles behind us, is that it? Do you believe in a new start? Should we even try to forget our loved ones once they have departed? And what if we can't? What comes after?'

I poured myself a much needed glass of wine from a decanter that stood warming in the hearth, when the white, one-eyed, greyhound trotted past. The slim, three-legged creature went straight to the forbidden chair. Once curled upon it, the dog flicked one flea-ridden ear at me as though some unseen hand fondled it rather roughly. By day it appeared thinner and more battered than ever.

Lord Hart smiled at his companion that, according to his butler, should not have existed.

'You're a hard man to read, Walker. Always were. That's it, drink up. It's claret from my own cellars.'

It would have been churlish of me not to have been charmed by his sudden volte-face, not to mention vintage, obvious tactic though it was to gain some advantage as yet unknown to me.

'I've written to my solicitors, George. According to a codicil in the will you have the right to continue to stay under my roof for as long as you live.'

'Please, Colin, I think we should talk about Lizzie first, don't you?'

*

I could not help admiring his directness and insensitivity. Given that I was the widower it was perhaps inevitable that my wife's uncle should seek to pain me with the one person who had brought about this very meeting. For as long as he made Lizzie a stipulation of our reunion it was likely that she would forever be the one condition that I could never fulfil.

I could think of no other way to explain the abrupt, unseen resentment that I felt rise up between us. It fell to me to strike first, so to speak.

'I'm sure Lizzie would want what is best for both of us now that she is gone,' I said.

'I think so, too, old chap. You might see only the dead hand of time here, but she didn't. This is where she came into the world.'

'So it's not, you know, possible that something about this place could have come back to haunt her as she lay dying?'

'Good God, Walker, is that why you're here? To ask me for forgiveness?'

'Would that be so stupid?'

*

I watched Lord Hart lean again on his cane. With a need less physical than psychological, he seemed weighed down by some burdensome presence beyond mine. When, however, he stood up slowly but thoughtfully from his wheelchair, he drew on unseen reserves of resilience.

'This room was Lizzie's favourite, Colin. As a child she would bounce up and down on the sprung leather seat of that very old chamber horse by your side. Most of all, she liked to sit cross-legged on the floor and draw its paintings. Believe me, this is the place where she first thought about becoming an artist.'

'That it? Her school considered her a weird loner, but in this room it did her good to be around hideous people? What are they, anyway?'

My restive host waved his cane at a circular gold-framed picture of a bare-breasted woman of exotic Arabian origin. A droopy ostrich feather adorned her dark glossy hair while she regarded herself against the sun's golden rays in her mirror. She was VISVUS, first in the row of Five Senses.

'Out of SMELL, HEARING, TOUCH and TASTE, it was SIGHT that was Lizzie's favourite. "So what are you trying to capture?" I once asked her. "Her eyes, uncle," she replied. "I want her eyes." '

I failed to see why my obsessive host should become so absurdly worked up about something so trivial.

'You and I both know that I'm not here to look at pretty

pictures,' I said, clicking my heels. 'So, back to business.'

'Isn't Lizzie our business? Isn't she the real reason you've come, old chap?'

'The legalities. Naturally.'

'Don't be a damned fool, Walker.'

I followed his rude, restless glances while he sank, over-excited, into his wheelchair.

'Lizzie's dead,' I declared. 'That's an end to it.'

'Not if you've brought her with you.'

*

There was no telling whose hypocrisy was greater, his or mine, but I scowled quietly to myself at his presumption.

'People will always say that I did it for the money.'

'I never said that,' replied Lord Hart. 'I never believed you'd do something so stupid, as such.'

'You must think you were very wrong to entrust me with her happiness, but it's the aftermath we have to contend with now.'

'The estate's, especially.'

'While sorting through papers to settle probate, I discovered that Coberley Hall had been put into a trust for Lizzie by her mother until she was thirty. How come?'

Lord Hart tapped his dragon cane, set its lucky black ball spinning between its fangs.

'Because Lizzie should never have had it.'

'How's that?'

'It's complicated. And personal.'

'That's not what you wrote me in your letter.'

'I've changed my mind.'

'Okay, but if everyone had come clean about it all from the

62

beginning Lizzie and I could at least have lived in Coberley Hall for a while. Who knows, we might have tried for another child.'

'You mustn't blame Lizzie, the devil you mustn't. For years, I actively discouraged her from returning here. I didn't want her falling under its spell again.'

'So much for Coberley Hall being her great inspiration.'

'Tell me, how do you tell someone that their father is mentally ill when others were so eager to label her the same?'

'Stop there. Yeah. Please do. You 'managed' the family secret all this time because you thought it best for us all. Really?'

'My brother was a very complex person, old chap. To see him shambling about dressed in ill-fitting clothes like a Wild Man made me want to scream, the devil it did, because at times I thought he would drag the rest of us to hell with him. Fact is, it was better for everyone if Philip and Lizzie had no proper contact those twenty-five years.'

'You mean you let her think her father had abandoned her.'

At which Lord Hart whipped off his glasses. His cool, blue eyes were two small dots as he fought to hold in his fury.

'Never speak that word in this house, it's too … dangerous. She was always someone's daughter.'

'Technically.'

His laughter rang bitterly off the coved plasterwork ceiling.

'When a father sacrifices what is most precious to him he does not necessarily do it simply because he won't hear or listen to reason, he does what's best for the other person whether child or adult, he puts motive and cause before his own unreasonableness. My brother did what he had to do because he had no other choice, he wanted to save her from himself.'

'Actually he didn't.'

'No, actually, I did. I kept the estate going for us all.'

'She deserved better. So did I.'

'And what good would it have done you to have acquired Coberley Hall any sooner? I didn't want her putting one life on hold because one day she would inherit another. I didn't want her to be that lazy. As it is, she became an accomplished art critic and portrait painter. You do know I followed her career every day?'

'You've been far too keen to keep everything to yourself. You've been that selfish.'

Lord Hart stared at the dog on the chair.

'They say absence makes the heart grow fonder but they don't talk of the heartache, they never imagine the consequences or choices that follow on.'

'At the end, Lizzie spoke of this place in a way that suggested she feared it, but not once did I hear her blame her father.'

'Lizzie might not have lived here after the age of seven but this was always where she belonged, body and soul.'

'No, yeah, I don't know.'

'As I said, Coberley Hall is where she came into the world, Colin. Her life began in the countess's room.'

'That explains one fucking thing at least,' I said ungraciously.

'What's that, old chap?'

'As Lizzie lay dying she was forever alluding to someone she called the countess. She was back in the room where she was born, I suppose.'

My host chewed one arm of his shades very slowly and carefully.

'Is it not wonderful to think that she wandered happily here on this very spot? She and Lizzie.'

'That her friend?'

'She called her Lucy.'

'Lucy who?'

'Didn't I say? She's the chatelaine, she's Countess of Downe and rightful owner of Coberley Hall.'

'You mean she once was, centuries ago.'

'I'm sorry, I don't know what I'm saying.'

'You seem to confuse Lucy with Lizzie.'

'It isn't always true that the people who have died or passed through a place haunt it the most, Colin, it can be the non-existence or want of something still felt by the living. That's what makes a house like this so special. Lizzie could have visited us if she'd wanted to. I wouldn't have stopped her. That's a fact.'

'Which is what I find so odd. What daughter doesn't want to be with her father, no matter what?'

'Why should you worry, old chap? You're the one who wished her dead. Are you even willing to talk terms?'

I threw down my poker before it grew too hot in the fire.

'Forget all that for the moment, I'm asking you if Coberley Hall has a bad past?'

'You and I like to call it the past, Colin. We say our prime is past or talk of a person's past life. Once upon a time people spoke of a woman with a past as though it wouldn't bear inquiry. But really 'before' and 'now' are not so different, they're like two sides of the same coin. For everything that is put away and buried there is room afterwards for doubt, don't you think? The unresolved walks with us.'

'Walks?' I queried nervously.

'Is it not our worst bogy man?'

'The past dies with the dead, I know it.'

'Be honest, Colin, you'd like your wife back. Would you?'

'Let's begin with the farm's accounts, shall we? If I'm to own this estate I might as well know the worst before I get started.'

At which Lord Hart propelled himself quickly at the door. Before riding off to some obscure part of the house from which I was to be firmly excluded, he spoke once more over his shoulder.

'You'll find most of what you want in the library. One other thing, Colin, do you believe in mediums, at all?'

'In a word, no. I've tried.'

*

Left to myself I paced awhile up and down feeling chilly on the room's grubby boards. Tall pilasters ran from floor to ceiling and divided up the walls into neat little bays that contained each of the Senses. Before I knew it, I had arrived at a place on the panelling where one painting looked very different against all the decorative squares and octagons. How I had not noticed it before I had no idea, but unlike the others ODORATVS did not turn her tense black eyes my way. Within her more intricately stencilled picture frame of petals and foliage, she was totally resolved not to be distracted from the bouquet that she was busy arranging in a small stripy vase.

Not for long could I resist her resistance. With heightened sensibility to my surroundings, I smelt the sudden scent of violets.

A whole lifetime flashed by me, I could not shake off my feeling of complete fixation with such a perfume. My soul did its best to pass out of my body.

I was in danger of floating…

It wasn't my life but Lizzie's.

Not floating, but flying.

I felt raised up. Violets had been my wife's favourite perfume. I was standing where she had once stood as a child and gazed at the painting perhaps for the first time. I felt her rapture for oils, if not her artistic inspiration. It was like revisiting the life-changing moment that had decided her whole future.

I shook my head and the vertigo faded. I rushed to sit down. Suddenly the agitated greyhound left its place by the fire and ran past my legs to the wall where it nuzzled frantically at the base of the thick oak panelling.

Clearly, it had detected a rat or mouse.

Instead it whined as if for someone.

It was not Lord Hart. I could hear him banging about in his wheelchair in the room next door.

I shooed the stupid animal away. Still it would sniff at the almost indiscernible crack in the wainscot. If I hadn't known better, I would have said that the silly thing would have me believe that someone had just passed by on the other side.

11

So lonely and peaceful seemed the house suddenly, so empty of my fellow human beings, so stale, sad and uncared-for the rooms, that I found myself coming to appreciate it like some strange afterthought.

I picked my way over fresh birds' droppings to arrive at the three-clawed, hermaphrodite sea-gods that guarded the door jambs in front of me. Back in the second-hand bookshop in Brighton, I had read alone in dark corners both enduringly and secretly. That way, I had tried to stay in my stepfather's good books by becoming invisible, but in his opinion it hardly mattered whether I lost myself in this world or the next because the death of my mother had left him both unwilling and unable to cope with the living.

It had been so long since I had breathed the rich smell of old leather and paper that I felt both nauseated and ecstatic.

'What the hell,' I cried and marched in as far as a silvered mirror above the fireplace.

Even a house that had been left as high and dry as this one by the current of events still had a heart or soul of sorts, I fancied. Framing Gothic alcoves and arches, lancets and trefoils were patterned by crisp pale marquetry that glowed like threads of gold. Here lay the legacy of personal choices and the result was both social and monastic. You could tell how much somebody had loved the world by what they left behind on their sagging shelves.

Otherwise things didn't look too promising. Heaped high on the table were disgusting piles of letters, bills and receipts that had begun to moulder. I could contend with my disgust at the dead flies but not all the muddle.

Had there to be some selfish reason why Lizzie had refused to tell me about Coberley Hall sooner? If so, in here I could perhaps unravel the mystery?

Frankly, the wretched room was less library than store or Evidence Room, that all-important depository for vital maps and papers that detailed the history of an English manor house. No one sat here reading books for pleasure. On the contrary, the totally inadequate fireplace had always been designed to discourage anyone from lingering.

Pretty much.

There was nothing like an inheritance to spur on a man in his inglorious intentions. Next minute the frisson of fear on my skin grew doubly prickly and chilly, I felt it freeze my fingers as I touched upon such delights as maps of the pasturage at Pinswell, the two farms at the nearby village of Upper Coberley, the Rectory in Coberley itself, its mill and land at Ullenwood.

I unfurled the document with exceptional distaste, then with curiosity. At the bottom of its very long greasy page that was every bit of three feet wide, several blobs of ugly red wax represented different seals, I noted. An odd shakiness spread through my body. Whereas, at its top, one red-edged page began THIS INDENTURE in elaborate script, another was headed LAND, being that portion consisting of Coberley Hall and farms 'brought to the 2nd Earl of Downe by way of his marriage'.

I felt sure I could count on the documents' veracity. After sorting rolls randomly by eye for a time, I estimated that I had before me papers relating to every signatory to the estate since the earl had sold up in 1657 to go travelling in Europe.

Which was all very well but every subsequent purchaser, whether they were the families of Castelman, Elwes or Phelps had had their names stabbed and blotted from the proofs of ownership. That was only part of it. When I held up the deeds' thick waxy papers to the mullioned window the winter light pierced sweeping cuts made with knife or fingernails. In places, someone had slashed paper like flesh off bone.

Frankly, the alterations looked like an attempt to abate someone's furious temper.

My hand travelled hurriedly back to the Boundary Book. There I traced the limits of fields, woods and tracks that had once been so much more extensive until I could see how someone might hanker after things they still considered to be theirs from long ago. In the pursuit of this adulteration, in the obliteration of successive ownership, Joseph Jones's name had been scratched through as well.

Whoever the perpetrator, they had altered things back to the way they had been in November 1638 when John Dutton of Sherbourne had first given Coberley Hall as a dowry to his daughter Lucy.

*

I was still asking myself why anyone would want to reverse three hundred and seventy-odd years of history when James came in with my tray of hot chocolate and biscuits.

'Thanks,' I said, clearing a space among the papers with a careless swipe of my knuckles. 'Do us both good to see this room a bit tidier. Definitely.'

'His lordship's father was the last to use this library, sir. He did a lot of research into the 1640's.'

'You know who vandalised these papers?'

James's response was to resume his errands with a shake of his skull.

'Perhaps you should get rid of that greyhound, sir?'

'Perhaps I should.'

*

The stimulating effect of the chocolate served to heighten my dream-like senses, I seemed to float with the strange, heady aroma of what I was drinking.

Whereas most of the library was a wreck, its shelves were exceptionally tidy and orderly. Protruding from many of the books, pieces of paper marked places like flags, I realised. When somebody recorded their search for something that methodically they did more than mark their progress from volume to volume, they left a trail that could be followed.

I pulled a book at random from the closest shelf and it proved to be a gruesome Jacobean revenge tragedy entitled 'The Duchess of Malfi' by John Webster. But the moment I read beyond its title-page a seething, living mass erupted in my hands – a plague of worms, no less, invisible to the naked eye at first, but scuttling and scurrying through my fingers, I fancied. I shut the book and they were gone – reopened it and they grew still livelier.

'The rottenness of it all!' I thought and put the play back on the shelf.

With my cordial I came to my senses. In its peculiar aftertaste of grated chocolate, vanilla and spices I detected an aromatized and sweetened cordial designed to stimulate the heart and mind like a medicine. I was drinking a concoction that had been grated and whisked with eggs in the way people had mixed hot chocolate after it was first shipped via Spain to England from Mexico. I was savouring the same bitter-sweet tang that this Hall's inhabitants had in the 1650's.

In my relief, my eyes settled this time on an album lying by itself on a chest of drawers. Inside it were carefully penned references to ancient newspapers whose stories were copied from contemporary accounts of the English Civil War. Our history sleuth had pasted together in a big scrapbook the reminiscences from various Parliamentarian commanders. One such account was a **Copy of another Letter from Lieutenant-Collonell Massey's Leaguer, London. 1644:**

'Here, in three hours' space, this Battel was extreme hot, where with furze faggots we were forced to set fire to a Gatehouse before we could get betwixt the court and the house, and then our men stormed and entered the breach and came to the hall porch and plied the windows so hard with culverins, that the enemy durst not appear except in the high rooms. But while they were thus busied, Captaine Digby and divers men did still make hot at us with great resolution from the Gatehouse where they were very profuse of their powder, until our grenadiers with scaling ladders did endeavour to fire the upper story, but without any touch of it they were forced to breach open the door with iron bars. Then assailing with their pistols they did do their utmost to vanquish the papists that were within, who although they knew they could not subsist, shot from out of all the doors and windows, but after all their bravadoes came meanly off. Captaine Digby did behave himself very gallantly, and was shot in the mouth, had one or two shot more, and had his legs shot under him.

'But Countess Lucy then crying shame that our soldiers were without mercy and complaining that she were betrayed, came to me that she might bind Captaine Digby's wounds lest he die forthwith, but I bid her leave us upon pain of death, that we would take the captaine with us in to Gloucester. But still she came after us with great treaty that he have his life spared. So little did she fear what the enemy could do against her that her love or grief cannot but work remorse and regret, and she cried out "God damne you" while we did drag the dead and wounded away when in heat one soldier did cut her greyhound's eye out and some other, the countess herself very narrowly escaping.'

No one spent hours sifting through the first ever printed newspapers to reassemble the gruesome horrors of war without some very good reason. They had to believe that what had gone before had some bearing on the hereafter.

*

That evening I sat at the high table in the cold, cavernous great hall while the painted Cavalier eyed me attentively from his lonely portrait. Having drawn his rat-coloured cloak tighter at his silver lace collar, he shot me sidelong glances that verged on the knowing. I had to fight off the feeling that simply by keeping him company I was inviting the occurrence of some awful personal injury or general disaster.

Inscribed on a plate at the base of the picture were a few words, I noticed:

As we are so shall ye be.

Now I had always been drawn to those macabre, if absurdly decorated, medieval chapels on top of whose tombs lay the perfect effigies of gilt metal knights complete with their scabbards and armour. Better still, below them were carved their other parallel selves but naked and nibbled by rats and worms, all lovingly chiselled.

With only my torch and books for relief, I had, hiding out as a boy in the bookshop in Brighton, found hope in hallucination and meditation brought on by hunger. I had swung from suffocation to ecstasy with the aid of my magnificent pictures of gaudy Gothic vaults and graves. Not until someone learnt to suspend one life could he look to another.

I pricked up my ears but the Cavalier's lips no longer spoke to me through their paint and varnish. In fact, the words penned on the plate below him came from a Medieval folktale whose riddle I had read long ago and whose story was entirely explicable: one day three rich lords travelling along a lonely road met three dead men who were their futures. No, really, it didn't explain a thing.

*

Afterwards, my disobedient greyhound followed me up to my bedroom, though I would have said for certain that I had closed the dog-gate at the foot of the stairs behind me.

From the end of my bed the wily sight-hound spied on me as I prepared for another cold, sleepless night ahead. My brazen stalker was not the slightest bit bothered by my reluctance to sleep lest I dreamt myself back to my wife's deathbed.

Day 9. March 31. 2014.

Looking very sick. Pain particularly bad today. In and out of consciousness. The poison continues to work at snail's pace.

I can barely make out what Lizzie says because she is as good as delirious.

Or dreaming.

'Hers is a sad face.'

'Why sad?' I ask.

'I can't say. It just is.'

No longer in a room with her own TV she is now back on the ward: Red Bay. Bed 8.

Stomach very swollen but it goes down immediately with more drugs administered while I am present.

Lucid, suddenly.

'Don't look now, Colin, but that woman in the bed opposite is 92.'

That's when I ask her again.

'Whose is the sad face you keep dreaming?'

'That'll be my friend.'

'According to the nurses, it's a recurring nightmare.'

'Long ago she had a daughter like me called Elizabeth.'

'Shush, Lizzie. Get some rest.'

'But she says she doesn't like to see me suffering.'

'Don't worry, none of it's real.'

'Then why does she want me to go with her?'

Hospital still a maze to me. Try taking the lift. Get lost. Is it left or right? Two nurses tell me left. Get there and it's right. Laughter all round since they actually work there.

I'll go out another, quicker way next time by the stairs.

That CT scan will almost certainly reveal the truth I'm dreading.

*

I woke up gasping for breath, to find that my canine attendant had crept much closer up my chest. Now he was peering into my face, watching and whining. His single iris burned as blue as brimstone. Meanwhile his other mysterious, stone eye remained totally unfathomable like a section of blank wall or canvas.

Never did like pets, particularly. But Lizzie did. Once she adopted a stray dog and placed food for it on our front doorstep in Clapham.

That might have been a greyhound, too.

I walked to the window and looked down on the formal front gardens. James was busy extinguishing the candles that lit little pointed stone niches set into the walls. He did it with frequent looks over his shoulder. I very much wondered whether, in removing all the attempts at some sort of vigil, he intended to forestall the perturbing consequences of someone else's actual rendezvous? I truly did not yet know, I literally didn't.

Therein lay another riddle. I could puzzle over things seen, yet see no end to my puzzlement. For what dire purpose would someone dare to keep doubt at bay but hope alive in their own sad heart, anyway? What lies? Who met at night with whom?

It wouldn't be until tomorrow that I had the slightest inkling.

12

At first light, with no definite belief that I was yet fully awake but with a sound in my ears that I couldn't positively identify, I jumped out of bed in a hurry to listen.

Doors slammed elsewhere in the house, the air growing smokier and sootier.

But that told me little. I blinked my leaden eyelids and clinched both fists to banish what I was convinced was still a dream. Instead, from room to room a dreadful cacophony of springs, weights and wheels burst into motion. All the house's roundhead and drop-case clocks began to strike with a clangorous disharmony of ghastly dings and dongs. I clamped my hands to my ears but the clanging left all my internal organs jangled.

That scream again.

Hurrying to my window, I scraped at the ice that had, overnight, fogged its panes. Still was I left in something of a quandary. When a man chose to throw his own household into total chaos then he had to be so inconsiderate as to constitute a real nuisance. Someone stood in the snowy courtyard directly below me, I realised.

Suddenly he fell as if hit, with a moan. It was Lord Hart.

'Look here, James! Footprints! Did that fool Walker leave the gatehouse open last night?'

Of my own shout he made nothing.

A sallow-faced James gathered up a Panama from the ground.

'You told me not to give him any keys, m'lord.'

'Someone did. Somebody let them in.'

'If his lordship will only go back inside?'

'Fetch Walker! This minute!'

When someone was that hell-bent on waking another with his ludicrous yells, when he half scared me to death by straining his larynx to breaking point in such cold air, it was a bit much to hear him try to place the blame on me.

'So what does he, like, expect me to do, then?' I demanded.

James and I met at the dog-gate at the foot of the stairs.

'This way, please, Mr Walker. His lordship wants you urgently.'

'Is there a fire or something?'

'Not a fire, sir. There has been an incident.'

'What incident?'

'You'll soon see, sir.'

7 a.m. stopped its appalling ding-dong. That was the marvellous thing about Coberley Hall: the chimes of its clockwork monsters all came together in one great crescendo and echo afterwards.

*

Nothing could have prepared me for the unexpected outburst of emotion with which Lord Hart greeted me in the entrance hall.

'Colin, thank God. Has James told you? We have a prowler, the devil we have.'

'So how do you know? They steal something?'

'On the contrary, old chap, they've left us something.'

'Where?'

He broke into a fresh litany of complaint, waving his dragon cane at the porch in furious pantomime.

I paid no real attention, nor did I believe him.

'Or maybe the fact that we will all freeze to death with the door wide open should tell us something?'

'Go see for yourself, Walker. Believe me, it's not pretty.'

'That bad, eh?'

Pinching the collar of my coat at my chin, I marched through the door's ancient archway. Lying on the doorstep was a severed head, I discovered. Obnoxious pink and red pieces of tough fibrous tissue that had once united muscle to bone were now ripped apart, since the neck had been so crudely detached from the body. One eye was a raw, ruptured socket and a large fleshy tongue dangled by a thread out the side of its mouth. Whoever or whatever had hurled the bloody remains at the door had done so with considerable venom. The eye bled all the way down the door.

It was the head off a stag. I gave the branched, horny antlers a desultory tap with my toe.

'This someone's idea of a sick joke?'

'It's worse than that,' replied Lord Hart. 'It's more sacrilege than sacrifice.'

'Doesn't mean we should lose our own heads over it.'

His gaze met mine. Some indirect meaning passed between us. I was left with the distinct impression that I was an idiot if I thought that what had just happened was some commonplace prank.

'Mr Walker and I can do a tour of the house and make sure everything is secure,' said James helpfully.

'No time! Hand him my shotgun.'

'You serious?' I said.

James straightened the Panama on Lord Hart's head. 'Let me call Rebecca. She'll know what to do.'

'Damn it, James, I don't need any more nursing. I know what this means, the devil I do. I saw someone from my bedroom window.'

'Are you quite certain it wasn't another hallucination?'

'Do stop going on about those!'

James glanced my way and narrowed his eyebrows. For all the frantic whispering, he would not have me hear what his master professed to have witnessed. He did not want me to know things I should not in a seemingly absurd cross-examination of his story.

'But surely you can't want Mr Walker to venture out so early on such a morning?'

'How else will we know anything for certain?'

James secured the shotgun in his grasp.

'If you're absolutely sure that you are not sending him on a wild goose chase?'

'Damn it, man, this head is no joke, it's a declaration of war.'

*

Soon after, a rider trotted a horse into the yard.

'This him? This our sheriff?'

'He's the one, the devil he is,' said Lord Hart. 'Gemma, meet DI Colin Walker.'

With that, the grey-haired groom slid down to the ground and stood there holding the reins. There was a gap in her upper jaw where there should have been molars.

'Met Sara in the lane. Came at once. You ride, Inspector?'

Rolling my hand with distaste over the animal's heavy black nose, I let him lick my hand with his wet rubbery tongue. It was like being washed by a gigantic, beslavering bloodhound.

'I once rode a donkey on the beach at Brighton.'

The cob returned my look and it was dark and deep and utterly desolate.

Gemma smeared a filthy hand down her thigh while she chewed gum.

'Those shoes you're wearing aren't very suitable.'

'H'm, well, no, I guess not. Then again, I'm only here to decide what best to do with Coberley Hall…'

'James, fetch my brother's riding boots,' cried Lord Hart. 'Get going, Colin, before any more snow falls and takes the trail with it.'

'Who says I'm going?'

'Don't worry,' said Gemma, altering the stirrup for me. 'You're the same build as Philip.'

'Philip? How come?'

'Didn't they tell you? This was his horse Sir Percival.'

So snug a fit did the boots prove, so right against my calves that they could have been made for me. Meanwhile, Sir Percival stood fidgeting by the stone mounting block in the yard, so eager was he to resume his ride out.

Even so, I made a great show of checking the saddle's girth before I struggled to climb on.

'Drop the gun in the holster at the front of your saddle,' said Lord Hart, getting me to fill my pocket with cartridges. 'It's a relief, in situations like this, to know that we have someone we can turn to.'

'So please, can you tell me who or what is suddenly our enemy?'

'You worried?'

'Don't fret, I'm trained to use firearms.'

James passed me the shotgun.

'Not that,' said Lord Hart, 'Sir Percival. My brother knew exactly how to keep him on the bit so you must ride with a light hand.'

I scowled. The great silver arms of my mount's tack in his mouth, complete with their interlaced rings of curb chain, chinked under his chin like armour. I scratched his unnecessarily enormous ears.

'It'll never happen but I'd better make the effort, hadn't I? Did you know that Lizzie wanted to keep horses?'

'Planned to come back after all, did she?' said Gemma.

'I beg your pardon?'

'Sorry, Inspector, but you're the subject of much gossip in the village.'

'Well, go on then,' said Lord Hart. 'Don't waste any more time. He's getting away.'

'You could be him on that horse,' said Gemma, whistling at me like a kettle. 'You could be Philip come back from the grave. He loved that horse to death, that he did.'

'Shut up, you old witch,' said Lord Hart. 'You don't know what you say.'

*

Only a fool would put on a bold front simply to satisfy his newfound friends, only an idiot would pretend that he was naturally courageous as he rode through the porte-cochere from one courtyard to another on such a nebulous mission. A man like me should at least keep up his display of sang-froid and not break into a total sweat before he was safely out of sight of all witnesses.

More muleteer than Cavalier, I coaxed Sir Percival's bulging sides with my heels and set off at a miraculous trot after a touch with my crop. I did my best to emulate a dead man's skills.

*

Somehow it was all down to me to track the prowler, except Lord Hart could not or would not give his suspect a name. I sympathised. That head on the doorstep was an insult to the man, a violation of his property, a blasphemy against everything decent and good.

Full of bravado, I rode along in search of footprints. In the bitter morning I dug my gloves from my coat and pulled them on one by one, but still a reptilian chill flowed through my blood. This coldness was not the general dislike, even aversion, to the chilly house that had so got the better of me last night but another, more specific resentment. Others might have called it a preposterous imposition.

13

In the otherwise virgin snow a thin line of footprints formed a dark and ragged row of holes. I could hardly explain it, but the black trail appeared profoundly lost in the white landscape, which made me feel alone, too. I felt like I had when I had bunked off from school because I had been too fearful to show anyone my burns and bruises. As my horse and I stumped along under a sky the colour of pewter, I kept glancing over my shoulder, relived my past like that of some frightful absconder.

'It's not my place to be a vigilante,' I remarked aloud.

Once hunted myself, I was loath to hunt.

There was little sign of life at Slack's Cottage and I didn't stop to inquire. When a man rode shotgun for somebody else he had best keep his business to himself.

Now and again I leaned low off my saddle. Where the ground had cracked and crumbled, the tell-tale indentations grew long and broad, even massive. Somebody had stopped here to empty a stone from their boot but the bare foot was so big it was truly bear-like.

'Yeah, yeah, it's just a bit trampled,' I thought and smiled at the harmlessness of snow.

Meanwhile far above me, jackdaws joined rooks and crows in the treetops by the hundred. Those pompous lovers of carrion posed like sooty fruit on the highest branches. I very much refused to feel that to ignore them was to deserve some grievous disaster or deadly misfortune.

Suddenly there rose from the wood's black heart a prolonged and plaintive cry. It came from beyond the edge of darkness and obscurity. So stricken was the sound, so painful and soulless and yet so ambiguous, that it filled my ears with a melancholic wail of regret that could have been man or brute. My response was to hurry along the wire mesh fence on my left flank. There, storm poles and stakes reinforced an impressive defensive work that cut one half of the wood from the other. Soon I was inside a great pen, in a dark, intensely private place where game-birds could congregate in large numbers at galvanized feeders that resembled enormous metal mushrooms.

A moment later, Sir Percival dug in his heels.

The more I tightened my grip on the reins, the more he shot backwards.

Then I saw why. Leaning against his Land Rover stood a stocky man who held fast to a leggy, black and white spotted pointer by his collar.

Piled in the truck's open back were bags of corn.

'You hurt, at all?' I shouted.

At first he barely moved, only continued to stare wildly into space. The entire bottom half of his best quality tweed jacket hung in tatters. Something had clawed holes in its white lining in spectacular fashion.

His brown eyes blazed at me.

'Who wants to know?'

I looked into his face and saw the utter exhaustion that came with unreasoning horror.

'My name is Colin Walker.'

'Doesn't explain why you're on Lord Hart's horse.'

'Doesn't explain why you're all bloody.'

He wiped his short grey hair with his hand, which made his scalp redder.

'I'm Peter Slater. I manage the shoots round here. Come carefully, or you might get caught up, too.'

But Sir Percival tossed his head, rolled his upper lip and snorted loudly. He would barely go another pace despite all my efforts.

Why he wouldn't move soon became very clear. Suspended above the blood-stained snow hung a fearsome sight, I observed. It was a man. His hair had that wild dishevelled look which could have belonged to a scarecrow, but was actually more representative of sudden abject fear. Both his socks had turned red where his boots had gone missing. He'd not long been killed.

I leaned off my saddle and spat violently.

Peter kept hold of his dog which was going mad.

'Steady Prince. Heel.'

I chanced a second look at the corpse. Mostly bald but with a very black beard, the flesh and blood bugbear did not look more than forty. The wound in his neck was still bleeding him dry. As a result, his flesh turned grey and papery. Vomit slimed his mottled green and brown camouflaged jacket and trousers. Where he had been pinned violently against the tree the circulatory shock had popped both his eyes like corks from their sockets. Much as a suicide would defecate at the end of a noose in their moment of death, so this unfortunate wretch had evacuated his bowels in one last humiliating human function.

I wiped my mouth on the back of my glove.

'Who is he? Do we know?'

'His name is Sullivan O'Leary.'

'What in heaven's name do you think happened here?'

Peter averted his gaze to the wall of dark trees, stared long and hard into their wider shadows.

'Ran right into his own trap, I reckon.'

It was true that the dead man had kicked a stick out of its slot that had triggered a branch bent back under tension. Stakes had shot through his neck and groin and left him dangling. But honestly, I found it hard to believe my own eyes. The resemblance to a butcher's carcass was ghastly. His belly was a raw, bloody slit from which the first portion of his small intestine had been torn immediately below his stomach. The spears that had clawed him open had not just performed some savage enterotomy but a terrible Caesarean. He had been made to give birth to his own guts.

'But from what was he running?' I asked.

My craggy-faced companion held on to Prince for dear life as some sort of comfort.

'Sometimes you find dogs running wild in these woods after they come up from town.'

I glanced at his pointer but it was hard to believe that any dog could be so violent, except to his jacket.

Looking round, I observed something else.

'See that? The trap is still baited.'

Peter drew madly on his cigarette and squinted at me through its cloud of blue smoke. He fidgeted like someone anxious to prevaricate.

'Maybe he used meat to catch wild boar? Perhaps that's what tore off his clothes?'

'Well, h'm, but is that likely?'

'Boar have been seen eating sheep in other parts of the county. Mostly they scavenge on road-kill, but very rarely have they been known to attack people with dogs.'

'Poor fellow. But is he my prowler,' I asked, 'because someone dumped a stag's head on Lord Hart's doorstep this morning. Naturally, we want to know who. Footprints brought me this far.'

'Some might say that's what poachers do in a quarrel.'

'Would you?'

'Who poaches people? O'Leary and his lordship haven't seen eye to eye ever since he was caught selling deer carcases for a hundred pounds a time to local restaurants.'

'So I've heard.'

'Then you'll know he was not a good person.'

'Well, I suppose his dispute is my dispute now. Worse luck. I'm the new owner of this estate.'

I leaned low to offer him my hand. He extended his long, thin neck tortoise-fashion as he raised his chin from the woolly rim of his Arran sweater. Blowing smoke between us, he clasped his bloody fingers on my glove. Really, by now I was in urgent need of a cigarette myself.

'You that lawman everyone's talking about?'

'In a way, yeah.'

'Sorry we had to meet in such adverse circumstances.'

As it was, O'Leary's skewered face pointed impossibly skywards. His mouth gaped after occasional snowflakes with parched blood-caked lips as though he were terribly thirsty.

'Hadn't we, you know, better lift the poor bastard down.'

'I think we ought not to touch him,' replied Peter.

'On second thoughts, leave me out of it. Honestly, I was never here. No, really, I wasn't. Right now, I don't wish to be involved in something so hideously accidental. I'm leaving tomorrow, anyway.'

Peter ignored my hurried protest.

'You looking for something?' I asked, swallowing hard.

'His hat. He always wore a big green hat with a feather trim, but I can't see it anywhere.'

'Did O'Leary say anything before he died?'

'He muttered something about meeting the Devil.'

With that, I left Peter to ring for help on his phone. When a man had bad news to deliver he had best get safely away before any more trouble.

*

'Sullivan O'Leary!'

The colour drained from Lord Hart's cheeks. If he was disinclined to believe me at first, it wasn't for want of evidence.

'I believe I can say without a shadow of doubt that O'Leary was your intruder,' I repeated, even as I propped my gun by the fire in the great hall. 'Clearly he bore you a grudge. That trap might have been meant for you?'

I pulled off my black gloves and unbuttoned my coat. After the icy woods, the flames felt almost too hot on my dead white fingers. At that moment I saw blacken the mullioned windows the querulous darkness which had pursued me all the way from Chatcombe wood. The shadows scratched at the leaded panes as I delivered my verdict. It was the jackdaws again.

'You meet anyone else?' asked Lord Hart anxiously.

I told him what I thought. About the wild boar, too. To which he said nothing at first, only sank lower in his chair with a brooding, unsettled frame of mind. He stared at the fire like a man afraid to trust his own decision.

'Post warnings all over the village. Tell people that something wild is loose in the woods. No one is to take any more stupid chances.'

*

If I deliberately went in the wrong direction when the police arrived, it was because I wanted to know how our trespasser had eluded notice quite so easily.

Frozen footprints led left through the graveyard to a slab of marble. Inscribed upon it in gold letters were a few words:

Treasured memories of Philip Jones 14.10.1964 - 21.11.2012. Aged 48.

**Let Fate Do Her Worst. There Are Moments of Joy, Bright Dreams Of
The Past, Which SHE Cannot Destroy.**

Whereas moles had left little mounds of earth elsewhere in the graveyard, here I found a whole tumult of subterranean activity had risen to the surface. Globules of light brown soil sat piled in little heaps on the grave where its contents had been turned inside out.

Nearby, two other headstones had been kicked clear of snow. Both **Sally Jones 10.1.1937 – 7.5.1981 and Joseph Jones 8.2.1917 – 13.8.1982** had seen snow scratched from their inscriptions by someone's claw-like fingers.

If nothing else, our visitor had done their best to call into question the dead's right to some well-earned repose.

*

Soon the icy wind froze the tip of my nose. How it was that the countryside in winter was so much less bearable than the city, I hardly knew. And to think, a brolly had once sufficed. Loud in my head was Sara's insufferable caterwauling. I'd had to sit her down in the kitchen, since Lord Hart had refused point blank to tell her about her father's demise. Now no one appeared on the winding narrow road or looked out of the school.

It was, I had to remind myself, still the Christmas holidays.

Nor, as far as I knew, had there been any reports of a big cat or bear escaping from a circus or zoo. It begged the question of what had really befallen O'Leary in the woods. Of what he had been up to I had no real clue.

Otherwise nothing outwardly looked very different. A fussy little plaque on the wall of Yew Tree Cottage in the centre of the village boasted that it had once been its bake-house and laundry. At the far edge of habitation, a diesel generator throbbed somewhere among the sheds of Dowman's Farm. Suddenly a dark-haired man who looked very Italian crossed the filthy yard on his way to a tractor. As he did so, he shouted me a loud 'good morning'. A moment later a police helicopter skimmed the trees with a most appalling clatter. Its searchlight was tracking the edges of the fields most diligently.

Otherwise, to my own dubious progress it appeared indifferent.

Reassured, I returned the same way I had come, but after the farm I turned right down a very steep hill to cross and re-cross the little river Churn. Beyond lay Close Farm. By now I had left only a few posters to distribute. I left the swollen stream behind me and progressed back up the road. With its elegant Palladian portico set behind its high garden walls, the rectory was up for sale, its itinerant rector no doubt administering to an enlarged benefice to save money.

'Now that an uncertain state of affairs has arisen there ought to be someone on hand to calm people's feeling of shock and awe,' I told myself. 'They ought not to be left alone to disbelieve or suspect the very basis of their lives without some spiritual guardian in the aftermath of such a terrible scare. They should not be forced to admit without his help the most unsettling possibilities imaginable.'

I seriously wondered whether or not to tear down my poster from the gate. I could justify my role of alarmist neighbour, but not of panic-monger. To credit the unknown with too much credence was to give monsters the benefit of the doubt.

Suddenly my phone bleeped in my pocket. The call came as a shock. Yet, wrong was I not and most clearly did I have a signal.

It was DC Jan Shriver, back at the office in London.

'Great night! You should have been there. WHERE WERE YOU?'

'Have patience,' I promised her. 'I will get back to you just as quickly as I can.'

Any sooner, and it was like asking a drowned man to fill his lungs.

*

Upon returning downhill towards Coberley Hall, I retraced my footprints in the snow. Behind me, the empty road led back past the metal ring on the post office wall once used to tether horses. Except now on the white ground my black prints appeared to stretch forever into the distance. For days I might have been travelling, without sun or moon. The village I had chosen looked literally devoid of all habitation. A great tiredness overcame me, not because I was footsore or hungry but because my own flesh and blood felt such a burden.

The abrupt realisation was unfamiliar. I stared down at my feet again to see my shadow mimic me with its thin, bony progress. With wasted arms and legs, with hideously distorted fingers which were so misshapen and wrinkled, it aped my every action with one of its own. Yet its chin was shaggy like a beast's and from its open mouth protruded fangs, but being mere shadow there were no eyes. Despite it being such a black, formless thing, it pursued me with exultant, greedy malevolence. It would drag me down, if it could, as if I were the right prey for such a great bloodthirsty animal. A certain intelligence in its black mass saw it seek to claw at what remained of my desire for life.

Furious at my brief feeling of unbelief, I was glad I had my shotgun to hand.

14

On top of a tomb in a quiet corner of Coberley Church of St Giles lay the full-size effigy of Sir Thomas de Berkeley, next to his recumbent wife. Although his chainmail and armour were a grim stony white, as were Lady Joan's wimple, hood and gown, to see the dead retain their features in their chiselled faces was vaguely disconcerting. The day was one week after Sullivan O'Leary's insufferable end, but that's where any similarity between knight and poacher ceased.

'Well, go on then,' Lord Hart urged us, leaning heavily on his cane. 'Set the bastard down.'

'Doesn't look as if he'll be much missed,' I hissed, glancing through the side chapel's pointed arches.

Most pews were deserted.

Fact was, I had fully intended to leave for London days ago when George went out of his way to convince me that, because I was now in effect the new lord of the manor, it was only right and proper that I stay on long enough to be seen to observe the barest of obsequies on my first appearance in public.

I helped shunt the coffin across the floor with a kick. When one man buried another he ought not to feel such a fraud in his borrowed black clothes, he ought not to strut about in his complimentary mourning like some sort of actor. I was dressed in more attire left behind by his lordship's lost brother Philip. Actually, the look of the dead suited me rather well.

*

Of course O'Leary's fate was a terrible tragedy, but what was a man to feel?

Even as I ostentatiously massaged my sore shoulder, the three other pallbearers seemed to think me unsympathetic.

But what should I have said after such an accident?

Meanwhile, Lord Hart led the rector to one side in the South

Chapel.

'I'm afraid, George, that I consider it most improper.'

'Proper or not, Canon Lacey, it must be done.'

'But how does that fit in with today's service?'

I began to feel that simply by being present I was hindering some repugnant plan.

Really, a burial was best done in a hurry.

But what mattered my obstreperousness to them?

Grumbling to himself, Canon Lacey bent over an odd little quatrefoil window. He crouched down rather stiffly to the cusped tracery of its unglazed, square hole that ran right through the limestone wall almost at floor level and made a very draughty exit to the outside world. Visible were the broken pins for the hinges where a door had once secured its missing contents. I did question why he saw fit to draw a hand bell from his robes, but once more was I subjected to a prim and sullen silence as I saw him proceed.

When a man's poor reputation went before him he could but bask in its afterglow.

'You do realise this bell was last used for mass hundreds of years ago,' said Canon Lacey. 'It belongs to the old religion.'

Lord Hart twice tapped his dragon cane hard on the floor.

'Doesn't mean you can't ring it now.'

'But it's an old sanctus bell.'

'It's a blessing, in a way, that you still have it.'

'I shan't answer for the consequences.'

'Damn it, man, I'll do it myself, the devil I will.'

With that, Canon Lacey shook the bell vigorously inside the hole in the wall.

Once more, I stepped forward to venture an objection.

Once more I was repulsed most sourly.

So I turned on my heels and took my place in the exceedingly chilly nave. There I tried not to shiver on one of the unpleasantly hard pews. Among half a dozen villagers, Sara sat snivelling in front of me. I passed her my handkerchief, motioned to her to keep quiet, or else.

Whereupon I saw Canon Lacey mount the steps to his very imposing, carved Jacobean pulpit. He would, I hoped, launch into an extempore discourse about the wrongs of someone who had thought they could get away with getting up to no good. I fully expected a fulsome spiritual condemnation of the wretch who had tried to poach my deer with such illicit and unsportsmanlike methods. I expected him to make up for the fact I wasn't already in London.

But it did make me shiver to sit so perfectly still, or otherwise put on a big show of respect for a nobody.

Personally, I disagreed that the living had much to say to the dead. That was like suggesting that they could, once the book was closed, favour us with some sort of afterword or forgiveness.

*

At first an unexpectedly tongue-tied Canon stared right over our heads. With resolute, robust yet distinctly defensive determination he addressed not us but those not able to be present.

> 'For the trumpet shall sound and the dead will be raised
> **and we shall all be changed.**
>
> The perishable must be clothed with the imperishable
> **and the mortal must put on immortality.**
>
> We shall not all sleep
> **but we shall be changed.'**

His round fleshy face grew redder and redder. Soon I thought he might faint from some agitated, inner battle that raged in his heart. At one point I saw him dab his white forehead with his sleeve most extravagantly.

His lordship nodded back very promptly.

I could explain the contempt but not the courtesy. For, Canon Lacey made clear that if we did not all pull together today, if we did not raise our voices as one in tuneful harmony, then how could we hope to lift our own spirits, let alone those of the dead? I did attempt to join in, with a few words somewhere between tenor and bass, did try to make the great effort.

Intercession was duly offered where we all replied dutifully *Lord, have mercy*. Then, following the Lord's Prayer, an increasingly agitated rector gabbled The Blessing. We were all keeping the customary time of silence when a young woman rushed up the aisle full of pathetic apologies. Dressed in a long black woollen dress and matching shoes, she set herself down in a pew alongside me. She had hidden most of her striking auburn hair beneath a close fitting black hat but not her fringe, which was ragged. The hat's flaps hid her ears, which given the sudden arctic temperature in the church was no bad thing. Sitting very upright, she exuded an air of irritating and strict virtuosity as she fiddled shiveringly with the white lace cuffs at the end of her sleeves. Then she retied her scarf very fussily, because, after her came the most frightful draught. It blew with the forced blast of a furnace, rushed into the church as if something suddenly rarefied the air from above or behind us.

Sure enough, there was a terrific bang of wood on stone.

'Damn it,' I said. 'You left the door open.'

*

I intended to sit very still, to be a model parishioner, but there I was, staring up at the roof. It did seem to me that the oil lamp above my head began to sway on its long cable from the rafters. Back in use in the absence of any electricity, the heavy brass reservoir full of oil gathered momentum. The wick soon trailed black serpentine smoke from its swinging white glass shade. Other lamps started to do something very similar.

At first I stayed as calm as I could.

'You will not see any reason to call me any less reliable than anyone else,' I thought.

Then the organist played a wrong note. Abruptly, everyone did as I did and turned their heads, we felt the blast of icy air uncoil past the pews in more or less rapid natural motion. It snaked up into the pulpit and blew away the rector's papers. My hymn book, too, opened and shut frantically. The chilly draught did a whistle-stop tour of the side chapel. That gale reared up into the roof where it blew ever more loudly and strongly before descending to snuff out the candles near the ancient communion table.

Few knew what it took me to rush to help pick up the coffin, bear it out of the South Chapel and still maintain a solemn fixed expression.

It was that sudden.

*

As for Lord Hart, he stood firm beside the pulpit, held his dragon cane aloft ready to command the air.

'Show thyself! I dare you!'

Immediately a bell in the tower began to toll.

'For God's sake, no,' shouted Canon Lacey, clasping his hands to his ears and fled through the vestry doors.

For a moment, I and the other hapless pallbearers came to a halt inside the porch.

'Whatever does he mean?' I cried, trying to rebalance the heavy wooden box straight on my shoulder. 'Where on earth has the rector gone to?'

A gap-toothed old man opposite me flashed me his gold fillings.

'Canon Lacey's in the tower.'

'How come?'

'Can't you hear? That's the tenor bell. It was cast in the seventeenth century and is never usually rung.'

'You certain?'

'I was church warden until very recently. You can take my word for it.'

The passing bell jarred my brain with its tuneless, deafening decibels. I heard it wail every time its vicious tongue struck its thick sound-bow.

At long last I dislodged the coffin from the doorway in order to steer a quick path to the graveside. Something else caused me to look up. Winged devils crawled about on hideous claws to hang off each crenelated corner of the bellowing bell tower. Their outsized, hooded eyes bulged at us from beneath their very serious brows while their gaping mouths vomited insults in stone. But they were just harmless gargoyles.

At which point I realised that Lord Hart was no longer with us. Instead, there came a high-pitched cry from elsewhere in the churchyard. This was not that ridiculous display of emotion shown by him in the church a moment ago but a joyous screech of excited disbelief. He was staring at his brother's violated grave, I observed.

It fell to Peter to rush over to comfort him.

Personally, I heard nothing beyond the word 'miracle'.

Then Canon Lacey returned at a brisk trot, even as the bell slowed to a more uniform stroke like a clock. Next, it stopped ringing entirely.

'Thank God,' I said to the warden. 'Much more of that and my nerves might have shattered along with the bell.'

It wasn't that,' corrected the rector. 'Didn't you notice: it was ringing backwards?'

*

The coffin came to rest crookedly in its frozen pit, when I saw Lord Hart depart for the nearby doorway in the wall.

I started after him at once on this, the most direct route back to the Hall.

'Can you please wait, George. We ought to talk.'

He leaned on his stick but kept stumbling along.

'Not now, Walker.'

Immediately, James rushed between us, pushing a wheelchair and blanket ready to scoop up his master and transport him indoors. He would have me believe that he had suffered too much to answer the simplest question.

'Where's Rebecca?' asked Lord Hart.

'She ran off to the lake, sir.'

'Go get her, Walker. Tell her to bring me my pills. Tell her it's urgent.'

'Got it.'

That was the trouble with the infirm, I thought, they could so easily use their affliction to their own advantage.

*

Someone was already pushing her rowboat into the water, I discovered. I gave her a wave. It was the young woman who had sat beside me in the church. I was surprised that she did not notice.

'Sorry to intrude,' I lied, 'but I didn't get a chance to properly introduce myself. I'm Detective Inspector Walker.'

'So I've heard tell,' replied Rebecca sourly and pulled off her hat to spill her long fiery hair down her back like lava.

Too late I came to a halt on the bank – she had rowed away from me. In profile her face was leaner than I remembered. She had a very strong jaw line, but her skin was a peculiar papery colour. Here was someone who stayed up too late or, like everyone else in Coberley Hall, never saw sufficient daylight.

'Please, do you have Lord Hart's pills, at all?' I asked.

'What about them?'

'He's having an attack of nerves, on account of the fact that I think he saw someone in the church.'

'Who was it?'

'I don't know.'

Easing her grip on her oars, Rebecca slowed her rowing.

'Is he seeing things now?'

'I don't think so.'

'Then he can wait.'

Tangled weed clawed and clung to her blades. There was definitely something malignant about how such a stagnant jungle could lie just below the surface.

Not that I cared.

'That business of the bell was very odd,' I cried. 'Did you see who rang it?

'It was only the wind in the tower, Inspector.'

'What about you? Are you all right? James said that you ran off suddenly. Or did you see someone, too?'

She paused to select a sweet from a bag in her pocket.

'Go away Mr Walker.'

'Give me the pills and I will.'

'No, I mean leave Coberley Hall, because after today you might not have the strength to do so.'

'Why would I? It is, you know, all mine from now on.'

Rebecca raised her face and her lips parted in a slight smile. Her sea-green eyes fixed mine both cynically and bitterly. Then unexpectedly, her indifference appeared to change more to a concern that I was not listening.

'It's too late for me, Inspector, but you can still keep one foot in the real world.'

'Please, call me Colin.'

'Let his lordship mess with your head and he'll cause you to go down the same path I have. There's something very wrong about Coberley Hall, but you still think that seeing is believing. Don't delay your departure too long.'

'Or maybe the fact that Lord Hart pays you so much to be at his beck and call says it all. I've read your name in the accounts.'

'Place yourself in his shoes. How much would you gamble to bring the dead back from the grave, Mr Walker?'

'You mean his brother?'

For a moment her look spanned the watery divide between us, gave me a dangerous stare in case I was, after all, beyond all hope of prayers or imprecations.

'Let yourself believe what he does, Mr Walker and you'll see and hear things that aren't there, too.'

'Me?'

'You can rely on it.'

'How does that make me different from you?'

'Someone has to help fight what else comes through the door.'

*

Perhaps because Coberley had no pub there was to be no wake, thank goodness. I would not have to play at being everyone's new suzerain over a few embarrassing beers or give some disingenuous tribute to the unrelated dead, after all.

That night I couldn't stop thinking about what Rebecca had told me.

Fact: when someone died they were flesh and bone in the ground or ash in a casket. Fact: who knew where they went after that? The earth dissolved us or a blast of wind blew us wherever it wished into everlasting anonymity. But we could not say for sure where we came from or whether we returned and so it was that Lizzie's face floated back into my head from her afterworld.

Day 8. April 1. 2014.

Sleepy after taking 2 Tramadol. Sick again. Needs liquid protein drinks and vitamins. Otherwise, too weak.

Straight back to hospital to stabilise her regime and give her anti-nausea drug. Doctor: 'We've not been doing our job properly.'

Day 7. April 2. 2014.

Body sicker but mind clearer. Holds my arm. Can't walk far. Afraid she'll vomit again in public.

'I know what she wants, Colin. She's told me.'

'Who?'

'My friend. She says I must go back to where I began.'

'Who is this friend, exactly?'

'I can't say yet. She won't let me.'

'So why does that, like, worry you?'

Again Lizzie's bloodshot eyes look away.

'I don't trust her.'

'Didn't I tell you, she is just a dream?'

'But she looks so lonely.'

'That it?'

'Whatever you do, don't ever ring Coberley Hall's sanctus bell.'

'No, but who would?'

'That bell summoned the lord and lady of the manor to attend mass in church every Sunday. Its rings carry all the way to the house.'

'So why should that matter?'

'Because she'll hear you.'

*

I sat up in bed and looked all about me. My tatty one-eyed greyhound heard it, too. It took a desperate man to feel ungrateful when a dog roused him from his slumberous torment. Someone was scraping a chair about or opening a drawer in the desk in the closet behind the red arras, I fancied. I sat with a sheet pulled close to my eyes, listened bravely. Next moment, my three-legged hound jumped off my counter-pane and trotted across the bare wooden floor as far as the curtains.

Heroically, later, I set off on tip-toe after him. I picked up a shoe

100

and waved it about as a preliminary to action.

'Who's there?' I cried.

Instead of a thief, the closet was deserted, a swan's feather already returned to its inkwell on the desk's otherwise bare surface. Yet dreaming was I not and absolutely was I not too drunk. One quill from a collection of old pens and paper had rolled on the floor, that's all.

But who was I to deny that the dead ever wrote to the living?

15

That I was hungry I could not refute, yet recognised the want of something in the hunger. At first I paid it scant attention, nor did I check my stride. Shielding my murderous eyes from the glittery hoar-frost that had left everything so white and ghostly after the night, but egged on by the gleeful prospect of killing something, I stole along the edge of a stony field with my shotgun at my shoulder. Dark thoughts took wing in my head.

It was the aim of my walk to unburden myself of another, equally physical but pressing deficiency.

After O'Leary's interment, I really should have left Coberley Hall immediately. Instead, here I was seeking to pinpoint a strange, sad lack which the after-effects of the funeral had infused in me – a seductive, pensive, but alluring deprivation whose attraction I should have been able easily to resist. I could only say that it had nothing to do with having missed breakfast.

I scanned the day's clear blue sky ahead, all the better to decide where best to begin my rough shooting.

What more indubitable feeling of the power of life over death could there be than to hold a still warm bird killed by my own hand? What clearer proof?

'Nevertheless, I am disappointed,' I told myself, looking along both barrels at my first crow. 'I cannot understand why it should be so incumbent on me to feel my wife is still alive when she is not. Like a hunger.' Of course, after ten years of marriage any man might have been expected to be so affected by his loss as to sense, almost bodily, the absence of another in himself, but since coming to Coberley Hall I had begun to feel strangely sick to my stomach with excitement. Was I then literally incapable of digesting that I had watched her breathe her last?

No medium ever told me any different.

*

Death birds, people called them, but cocky, black harpies would have been more apt since those crows were soon on to my little game. The cheeky scavengers strutted about the frozen earth with ungainly hops just out of range.

As for rabbits, they were gone in a flash of their fluffy white tails.

I was feverishly ejecting two spent cartridges from my hot gun when I saw a familiar red Land Rover with a white roof turn my way onto the headland. Bumping about in the truck's open back were the usual white plastic bags of grain, I observed, as the driver drove madly along. He was going from one feeding station to another around the edge of the field. It was Peter Slater.

Fancying myself as a man of the land, too, I hung my shotgun over my arm and strode casually but not unimportantly down the track to bid my fellow sportsman good morning.

'Get in the truck.'

His shout was so horribly imperious that it was not unreasonable to suppose that he was talking to his dog, not me. As a result, it was a moment before I did what Prince did, obeyed and climbed into the cab.

Peter spat out his cigarette but kept hold of the door for me.

'You shouldn't go around scaring the birds like that, Mr Walker, I'm damned if you shouldn't. There's only one more shoot before the end of the season and that's for the beaters. They won't thank you for ruining their big day.'

'Sorry, I'm sure.'

On my very own estate, it turned out, there was a rigid date about what to slaughter before and after. I would have to bag my melancholic crows some other time, it seemed.

'We going somewhere?' I asked, as the door slammed shut in my face.

'You and I need to talk.'

'What about?'

'Sullivan O'Leary.'

A few seconds later we drove off at high speed. I could swallow the peremptoriness of his demand but not my pride. Hanging on to the loose door handle for the sake of my guide's greater and more urgent mission, I gritted my teeth. With Prince on my lap and two paws in my groin, I rode on very bad springs at some sacrifice to my bladder.

'Who lives there?' I inquired when we sped by a bungalow at the top of the field.

Peter swung the Land Rover round a sharp corner. Then he stopped by a gate to look both ways at the lane.

'Joseph Jones's brother moved there after his premature retirement from the priesthood.'

There was always something gloomy about an abandoned building, I thought, as though the soul had been sucked out of it. But coming with this outwardly intact, although thoroughly empty home, was the uncomfortable suggestion of restless regret and unfinished business. It was the sight of all the ivy that had subsequently come to choke its honey-coloured chimneys, I supposed. I wanted to stop and tear it all down.

But not long was I allowed to stare.

Before I could peer past the fir trees at some rusty red barns and long wooden sheds within the gated yard, my impatient trucker roared off down the lane.

'It's a strange place for a priest to end up,' I said, looking back.

Peter smiled.

'Father O'Connell was in an unbalanced frame of mind when he holed up there. They say that he had an altogether stubborn inclination to disbelieve in the certainties of life and death. In the absence of full proof, he refused to believe that someone's feelings entirely passed away with their body. Although of uncertain meaning, the character, truth and emotions of the deceased could live on after them, if only in the one who had last loved them most. In short, he doubted if the dead always died.'

'What happened to him?'

'The Vatican took exception to his heretical writings. The Church mistook his interest in the aftermath of death for something truly monstrous. But that's another story. Right now I need to show you something.'

*

Peter's bumptious behaviour did little to allay my feeling of having just been kidnapped. Any man who drove so recklessly with no consideration for his passenger's coccyx did it not because he was strongly desirous to reach his destination, but to relieve the storm in his own head.

'This it?' I asked, as we skidded to a halt at the crossroads in the middle of Chatcombe Wood.

Least of all did I expect our chance meeting to evoke in my friend some grim compunction or otherwise useless pricking of his conscience. We were back at the scene of O'Leary's tragic accident.

Peter lit a fresh cigarette.

'After you left me with the corpse, Prince and I found more tracks in the snow, Inspector, I'm damned if we didn't. I took a photograph to show you.'

With that, he reached in his pocket and brought out his phone. On its screen showed the bear-sized outline of heel and instep.

'Are those claws or toes?'

'O'Leary left a trail of spent cartridges among the fir cones and needles. No wild boar survives a man with a gun. He set his trap for something bigger.'

Since I was hearing something that I had already decided myself I had to be forgiven for appearing ungrateful.

'How can you be so sure?'

'Because I've seen it before, years ago, Inspector.'

I looked him in the eye.

'Yeah, no, I don't know. I'm afraid you're going to have to be a bit more specific. Come to that, why wait a whole week to tell me?'

'Lord Hart would prefer it if I never told another living soul.'

'So inform the police, not me.'

'You are the police. I even think that is why George is determined to have you stay on in Coberley Hall.'

'No he isn't. Is he?'

'Hear me out and judge for yourself.'

'You talk as if you two share a secret?'

'Doesn't mean his lordship can force me to stay quiet now, does it? It's been over thirty years.'

'So tell me, why have you?'

*

'It was a very hot August in '79 when George invited me to visit Coberley Hall. I'd never stayed in the country before and so I didn't know what to expect, but let me tell you, Mr Walker, nothing could have prepared me for the state of that house or him, I'm damned if it couldn't.

'Dressed in grubby black trousers – part of his school uniform, no less – he held a bloody rag to his freshly cut lip. He urged me to enter ever so quietly.

' "Sorry, old chap, but Pater's in one of his moods."

'I'd first met George and his brother the year before at the local Grammar School. Two fresh-faced fourteen-year-olds, they had been transferred from a private college because their stepfather had decided that they were both a total waste of his money. In the beginning, I thought them country toffs with silly affected accents, but when George and I came to sit next to each other in Latin class we discovered that we both loved guns.

'Upstairs, the house was filled with an odd afterglow. Each time I paused by a window to peer outside, my view was blocked by a thin white sheet that shut off the outside world with its dim translucence.

' "It's on account of weed killer and insecticide spray off the field," explained George in a hushed voice. "Pater suffers from Chronic Obstructive Pulmonary Disease. His doctor has told him that he might not live another five years."

'We had to glide through the house like ghosts, which wasn't easy when every bare floorboard creaked and groaned. We had to avoid offending Joseph Jones at work in his office. Passing from one shabby room to another, everywhere I looked was covered in cobwebs and dust.

' "Doesn't your mum look out for you?" I asked, zipping up my new blue anorak right up to my chin because, despite being summer, the house felt horribly cold.

'George licked his split lip.

' "Mater ran off with her lover a month ago, old boy. Pater's been absolutely beastly about it since."

' "But that's not your fault."

' "Just got to soldier on, old chap. That's what I say. Had a bad effect on Philip, though."

'But all that was forgotten when we set foot in his bedroom. In the middle of a table stood a fully reconstructed skeleton of an animal.

' "Wow, what a monster!" I said.

' "Philip knows a cave where there are all sorts of bones."

' "It looks like a dragon's head."

' "It's a badger, stupid," replied George proudly and began to articulate its jaws and claws. "See how it has all been wired back together."

'What surprised me most was how delicate all the bones looked, each poised in the same relative position as in life. He would have breathed his own breath into it if he could, Mr Walker. As it was, he used a drop of blood off his lip to smear the badger's teeth with a semblance of being.'

*

Peter struggled to hold his shaky cigarette to his mouth. I feared for a moment that he might stop before he'd truly begun.

'So Philip was a budding palaeontologist, too, was he?' I asked.

'Really, to me and everyone else, he was a bit of an enigma, Mr Walker, I'm damned if he wasn't. I used to pass him in the school corridor on our way to and from biology classes but more often than not he would be laughing and talking to himself. Naturally such eccentricity did not go unnoticed. Other boys were soon saying that he was possessed by demons. But for his brother he was alone.'

'Considered them inseparable, did you?'

'I mean they lived in a world of their own.'

'Go on.'

'Once we had entered Chatcombe Wood George and I approached a line of poles. The fortified position was further strengthened by a ditch whose counterscarp we had to traverse before we came to its entrance. At the centre of the fort were the remains of a fire.

' "This is where Leslie the woodsman lived," explained George. "He cut the underwood, stripped bark and dug holes for new trees. He did the ditching and hedging and maintained the ride for the lords of the manor just as the 'woodward' did for hundreds of years before him."

' "Where is he now?" I asked.

' "He's dead, but some nights he haunts this shed, I'm sure."

'Peering into the ruin's entrance, I saw how someone had indeed recently attempted to make a bed from old faggots of brushwood among all the axes, spokeshaves and saws.

' "It's a tramp, more likely," I declared, dismissively.

' "Whoever it is, they are living wild in Chatcombe Wood."

'I looked around. Near the wooden shack stood a large steel tank sprouting weeds over a brick hearth that still contained wood ash and charred logs. Several fence posts, the last that Leslie had left to soak and simmer in creosote for days at a time, floated ready in their bath, as if he were about to return for them at any moment.

'Suddenly a voice challenged us from among the trees.

' "Halt! Who goes there?"

' "It's me, George."

' "Password?"

' "The countess."

'I whirled round. Draped in a green blanket pierced with twigs and leaves and wearing a Grammar School cap adorned with bird bones, Philip held a homemade pike at the ready. Of course he looked absolutely ridiculous for a boy of fifteen but there was something about his wild, staring eyes that persuaded me to give him the benefit of the doubt. Rather than dismiss him as simply childish, I supposed that he was playing some sort of game to distract himself from trouble at home.

' "Who's that with you?" he demanded.

' "You know Peter."

'Like his brother, Philip was wan and thin. His bright blue eyes shone in two saucers of dirt through his camouflage.

' "You bring father's gun?"

' "No, why? Have you seen something?"

'He barely responded. I had the impression that he was terribly disappointed not to be able to report anything substantive.

' "You've hardly been back to the house for days," said George. "Have you even properly eaten anything?"

'Philip shot us a glance that was neither confiding not trusting.

' "I've been busy making more bayonets – to get ready."

' "I thought you said you hadn't seen anything?"

'At no time did the brothers really discuss what they were planning, they simply moved like animals through a terrain they knew like the back of their hand. I was the one who tripped, fell and scratched myself on long trailing brambles, I'm damned if I didn't. Suddenly the view opened out and I could see pretty coloured Polo ponies grazing nearby on the next hill.

'Philip led us to an old quarry.

' "Quickly, look for rocks. Not too large. Fossils make the best missiles," he suggested with his eyes shining brightly.

' "I favour Devil's toenails," said George, suddenly warming to the task. "They sit in the palm of your hand like fat little marbles."

'Already Philip was clambering over old refrigerators and rusty ploughs. He was looking to retrieve pieces of metal from what turned out to be a farmer's illicit scrap heap.

' "Look here!" he declared, angrily. "That coil of wire that we put by last time is missing. I left it under that tyre."

' "For sure, someone's taken it," agreed George.

'Meanwhile Philip extricated a large, cast iron pot from a seemingly intact oven. He placed it on his head like a helmet.

' "Look," he said, "I'm a Roundhead in Cromwell's New Model Army."

'Half an hour later we marched back to the beech wood laden with spoils.

'But it made no sense to return to our fort too soon so we deposited our finds by a newly felled tree and sat in a circle to confer.

' "See, this is how you make a bolas out of cloth and stones," said Philip.

'It was the first time that he had really acknowledged my existence.'

*

With that, Peter turned the key in the Land Rover's ignition.

I did not expect him to break off his story quite so abruptly.

'That it?' I objected. 'You hijacked me all the way here just to tell me how to catch rabbits?'

He frowned.

'Not rabbits, Mr Walker. What began as a game became increasingly feverish and frantic.'

'So, please, can you tell me what else there was to chase in Chatcombe Wood thirty-odd years ago?'

'None of us quite knew. That was the thrill of it.'

'You mean you *chose* to imagine something exciting to get you started?'

'Or someone.'

'Honestly? A manhunt?'

'We set about tracking whoever it was who holed up in the woodsman's shed at night.'

'H'm, yeah, but that was just a tramp, surely?'

A frown became a scowl.

'In our eyes he was a bogy man. Next minute we were on a heroic mission to rid the woods of some unbelievably evil ogre. We were Saint George in pursuit of the Dragon.'

'But it's not, like, you ever actually met a real bogy man.'

'You misunderstand, Mr Walker, it was the monster in us we wanted. Nothing less would do.'

'Okay, okay, yeah. But do we believe in monsters any more? No, literally, we don't.'

'You not got any beast you need to feed, Mr Walker? You not felt its hunger?'

I fidgeted in my seat as he revved the engine.

'You're beginning to sound like that mad Father O' Connell you mentioned.'

Once in reverse, Peter swung the Land Rover round to face the way we had come.

'Hold onto your gun, Inspector, we're not finished yet.'

'Now where the hell are we going?'

'Back to the place where I first discovered what it means to feel cursed.'

16

Peter's remark I received with a smirk, which seemed not inappropriate for such an old-fashioned word as 'cursed'. It was beneath me to gild his specious ghost story with a sinister significance it did not deserve.

Meanwhile Prince dug his claws into my lap.

'Er, is this, like, the same way we came in?' I asked, bumping up and down inside the pitching Land Rover.

It seemed completely wrong that I should be invited to go down paths entirely unknown to me in directions not of my choosing. The ridiculousness of it all deserved to be challenged. But no sooner had I spoken than Prince and I were shot against the windscreen.

'What the hell!' I cried, peering over the truck's road-splashed bonnet. 'Why have we stopped?'

Squirming about on the seat, Prince whined at his master not to wander too far from the vehicle. I did the same.

Peter took his gun and strode over to the pheasant pens. Fox-proof electric wires had been flattened and stones kicked aside where something or someone had crashed through the defences, I noticed. My wary companion trod spiky green bluebell leaves to do a quick survey of the damage. Next minute, he climbed back into the truck and handed me a brown leather pouch.

'Whoever broke down the wire must have paused for a drink,' he said, driving on.

It entirely baffled me to see how it was in any way significant. The fence bothered him less than his find.

'H'm, well, yeah,' I replied. 'It's like holding a big dried up prune.'

'That's because it's made from deer hide.'

The disgusting object was a canteen in the shape of a gourd. Over time it had grown stiff and unyielding, even shrivelled. When I sniffed it, a cold earthy smell met my nostrils, an odour that pertained rather disagreeably to the dank leaves and beechmast that littered the wood's blackest corners. It was hard not to think that, through his overreaction, my madcap driver would have me believe that I was touching something of calamitous significance? At its top was a loop where it had once hung from belt or saddle.

'Seems very, very old. So whose is it, do you think?'

Suddenly Peter accelerated the Land Rover up the track at full speed. That business of who or what had damaged the defences remained unsettled for the moment. But before I could protest, I was ordered out of the vehicle. Next to a brimming, green-blue lake stood a disintegrating wire mesh cage, I discovered. The roof of the pen had fallen in long ago and grass grew through a wooden hutch built half out over the water. Nearby a perforated wooden crate, that lay with its lid off, was lined inside with rotting feathers.

At that moment, neither my presence there nor my present company pleased me in the slightest.

'Honestly? A pond is what you want to show me now?'

I tripped on the broken stump of a giant hogweed. We were outside Chatcombe Wood but not its atmosphere. Behind us, the wall of trees bent and scratched branches in the wind that blew off the open fields. If I clung to the Land Rover's ill-fitting door it was because I was determined to dismiss my fears. *No branches ever grew claws.* Still I had to force myself to be all ears in case I missed something. It was always a relief to leave a wood – I couldn't bear not being able to see past the shadows.

'Just hear me out,' said Peter, taking my arm. 'Let me tell you what happened here years ago.'

'Not before I get back in the truck.'

*

'You're looking at Bert's duck pen,' said Peter, leaning on the Land Rover's steering-wheel. 'Back then, he was the cantankerous old gamekeeper who lived in a funny little round house not more than a mile from here as the crow flies. Philip knew when Bert toured the estate each day which gave us time to prepare out ghost hunt.

'Never before had I seen such bright stars. In town you never get to observe the night sky properly, do you Mr Walker? It was a revelation. In those days I believed in neither the spiritual nor the supernatural.

'After an hour I could barely tolerate my own nervousness, but fancying in every shadow some fresh phantom I soon began to discount any notion of meeting a dead woodsman.

' "Wait!" warned Philip. "I hear something."

'He was right. What sounded like a smoothly continuous flow of water started our way. With the gentle, lively ripple I soon distinguished hundreds of squeaks and squeals.

'Philip parted strands of oilseed rape in the field where we were crouching and pointed further up the track. Trudging along the edge of the wood was a large, powerful figure and with him came hundreds of rats. The spring in his step was sprightly for one who limped a little. The long grey hair that protruded from his floppy, wide-brimmed hat pronounced him old, but not from time elapsed or length of life. Indeed, something about him struck me as remarkably ageless.

'From one gauntleted hand swung an oil lamp, in his other a blade.

' "Bet you he stole that lamp from the sheds at Father O'Connell's bungalow," whispered Philip. "They use them by the dozen up there to help incubate the pheasants' eggs. He's a thief as well as a ghost."

'A violent shock set my cold blood on fire. With no real predilection for the unnatural, I was less inclined to cast him as a spectre than some strange wanderer or pilgrim. I never before saw such fine leather boots, even if their turn-down tops and toes had dried out and cracked with excessive use.

'I was unsure which part of me burnt hottest with embarrassment. I felt it more as a total assault on my entire nerve-system, the result of perceiving or being asked to perceive a distinctly maleficent and hellish presence. Exiled from one world, he found it hard going in the next.

'We watched him dip his old deerskin canteen in the pond. Hunched and hideous in his rat-coloured cloak, he screwed tight the gourd's stopper, then sniffed and hissed. Bad lungs were enough to edge each breath with a wheeze. To me, every one came across as a snarl.

' "We should go," I murmured, "in case we get into trouble."

'But before we could call off the whole silly venture, the stranger began to raid the ducks in their duck-house. He made the devil of a racket. He severed one bird's neck with a slash of his silver dagger. That's when I caught a glimpse of his face. As I'd thought, despite the silvery hair, moustache and goatee, he was no more than forty or so years old. One bleak, sunken eye gleamed in the moonlight with a steely, battle-hardened fury, but the other socket was a wall of white caused by disease or injury. Below the dead eye, half his cheek had been sliced by some sharp, angular edge drawn breadthwise across his face. The ugly scrape had cut to the bone that framed one corner of his jaw. He would never kiss a woman properly again where his mouth was so deformed.

'In attire he was still proud and strong, almost noble.

' "He has the air of a soldier," declared George.

' "Or he's the vision of one," said Philip.

' "You serious?" I said.

' "I mean he could be a phantasm of someone dead and buried long ago."

' "Seems flesh and blood to me."

' "If Father O'Connell were here he'd say we were looking at a bogle."

' "So, please, tell me what in hell is a bogle?"

' "It's an old word for bogy man, bugbear or phantom. Sometimes it is the Devil himself."

' "Er, well, yeah, I never saw a poor lost soul look so human?"

' "Don't you see?" said Philip. "Bogles go about the world disguised as men."

' "But what man is he?"

' "Doesn't he remind you of a Cavalier in that high-crowned hat with its feather? He could be a survivor on the run after being defeated in battle or else an escapee from prison."

'I could no longer think rationally, Mr Walker. Maybe it was my lack of imagination, but for me the rats appeared to gather in a circle around us.

' "For God's sake, run!" I screamed. "Run for your life."

'But when I glanced behind me, I saw Philip delay. Fascinated by the dishevelled figure, he had stopped to whirl his bolas behind him.

'Back in Coberley Hall we convened a summit of war.

'Philip held up rope and wire.

' "We have to capture and kill him," he said.

' "But what if he's only a tramp? Or a real-life soldier back from a war?" I objected.

' "We have to hang him up and skin him alive. Before that, we'll hold a saucepan to his slit veins and make soup with his blood."

' "Do you even know how to gut a bogle?" I asked.

' "Like a deer."

*

'Next morning, on the way to Chatcombe Wood, I detected a change in Philip. He was no longer the diffident, shy schoolboy whom everybody avoided at school, he had acquired an electrifying sense of purpose which gave him unnatural energy and drive. He was, dare I say it, entirely happy.

' "First smear your hands with mud. We mustn't leave our scent on the trap or alert the beast to our presence."

' "All this for a figment of his imagination," I whispered to George, who agreed.

'Philip drew out his knife and cut a notch in a stake. This was no

117

more than a piece of kindling but he drove it half into the ground with a stone opposite a beech sapling.

' "This way, he has to pass through a gap between tree and pond."

' "See how blurred and out of line these prints are," I said. "I reckon you winged him with your bolas. He really is hobbling now."

'One loose, torn sole had split into two where it had left cloven ridges of soil among the many deer spoor. Here and there were great, bear-sized holes, trailed by a spur.

'Thanks to our peg in the ground and its trigger, the top of the sapling stayed where we lodged it. Its tip bent right down to the ground ready to trip its snare. Then we returned to Coberley Hall to wait for nightfall.

*

'All that evening I listened out for any scream that might arise from the wood. Of course, in reality, Chatcombe was over a mile away, lost in the black landscape. At midnight three of us set off for the duck pond, each armed with bolas or pike.

'We arrived within sight of the trees when we heard shouts. It was a shock, Mr Walker, I'm damned if it wasn't, because until then I'd had no faith in our wild scheme. The beech sapling had sprung high, higher than I'd imagined possible, I'm damned if it hadn't. Our captive dangled upside down by one foot from the snare so that his coat had fallen down over his head which now rested at a dangerous angle to the ground. With one great hand he was trying to claw blindly at the noose round his ankle.

'We raced out the field and across the stony track where I grabbed the captive by his waist. Philip danced about with his knife poised in the air while he tried to decide where best to strike him. He favoured the heart.

' "Wait!" I said. "Shouldn't we offer terms?"

' "Are you mad?" cried Philip. "He's the enemy."

' "No, he's right," said George. "We have to observe the conventions. Uncover his head. In the English Civil War besieged garrisons were more often than not given the chance to surrender their weapons."

' "Oh, so we're soldiers now, are we?"

' "Shine that torch over here!"

'I gave a kick. Off came the cloth to reveal the incandescent, pugilistic face of Bert the gamekeeper.

' "You!"

' "Not me," cried Philip.

' "We didn't do it," said George. "Honest, we didn't."

' "Cut me down, you bastards, before I give you all a good thrashing."

'By torchlight the gamekeeper's mean little face was a ruddy mixture of bright red and purple with rubicund veins set to explode across his temple.

' "It's lucky we came along," I blurted, desperate to think of a lie in time. "You could have died."

' "What are you doing here, anyway?"

'None of us said anything at first. Bert sat rubbing his bloody ankle with a groan as we pulled off the loop of wire.

' "Well, if it wasn't you who set that blasted trap, who was it? I've been hanging upside down for an hour."

'Philip stepped forward to pat poor Bert on the shoulder.

' "It was that tramp who lives in the woodsman's shack."

' "What tramp?"

' "He's been there ever since Leslie died. We saw him stealing your ducks."

'Bert dusted dead leaves out of his grey hair and straightened his jacket. It took the three of us to lift him back on his feet.

' "How do you know about that?"

' "It's all over the village."

'He looked aghast.

' "Okay, boys. Now scram. Go to bed at once."

'We marched back along the track and kept up the charade until the gamekeeper was safely out of sight.

' "We've done a terrible thing," I said. "Now we'll have to make amends for interfering in something we don't understand, but it's not too late. Please God, don't let anyone be hurt. He cannot be what he seems."

'From then on, we slouched back to the house like cowards. We left the wood which had grown darker behind us.

' "Who cares about any tramp, anyway?" said Philip, his chest heaving with disappointment.

'That was all he said, which soon came back to haunt us.'

*

'Yeah, yeah, yeah,' I said, gazing at the wrecked duck-house. 'You boys turned a tramp into some Gothic fantasy so you could go on a mad manhunt? But what harm could come of it? Honestly?'

'Soon afterwards word got around that a tramp really had died in Chatcombe Wood. He had no identification on him, no tattoos or anything to say who he was, I'm damned if he didn't. What struck me most, Mr Walker, was how little it took for a man to vanish off the face of the Earth, so to speak.'

'H'm, well, you know, it's not easy to keep body and soul together. Anyway, was it not his decision to live like a wild animal?'

'But not to die like one."

'No, but who would?'

'The thing is, after being strung up by a tree he had been gutted in the same way a deer would have been. His butcher had inserted a claw or blade at the penis and then sliced him all the way up to his chin. By splitting apart his chest somebody or something had pulled out the entrails, but not before they had slit open his veins and drained all the blood. It was an act of such despicable callousness that people said he must have been clawed to pieces by a fiend. Of course the police scoured the woods for a weapon but found nothing. Officially the coroner returned an open verdict which still stands to this day, but unofficially the police attributed the killing to another tramp. They came to the conclusion that some powerfully built drifter had quarrelled with him over the use of the shack that night.'

'You literally saying what I think you're saying?'

Peter rolled his eyes at me.

'You saw what happened to Sullivan O'Leary. He was missing his boots, too. Back then there were no escaped wild boars, but that killing was by someone or something equally cruel.'

'You serious? Some *thing*?'

I could barely stomach his gall and impudence. For me to share his childish and grotesque world, he would first have me believe in some poor soul whom he had not the slightest compunction to liken to a dead Cavalier, it seemed.

Suddenly I heard Prince whine and whimper in the cab of the Land Rover. He rubbed his ghastly wet black nose round mine and sniffed bad things I couldn't.

'We should leave this place at once,' I said, urging Peter to restart the engine.

It seemed to me that he would have me speculate wildly with reckless incaution about some imminent danger that could not possibly be true. Bafflingly, he spoke as though such a malign presence had first cast its shadow over the estate years ago.

'All I know, Inspector, is that the bogy man we imagined came to life, I'm damned if it didn't. But I can see I've stretched credulity too far for you already.'

'In a way, yeah,' I said, as I suffered appallingly on my badly sprung seat. 'Who found the tramp's savaged body, to your knowledge?'

'Bert did. Shortly afterwards he completely lost his nerve. It was the shock of it all, I suppose. He had to leave Coberley for ever because he couldn't bear to set foot in Chatcombe Wood again. He said it was cursed.'

'By your lone dragoon? I very much doubt that.'

Peter glanced at the seat and the old leather gourd at which Prince kept sniffing and growling.

'We won't know until we meet him again.'

17

Unsettling as Peter's story was, I bade him convey me post-haste back to Coberley Hall. There came into my head a strange dizziness and my chest felt fit to burn. Even as my brain worked my pulse too hot and hard, I did wonder, with each successive jolt of the Land Rover, how many beats per minute my heart could bear.

It was that unpleasant.

Ten minutes later I braced myself for the final skid on the forecourt.

'Thank you, my man,' I gasped, groping for my gun. 'It was kind of you save me the walk.'

As best I could, I eased my bruised buttocks off my seat to fall out the door, tried to do it with proper dignity.

'Tell me, Mr Walker,' said Peter, hunching his heavy shoulders over the steering-wheel, 'as a police inspector would you consider yourself good at getting to the heart of the matter?'

Just because I had listened to his absurd anecdote about a killer years ago, he seemed to think that he deserved yet more of my precious attention.

'H'm, well, yeah. When people confuse facts with hearsay they soon arrive at an irrational explanation for the merely criminal. Curses and monsters are a misuse of our imagination, I'd say. Such credulity leads to an irrational fear of some very odd things, but it does no one any favours to treat the supernatural as real.'

'Come now, Inspector, when you looked into a murderer's eyes was it not some other malevolent power that you deplored? The desire to do evil to others is a universal force which we can barely grasp mentally or emotionally, only marvel at, with awe. Admit it, you've been amazed, too?'

'Naturally, as a policeman, I've had to look into a killer's eyes, have had to try to see what lies behind their malignant coldness. Yes, you can call it 'evil', be that biblical. You can resort to medieval ideas of sin and the Devil. No, honestly, you can't. In the end it all boils down to selfish, petty desire.'

'So what else do you call it?'

'My fucking job,' I said, smearing Prince's muddy paw prints off my coat.

'Really, Inspector? That it? Or did the Devil never come knocking at your door?'

'Do you good not to read so much horror fiction.'

'Who says all vice and passion die with the deceased, *every mystery*? Things get left behind that the dead want resolved. What will it take to persuade you to accept that there are more things to answer after we die than are ever told?'

'I'm hardly a fit person to do anything any more.'

'I don't mean to be like your detractors, Inspector, I don't mean to demonise you or to make you out to be a monster, I don't want to think that small. Take that stone face mounted high on your gatehouse wall. Why do you think the builders of Coberley Hall chose to place it so prominently over the entrance?'

I glanced up. What I had so far dismissed as a sleepy, clownish head today regarded me with a barbaric stare from which I instinctively recoiled. The face was sufficiently human to mimic my fears and emotions, it was a ludicrously and insulting version of my wildest self. In that respect, it harked back to ancient giants and club-wielding ogres. It had the frightening aspect of the biblical Gog and Magog, supporters of the Antichrist. This was the head from some naked Wild Man seen in heraldry and medieval Lord Mayor of London Parades years ago.

'I see a hideous stony excrescence.'

'A bogy man like that is the personification of a powerful idea, Inspector. In similar fashion, the roof gutters of Coberley Hall are lined with winged gargoyles. None is there because the house contains any evil, quite the opposite. They are there to keep evil out. They're no whimsical folly but a rational way of fighting an itinerant, malevolent force that is consonant with religion.'

I studied the deep furrows on the head's intaglioed cheeks and it did appear to be a countenance that had been carved in somebody's idea of a man-beast. The stiff coarse hairs about the mouth and nostrils were more like the vibrissae of a wild pig or other fierce animal that once ran free in the forest.

'Yeah. Probably nonsense. But you have to admire people for choosing to fight demons with demons.'

'Good morning to you, Mr Walker. We'll talk again soon, I'm certain.'

I smiled. I appreciated the offer of goodwill, but wanted none of the goodwill offered.

*

Dinner was yet another dubious olio of scrawny pheasant and carrots. I picked at the bones while I tried not to submit to the humiliation of eating alone in my very own great hall. I began seriously to consider that Peter Slater's macabre admonition did, for the most part, account for my disinclination to eat much at all? In truth, my gloomy theosopher's belief in demons did unnerve me a little, I who would specifically disprove the dead's ability to dwell in the hereafter, I who took comfort in the fact that my nightly visitations by my deceased wife were only dreams' psychical phenomena and therefore outside the domain of the physical. 'Am I really to discount all my years of professional policing and allow someone else's puerile fancies to take possession of my mind?' I asked myself. 'I think not.'

That moment, my food lodged in my gullet. I went to vomit but could only choke, not regurgitate. In the beginning I thought it was a bone. Instead, I was in the grip of a sudden convulsive wrench or strain, could not release the invisible grip on my windpipe.

My wheezing and whistling did not go unnoticed.

'Are you quite well, sir,' asked James, relighting the candles on the table with a spill from the fire.

I remained very still. All but one wick on the candelabrum had blown out in an instant. Emphatically, undeniably, I felt brush my cheek an empty stroke as of air. Caressingly, it stole by me, thief-

125

like. A moment later a door slammed shut somewhere in the screen's passage.

That was the trouble with panic attacks, they left a man's chest heaving for every last breath.

'Oh no, it's fine. Yeah, I'm good, totally,' I replied. 'Tell me, is that awful portrait above the fire really the current lord's father?'

'It is, sir,' replied James, performing the roles of both pantler and scullion. 'As you will be beware by now, sir, Joseph Jones loved to dress up as a royalist captain in the King's dragoons in order to take part in re-enactments of English Civil War battles.'

'Doesn't mean we know what started his ridiculous obsession.'

'Obsession, sir?'

'Him, well, yes. Passion, then.'

To the portrait's blue eyes and face fixed in cold detestation there was added a slight grin.

That was another thing, that hideous painting had to go.

'It's all on account of the chest that he found in the cellars, sir.'

'Why? What was in it?'

James posed for a moment like someone who could envisage events preserved forever in time, position and resemblance.

'He found letters and possessions which sparked his interest in the countess.'

'That would be Countess Lucy?'

'There has never been another, sir.'

'Please, can you remember what was in those letters?'

James's breathing quickened. Suddenly he was now a diplomatic plenipotentiary invested with full powers over Coberley Hall's special history. At that moment he could have been as old as it was.

'I would show them to you, sir, but Mr Jones made me burn every last one in the garden.'

'I literally can't think why he would do that unless he mistook them for rubbish.'

'No, it was never that, sir. When I walked into the library one day I found his lordship very excited. He had broken out in a cold sweat and his hands were trembling. I was struck at once by his pallor.'

'So, quickly, can you tell me what was written?'

'Does it matter?'

'Might do, yeah.'

My slightest movement, the chink of my spoon, the sliding of my tankard on the table, sparked in James a nervous reaction. I rather thought it was something akin to dread.

'The thing is, sir, I only have the story from Mr Jones's own lips.'

'How does that make a difference?'

'What I will say, sir, is that Mr Jones took past events and reconstructed them to give the countess back a semblance of life. In the absence of much official history, he gave her the best biography he could imagine.'

'You mean he was more interested in her becoming his personal beloved re-enactment than the truth?'

'Is not history what we choose to remember, sir?'

'Surely you can tell me something more. Can you?'

He gazed emptily at the floor like a man fearful of his own power of speech.

'Quite possibly Royalist soldiers were billeted at Coberley Hall during the Civil War, sir. If so, that's when Lady Lucy would have come face to face with Captain Digby. They would have lived cheek by jowl under the most extraordinary circumstances for several years.'

'They came together to defend the house?'

'Desperately so.'

'Er, was not her husband, you know, at her side?'

'Oh no, sir. The 2nd Earl of Downe was away raising a troop of horse for the king in Oxford.'

'From an account I read in the library, Lady Lucy was lucky to escape with her life.'

'As I was told it, sir, in 1644 things weren't going well for the Royalists. Littledean Hall in the forest of Dean had been taken and its garrison all murdered. By September 10th it was the turn of Coberley Hall. Colonel Massey, commander of the Roundheads and fresh from his successes in the forest, sent a messenger to beseech Lady Lucy to surrender her men and property, but she burnt his letter at the gate and told him 'insolent rogue that he is' that 'he shall neither have men, chattels nor house.' She vowed to set fire to everything and herself rather than surrender.'

'A brave lady, indeed.'

'Like the Countess of Derby who defended her Lancashire home of Lathom House for nearly two years, she was the sort of chatelaine who feared neither chain-shot nor cannon balls through her bedchamber window.'

'Poor Digby was severely wounded, right?'

James said nothing.

I felt another shift in the air as the fire in the grate suddenly roared and flickered. I could feel my bad lungs bubble as escaping, acrid smoke did its best to poison the atmosphere. Really, it had to be possible to do something about such a draughty chimney?

'Did Lady Lucy discover what became of the captain afterwards?' I asked.

'Rumours reached Coberley Hall that he was still rotting in Gloucester prison a month later, sir. So Lady Lucy ran away to find him, only to return a few days later with nothing to show for it except a new ring on her finger.'

'Yeah, no, I don't know. Without the letters we can't prove a thing.'

I was being offered truth and lies in equal measure. The one had a few verifiable facts, the other an ingenious, theoretical proposition devised by a man I now knew to have been a zealous and fanciful devotee of romance. That is, a violent liar? Unfamiliar with such romanticism, I scarcely knew how to judge if he had been excessive or inspired. I could not correctly decide the force directing the enthusiasm.

'So, please, can you tell me where the chest is now?' I asked.

'Miss Elizabeth's mother had it put back in the cellars, sir, on account of the fact that she didn't like Miss Lizzie dressing up in its clothes that were so old and fragile.'

'Okay, okay, yeah. You're saying my wife played with ghosts?'

'Children can live in more than one world at once, can't they, sir.'

'For there to be a countess there should be a grave. Yet I don't see hers in the churchyard. So where is she?'

James broke me more bread from a trencher.

'Many a plaque and headstone have gone missing over time, sir.'

'We know anything factual about her, at all?'

'We know her father forced her to marry Thomas Pope on 26th of November 1638, sir. The earl was only sixteen.'

'And she? How old was she?'

'Fourteen.'

'Not very, then. Nothing else?'

'In Coberley Parish Records it states in faded brown ink that **Lucy Countesse of Downe was buried the 8th day of Aprill. 1656**. Underneath, in another, blacker ink, someone has added: **She fasted from eating or drinking before her death ten dayes**.'

'Not unlike my own wife, then?'

'Exactly, sir.'

'Except Lizzie's stomach was so swollen that no food could physically pass through it.'

'I don't suppose Lady Lucy's starvation was in any way

voluntary, either, sir.'

'I'm sorry, but you seem to be implying that Lucy and Lizzie have something else in common?'

'When the present revisits the past so clearly, sir, people will draw parallels?'

'Are you suggesting murder?'

'Forgive me, sir, I've said too much already.'

'Damn right you have. We're talking about three hundred and fifty-eight years ago. How can one woman's pain ever be another's?'

*

I had spoken with unexpected and unwise confusion too full of emotion. I found it most alarming that such feelings could still rise to my throat. The realisation of that soft, cold touch to my cheek reoccurred. In hearing James's reference to Lizzie's former presence, it seemed to me that I was inviting mere words to endow her with flesh and blood, so vividly did they invoke her image.

Turning my eyes hurriedly to the table, I bade him quickly scrape my leftovers into his voider dish and fetch my hot chocolate.

'Tell me, what befell Lady Lucy's husband after his wife passed on?'

'Thomas Pope sold up and left Coberley Hall forever, sir, only to die in a coffee shop in Oxford a few years later.'

'Really? Perhaps this gloomy old pile is destined to curse us all, after all?'

'I'm sorry you see it that way, sir.'

Our eyes exchanged looks to no avail.

'And yet poor George becomes sicker and sicker?'

'Perhaps your presence will revive him, sir.'

*

'Talking of revival,' I said upon James's return, 'I plan to repaint this hall's dreadful panelling in some bright colour.'

'I trust you will be the soul of discretion, sir?'

'You disapprove?'

'His lordship wouldn't want you to do anything too hasty.'

'Honestly? This gloomy place? But whoever chose so much dark Jacobean wood anyway?'

'Why, its chatelaine, naturally.'

My once more lugubrious butler turned to go. Meanwhile the white greyhound sat down by me like my acolyte. I placed my hand on its head to encourage it to acknowledge me, but the spiteful ingrate bit me instead. It raked my hand with its teeth while its eye grew wicked and luminous.

Of my pain I was quick to complain. I beat a retreat to the fire to lick my gashes. This was the spot on which Lady Lucy had once stood warming her palms on a cold winter's day, she would have poked the logs with the same black wrought iron tongs I did, between savouring her hot chocolate. The aromatized, sickly syrup excited my heart with its delicious but very sweet old cordial as drops of blood seeped one by one between my fingers.

'Did you really starve to death when your beloved dragoon failed to rescue you? Is that why you forever pray, wait and hope, *here*? I don't think so. I don't believe you'd hang around that long. Would you?'

For a moment she was less fanciful revenant restored to life by some fanatical English Civil War enthusiast than my very own familiar.

After all, she knew Lizzie.

18

'Damn it, Colin, you're the spitting image of my brother, the devil you are,' cried Lord Hart, admiring my borrowed jacket and breeks. 'Who cares about a bit of snow on the ground when you can dress the part so well? I told you it was worth staying on one more day.'

'You don't think me a fraud, George?'

He watched as other men gathered in front of Slack's Cottage and his eyes grew moist for a moment. In his blue irises there burned that unsightly passion born of regret and loss that I was beginning to think suited him so well. It was beaters' day and my task was to help drive birds out of the wood for the guns to shoot.

'What is this existence but a dress rehearsal? Taedium vitae, Colin. Our days are numbered in this life, but it's what comes after that counts. Aren't you glad you decided to join us?'

'No, well, I don't know. Glad I pass muster,' I replied, hastily fastening a button at my throat.

His eyes drifted towards the woods, somewhat nervously.

'Really, old chap, you could be Philip.'

Revenant I was not and most certainly did I not revel in it. In fact, my plus-fours were a little too tight for me. Also, whenever I flexed my arms I smelt alarmingly of mothballs. Stamping my cold feet on the icy ground, I was a mannequin who modelled the costume that he had exhumed for me from his dead twin's lovingly preserved wardrobe.

*

Eight guns, a few pickers and I walked up the lane with the dogs padding along happily beside us. Each gun paid for the bird he shot, every kill to be recorded on his game-card. Anyone lucky enough to have a loader to pass him his weapon could shoot twice as fast which was, of course, better business for the farm. George brought up the rear in Adrian's shabby green Toyota.

'Merlin! Heel!' cried Patrick McGuinness, when his retriever suddenly ran into a field.

'Keep that bloody dog under control,' ordered Lord Hart as he rode by. 'Or I'll shoot him myself.'

'Sorry m'lord. He's young.'

A short, rotund man in a wax jacket, Patrick was the village electrician who had helped carry the coffin at Sullivan O'Leary's funeral. Frankly, it amazed me how people with perfectly reasonable but hardly spectacular jobs felt obliged to elevate themselves to the status of VIPs. But that, for some, was what beaters' day was all about.

'You been bothered by Peter Slater lately?' said Lord Hart to me from his seat in the truck. 'I heard you and he had a bit of a chat?'

'Yeah. Do me good to shoot some clays at his school. I need the practice.'

'That it? What else did the friggin' bastard tell you?'

'Oh, this and that.'

'He didn't talk about me, did he?'

'Not at all.'

'Take my advice, Colin. Men in our position should never be seen to listen to the tittle-tattle of those who can't be trusted not to gossip.' He toyed with the dragon head on his cane, gave its neck a sharp, lethal twist. 'Drive on!'

I was left to feel that to go behind his back was to expect some particular bad luck or universal misfortune. I understood the hint, but not everything hinted. Behind me walked a badly shaven individual called Matt. Apparently he sold Ferraris for a living and was deep in debate about the current emergency.

'They say it could be weeks before the floods go down in the valley. More soldiers are on standby with sandbags at the electricity substation next to the Severn.'

Patrick agreed.

'My aunt in Gloucester has to collect clean water from a road tanker every morning.'

'At least on the hills most of us have diesel generators and can pump our own.'

'Never known such cursed weather. Did you see the ring round the moon last night?'

'Maybe it's a sign of worse to come?'

*

Talk graduated to rams and septic tanks, but I found myself strangely impervious to everyone's boring concerns. When my companions mentioned that the Thames had now flooded Chelsea, the news appeared to relate to somewhere far off in place and time. Never had I felt more withdrawn from the city that I had, until a few days ago, called home.

As for the beater beside me, he was a sad, sallow sort of chap. An old friend of Adrian's, he had grown droopy moustaches in the style of Genghis Khan. Paul Mitchell was his name and he had once driven tractors for Joseph Jones.

'This hill gets steeper every year.'

'You can say that again,' said Patrick, struggling to regain his breath in the bracing winter air. 'Doesn't do any man's heart good to be so cold.'

*

Frankly it was a relief to leave the guns behind.

I watched them take up position one by one along a line of lonely little wooden posts set in a field as I trudged on up the hill. When killers joined forces for a jolly day out each man still stood alone. I could join in my comrades' brief attempts at conversation but not their camaraderie.

'This way,' said Adrian. 'We'll take a short-cut by way of the old piggery.'

Once past the signs saying KEEP OUT, NO COLD CALLERS and strictly NO JUNK MAIL, we were in a yard half left to go to rack and ruin. Great coils of razor wire snaked over redundant galvanized water tanks while empty plastic carboys of creosote and rusty wheelless wheelbarrows rose like demi-bastions of rubbish to keep out or corral something. It seemed highly likely that the tenant's otherwise ignorant blindness to the steady neglect of their lonely outpost, since that was how it appeared, did greatly facilitate the neglect itself.

Treading a sea of mud, I tip-toed disdainfully by a row of ruinous sheds. From a doorway, Sir Percival poked his big black head out next to the chimney of a rusty barley boiler. Beside him, a pretty coloured mare box-walked in fretful circles. Both hoped that we had come to release them back to the field.

'Who lives here?' I asked.

'Every day his lordship has Gemma pick out the horses' feet and brush their tails.'

'So he really does keep them to do nothing?'

Adrian hitched his camouflaged trousers up his skinny buttocks and spat in the grass as he led me round the corner of a decaying barn.

'Just because a man has lost a life one way doesn't mean he can't relive it another, Mr Walker. When his brother stayed awhile in Salterley Grange Sanatorium, George would bring him home to ride his horse whenever he could.'

'Er, sanatorium?' I exclaimed. 'What sanatorium?'

'Former sanatorium, to be precise. It was rebuilt into flats after it closed in 1969. As the crow flies the grange is one and half miles from here.'

'Sounds serious.'

'It was the sort of establishment that nursed convalescents and consumptives. Its hilltop position made the air better to breathe.'

'So Philip had some kind of pulmonary disease or phthisis?'

'I can't say it was entirely that, Mr Walker. Absolutely I can't. True, it began with panic attacks when he couldn't breathe as if he

135

had asthma or something, but really it was a progressive wasting disease brought on by an acute stress disorder which affected his lungs. Finally, he wouldn't eat a thing. Doctors supposed that he was anorexic but he insisted he was damned.'

'Yeah. I mean should I be worried?'

'In the end Philip died alone at home.'

'Doesn't mean the end of groundless rumour. That sort of thing can dog a family's reputation forever.'

Adrian's taut, thin lips tightened and his eyes grew colder.

'Some people say he went mad.'

'So tell me, what is the point of preparing someone's horse for them every day when they don't ride anyway? Why bother with the pretence when you know you can't bring them back from the grave?'

'You wouldn't say that, Mr Walker, if you thought you could.'

*

I had my stick to beat the birds, if not the knowhow to do the beating.

But not long was I allowed to linger. From barn to wood, Adrian had us fan out quickly. I glanced round, not trusting my shattered senses. Those first volleys from the guns soon bruised my ears. Frankly, it was less a battle than a firing squad. Startled pheasants took wing with a whir. Their beaks issued such peculiar registers of alarm as to laugh at sounding their own alarum.

That's not to say that my finger did not itch to pull a trigger, too. A second volley followed. Several birds crashed on to the roof of Gemma's wooden bungalow where loose shot rattled down plastic gutters. Other birds climbed as fast as they could into all four corners of the sky, but being so inordinately clumsy they were far too slow to outfly every hail of lead. One after another they lost wing, head or tail to drop to earth like silent baggage.

Pretty much.

After the guns fell quiet the dogs rushed to retrieve. Which was when I saw Patrick McGuinness slip quickly through the trees with much whistling and swearing.

'Merlin. Get back here! Bloody dog, I'll kill you.'

Not content to toss dead birds about in the field, the Labrador had the scent of something. Patrick was livid. So was I. As a consequence, I was more incautious than I should have been when following, because this was no longer about a retriever too excited to retrieve, it was about its owner's sense of his own rage. Merlin was making him look a fool in the eyes of his peers.

Seconds later he loosed off a shot.

I let out a cry.

Where the snow had been trampled so there was a drop of crimson. A few paces on, there was another one. The slope up the hill was no different. It was blood.

At last I arrived at a crumbling three-foot high dry-stone wall that divided the wood from the fields. Against it, my incensed companion sat very quietly and still.

'Patrick, what the devil have you done?' I demanded, but he had not the manners to reply.

I went closer, grumbling. Whereas his short, stout figure had earlier made him appear outwardly benign, he had shrunk and shrivelled to a shadow of himself. His face was pinched and sallow, his mouth twisted and ugly, his startled brown eyes without movement. My first thought was that he had suffered some sort of fall.

I tried whistling Merlin.

Distinctly discomforted, I decided to raise the alarm when I heard a snarl close by me. In the beginning I could not believe my eyes. There was a deer hide in a nearby tree, at the foot of which the dog sat growling. Yet deceived was I not and not for nothing did I dither. A man was crouching very low on the sniper's wooden platform. I could see instantly that he was not young, though he did not look in any way enfeebled with age or infirmities. His hair was pure silver. Being on the road for so long had stained his dirty leggings, jacket and long rat-coloured cloak, bent his shoulders and reduced him to a scarecrow. Something in his severe abasement caused me to shiver, a shudder that was reinforced when he used his agile fingers to descend from branches among which he was so adept at clambering.

Of my own movements I made not one.

Next moment, the vagabond leapt from the tree and ran. With huge strides he covered the ground all too close in front of me, swept me aside with the sheer physical power of muscle and bone. At every step I heard him sniff and snort to get the measure of me. Suddenly there came a crash and a piece of wall flew through the air as he hurled it behind him with great fury at Merlin.

The stone struck the dog's shoulder and knocked him sideways. It was an ill-judged blow but still managed to bowl him right over. I clutched my head and fell on my knees. For a few seconds I was left reeling. My cap went flying. That stone had grazed me, too. I gasped and wheezed for breath, but I did, before I panicked and almost blacked out, see something hideous stare me in the face.

While a large green hat trimmed with a buzzard's feather tipped off his brow, his one dead-alive eye flashed white as bone. The other eye, peculiarly sore and feverish, burned with a red-rimmed glow that was equally uncanny. I breathed his foul breath.

'I see where you're at,' I said aloud and watched him bound across the field and beyond.

My heart beat at bursting point until I could barely stand at all. But at least I'd fared better than Merlin. He was dead.

*

Raiding Patrick's pockets for live cartridges and relieving him of his cigarettes, I at once snapped shut the breech on his shotgun and set off in pursuit of my quarry.

'You'll not get the better of me that easily,' I thought.

I waded up to my shoulders in the cover of dead maize where bright yellow corncobs lay rotting on the snowy ground. This was not rich land, but it was extraordinary how different parts of the estate could change from flood to desert in a few days, as if some great subterranean labyrinth of caves leaked rain far beneath all the earth and stones.

Suddenly I felt very alone and exposed. Two noisy lapwings performed dramatic acrobatics in the sky directly above. They soared very high and wheeled very low each time they wove their tight formations against the wide horizon. They were both harlequins clowning about and magnificent daredevils putting on a show. So skilfully did they spin at the point of a feather that they flagged their black and white wings in semaphores all the time they whistled to me far below. As it turned out, their piercing, high-pitched 'p'weeting' only emphasised an awful preternatural calm.

I came via the lane to the claustrophobic line of twisted, gnarled trees known as Mercombe Wood. It was mostly oaks and ashes, within which the winter sun hardly shone. Beads of bright orange fungi clung to rain-soaked green trunks like miniature lamps in fairy patterns, alluring but deadly. The most I could hope for was the sound of my own boots each time I put one foot in front of the other.

Sooner than expected, a little white house stood guard at the place where my track divided. Its three-sided, almost circular front was topped with a stone-tiled roof shaped like a witch's hat. Built of rough stones and crudely cemented together, there was something faintly absurd about its situation which was so secluded.

Once upon a time, an obstreperous turnpike man would have blocked the road junction with his picket fences.

A confusion of muddy bicycle tyre marks went to a gate that led up the former tollhouse's garden path. Smoke blew about at the top of a chimney, I noticed, but when I banged on the front door, no one responded.

'Open, damn you and answer for your crime!'

I peeped in at a pointed window and saw a shelf hung with disgusting dead rabbits and pheasants. Various knives lay on an equally unpleasant, blood-stained wooden table where an octagonal lantern contained a candle ready for lighting. Beside the very old lamp rested a vase of fresh flowers bought from some shop or garage. Also on the table I could make out something lettered with the alphabet and signs. Like me, someone considered the dead their unfinished business. It was an Ouija-board.

I was outside the house that had once been lived in by Bert, the deranged gamekeeper, I realised. But no matter how craftily or secretly I stalked them, I met not another living soul. Instead I did, by a circuitous route, only end up back at myself.

*

By the time I arrived at the shoot the other men stood over Patrick's lifeless form. He still lay where I had abandoned him. Despite the general level of confusion, somebody had thought to close his pitiful eyes, yet even so his lids seemed restive. I could see how he was lifeless but not at peace. I found myself scrutinizing the greyness that crept into his skin for longer than necessary. I really did have to make doubly sure that he was dead.

Moments later, I saw that the one observing me most was Adrian. Since he was being so unbearably attentive, I had to assume that my face registered more ambivalence than I thought. I forgot I was bruised from that stone.

I gave him a hasty, if frosty smile. When someone had just gone head to head with some blundering theropod or Sasquatch in the guise of a man, he owed it to himself to show some restraint in the face of suspicion. It would do me no good to run about yelling and screaming that I had met a bogy man since most men deemed such things not to exist.

I did not want to suffer the same ignominious fate as Bert. Other lesser souls were unlikely to take the time to see the difference between an imagined monster and a real one. Frankly, I had no intention of giving any of those present the slightest excuse to label me a lunatic like he was.

'Poor Patrick fall off the wall, did he?' I remarked, lighting another of his cigarettes between my bloody fingers. 'Those loose stones look lethal. A man could soon break his neck.'

Adrian's squint was not at all helpful.

'Where were you when it happened, Mr Walker?'

'Me? I went in search of Merlin.'

'Doesn't explain why you have Patrick's gun.'

Thankfully an ambulance and police car drove up the lane. At long last the deceased could depart to great relief all round.

A few of us bowed low to the unfortunate man in respectful silence.

Only then did I set my cap back on my head, because after the thrill of the chase came the chill.

19

When a man dropped dead so inconsiderately, it did more than ruin the day for the rest of us, it meant good food went to waste.

'I'm sorry, gentlemen,' said Lord Hart, 'but it's past two o'clock. Since none of us is in the mood to eat any more, I'll stop at Upper Coberley and tell Laura Simmons to cancel dinner.'

I disagreed. Should I ever choose to assume a permanent place of honour in such a small community, it was only right that, as someone of consequence, I should see fit to use every occasion, however egregious, to set an example to the locals.

'Would it not be better to treat our meal more as a wake than a party?'

'Well, Patrick was Irish,' declared Lord Hart, about to ride ahead in Adrian's Toyota. 'I say we have a drink in his honour, at least.'

Everybody decided to follow my lead. After all, it was not only about the food but the money – the Coberley Estate had already paid for a lavish banquet. Also, had I not kept a stiff upper lip my flighty companions might have mistaken my lack of fortitude for sentiment. On the run from remorse, I was not about to let sorrow, no matter whose, bring me to book, which was not, of course, to say that there was no case to answer.

I had not fled London to suffer someone else's tragedy.

*

I was trying not to do a slalom down the awfully icy lane when there rose up before me a very old, three-storey farmhouse. If a building had to be too tall for its own good, too overbearing for the tiny country lane that was still only a badly paved farm track, then its entrance could not have been meaner. A little pointed porch adorned the frontage where village cottage met town mansion. I refused to be resentful towards such a fine house on account of its elegance when it was not a patch on Coberley Hall.

'You all right, old chap?' asked Lord Hart at the garden gate.

I tore one hand from another and patted my chest.

'Hem, it's nothing. I'm good, yeah. I'm fine. Definitely.'

Before me were two rows of flaming torches. The narrow, fiery channel of flambeaux down which I had to pass formed a path as though for some feudal procession.

'A word of warning, old chap,' advised Lord Hart, watching me wheeze and gasp in a panic. 'Laura is lovely, but do avoid her husband. He used to be a university don and is positively vile, the devil he is. Not only is he stone deaf but he won't admit it. His whole life is not exactly a direct lie yet still a positive misrepresentation. Suggestio falsi, old chap – some people pretend to be nice. Better hope he doesn't decide to play the trumpet.'

The man in question was a seventy-year-old, tedious looking individual with a very loud voice who was holding forth about his glorious career next to a roaring wood stove.

'Oh yes, Oxford nowadays is a factory. Had a graduate come back to see me once. Said he'd been one of mine but I hadn't a clue who he was. There are so many of them, you can't possibly remember any of them afterwards.'

I avoided this ghastly academic ichthyosaurus and helped myself to a glass of chilled champagne. For although part of the house had been too brashly built for my taste, with a stylish mezzanine floor and a great glass window for an enviable view down the valley, I was standing on stone flags that echoed like a great mead hall. I found it easy to despise its fashionable décor, but not its comfort.

'Dear me, poor Mr McGuinness. You see it happen, at all?'

A woman dressed in a long coralline dress and adorned with real diamonds made a bee-line straight for me.

'Yeah. Probably a heart attack but we've all got to go some time, haven't we?'

'Pleased to meet you,' she exclaimed, fixing me with her busy, hazel-coloured eyes. 'I'm Laura.'

'DI Colin Walker. I've inherited Coberley Hall. I'm here for a short while, looking into boundaries and deeds and things.'

'Then you and I are neighbours.'

Twenty years younger than her grizzled husband, she displayed the fine cheekbones and long dyed black hair of a still very beautiful woman.

'Yes, no, I don't know. Can people be neighbours when they live in two different Coberleys?' I asked, smiling. 'We must be a mile apart at least.'

'In the country a mile is nothing.'

'So sorry we had to meet in such trying circumstances.'

Laura shot a look at her husband.

'The ones who should go never do, do they?'

Suddenly she sailed away, resplendent in her figure-hugging dress and high heels.

'I love your house,' I called after her. 'Have you, like, lived here long?'

She shouted to me over her shoulder.

'Lord Hart sold it to me when his brother died. He said it brought him nothing but trouble.'

'Er, in what way, exactly?'

'Most houses this old are a bloody nuisance, aren't they?'

*

Because the stone floor echoed right up to the rafters, one unintelligible word soon repeated itself in close mockery of another. The room positively flooded with gibberish until I seemed to sink deep underwater. Empty black mouths gaped at me as if we were all sinking. 'This is how it would be if our dearly departed could attend our parties,' I told myself. 'Because the dead outnumber the living, would they not soon drown us out with their hellish babble? Come to that, who then would dare talk at all when they could be our witnesses?'

A moment later, there came a touch on my elbow. It was Laura again, peering at me intently.

'Come, the roasted pig is ready. Listen up, everyone! You'll find plates and food laid out for you in the marquee in the garden. Grab and go. Grab and go.'

'So where's Lord Hart?' I asked, joining the awful throng.

'Oh, he never stays long. Won't eat a thing with other people. Ever.'

Of my own hesitancy I said nothing.

*

Laura led the way into the pyramidal white tent from the top of which fluttered a red pennant reminiscent of some courtly tournament. With Lord Hart absent, I maintained a certain hauteur by suitably expostulating and intoning after his manner. That's to say, I paused before replying or simply ignored what was said should I deem the topic of conversation too far beneath me. Unfortunately, there was much dark muttering about a boundary dispute between neighbours.

'What do you say, Mr Walker?' asked Matt, twiddling a glass of wine in his hand. 'Would you go to court to settle a line in the sand? In olden days the local lord would have decided all such disputes in his great hall. Your word would have been law.'

I was about to extol the obvious merits of feudal ownership when my gaze came to rest on a woman wearing a greenish-gold gown in the tent's narrow entrance. Only I seemed to notice her. Otherwise she stood awhile trying to decipher or interpret the significance of the signs, movements and conduct of all those who passed right by her without a word. With dark, sunken eyes and almost lipless mouth where its flesh had shrunk from her teeth, she resembled someone whose face was literally wasting away to nothing. The opportunity to join us induced in her an insatiable hungriness for our company, yet any celebration was uninviting when insufficient courtesy was shown to the invited.

It was the same woman I had glimpsed at the roadside near Slack's Cottage when I had nearly been run down by the National Express coach to London, I realised. Since then she had torn the gimp lace lining of her worsted petticoat so that its braid of black silk unravelled behind one of her green velvet shoes.

Still she would open and close her mouth like someone who would remember how she once needed food.

'No!' I thought. 'It can't be.'

As I started towards her, I saw her wobble. With her face turned away, she hid her features behind the long curls of black hair that she kept brushed forward from her brow. The dress she was wearing was very old. She trailed its beautiful silks through the mud. Otherwise the gown looked as it might have done, unimpaired and magnificent for centuries, except for the gaping, frayed edges where perspiration had rotted holes under her armpits.

But she rallied.

With skeletal fingers now resting for support on one of the tent's guys she left me in no doubt that it was not necessarily my help she was seeking. She easily stayed upright like someone who had only just realised into what world she had stumbled.

'Wait,' I shouted.

Even as I spoke the chef revolved the stuck pig on its spit and everyone cheered. I was drowned out. In a cloud of odorous smoke, the meat spat and steamed. I had to jump aside but not before I saw the apparition make a motion to vomit. She kecked at the sudden smell of hot, meaty juices that dripped on hot coals, then choked in the fumes. She revolted at the scalding stench of an animal being basted with its own sizzling juices.

Lizzie had never been able to tolerate the smell of meat much, either.

But this was not that revolt.

Sure enough, her lips mouthed some other protest.

Fanning hot steam out of my eyes, I rushed out the tent's exit and gazed up and down, stood there feeling sick on the ghastly, noxious vapours that rose from my stomach to my brain. Too late. She was gone, leaving me to feel gutted. Yet, despondent was I not and for certain did I not despair.

Torn in the tent's thick, white canvas were nine long rents from her sharp fingernails.

*

'You leaving already, Inspector?' asked Laura, tapping ash off her cigarette.

Looking about me, I had come to a standstill in a cobbled courtyard next to an old scullery and washhouse, I observed.

'As you can tell, it's been quite a day.'

Laura clutched a warm shawl round her shoulders.

'I hope it wasn't the bacon, I'm sorry if it was rock hard.'

'Not the food, not at all.'

'You look as if you've seen a ghost, Inspector.'

'Didn't you notice? A woman came to the tent and looked in. She was very pale and dressed in fine but odd clothes. I went to speak to her when she vanished.'

'Most likely it was Marigold.'

'You know her?'

'Everyone does.'

'Doesn't explain why she goes about in rags.'

Laura shrugged.

'When young she was a talented but anorexic actress. She gave up her career to live with Lord Hart. He saved her life, some say, except now they don't live together any more.'

'Lord Hart? I had no idea.'

'Ever since they separated recently she has taken to living in the old tollhouse in the woods. Everyone calls her the countess.'

'You think she's crazy?'

'Not crazy, Inspector. But how do you live with a man who has grown sick of living?'

'Please, call me Colin.'

Her touch broke the spell.

'Poor Patrick, I feel so sorry for his family, don't you?'

My hostess's eyes met mine with all the force and stricture that went beyond casual concern, she really would have me banish whatever it was that still caused me to peer so anxiously all around.

'Will the dead not rest if no one will mourn them?' I wondered, nervously.

'Dear me, what an odd thing to say. Why do you ask?'

'H'm, well, no reason,' I lied, then sought to distract myself further. 'My stepfather has no idea if I'm alive or dead. Nor I, him. So what are we to each other now? Ghosts?'

'We may try to be dead to one another, but the living can't ever make ghosts of the living.'

'No? I wonder? When a man denies himself all feeling for long enough does he not become dead to himself?'

'Come, Colin. Walk with me. Some fresh air will do you good.'

'Seems sensible. Have you, like, ever felt haunted by anyone?'

'You're talking to an archaeologist. I deal with the dead all the time. Consider this house, for instance. When I had it remodelled I discovered that the cellar had been built by the Normans. Left behind were several old floor tiles. Would you like to see them?'

She shot me a winning smile, knew how not to appeal to my vanity in vain.

*

'Talking of finds, I have something to show you,' I said.

'Allow me,' said Laura, examining the forged spike in my hand.

It was big enough to pin a man to a cross.

'Adrian was burning the last of some very large, very old timbers in the farmyard at Slack's Cottage when this nail shot out the fire at my feet.'

'From a medieval tithe barn, no less.'

'It's sad, in a way, to know.'

'Thing is, Colin, that barn was bulldozed before I arrived, so I never saw it in all its glory. But go back centuries and the farmers round here would have stored grain in it for the benefit of St. Peter's Abbey in nearby Gloucester. The monks owned the land, you see, and made the tenants pay them a tax of one-tenth of their crops each year.'

'So why wait until now to burn the last of the timbers?'

'I can't say, but for as long the past is forgotten it stays a shut book. Then, one day someone arrives to add an afterword.'

'Don't look at me.'

She handed me back the nail.

'Not me,' I repeated.

*

With each long and short skip, we danced hand in hand among the icy puddles. Laura hooked up her dress so that she could step from brittle floe to brittle floe and not lose her balance, led us to a stone shed where she unlatched its stable doors, top and bottom.

'I didn't know anything about the tithe barn until I met Paul Mitchell,' she said, moving fat, plastic bags of Happy Hoof from our path.

I dodged a rat that ran over my toes.

'Seriously? That awful little man with the ridiculous moustaches like Genghis Khan?'

'That's him. He lives in a caravan where the tithe barn once stood.'

I held up my trouser bottoms as high and tightly as I could.

'Must you dig in such dark corners?'

'Forgive me, Colin, no one before you ever asked.'

She squeezed past other bags of gnawed horse feed.

'What are these blue pellets on the floor?' I asked.

'Don't worry, it's only rat poison.'

'Perhaps you should try something else?'

Laura had to bend almost double between the shed's low sloping rafters on her quest for her archaeological treasures.

'What are these pictures doing here?' I asked, by way of distraction.

'That's her. I forget her name, but she's the one Paul found dead on a pile of firewood in the tithe barn all those years ago.'

Steel drawing pins had corroded virtually to nothing, but two postcards and one photograph hung off a beam, I observed.

'Dead, you say? How come?'

'She was clutching a postcard like that in her hand when he found her. No one had written on it. She must have brought it with her as some sad reminder of home. Everyone hated that barn ever after.'

'Honestly? That it? You think the tithe barn was bulldozed because of a few bad memories? Adrian told me that it was to be a listed building and *that's* why it was knocked down – no one wanted the expense of repairing it?'

'I can't rightly say. I don't know much more about it.'

*

In this most inaccessible of places the dark-haired girl in the picture looked to be just a teenager, in my estimation.

'Been here a while, has she?'

'Since 1979, by all accounts,' replied Laura. 'That's when she fled Communist Poland, the same year the Pope visited Gdansk. Their uncle worked in the shipyard and thanks to him she stowed away on a ship to Sweden. How she reached England, Paul didn't say.'

'Who's that with her?'

'That's her brother. I remember him, he's Viktor.'

Sweeping aside appalling cobwebs, I could make out a young man whose fair hair was closely cropped and very militaristic. His smile was more effusive than his sister's and more reckless. He had tight hold of her arm, I noticed. Brother towered above sister until, with his broad shoulders and massive hands and feet, he could have been a giant. His mouth twisted somewhat oddly to reveal one very sharp canine but given the modest size of the photograph, it was hard to say if this was due solely to the malformation of an unreconstructed hare lip or whether he hated smiling for the camera. Both siblings had been snapped against a background of old-fashioned trams and brutal skyscrapers whose concrete monstrosities had come to dominate so many European cities rebuilt after the devastation of the Second World War.

The girl in particular looked like someone on a perpetual diet whereas in reality good food had often been expensive and hard to come by during the Communist era. Angular and lean, she could have been a model on a catwalk. It was the dark, sunken eyes that betrayed how hard her life had been. Her smile was infectious, though. Clearly, when the photograph had been taken she had already made the decision to make a run for it.

'You say she's sad, but she doesn't look sad to me.'

Laura leaned over my shoulder to peer at the print.

'You're right. Strange, she is smiling. I see it now. I must have been thinking of what happened later.'

I dabbed dust off the photograph with my fingertip, while I fixed my eyes hard on the girl's face. Not only was I wordless, I was an actor in a mime show. I was pointing and poking, yet had to look twice to be certain, had to see for myself the stretched, skinny and angular face from whose nose, chin and eyes more familiar features were descended. This was no chance photograph but the dream in my head. She was every question and every answer. Ghost of my ghost, was it not her body I had seen rest so recently on her deathbed? For a moment I signed with my frantic deaf and dumb alphabet, pressed the heel of my hand to my mouth to deaden the gasp. Only then did I dare trust myself to admit out loud the

151

blindingly obvious.

'Lizzie looked just like her.'

'You know her?'

'H'm, well, yeah, this is Esti Dryzek. She's my mother-in-law.'

*

Otherwise I was literally speechless. A picture from so long ago should not have evoked so much present emotion. That way, everything and everyone had a place in time, but what if somebody refused to stay put in a sequential past or particular period? What if they should resume their story after a long pause or provisional ending? When someone defied any continuous methodical dating and recording, did they not become timeless and endless, even animistic?

Laura smiled.

'Do you believe in astrology, Colin? I do, I'd say the stars meant you to find that picture for a reason.'

'Perhaps it is all connected.'

'In the short term things worked out better for Esti than Viktor.'

'Stay long in Upper Coberley, did they?'

'Dear me, no. Once Gerald Turner was gone, they were, too.'

'Gerald Turner?'

'The farm manager. Now are you ready to look at these tiles or what?'

'Later,' I replied and fled back to the party.

*

'You seen Paul Mitchell, at all?' I asked, the instant I burst into the marquee.

'Paul went home a few minutes ago. Said he felt funny in the head,' advised Matt, who otherwise proved quite useless.

I conducted a thorough search of house and gardens but the

illusive Mitchell was nowhere to be seen. Nor did any woman dressed in rotting clothes stand looking for someone in the marquee's chilly entrance.

I made some excuse and departed.

Terrified myself, I refrained from terrifying. As I scurried along the lane, grey clouds massed low in the sky. Nothing could diminish the chilly sensation that, in the otherwise empty road, somebody else trod close on my heels. But it was nothing. My eye simply retained an after-image of that odd woman at the party. Any revenant could only be less consequent that antecedent? They would have us believe that they were the conditional proposition on which life following death now depended? But Laura was right, no one should expect to feel more alive with the dead than the living.

Of what else had I to be afraid? The afterlife?

I refused to call it conscience.

After*love* was more like it.

20

'Colin, you look like shit.'

'So nice to see you, too, Sergeant.'

Chilled, I tried not to let my real thoughts dwell on the charnel-house that once housed displaced bones in the crypt beneath my feet. We had agreed to meet in the Lady Chapel of the Parish Church of St. John Baptist in Cirencester. At least Jan had answered my cri de coeur, only now I felt a bit of a fool.

Shunting me sideways on my pew, she hooked a curl of blonde hair out of her face in order to plant a quick kiss on my cheek.

'So what have you, like, done to yourself, then, Colin? Apart from not shavin', that is?'

'Seems harsh.'

'I mean, where did you acquire that awful tweed cap and coat you're wearing? What is that funny smell?'

Hastily I turned down my moleskin collar.

'Er, everything belongs to Lord Hart's dead brother Philip. Sorry about the mothballs.'

'No, not that. I smell nicotine. You aren't smoking again? Are you?'

'It can be as cold as the grave on the Cotswolds.'

'Then thank your lucky stars that I have in my car a suitcase full of your clothes.'

'I never intended to stay this long.'

Jan uncoiled her slim leg into the aisle and admired her new red shoes at the end of her grey cashmere trousers.

'Seriously, Colin, why a church? It's freezing.'

'Somewhere like this has to be so much quieter and calmer.'

'You think? I just researched this place on my phone. Says here that when Prince Rupert stormed the town in 1643 he used the nave as a prison. So desperate did the captured parliamentarians become that their loved ones smashed the stained glass windows to pass food and drink to the sick and wounded.'

'Do you good to learn a bit of history.'

'Right now what I need most is a coffee.'

'No, honestly, thanks for coming.'

'I nearly didn't. I had to drive through two feet of water round Oxford. You working a case, or what?'

'Yeah, no, I don't know.'

Such, however, was the reality.

'I thought I recognized that cold look in your eyes. But you can't. You're in limbo. That is what compulsory compassionate leave amounts to, i'n't?'

I corkscrewed my buttocks on the excruciatingly hard wooden seat. A moment later, I directed my gaze at the nave and back again.

'Ever wonder how the men who built this church married devotion with geometry? How did they devise and draw all its fussy Gothic windows to let in the light so beautifully? That way the secular expresses the divine.'

'Since when were you an expert on the spiritual?'

'Perhaps we overlook all hope at our peril?'

'Really, Colin? Everyone at the Yard takes you for a total sceptic. When did you ever believe in any accepted doctrine on any subject? You're too battle-hardened, not to say heartless.'

'Didn't say I came here out of faith.'

'You look like hell, you're so thin and pale.'

'Suppose we go for that coffee, instead?'

I could ignore the aspersions on my body but not on my mind.

Jan shook her head.

'You can't fob me off with a latte. I was Lizzie's best friend, remember. She and I met at college.'

'I don't know. What good does it do to make so much fuss over so little?'

'Really? Now you tell me? Where is this God-forsaken dump that you're staying, anyway? Does it even have a name?'

That was the trouble with police officers, they didn't miss a trick. Meanwhile, on the south wall of the church there were to be seen the sad, washed-out remains of a late medieval painting, I realised. There, at the Last Judgement, the Devil watched me fidget as poor, lost souls were tipped into hell.

'That reporter is sniffing round the scene of your car crash again,' said Jan, after a while. 'He's trying to find a witness to what really happened.'

'Fuck him. I wasn't trying to kill myself because of any guilt, I really did swerve to avoid what I saw in the road.'

'As for that other business, the Commander keeps hinting that he wants to take things to another level, but with a change in the law in the Lords so imminent everyone's holding off. It's all down to the CPS to see if they still have a case against you. But then who wants to damn one of their own?'

In the chapel's east window, I winked at sun not shadow. Only by turning a blind eye could I feel I was capable of outstaring the horror.

'Did you speak to Maria? Did you have time?'

Jan planted her hand very firmly on my knee and her diamond ring dug into my trousers.

'You know, as a doctor, she works incredibly long shifts.'

'You two actually getting married, at last?'

'Come to the wedding, won't you?'

'Just as soon as I'm back in London.'

Jan leaned sideways and her eyes probed mine with surgical precision.

'Okay, now tell me in church what you can't in Costa's?'

'Since arriving in Coberley Hall I've come to doubt my own senses,' I confessed in a whisper. 'There's no electricity and I have to grope my way about day and night with a candle. Half the time my phone won't give me a signal and I daren't mention the sanitary arrangements.'

'Serves you right for skipping town so clandestinely.'

'I can tolerate the longing for basic comforts, but not of nightly disturbance. I can't seem to get any proper rest.'

'Maria says that when someone has a night terror they will open their eyes but they're neither completely awake nor asleep. Nor are they aware of what they are doing.'

'So, please, Jan, can you tell me why the apparitions should appear by day?'

'She has a patient who dreams that someone has broken into his bedroom. This intruder persuades him that he must leave his bed, kneel on the floor and beg for mercy, it's all so convincing.'

'Really? Me? A *day*dreamer? But you're right, I do sometimes 'wake up' and feel that I'm due to pay for my crime, that there never will be any salvation or forgiveness, only reckoning and revenge ever afterwards.'

'Maria believes that you're trying to cope with an acute traumatic stress disorder triggered by your part in Lizzie's death. As children we often suffer really bad dreams but only relatively few of us go on to have them when we're adults. However, the older we are the more dangerous the nightmares become. You still terrified of confined spaces?'

I promptly looked up at the chapel window and, blinking hard, stared at the red and blue biblical figures which were clearly illumined by the bright world beyond.

'Yeah, well, okay. As a child my stepfather shut me in a cupboard.'

'When the mind is occupied by one idea it can lead to a morbid state of nerves that Maria calls nyctophobia.'

From the south wall, the Devil laughed at more of the damned who fell into hell.

'Doesn't really explain why I've started to see things at other times, does it?'

'Maria advises keeping a journal.'

'I'm doing that already.'

'You look exhausted, Colin. Your brain needs to rest. Who knows what tricks it is playing on you, otherwise, all the time?'

For once I agreed. But for a man to sleep well he had to make a clean break with each day. To make a clean break with each day he had to surrender himself to the night that came after. To surrender himself to the night willingly he had to believe he was breaking with the continuity, sequence or course of his very existence. In the north-east corner of the chapel stood a hideous but imposing memorial to a man and wife dressed in early Jacobean ruff collars. Their awful, sculpted figures lay face up on top of their tomb where they rested their preposterous heads on hard red and black pillows. For hundreds of years the loving couple had lain together for all to gawp at and yet I distrusted their smug serenity. I wanted to know that the sleep they slept was forever dreamless.

'Colin?'

It was Jan, bringing me back from my reverie.

'Sorry.'

'So tell me again what you said on the phone. Who is this woman you see who reminds you of Lizzie?'

I felt the charnel-house beneath my feet grow chillier.

'Yeah, no, I don't know. Her whole self revolted from me, but it was me she seemed to want. They call her the countess.'

'What did she ask of you?'

'Not a thing. Why would she? Yet I did feel like I did when I crashed my car. Can it be that someone else sends her?'

Jan could not believe what I had just said. Had I really meant anything by it? Had she? In the end I believed in one sort of ghost and she another.

By now we were walking together towards the south aisle.

'Please, Colin, who else would use Lizzie to get at you from another world?'

*

'Wait,' I said, halting in mid stride. 'Did you bring what I wanted? Hand me your bag at once. Is it in it?'

'Really, Colin, you're being very abrupt and jumpy.'

'Until now I've thought nothing of it.'

Reacquainted with a gold ring in my hand, never before had I felt it invite so much presentiment of material harm or even evil.

'Can't say I ever saw Lizzie wear it,' said Jan.

'She didn't.'

'Do you know why she wanted such a spooky old thing? I don't.'

'As I thought, it must date from the 1640's or 50's.'

'So how in hell's name did she come to own it?'

'She didn't tell me properly. It may be that it started life as a keepsake, souvenir or legacy, but later somebody had it made into a mourning ring to show loyalty to King Charles I, not long after he was beheaded in 1649.'

'That's the king's image, then?'

But of that I could not be certain. Blowing hard on the ring's shiny concave surface, I rubbed a man's miniature portrait back to life on my sleeve. Set in a circle of deep blue enamel, his boyish pink cheeks and heavy black eyebrows exuded an elegiac aloofness, suggesting that it was his duty to safeguard the future of a whole kingdom. Here and there the gold had worn away to reveal black metal underneath.

'Let's face it, most Cavaliers look alike.'

'If you literally can't put a name to him why do you want it?'

'I still think it might be significant.'

*

Once in a restaurant, but holed up in a corner away from the noisier tables full of unbearable busybodies, I set aside my knife and fork to watch my ravenous companion bone her salmon.

'Haven't dined out for ages,' I admitted anxiously.

'Already you're forgetting what life's all about,' said Jan. 'You know we all miss you, Colin, even that bitch in HR whose psychological test got you suspended. You know that if she finds out that you never disclosed your panic attacks, she'll go mad. It's a serious breach of police protocol.'

'Until Lizzie died I thought I'd left them far behind.'

'You need to get your act together. That means not lying about your health to anyone. Me, included.'

'Perhaps I really am not well?'

'So come back to us?'

'Soon... soon as I can.'

'Don't tell me you're starting to see yourself as lord of the manor? You, who always lambasted the ruling classes? You, who vowed never to send any child of yours to private school?'

'If the baby had lived we would have called her Lucy.'

'DCI Hopkins asks how you are.'

'Tell me, did Lizzie ever mention anything about her upbringing, at all?'

'You're not listening to a thing I'm saying, are you, Colin?'

I reached for a glass of water.

'Fact is, I didn't know my real father and I took his absence for granted. I thought Lizzie did the same.'

'She did say that it was one reason why you and she first got together.'

'Since chatting to people on the Coberley Estate, I've begun to doubt her whole story.'

'There never was anyone more honest than Lizzie.'

'So why did she lead me to believe that her father was dead when he wasn't? Why put herself through so much for nothing?'

'You know she loved you body and soul, so why doubt it?'

'Since then I've discovered that he was hidden away by his brother in a former sanatorium.'

'Sounds dramatic.'

'I see the significance now. For years, on Lizzie's birthday, a small present arrived at our door, no matter where we lived in London.'

'So what if she didn't want you to know that she had been fathered by an oddball? It's her life, Colin, her choice, i'n't?'

'That's just it, I'm not sure Philip was mad, entirely.'

'What then?'

'Maddened is more like it. Or cursed.'

Jan pointed to my redundant cutlery.

'For God's sake, Colin, please do eat something, you're making me nervous.'

I shrank from my own verbal clumsiness.

'When Lizzie lay dying the painkilling drugs caused her to call out all sorts of strange things in her opium-tinged delirium. She cried hell and Coberley Hall in the same breath.'

'How is one at all like the other?'

'She said that it was a place I had best not go alone.'

Jan spooned thick toffee pudding into her mouth.

'So why bequeath you the damned place if she was so dead set against it?'

I skipped straight to the coffee.

161

'That's what I have to discover. That's why I've stayed on to investigate.'

*

'Perhaps this will help,' said Jan and deposited a black notebook midway between plates on the table.

'What is it?'

'I found it at the bottom of Lizzie's jewellery box. To be honest, I don't know what to make of it.'

The notebook's cover flipped open against my saucer.

'Seems she sketched things on every page.'

'One thing, actually,' said Jan, as her eyebrows almost met in the middle. 'Every picture is a pencil drawing of a house with three gables.'

'That's Coberley Hall.'

'She has drawn it so many times she ran out of paper. But see here, Colin.'

My eye followed the tip of Jan's long red fingernail while I studied the heavily drawn lines that represented the house's roof and walls. Scratching up and down with her pencil, Lizzie had executed what appeared to be a series of childish or unfinished pictures but in everyone there was, to my amazement, the outline of a figure at a window.

'Is it Lizzie?' asked Jan. 'Has she drawn herself?'

In that moment, I felt the same hurtful presentiment that had come with the ring.

'The thing is, I can't be sure.'

Whoever gazed straight at us through the leaded panes of glass had been captured with a few amateurish dabs and dashes. Beyond the slight resemblance to an actual person the observer, being black on white, had the appearance of somebody seen against the light so that only their basic outline was distinguishable. As for the face, that was lost in a caul of shadow.

162

'To sketch the same house over and over with only very slight variations would suggest it was in some way beyond her control,' said Jan. 'She was drawing it like an automaton as it resurfaced from her childhood, I guess.'

'Or like a medium.'

'Whoever it is, she must have meant you to see it, Colin, I'm sure.'

'Why do you say that?'

Jan pointed again at the oriel in one gable. There, the tiny figure could be seen scratching something on its window.

*

Half an hour later Jan and I unloaded my suitcase from her grey Volkswagon Golf in the nearest car park.

'Are you quite certain you don't want me to drive you back to Coberley Hall, Colin?'

I shook my head vaguely. Yet undecided as I was, very firmly did I demur.

'You get off to London. There might be more floods.'

'What's a few extra waves?'

'Tell the landlord that I'll sort out any rent I owe very soon.'

'In the meantime, Colin, no more going off grid. That means no 'ghosting'. I want to text or call you whenever I wish.'

I smiled. She had forgotten what I had said about no signal.

'I mean it, Colin. That notebook of Lizzie's is really strange. I literally think she meant something urgent by it.'

'I'm not so sure.'

'Why cry for help from the very place she intended to leave you?'

'For as long as she really is dead how will I know?'

Jan waved me off. She thought I was joking.

For someone to define a fear so graphically explained little when the reason for that fear was so indefinable. Rather, Coberley Hall, as sketched, constituted a parallel world with super-symmetrical shapes that were a mirror-image of the house as I knew it. Such a blind, black world did, for all I knew, constitute half the universe, yet it remained dark matter to most telescopes.

*

Ten unbearably stuffy miles later, I banged my buzzer repeatedly in order to persuade the stubborn driver of local bus number 51 to deposit me at the lonely roadside halt near Coberley. The fiery sun rolled low like a ball over the hills. I tugged my tweed cap flat on my head and once more turned up my collar. So dazzling was the white-hot furnace on the horizon, but so neutral, impartial and indifferent that the hairs on the back of my neck rose up and prickled.

Meanwhile, each griffin tightened its talons on its pillar as it watched me pass by, very intensely and closely. If surprise could move stone to smile, then both birds were so gratified as to greet me with broad grins at my return along the lost driveway.

I gave a second shudder. When the whole sky turned a blind eye on someone he could be forgiven for wondering how so many blistering rays appeared to decompose before they reached him.

I had the comfort of sufficient day to light me homeward, but not yet the comfort of being home.

21

Upon arrival at Coberley Hall I was intensely nervous and watchful. I distinctly felt the ancient house's dark interior prepare to enwrap and enclose me, yet secretly thrilled to the promise of its strange tranquillity. Greeting me in the candle-lit entrance hall, a censorious James offered to relieve me of my coat and suitcase. To him I tried to pass off my excitement as guilt.

'So, please, tell me I'm not too late. Am I?'

'Supper was served ten minutes ago, sir.'

'H'm, well, yeah. The buses only run every hour.'

'Pressing business, was it, sir?'

'Please take my case to my room at once,' I said, removing my gloves in a hurry.

I thought it highly unlikely that he had not already reported my absence to his lordship. However, when I stared into his slate-grey eyes, I received no response. Which was to say that he was a past master at observing the niceties by affecting disinterest.

As was I.

A moment later, I strode straight into the great hall with a smile and a swagger. There, I was delighted to confirm that a place at the top table had been laid for me. I lifted the lid to a pheasant and cereal broth that steamed in its solid silver porringer, then sat down on the best chair. I positively smacked my lips in keen anticipation. Faint with hunger was I not, but most resolutely did I feign being hungry.

For I was all goose-flesh at the prospect of what I had to do next, the moment I finished dining.

I relished the risk of the thing to be detected, if not the risk of detection.

*

The fretful, one-eyed greyhound overtook me at the dog-gate. Together we proceeded up the unevenly worn oak stairs past the hideous catarhine monkeys whose long impudent tongues slavered at me from atop their newel posts. Meanwhile from her empyrean abode in the white alabaster ceiling, Venus welcomed me ecstatically with her milky blind pupils. A look as empty as hers forever posed a puzzle: could any man be a true arbiter of love? Could I? Never before had I asked who or what that might mean, only whether these were normal reactions to the unknown.

No sooner did I reach the gallery and approach its row of candle-lit portraits than the greyhound began to yap and whine. The irritating animal ran along the landing and sat down in the open doorway, waiting and hoping.

In this it was remarkably insistent.

'Be quiet,' I hissed. 'You'll bring James.'

Starting forwards, I went straight to the first in line of the eight Cavaliers seated on their horses. There was something wry or mocking about the manner in which each man skewed his face at my approach. One after another they inclined their brows in mirrored mimicry of my movements, they unstuck stiff arms and necks from globules of varnish as though they would rediscover from me their precious ability to perform certain punctilios. Each took it in turns to give me a slight bow as if he were about to sweep his feathered hat with a single swipe past his saddle.

My animated presence sparked an odd enlivenment.

Because the Cavaliers were painted in the same style, fashion and colouring, their congenerous similarities showed all to be allied in nature of origin. Thanks to the crazing in its deep blue enamel surface and those patches where gold had worn back to silver, there was no doubt in my mind that the ring that Lizzie had come by so mysteriously did genuinely represent the era that the portraits depicted. And more. For, while the picture frames might be from different centuries, all the men had the face of the captain on my finger. Here were the long black curls, goatee and moustaches of a Cavalier in scarlet from whom everybody else had taken their likeness. That went for Joseph Jones's self portrait downstairs in the great hall, too.

With a mourning ring you could be reminded of a person

otherwise too readily forgotten. You could literally keep hold of that distinctive laugh in their voice, that certain look in their eyes, as well as the touch, smell and taste of their skin. Did we not speak of a man or woman giving up the ghost? That's to say, his or her apparition was a principle of life or living spirit. It could survive? But for how long?

The ring identified the man's features but not his identity.

Notwithstanding the mystery, I felt very content with my little piece of detective work. That's because I now thought I knew who he was.

22

It was mid-evening when a violent gale blew from the north. I felt obliged to cover my face as insufferable clouds of soot fell down the chimneys to fill my throat and lungs. They reduced me to fits of coughing. Each annoying, sickly blast shattered the house's already peculiarly fragile frigidity, yet in no actual breakage did the threat materialise. Doors remained on their hinges, windows stayed shut and portraits hung straight on the walls as Cavaliers and I rode out the storm.

I fled from room to room past the quivering flames of dimming candles and deafeningly loud as the awful wind was, I thought I heard coming from Coberley Hall's ancient porch the rat-tat-tat of someone knocking.

The raps sounded intermittent but inescapable. It was on such a day that I had once been forced to brave thunderclaps that burst over the sea at Brighton. Then I'd clutched both hands on my penknife – I'd felt rise inside me a savage self that belied my age. Resisting my drunken stepfather's curses and growls on the other side of my bedroom door, all I had had to do was to turn the key to meet the monster. Back then I was alarmed by those first, murderous thoughts. I was five.

'Okay. I'm coming.'

If I had grown up to become a policeman it was because I had chosen to use my sense of injustice to fight my hatred.

*

The moment I twisted the heavy iron ring on the porch's thick oak door, it blew back on me most violently in the blizzard. Above me, a fiery white ball of lightning set the window's garish family shield ablaze. Its nine awful crimson lozenges, more hideous drops of blood than hearts in this light, reflected red on the diamond slabs on which I stood. Each dazzling discharge looked set to connect house to heaven.

'Anyone there, at all?' I cried.

My desire to quell someone's impatience was of paramount concern to me, but when I turned to re-enter the porch there was no one there. Something about this out-of-body experience left me feeling foolishly light-headed. I could not tell what or why. Regardless of any childhood nightmare, no one swept by me in the hallway's chilly glow.

The whirling air was cyclonic, not preternatural.

Beside me, a door stood open to some stone steps down which a few wet footprints slimed. I decided to follow.

'Sara?' I called into the gloom. 'Is that you?'

Once in the bowels of the house, the air blew doubly cold, I discovered. Mortar in the thick cellar walls exuded the ghastly smell of oysters mixed with lime and sand where walls were as dry and dusty as a crypt. Awfully winding stairs exited from rooms far above me down which the necessary girl had once carried people's night soil from bedchambers to the fields. I raised my cigarette lighter to illuminate the dark curves of fat wooden barrels that reeked of very old claret. Mounted on pale red bricks, each cask had a tap at which James could fill his stone bottle ready for his lordship's wine-cooler in the great hall.

Really, I should have been upstairs in the library, should have been studying heraldic cartouches on every ancient enfeoffment at my disposal in order to document my actual and mental reinvention as Coberley Hall's new owner. Instead, all my immediate ambitions fell away. My toe nudged something. On the stone floor lay a book.

Judging by such words as I could decipher on the brown leather binding, the vellum pages contained sailing instructions and a description of harbours in the new colony of Virginia in the Americas. When someone dropped something in such a hurry they were being more than inquisitive, they were looking out of desperation and frustration because over time there were other things they might have mislaid? It was an ancient portolano.

Whoever had just visited the cellars had left open in a dark corner the heavy lid of a large, iron-banded chest, I noticed. The closer I inclined my head to see inside, the more I inhaled the faint aroma of some sweet fragrance. Hundreds of years ago, the oak interior had been stained purple with a perfumed dye or juice recommended by an herbalist to deter insects. I was looking at the chest that Joseph Jones had once seen fit to remove to his library. This was the coffer that had started him on his perilous journey back to the past. It smelt of thyme and cypress. Of my own possible embarkation, I was nothing if not sceptical.

All the same, I dared to touch somebody's personal belongings, tried to control my terrible inquisitiveness. 'Of course, I should simply throw out any old clothes, shoes and jewellery that appear at my fingertips,' I thought. Suddenly there swept over me a chilling sensation, a black superstitious fear of something not unfamiliar, so that I, perfectly aware of my mistake and wary of the impossibility of it, recalled the feel of my own wife's wardrobe. I was stricken by remorse, but did not suffer a tear. My stab of consciousness, not conscience, lasted but a few vivid moments.

Seconds later, the intervening fabrics and textures, through whose touch such impressions had been conveyed straight to my heart, again smelt of someone else.

Thankfully.

Tucked into the side of the chest lay a woman's white velvet face mask once worn to hide the ravages of smallpox. Since it had been made to conceal ugly pustules while they healed, the slender moulding gave a clue to its wearer's true shape and profile – it was more lifelike than death-mask.

That's where I should have left it, but could not. I felt able to disown a few pangs of curiosity but not of desire.

So it was I rushed to run my hands almost involuntarily over the fine, soft silk of white sarsenets and starched gauze muslin tiffanies. I kissed silky lawn sleeves on a beautiful, deep blue gown and admired point lace handkerchiefs made wholly with a needle.

Laid on top of a dark brown dress with wide ivory-coloured sleeves was a bag as big as my hand. This was no ordinary pouch with its brown velvet top sewn with pretty red thread but an almost grotesque thing of skin and scales. Its lizard-like surface was grey and white and tautly stretched across three long toes, at the end of which hung an equal number of polished gold claws.

Although the pouch had lost its lustre, there was no mistaking what I was holding. Swinging from its loop of plaited silk string was the webbed foot of a bird. I turned it over and out tumbled a few black and silver coins. Stamped REGINA ELIZABETH around their edges, most were groats worth pence, not shillings. Was this all the money the owner had been able to muster at the last minute, I wondered? For if this had been her travel chest, it looked packed and ready to go.

Hidden in the clothes of the dead was a bundle of papers, on the cover of which was penned in thick black ink a title: THE QUEENE-LIKE CLOSET or RICH CABINET of the Countess Lucy Pope. OPENED: whereby is DISCOVERED Several ways for making of Metheglin, Sider, Cherry-Wine, &c. TOGETHER WITH Excellent Directives FOR COOKERY: As also for Preserving, Conserving, Candying etc. Unfolding the ribbon-bound pages very slowly, I found Lady Lucy's writing to be very florid but elegant, whose 'd's and 'p's were all curly tops and tails and each swanlike 's' was stretched and slender like a modern letter 'f'.

In July 1644 she had written down in this, her 'receipt' book, a list of 'victualle and other necessaries needed to feed his Majesty. *Item* for one doz. gulls. *Item* for VJ signettes. *Item* for VJ doz. Pewettes. *Item* for ij doz. Egrettes etc.'

It put me in mind of the purse again. Since from the 12th century all swans had been owned by the monarch and were hunted only with royal permission, it had to be assumed that the king had not objected to dining on Coberley Hall's own birds? Had Lady Lucy had the swan's foot made into a souvenir for such a significant visit or had Charles I later sent it to her as a present, I wondered?

It was but a conjectural reading of a significant moment in someone else's history, yet long afterwards when a man read about things dearest to someone else's heart, he could still enter her confidence? When he became her confidant he became her bold, impudent sharer of her successes and failures, he could see beyond the mask.

Twice, by way of afterwords, she noted that the green parts of soapwort, when bruised and boiled in water, could help wash her delicate hair, while common centaury might yet cure her freckles though the bitter herb was 'very wholesome but not very toothsome.' Since I was reading the countess's innermost thoughts I encroached upon her wishes, ambitions and secrets. Because I thrust myself into her privacy uninvited, I came into her company, so to speak, I could begin to hear her long lost voice. She was particularly concerned to find a cure for the staggers in 'my deare horse Abby'.

I felt it my duty to keep the book safe, felt a jealous need to depart with it at once under my jacket. Accordingly, I slammed shut the chest, ready to skulk from the tenebrous cellars, when my burning gaze fell upon the lid.

Gouged between heavy iron bands were the words: **'Let no pittifull soule for evere more open this damnable chest without they wilt bring great greife upon this house. T.P.'**

It was only after I had taken a horrified step backwards that I was able to relight my cigarette lighter and shine its flames at the initials. They were Thomas Pope's. I felt nothing but outrage, and that not entirely clearly. It was as though a vision flashed into my head – I could not in any way prevent it – then took charge of me, heart and soul.

So it was that the 2nd Earl of Downe had come across his wife before she could leave Coberley Hall to set sail without him for America? He had caught her red-handed?

*

What seemed like a very long time ago, my descent into the netherworld of the cellars had been surprisingly easy. I had simply followed in the footsteps of Joseph Jones. But as the picture of the Sibyl in the great hall had warned me, while the gate to the realm of the dead stood open night and day, to retrace my steps and return to the upper air to breathe again, that was the real toil, *that* already felt more arduous. When I arrived panting at the great oak staircase I saw how its spiky wooden dog-gate stood open and the steps dripped fresh drool.

Sure enough, back in my bedchamber, that flea-bitten white sight-hound lolled lazily on my bed, I discovered. I went to the window to watch dusk creep across the formal gardens' grass parterres and topiary all the way to the orchards. From there Lord Hart followed the flagged walk that led out of the rosarium, I noticed. This was less someone trying to exercise himself back to health than a man who feared he might again miss some vital appointment. With his grey hair falling over his shoulders, he came to a halt on the icy grass directly below my room.

He was wearing his wholly unsuitable white suit but had pocketed his tinted glasses as he turned his face to the horizon. There he gazed west at the spot where the moon rose with defiance and impunity. He let its rays play over his rather inelegant nose and thin bloodless lips like someone who had forgotten what warmth really was. In his other hand was his dragon cane on which he leaned very slightly.

Like a man on tenterhooks, he waited impatiently by the garden's statue of Venus, peered, as I did for a while, into the dark side of twilight.

*

So it was that I chose to wrap myself in my bed's white and gold counterpane and clutch my black leather bag close to my chest. Suddenly that odious smell from the fields arrived to fill my reluctant nostrils with its taint of organic, rotten matter.

Not that I cared.

When someone like me closed his eyes at night he wanted to draw a veil over his memories, not have them come to him by some afterlight.

Yet still my dreams drifted where it was darkest.

Day 6. April 3. 2014.

Biopsy not done yesterday. Hopefully today. Sickness cured with anti-nausea drug. Lizzie better – brighter. Of course they haven't said it is terminal.

They don't have to.

'Did you bring my clean nightdress?'

'Yes.'

Didn't take much to A& E.

'What's on the news?'

I don't know. I can't bear to know, as if the world has shrunk to one bed in hospital.

Her face grows ever tauter and bonier, her skin colder and paler. Dry lips crack terribly. Her blood-shot, ebony eyes, robbed of clear sight by a dark curtain across her vision which frustrates her endlessly, still shine with a resistance that is quite heroic. Like an afterglow.

'She came to me again last night, Colin.'

'Please don't trouble yourself with such silly nonsense.'

'She says she can't wait to show me her dresses.'

'What dresses?'

'The ones she has kept for me since I was a child.'

'You can't go on like this, Lizzie. It's not helpful.'

'But she'll be so disappointed.'

Day 5. April 4. 2014.

Back home briefly. Pleased flat is so neat and tidy. Stomach still very swollen. Can't do up skirt. Not enough Tramadol to ease pain.

*

I woke at dawn and walked into Lady Lucy's closet to look out the window. Overnight more dreadful snow had fallen to entomb the house and my hands and feet felt absolutely frozen. Slowly, the white courtyard below was becoming a spider's web of thinning shadows while the sun crept over the rooftops. It promised to be a good day, however. Had the Countess of Downe stood here like me? Had she, too, felt real hope rise with the sun through this same fixed window? I traced the trite script scratched on the little iron ventilation plate and read it aloud again:

It is part of Virtue never to abstaine
From what we love tho it shall prove our bane.

I'm transcribing the words to my journal, I'm making sure to account for them in the ledger that I've taken from the library. I'm doing it before I lose track of which month it is, I'm continuing to write down an account of everything I've seen and heard in Coberley Hall since the first day of my arrival. I'm penning it the same way Countess Lucy did in her receipt book.

I rest the ledger on my black leather bag which I have on my knees. Nevertheless, the curious greyhound sniffs its soft sides most annoyingly. It takes a dog's nose, so attuned to the smell of meat, to respond to the almost carnal odour.

But it is all right, all locks and catches remain secure. A house this cold can preserve things forever.

Should anything happen to me, someone needs to know why I didn't leave here while I still had the chance.

23

Still I rocked wide awake on the edge of my bed. I tried not to breathe too deeply but really thought my stomach would never settle. It was thanks to that noisome smell off the fields again. But who was I to worry if there was something physiological about such an old house's nooks and crannies? What ancient abode did not wreak of rottenness, I told myself happily. Just because something vilely decomposing floated in the air, should I literally be so foolish as to lose good sleep over something not in the slightest incorporeal, supernatural, let alone metaphysical?

At that moment I detected the sound of music. Since there was no electricity in the house I hesitated to suggest that anybody was playing such an unusual composition on disc, tape or vinyl, could not see how this was somebody's bizarre download.

The tune sounded reassuringly remote, yet defied all sense of distance. The more I listened the farther away the music drifted – the less, and it permeated closer and closer. 'What the hell!' I thought and my temple throbbed. For, above the twang of viol and theorbo came the whistle of a flute which poured through walls without visible interstices. Never before had I jibbed at such a lovingly and mellifluous melody. It was coming from the direction of the long gallery, I decided.

'Damn it,' I cried, 'I can't bear your infernal racket any longer.'

Fuming at this most unexpected intrusion, I heard heels skitter elsewhere along the landing. That they did not sound like footsteps exactly but more of a slither, I could not rightly explain. By now I was in the withdrawing room. But should I follow, into the obscurity? I briefly returned to retreat to my bed. Then again, why should I delay a single second? I felt my stomach begin to churn once more. I had to lean on the doorjamb and open my mouth to stop panting before I could summon up the necessary courage.

Moments later, the greyhound overtook me, inquired after the footsteps, too. A patch of spilt darkness deepened into something altogether more solid ahead of us.

'What the devil is it, old chap?' I whispered.

Whereupon the shade before which the dog stopped to fawn grew longer and less distinct as troubled candles burned dreadfully low in their sconces. The greyhound sniffed the air which still stank of the fields. But this was not that smell. Rather, there floated with the adumbration the less sickening, metallic odour of dirt, decay, oil paint and old varnish. The odour floated pungently upstairs after which my indefatigable companion chose to run. I did the same.

Whatever it was it wafted all along the landing. I slowed by the Cavaliers and looked for Lady Lucy in her picture. A candle guttered. She was gone.

*

In a dismal old pile like Coberley Hall, all notion of a party felt like the betrayal of a secret. Yet I did definitely hear, high in the west wing, the commotion of bothersome guests about whom I knew nothing. To ruin the occasion simply because nobody had had the decency to invite me was rather mean-spirited. No, really, it wasn't.

The greyhound sat whining at the door to the long gallery while I lifted its black iron latch with a soft bang. That meant a gap to which I and my companion could press our crooked noses somewhat obtrusively. At once, the objectionable music assaulted my ears. This played so livelily and heartily that I had not the courage to go in. With my hot eye all bloody spots and cobwebs, I blinked at the glow from the room's innumerable candle-lit brackets and the logs on the fire. Wild reflections played over the plaster chains of flowers, leaves and scrolls on the dirty, coved ceiling.

My attention soon fixed on a tall figure who, with a swish of long hair and a sweep of her green gown, laid a cushion flat on the floor at her toes. It was astonishing how dazzlingly her eyes gave off a glint of gold.

Nor was her very old dress at all shabby but mixed gilding with silver as a seventeenth century embodiment of Spring. Beneath such finery she wore a white petticoat whose edge was worked with wild flowers. Her very dark curls tumbled down her back and carefully contrived lovelocks framed her forehead and cheeks, so that not a hair strayed out of place. Adorned with dropped pearl-earrings and glistening necklace, she had a way of considering Lord Hart as her subject with each sensuous smile. It was Marigold, dressed for a royal masque, at a guess.

Meanwhile that stupid dog at my feet was going quietly crazy. I made to move but at once, as if on cue, a flute player blew furiously on his wooden pipe in my ear. Next up, Marigold started to pray. She thanked everyone for coming and announced that it was time to begin.

'Come, spirits, join us.'

James, Sara and Lord Hart sat on cushions on the floor in a ring before three differently coloured candles that burned on a cloth at their knees. Then Marigold spoke again.

'We pray for protection from angry ghosts or demons and ask only that well-intentioned spirits join our circle.'

Immediately Lord Hart leaned forward. His breathy lips disturbed the nearest flame. 'Please ask her to call Philip.'

Marigold closed her eyes and rolled her head. Given the strong smell of incense in the room, she seemed to be in a trance already.

'Lady Lucy, we gather here tonight in the hope that we will receive a sign of your presence. Please feel welcome to join our circle when you're ready.'

There came no immediate answer. Then, on the Ouija-board an upturned glass moved from one letter to another.

Sara gave a giggle but James looked serious. Neither appeared frightened or cynical. Obviously they had done this before, I decided, or they knew that if only one person was sceptical the power of the séance would be ruined.

'Ask her to call my father,' said Sara, impatiently.

Again Marigold squeezed hands to harness the collective energy of the participants.

'Are you with us?'

She shivered and threw her head right back. Suddenly her eyes stared straight into space but appeared confused.

'Is it him?' asked Lord Hart. 'Is it my brother?'

'What about my father?' objected Sara.

But Marigold, being psychically gifted, only mediated the séance in silence.

Then the candle for 'NO' flickered and went out.

'What's happening?' demanded Lord Hart.

'Yeah, does that mean that dipstick father of mine isn't here, after all?' asked Sara.

'Is that you?' repeated Marigold, in response to someone only she could interpret. 'Lady Lucy, is that you? Do you have a message for us tonight?'

The music in the room took on fresh significance for her. Her voice changed and she began to exchange ripostes with somebody:

'This dance I can no longer go.

Pray you good madam why say you so?

Because George will not come, too.

He must come to, he shall come to,

And he must come whether he will or no.'

His lordship made no protest and neither did I. To deny the request to dance was to invite, if not ire exactly, then censure from the other participants.

Soon the songstress resumed her ditty:

'Welcome George, welcome, welcome.

Shall we go dance this once again?

Welcome, welcome, oh welcome dear,

And thank you so much for this dance.

Kiss me, kiss me...'

Next minute, I saw Lord Hart open his mouth to speak. With his partner on his right side he inverted his hand to touch the tips of her fingers, bow and honour her, I fancied.

'Madam, what good does it do the dead to dance with the living?'

Marigold yielded to the voice within her. She could speak but not own the words spoken.

'Sir, you are the cheefe architecte, overseer and Mr of my works for the pfecting of my heart's desire.'

'What about my love?'

'Sir, I would have that thing without which I cannot live.'

'Just tell me it isn't Philip.'

'Without sum acquaintaunce with astronomie and the courses coelestiall you shall not enter into my depe secretes.'

'Damn it, madam, did you not make me a solemn promise?'

'As did you, to procure my captaine.'

'Forgive me, countess,' replied Lord Hart hastily. 'How in heaven's name can this be in any way Christian?'

'The worst I know and feare not.'

'You'd cheat a man of his own soul?'

Which was when I became aware of Marigold's bizarre behaviour. She began to roll her eyes most wildly. From one earlobe dangled a drop-pearl earring with its tassel of human hair. As she lifted her gaze to his lordship and smiled, it gleamed and glistened. Then again, the ring looked less like a love token than a trophy. By wearing the clothes of the dead she could better voice their spirit.

'Sir, it is the subversion of good order, of all equitie and justice to bring someone back from the grave.'

'God knows, I never imagined that you would use my own loss against me,' said Lord Hart.

'The human heart does not receive its disturbance from the heavens.'

'Is it even in some small part my Philip?'

'Are you saying you do not value derely what I have already given you?'

'I can't bear the thought of some bogy man.'

*

It had to be approaching midnight. Already a wearisome foreboding and morbid fascination started to weigh heavily upon me at the progress of the séance. I could disregard my shudder of fear, but not of repugnance. That Lord Hart's denial and longing were in tune with his illness was obvious, but less so his bitter disappointment. It seemed that Countess Lucy had failed to effect some purpose, though what the exact nature of that purpose might be I found it hard to countenance. At the same time, the possessed Marigold had his full attention when she turned to mock him in the voice from 'the other side'.

'Better that you lock all doors. When finding here an impossibility of entering, this bogle or bugbear will go away, God willing?'

'Not that! Not ever!'

'Sir, think againe on the acts that were donne in your name, lest you deny me once too often.'

'What good is one man's likeness in the shape of another? He's a monster!'

'Sir, grete greif frees many a demon.'

'Damn it, I must know if he's human?'

'Sir, none of your stakes and pitfalls can help you now.'

'Do you even know the difference between accident and design, good and evil?'

'The Divel would have of us our souls for his paines only to survey and restore our lovers in the forms we conceive and plot them.'

'As I thought, you'd cheat me?'

'Sir, this daie long ago when I viewed Captaine Digby's face on a ring, since stolen, I made a rude tricke thereof, in a manner of a portrait with mine own hande, at which time the Divel being present, and being a soldier himself, as I remember, did offer me to make the same more parfitlie. Never would such a man in his sky collared gowne and his sylke doblett better adventure the practising this art.'

'Should I even give a damn about your lover? Give me back my beloved Philip!'

'And if he should have no harte, either?'

'Did not the Devil keep his promises to you, then?'

'Sir, I understood not them all, nor looked for so many, nor of that sort.'

'He forgot to tell you that the dead can't remember the dead or the living?'

'Sir, he who has no harte is nothing pleased with love, he is but a fetch of the one we loved.'

'Then the dead *are* lost to us forever?'

'Though my harte is upon the rack betwixt hope and despair, I am proposed, God willing, to still hold out for more.'

'Liar. You'd have this fetch of yours haunt me in the likeness of my brother?'

At that moment the flautist blew furiously for the invisible dancers. My own head whirled to keep pace with the abrupt change in tempo.

'What are a few Divel's delusions?' said the countess. 'What is it when a man is forced to make windows into his own soul, to remind him with whom his salvation doth lie?'

'I didn't ask to be damned by my own flesh and blood,' replied Lord Hart sourly.

'Now it is nothing in comparison to what it will be if you don't give me your love.'

'All I ask for is a living, breathing Philip.'

'And blind you to each other in a world that is everafter darke, like mine?'

'Madam, what manner of person are you?'

'Sir, a woman may only view in a mirror what she already is.'

'You raise ghosts, not men.'

'I think you doth find me unfeminine and fearsome.'

'Still you taunt me with your impossible scheming.'

'Still I allow you to live in my house at my convenience.'

His lordship slumped forward on his cushion. Reflected in his eyes was a terrible panic.

'I think you love to see grown men cry. Would you bind us all to your own sorcery?'

The countess spat and hissed furiously.

'Would *you* call *me* witch? I hear so many credible words of such from you, as alloweth not reason to doubt of it.'

At that moment the greyhound pushed open the door at which I spied, then trotted across the room as far as the séance. There, it sat regarding the proceedings with fresh interest. As did I.

'For God's sake,' said Lord Hart. 'Take someone else. Take Walker!'

'And if he proves repugnant to my nature?'

'But his loss is as great as mine.'

*

I leaned past the door foolishly much further, forgetting to silence its creaking hinges as I listened. Even a doomed man could not easily hold back when the exact nature of his doom was a mystery to him. But the séance was far from over. Marigold laughed. It was a laugh whose icy melody cut me to the quick with its exultation and scorn. With that one brief response to the mention of my name she showed a revulsion from any human joy or amusement. Again she spoke with the voice of another.

'To what sort shall you rank me? Would you have me tell him

of those stolen and lost, or shew him again the face of his pretty wife in a glass, and cause his beloved to be brought back at his command, as would you your brother? Did I not warn you of the price we must all pay? Better I kepe both your most mournful, loving hartes for eternitie.'

'Let Walker do your bidding, not Philip,' cried Lord Hart angrily.

'Sir, I ought to expresse, what man or woman I would have to be allowed my bedfellow. For, I will not bring in place a person ignorant of depe and violent loss, or skill of paine and hartache. They must understand adversity and be well instructed in the answeres of regret and greif…'

'To hell with your necromantic experiments. How can one broken heart mend another?'

'What nobler love is there than sorrow?'

'Madam, no amount of heartache will ever be sufficient for your foul transplant. Are you strong enough yourself?'

'Sir, would you do as I did and sign in your own blood a contract with the Divel and so grant him your soul in exchange for some arcane knowledge of love after death?'

'No, I wouldn't. I can't. I won't.'

'You grow sick and discontented and yet still I will persuade you to weep for me.'

'If you're not a witch then what are you?'

'Sir, if you pursue this wrong course you prevent that which I might, upon good reasons, do myself. So, I shall make of you such a precedent as your traitorous soul shall repent.'

'I have no more grief to give you. Let me die and be done with it.'

'Sir, only the living can weep for the dead.'

*

An exhausted Marigold slumped forward, said no more. But I did, I swore. Every man had a right to feel outraged when he overheard himself being bartered like merchandise, the more so when the reason for that barter was some phoney séance. The flautist began to blow a fresh tune even as I burst in.

Instantly the group broke circle. The moment they stood up and turned to flee, the spirit energy was lost completely.

James and Sara dodged by me with embarrassment written all over their faces.

Startled myself, I tried not to startle. I set my eyes firmly on Lord Hart. If vaguely the ancient planks beneath my feet protested, I paid no heed. His face was a mask of deceit and clever stratagem in the presence of his adversary. Clothed in his white suit, he stood before the fire where he coiled and uncoiled his long thin arm to conjure fantastic shapes with a poker.

'Oh, there you are, old chap. Come in. Don't be alarmed. We were just trying to contact our loved ones.'

I was still looking everywhere for 'the countess'. Now, no matter how obvious the proceedings, I urgently needed to discover what he had done to become so in thrall to any medium. I needed reassurance that he and I were not in anyway bound together other than in this world since no longer did I dare doubt the truth to nature of our shared vision.

'You haven't nearly told me what the hell is going on, George. That was your ex-mistress, wasn't it? If so, where did she go?'

'Oh, she knows every hidden door in these walls.'

'Because this house is haunted, Marigold thinks she can use Countess Lucy's spirit to make contact with your brother. Isn't that rather dangerous? You should be careful when opening a portal – it enables the dead to return to the realm of the living.'

'Oh, she's forever taunting me with her silly antics, the devil she is. Please don't take on so. She only does it to impress. She thinks she can scare me with her jealous rendition of the countess. She's provoking me with the ghost she says has come between us.'

I had been wrong about any ethereal music. In one corner an

ancient wind-up gramophone squeaked to a halt at the end of its recital.

With that, Lord Hart jerked his arm at me quite involuntarily. Slow to react at first, I nevertheless caught tight hold of the poker before either of us got hurt. By bursting in upon him like that I made the situation very awkward for us both. For a second, he seemed likely to unleash a tirade. Instead, he stared at me with his saucer eyes like a frightened child, only to be seized by violent, successive muscular contractions. Shouting his name did me no good. No matter what I did, he started fainting and fitting.

I managed to sit him back down in his chair by the fire where he spat and panted.

Pretty madly.

But not long could I gain his attention. He was lost in some spasmodic horror he alone could imagine. At the same time, the greyhound sat observing us curiously from the foot of the other, empty chair. He growled and guarded it closely, as if commanded.

Really, I could not waste any more of my time. I ran out the room and, leaning over the stair rail, bellowed to James and Sara to come quickly.

24

The most unreasonable man would have retired to bed with less fuss. Instead Lord Hart refused all help and shut himself in his room for the rest of the night. I did likewise, but not before I fetched a bottle of claret from the cellars. The greyhound returned to keep me company and watched while I drank myself into oblivion. It was two a.m.

In the darkness I could sense eagle-eyed wyverns eyeing me from the bedside curtains. When a man was guarded by such grotesque tapestries he could be forgiven for having a few reservations about such horny-toed friends, he could find it hard to believe that anything that grim could choose to owe him any allegiance. Not that I drew the drapes quite shut all round me. Of proper sleep it was too pointless to think.

I could estimate the increased warmth that came with my confinement but not my apprehension.

So it was I drew on my cigarette to muse on Lizzie.

Day 4. April 5. 2014.

Very woozy. Sick when she left her bed. Lethargic. Given up? Won't eat. Try tea and biscuit. Negative. Not like her usual self at all. Hits me that she really is wasting away. Impatient with her. Won't help herself. But how can I tell what it must feel like to be told that no one can save you?

Day 3. April 6. 2014.

Pukes dark brown, soupy liquid into her disposable grey cardboard bowl. Before she's sick she rocks like a child and gives a soft moan. Doesn't want to talk. Too sleepy. One eye permanently closed. Can't see very well anyway, not even with her glasses on. Can make out vague shapes only, she says. They cross her retina day and night, like cobwebs, blood and ghosts.

Smacks her parched lips and manipulates her mouth in dry, parched way. Water tastes awful. Can't settle – neither happily asleep nor out of pain.

No longer wired to an overnight drip. Skin looks loose, wrinkly. Deceptive because legs are so swollen. She would like to go into the garden one last time. Too ill. Too weak. Face only a shadow of what it was. Bony. Angular. Like a man's. Like her father? Lips unsmiling – tense. Inner battle going on. At one level she has given up and yet wants constant reassurance.

Suddenly she touches my arm very softly yet urgently.

'Please, Colin, be careful. Don't let me lie where I can be found.'

'Haven't I said? I'll bury your remains wherever you wish.'

Whereupon she grips my arm quite savagely.

'Not in the air and not in the ground.'

*

I woke up shouting.

Throwing off my counter-pane, I rushed to strike a match and light a candle. But wrong was I not and most definitely was that scream not mine. The clocks struck six in the morning. I pulled on my slippers and dressing-gown and made my way shiveringly on to the chilly landing. That cry had come from the direction of Lord Hart's bedchamber. Clearly the séance had given him bad dreams, too.

Better mind my own business, I thought, or else invite more embarrassing scenes on his part?

Yet something in his voice sounded so real, so unlike any night terror. Following the eye of white light cast by my candle along the panelled walls, I disturbed mice and spiders. Not even Sara was up and about yet, remaking fires. Otherwise the house was a silent maze of impenetrable gloom.

I entered the great chamber. There I rocked on warped oak floorboards whose unseasoned wood had long ago dried out so unevenly. The room felt chilly and unloved as if the soul had gone out of it. Sure enough, its fire was cold, white ash in its grate. Pompous, plaster pomegranates bulged like boils along a frieze, as did several grotesque jackdaws wearing cock-eyed gold crowns, if only to comment on the vanity of men.

'Really,' I said, giving myself a scare, 'it's too much. Why can't the stupid fellow simply shut up?'

Framed in misty mirror-glass that was set into the painted wood above the chimney piece, I seemed to float and revolve. I felt drugged, not drunk suddenly. On one very large table lay the remains of a meal but on another, smaller one his lordship had set out his board, draughts and dice ready for a game of backgammon. The pieces gathered dust where someone had yet to move them back or forwards. Clearly this was where George sat in a room still reserved for the best of occasions. Between this and the bedchamber lay another of the house's small, but elegantly furnished withdrawing rooms, I discovered. A dreadfully musty smell came from its faded tapestries as I crept closer to all the interminable moaning and groaning now coming from beyond the next door.

I could make out the wail of words, but few of the words wailed.

I went to lift the latch on the door somewhat gingerly when through it barged a tall, powerfully built figure. Dressed in worn-out clothes and odd boots, he barred my way. In his hand was a green, floppy hat trimmed with feather, I noticed. My candle lit his sore, red-rimmed eyelids. One stone-blind pupil blanked me totally. The other, shiny iris reflected my own in a film of blood that was streaked and spotted. It could have been the eye of a lunatic.

But deceived was I not and very quickly did I scream. The pace at which the dishevelled figure moved verged on the manic. From his harelip protruded a sharp tooth between incisors and molars like a fang. Its matching canine was missing. Round his neck was a priest's humeral veil whose oblong silk corners he clutched like someone who felt perpetually cold. My mind ran riot. Those could have been my stepfather's broad, rubbery lips, the day he half bit my ear off. So much larger than life did he appear that it was like coming face to face with a Wild Man from Ancient Britain. He was a child's worst bogy man, bogle or boggard.

'What the hell!' I cried. 'What have you done to Lord Hart?'

At which he seemed genuinely puzzled. When two strangers

gazed at each other it had to be because there was somebody or something that joined them together. One of us was looking for a missing link or he had simply forgotten. Some foul thing from hell he might have come to resemble, but in painful slow motion he struggled to mouth remnants of his mother tongue. He tried to remember what words to use from his former existence, I fancied:

'You do mistake me, sir.'

I went to seize hold of him but was instantly throttled in return. I was face to face with the man I had seen at the scene of Patrick McGuinness's death. But that revelation afforded me no comfort. His scornful eyes were such a shock to me that it posed a challenge to my own humanity. How had the dreadful loneliness in his face not struck me before? Gasping, I fought against such feelings of heart-felt pity, sympathy and general concern – my own.

Next minute he dashed me aside. I heard heavy boots tread the floors and flee upstairs, back to the long gallery or attics. I listened for jingling metal, like spurs.

All candles in the bedchamber had been knocked over and I was forced to use the light on my phone. Lord Hart sat bolt upright in bed in a mess of black pyjamas and blankets. He clasped his hands tightly together in prayer at the tip of his chin, his wild eyes stared straight ahead. He appeared to see right through me.

Of my own pitiable look he was oblivious. Raising one of his arms, I used his wrist to dab drool from his mouth with his sleeve.

'Did you think that man was your brother?' I asked, still choking and coughing.

He made no reply, but horror continued all over his face. His cheeks had gone deathly white and his lips were grey.

'Er, did you recognise him, at all? Was he even *like* Philip?'

He gave a brief nod. No blood spattered his bed, no obvious wounds lacerated his chest or arms, yet he had been struck dumb as if by some terrible blow.

'I have an idea he's still in the house,' I said and left him to relight his own candle as I took one for myself.

Little else could I do when he still suffered from such a compelling and disturbing mental impression. To say of him that he had simply mistaken one man for another was insufficient.

*

The higher I mounted the great staircase, the more the sharp-toothed monkeys and priapic beasts crawling up the banisters gaped at me in wonder. Perhaps they were not trying to amuse anyone after all, I thought, perhaps they were frozen in a pain of their own. It took my own shock to see it: their exquisitely carved eyes, teeth and tongues captured a terrible moment frozen in time long ago, on the day the house had first sunk into sorrow?

There was no sign of anyone in the long gallery but the stairs, it turned out, climbed further. For steps to be so widely and so beautifully fashioned from best oak this high in the house was clearly unusual. The builders had intended guests to climb all the way to the rafters.

When one man had another's nightmare rudely visited upon him against his will he could no longer dismiss it as an illusion of illness, not even his own, he had to admit that it might have some objective existence. When ghosts inconveniently ceased to be merely apparent or nominal, the most entrenched sceptic had to face facts about life and death free from prejudice and convention, he had to try to see what actually underlay any comparison.

Besides, I owed the bastard a punch in the face.

The staircase led nowhere. Baffled, I turned to retreat when the light from my candle lit up the wall at which the steps ended so abruptly. Etched into the stone was the definite outline of a door, long since bricked up and painted over. By calculating where I was on the west side of the house, it was possible to imagine that this door had originally been designed to give access to the roof. Beyond the blank bricks I should have been able to enter a flat-leaded walkway to give myself splendid views over the walled pleasance garden and clear view of the stars.

Except the extension to the house had never been built. My quarry could not have escaped through there, I realised.

How many other hopeful promenaders or astronomers had stood before this door to a world forever beyond reach?

Perhaps Countess Lucy had simply run out of money?

*

Back in my icy bedchamber I swept aside the heavy red arras that led into the closet. To my alarm, a chair lay on its back close to the desk. My eyes settled on a battered leather-bound volume of an old book newly fetched from the library. Hastily abandoned lay a pair of clumsy looking glasses with round lenses. I picked them up and tried them on. Mounted in a double spectacle frame made of bone, the lenses were thicker in the middle of the glass than the edges and although useless for distance viewing could enlarge the sight of print on a page. An ingenious semi-circular spring kept these ugly monstrosities on my nose while two green ribbons secured them with loops round my ears.

On the desk sat a woman's spectacle case engraved with Madonna and child and four ugly angels. Whoever had just been reading the book had been rudely interrupted, but not by me.

Written by Christopher Marlow and Thomas Nash, its crinkled vellum pages stood open at the suicidal lover's lament for Aeneas in 'The Tragedie of Dido Queene of Carthage'.

Fresh underlining sparkled where a Dutch quill had been used to draw attention to Dido's last words both passionately and violently:

> **'Here lye the Sword that in the darksome Cave**
> **He drew, and swore by to be true to me.'**

Still dissolving in the black ink was a tear.

*

A moment later, I felt a fresh chill on my neck. The window's blank metal ventilation panel stood open to let in a blast of winter.

I marched over to shut it and in doing so looked down onto the four grassy squares of formal gardens that stretched directly below me into darkness. For my own trepidation it was at first impossible to account. Then I saw *him* limping along a pale gravel path in the thickening mist close to the house, a hunched, brooding figure who buried his head in his rat-coloured cloak as he escaped through the gate that led to the church and its graves.

I cupped my hands to my mouth and shouted even as he passed behind the veil.

'You're no wraith, you live and breathe.'

*

With daylight came a decision. The mist clung to the crenelated battlements of Coberley Hall, mischievously adding to its promise of seclusion and secrecy. It was not a menacing brume, entirely. Yet neither could I delay but a sense of menace seemed to grip me.

A few roseate tints of pale sun, instead of lighting my progress, reddened the lime render like bruises on the courtyard walls. Such livid contusions in the cement were the surface manifestation of some internal wound. Each rosette bloomed bloodier and bloodier as I went by.

Hazy myself, I tried not to stray in the haze. Nor was I too drunk, though surely could I not deny that I had drunk too much last night.

As for his lordship, I left him a ludicrously, cantankerous bore. Locked in his bedchamber, he sat on a chair and levelled his gun's thirty-two inch barrels at anyone who tried to enter.

Frankly, I was not sorry to unlatch the postern door and set foot in the lane. Out here at least, the day was slightly less grey, the sun less dissolved behind so much vapour suspended in the air. On glancing up I glimpsed a figure seated at the gatehouse window.

To the best of my belief it was the same face as before, although my eyes scarcely discerned any actual features. I waved, cautiously. Such intense scrutiny of my departure could but speed the departure itself. Then I rolled back my cuff to uncover my watch. Only now, when I was safely outside my own walls, did the seconds and minutes consent to turn past four p.m., that first recorded moment of my arrival. I tried my phone. It did the same.

Half way up the hill I paused again in order to ring Peter Slater.

'You want me, Inspector?'

'H'm, well, yeah. You were right. Something's happened.'

25

Inch-long thorns clawed at me from black hedges along the lane, hideous branches leaned low from bare trees to pluck at my progress. Where one shape shifted to another in the fog the road disappeared into virtually nothing. I was literally my own compass in so much empty whiteness.

Straightening my heavy cap on my head, I soon felt my face acquire a rawness and coldness unacceptably numbing. Hardly ever did I avert my stare from things I saw or expected to see at any moment. Although I still held out hope of explanations that were positive and rational, it took considerable concentration not to let the smirking miasma prey on my mind. Actual fear linked arms with the archetypal. Unseen fields had a grave stillness about them, especially when my boots were the only sound in the silence.

Not a single bird sang. It was ridiculous but true: never was a man more frightened than by himself.

I stopped dead. Something about the size of a small dog hopped about in the lane not far in front of me. Armed and clothed as I was in a dead man's tweed shooting jacket and dark olive moleskin breeks, I felt obliged to show what it took to maintain nature's natural balance. For, was I not now steward of this land and arbiter of all that lived or died within its bounds?

Deftly, I pressed two orange cartridges into the breach of my gun. The greenest of countrymen should be able to blast this over-sized rabbit to pieces, I thought. I took time to take aim.

I was not in the least unnerved, except in so far as the fog made mysteries of everything. Damp, white air silvered the creature's delicate whiskers and sprinkled its reddish back with pearls. Its every breath dissolved in smoky clouds, much as mine did. Revolving its long black ears my way, it suddenly rose to attention. I saw it sit up like a stiff little soldier to fix me with its gaze. Still it went on chewing green shoots stolen from my field. Never had a look been so brazen and unflinching, but honestly there was something else in that gaze that spoke where words failed.

That was no rabbit, it was a hare.

Then it vanished, before I could tighten my finger on the trigger. Together with the Devil's assistance, it raced in leggy bounds too fast for my befogged eyes to follow. With its escape came deliverance. In Countess Lucy's time such a red-eyed pest would have been regarded as a messenger or spirit.

*

Oddly, no one was there to meet me at Father O'Connell's derelict bungalow. The heavy, rusty chain round the gatepost indicated that although padlocked, its days of guarding something were at an end.

That said, I climbed over.

I began my advances cautiously. When someone went in search of an ogre that had the strength of a gorilla, the most sceptical man had to credit such a creature with some physical or practical qualities. Thanks to my own bruising experience, I did for a moment try to set aside my former uncertainties to explore a different sort of logic. Of heaven and hell, I was not yet persuaded. Nevertheless, I had to remind myself, soberly and not in some phantasmal way, not to envisage the face of my stepfather. I said it again – we scared ourselves most.

*

In starting to poke about like this, I was soon ankle-deep in things left behind. Resembling a long row of stables, rickety wooden sheds had seen their upper doors torn off by gales since the great abandonment. They lay in a line at my feet like broken sails. I was looking at a place once used for rearing pheasants on an industrial scale. The shadow of death still outdid the decay.

Even so, for a moment, I had half a mind to survey the priest's former home, take this occasion to assess its real estate value. While I was rightful lord of the manor, my future remained contingent upon the rapid acquisition of some serious cash. Throw in a field or two and I might yet put New Farm, as it was once called, on the market for a million.

If all the paraphernalia of bird breeding had been discarded in the overly hasty departure so, too, had somebody's books and

196

clothes. A man's belongings rotted among a tangle of spare, bone-white ceramic heating elements for the sunlamps that had incubated thousands of eggs. That I could hear rats was not encouraging. At the same time, that unpleasant sensation of not being alone got on my nerves. Snapping shut the breach of my gun, I felt spied upon and spun round.

Sitting sentry-like on the grass by the gate, the red-eyed hare observed my foggy peregrination from afar.

*

Rats or no rats, I had to give that noise due credence. It was coming from somewhere inside the barn next door.

On my way there I tripped over a Bible. Tossed violently aside, it lay among a compressor, empty gas cylinders, rusty tools and several half-full jerrycans of fuel. Somebody had dragged a vinyl record player and washing machine from the bungalow, it seemed, in an act of supreme carelessness. I gave the Bible a gentle flip with my toe. Nothing so singular and mysterious could be regarded without some fascination.

Inside the front cover was a name. It was Father O'Connell.

*

As soon as I entered the very long barn I found myself among various wooden stalls, piles of creosoted timber and rotting haystacks. This far into the interior, the roof turned everything into a tunnel.

'Who's there?' I demanded, none too happily.

Still fighting the dictates of my imagination, I hardly dared suppose who it might be that moved beyond the wall of darkness.

Surely that was someone climbing down the wall?

Then I heard it, that pattering sound of claws or spurs against the rafters. They were restless, agile, prehensile, as of some creature whose fact I no longer regarded as fiction. I edged nearer. That was to challenge whatever obscene tactics my mind could yet muster. It wasn't just a few birds. I still actually hoped that, with the light behind me, this hideous awakening was somehow myself projected in shadow. That said, there was no denying an all-seeing and mindful malevolence.

'Come out or I'll shoot!'

But not long was I in suspense. Next minute I jerked my gun up to my shoulder and let fly.

My shots gave the tinned roof an awful battering. I heard a yell – someone had dived behind a pile of wood in a corner.

Then reason deserted me. I burst out laughing, I who was in the grip of a morbid excitement, I who would so insist on joining the dead to lurk among the detritus of someone's former existence. Now I skulked here more in cowardly than murderous intent, I who had sneaked away from Coberley Hall to give credit to the incredible, or so I'd hoped. Instead, I was in disbelief at myself.

A second or two later, one shadow detached itself from another. Ignoring my smoking gun, a black and white animal rose up vertically in order to place its front paws on my shoulders. Try as I might, I could not stop him licking my face with his slobbering tongue round my chin. It was Prince.

'You trying to kill me, Inspector?'

Now it was my turn to stare down the barrel of a gun.

'Yeah, well, okay. I had it in mind you were someone else.'

Peter dusted his large leather hat where lead pellets had just rained down on him from on high.

'I left my Land Rover up the lane so as not to announce my arrival.'

'You hear anyone,' I asked breathlessly, 'on top of that great pile of timber?'

He lowered his shotgun and felt inside his padded wax jacket for a cigarette.

'When I said come prepared I didn't mean you to blow his head off. You scared him shitless, I'm damned if you didn't.'

There came an ominous pause while we considered our best options.

Suddenly Peter began to examine the soft earth floor of the barn. He worked his way inch by inch back into daylight. There he crouched on the ground like someone examining the spoor of a wild animal.

'What d'you say we both search the bungalow?'

*

It was but a few yards from the barn to the side of the creamy Cotswold stone ruin. Now that we were two guns instead of one, I had little hesitation in kicking in a flimsy wooden door that led in through a conservatory. Along with the dereliction, the once domestic character of someone's home still lingered. However, ivy grew rampant through cracks and a garden rake stood rotting against a wall beneath smashed panes of glass.

When someone burgled a dead man's house after many years he did more than intrude upon a sickening emptiness, he soon felt sick at himself. If the dead were ever more than mere dust then who was I to say that they did not exist as they had always done, that it was not their books, their music, all their personal things that they still loved? 'What the devil,' I thought. 'How infuriating it would be to return to a place you knew so well only to find it all flung to the winds.'

Peter was too busy to notice.

'Milk went missing this morning from outside the Shooting School, Inspector.'

I unscrewed the top from a plastic bottle that stood half empty on a window sill and gave it a sniff.

'I believe you.'

'You see him, too?'

'Last night, in Coberley Hall.'

'You get a good look at him?'

'He's a beast of a man, that's certain.'

Triumph paled into fear as my gun-toting friend tightened his grip on his weapon.

'Keep searching, Inspector. There could be more clues.'

A distinct urinary odour filled my nostrils. More man than fox or cat, I remembered how awful Jan had declared I looked and smelt. Like someone down on my luck, she'd implied. I spat phlegm on the decayed carpet. Perhaps all men on the run came to smell the same. I could stomach my gut reaction of disgust but not of desolation. Everything else exuded damp like a cave. A hideous brown sofa faced the fireplace on which an unpleasant pile of animal bones resided – rabbit skulls, mostly. In addition, the floor was littered with hundreds of dead wasps. Curled into tight little black and gold balls, they crunched underfoot in drifts like shingle.

'Whoever visited George last night absolutely terrified him.' I declared. 'They knew each other, all right. It's not all in his head. He wants his dead brother to come back for him. Yet that's what scares him most! It doesn't make sense. Did he literally think he saw Philip? Was it even a man?'

'Man-like, at least,' replied Peter. 'In our mind's eye grief can take the strangest form, I'm damned if it can't. Abnormal. Huge. Atrocious. Of the nature of an autonomous beast. I guess it comes as a shock to see worlds that are best left an invisible, mirror-image of our own?'

'You mean our minds will go where we won't?'

'I really don't know any other way to put it.'

'What can anyone want with George?'

'Consider fear our worst enemy.'

'Yeah, well, maybe, but that's not massively helpful, is it?'

'That's only because in general we have stopped believing in the unbelievable, Inspector.'

'Is there a difference?'

'Some hold that long ago the human imagination simply

invented God and the Devil. Compared with our forbears we consider ourselves enlightened, but are we really so very different? Accursed manifestations revisit us in our dreams.'

'Accursed, no. Day and night terrors, possibly.'

Peter took a peek into a cupboard.

'You tell me. You met him.'

'We should agree a strategy.'

'First let me tell you how Father O'Connell met his end, here, in this room. You up to it, Inspector?'

'Oh yeah, I am. No, honestly, that's fine. Totally.'

He was really asking if I still trusted him.

26

'It was August, 1980. To step back through Coberley Hall's ancient porch after a year was to re-enter its peculiar hermetic mixture of neglect and sadness. The thing is, Inspector, I didn't dislike it, all I wanted was to have some fun. I was sixteen.

' "Pater's in his office," said George, peering at me round the edge of the front door. "Pax vobis and all that. Better come quietly."

'A big purple bruise darkened one cheek, I noticed.

' "How is your father?"

' "Cancer tests came back negative."

' "I'm so pleased."

' "Glad someone is, old chap."

'I only saw Joseph Jones at a distance. He was a thin, introverted little man with a vicious face who paced about with his head permanently bowed as if he could think of nothing but his own problems. But I soon forgot all that when I saw how many skeletons had been assembled in the otherwise abandoned nursery. As well as a set of badger's bones, there was now a fox and a hare, all wired together on special frames. Since my last visit, he and his brother had become remarkably adept at physical anthropology. Lying in an open red box, something marked 'Exhibit A' caught my eye straightaway.

' "Is that what I think it is?" I exclaimed, going to finger its bony crust.

' "Don't touch that! That's Philip's most prized possession."

' "It's huge."

' "See how the biting surface is worn away. That shows he lives wild and eats gritty foods."

' "He?"

' "The tooth-fang has both roots still attached, you'll note."

' "But where in hell's name did he find it?"

' "You ask him, old chap."

' "Where is Philip?"

' "In Chatcombe Wood. The fool didn't come home last night."

'Neither George nor I heard anyone return that evening. We only met Philip at breakfast in the great hall next morning. Remnants of mud caked his face in tiger stripes and fingernails were black with dirt. It was hard to persuade him to eat a single piece of toast, let alone sit long at the table.

' "Must we leave so damned early?" I protested. "The sun has hardly come up yet over the hills."

'Tucking his knife into his belt, Philip settled a hat pierced with ivy leaves on his head. Then he reached for his spear.

' "You want to hunt the enemy dead or alive, don't you?"

' "What enemy?"

' "What do you think?"

' "I thought we gave up that silly game last year? After all, someone died."

' "Who says it's a game?"

*

'Once past Slack's Cottage, we marched three abreast up the lane. On our left, a dense line of trees and blackthorn topped a steep grassy bank all the way to the brow of the hill.

' "Well, in you go, then," said Philip and peeled back several spiky branches that had been carefully bent, not broken.

' "So how do you know this is right?" I asked, licking a bloody scratch on my hand.

' "I've seen him come and go."

' "Doesn't mean we should."

'A deep litter of dry twigs, the debris of countless violent storms, snapped like glass under our toes.

' "See, this is where he shits and pees," announced Philip proudly and pointed to a freshly scraped hole filled with shiny brown excrement.

' "Our enemy have a name?" I asked.

'Philip gave a laugh. An unkind one.

' "And this is where he scratches his back. Look how the moss and lichen have been knocked off the bark of this tree. That's his clawing post over there by his den."

'What was so extraordinary, Inspector, was that we were only a little way from the busy main road. It was a place hidden in plain sight, so to speak. I exchanged glances with George, but he only winked. To please his brother, he wanted me to play along, I suppose. That meant giving in to his wildest whim. So far, this other world, so close to and parallel with our own, had been a bit of a lark but I was right to think that things were about to take an unexpected turn.

'George placed a hand on his brother's shoulder.

' "Steady on, old chap, you know what happens when you get too excited."

' "I'm all right George, really I am."

'The sun shone through the trees and gently warmed a large black hole among the trees roots. Naturally, Philip was first down. I had no lamp of my own, I had to rely on brief flashes of torchlight far in front of me, I had to claw my way into the entrance like a mole, Inspector. The slope seemed to go down forever as if we were descending into the bowels of the Earth. I had George's heels in my face and stones up my nose.

'Then, without warning, I stopped scraping my scalp on rock any longer.

' "Look here," said Philip, shining his light all round. "Spoons and tureens."

'We were in a cave of some sort.

' "What the devil! Isn't that our silver cake-stand?" declared

204

George. "Last saw that drying next to the sink in our scullery."

' "There could be a whole network of tunnels down here," I said with wonder. "I bet they go all the way back to Coberley Hall."

' "Keep exploring," ordered Philip. "This will be where our bogy man hides his maravedi and silver reals."

' "Our what?" I said, startled.

'His eyes flashed blue in the torchlight.

' "Treasure, of course."

' "Not that, the other thing."

' "You know, a bugbear, boggard or bogle. Every fiend loves to hoard shiny things, like a pirate."

'He would have had us search for stolen loot all day, Inspector, but I saw nothing else except a goggle-eyed hare lying stiff on a slab.'

*

Peter stubbed out his cigarette on the leg of his chair. After selecting another he slid me the packet, but his hand was as diffident as my own and he retracted it. Instead he left the offering part way between us on the table. In the end I gave in and helped myself.

'H'm, well, yeah,' I said. 'So how far did the warren extend, to your knowledge?'

'Never did venture all the way underground, Inspector. Never did go that far, I'm damned if we didn't. The batteries began to fade on Philip's torch and we very nearly got lost in all the darkness.'

'That it? You chickened out?'

'Not exactly. We decided to...'

But before I heard any more I had to go outside for a pee. A few minutes later I was back in my place at the table, in part because Peter refused to bow to my petulant protest. During my brief absence his look had grown solemn and his cheeks more ashen. One thing was obvious beyond his tiresome desire to unburden himself, in talking to me he somehow hoped the benefit would be mutual.

*

'In those days everyone knew that Father O'Connell had been quietly removed from the priesthood for indulging in the occult, Inspector. He had become very interested in seventeenth century witches. Already he had lured Philip in for beer and biscuits to discuss the existence of devils and demons. It was in him that we decided to confide our ghostly mission.

' "Stick together," George hissed in my ear when we opened the gate to the bungalow. "Whatever you do, don't trust his wandering fingers."

'The Holy Father was scraping up weeds in his garden, we discovered. His bony face had a very red nose, while his cheeks were horribly sallow. Every now and then he would stop to clasp his chest and sigh for breath. He wore his divine vestments to do his hoeing, but he did not look to me like a maniac. Stooped and hooded in the hot sunlight, he was someone whose arthritis slowed his progress. Only his weariness was more spiritual than physical. I felt sorry for him, Inspector, really I did, but I took an immediate dislike to him.

' "Top o'the morning to you, Father," said Philip and was the only one who walked straight up to him.

'Father O'Connell greeted him with genuine charity and kindness. Cupping his crabby hands round his smooth neck, he looked him straight in the eye quite fondly.

' "You've brought help, I see."

' "The others don't believe me, Father."

' "Ah, history is full of doubting Thomases, but you and I know the truth, don't we, Philip? *For the trumpet shall sound and the dead will be raised/and we shall be changed.* Come inside, all of you, and we'll crack open some beer."

'Now the temptation of free beer was too much for me, Inspector, I have to admit and so into the bungalow we all trotted. We sat on the edge of the new brown sofa and Father O'Connell brought us a whole crate of Budweiser until it wasn't long before we were ever so slightly drunk, to say the least. The old man reeked of incense, perhaps to cover up equally intoxicating odours. An altar cloth lay on a bench in one corner where the waxy scent of smouldering candles made me feel doubly groggy. The crucifix had come loose on its nail and hung upside down. Dressed in his sleeveless chasuble, he treated us like celebrants but really he was more interested in our brawn than our brains.

'In those days the Coberley Estate bought surplus railway sleepers by the hundred from British Railways. Joseph Jones used the wood to make gateposts and fences. A great cliff of the smelly things stood in the barn by the bungalow, stinking of creosote. Some still do. It was from these that Father O'Connell tasked us to construct a deadfall trap.

'Philip was enthralled.

' "It's so dark back here he won't know what hits him."

'Father O'Connell, looking wan and exhausted, not well at all, finished tying the trip cord to a bottle of milk to trigger the avalanche of timber.

' "With the day so dry the beast will be thirsty."

*

'By then it was already seven p.m. Father O'Connell cooked us sausages and bacon and we settled down in the conservatory at the front of the bungalow to watch the yard outside. I'd twice fallen asleep when I heard something creep down the side of the pheasant sheds and hatchery. Like a wave rolling stones up a beach, the noise rose louder and louder. Shadows grew longer and played tricks on my senses. Then the hairs bristled on the back of my neck, I'm damned if they didn't.

'Which was when I knew that I had seen something like this before, Inspector. Hundreds of rats were on the move. Their bodies melded together into one long, slithering river as they flowed right by our window. Of course, the grain feeders had just been filled in the woods to help fatten the pheasants, which had sparked the migration.

' "Won't the bogy man howl if we hurt him?" I asked, shivering inside my anorak.

'Philip gave a snort.

' "Who cares? He's not human."

'Without warning, Father O'Connell, his resolve strengthened by the beer, flung open the conservatory door. He held before him the cross that hung by a chain round his neck and sang the canticle deus misereatur from Psalm 67 as he rushed off to the barn.

'A moment later there came the sound of his voice, loud and clear:

' "*And if ye be evil ye are consigned to an awful view of your own guilt and abominations which doth cause ye to shrink from the presence of the Lord into an awful state of misery and endless torment from which you can no more return. Therefore, ye have drunk damnation into your own soul. Oh, that ye would awake! Awake from a deep sleep, yea, even the sleep of hell.*"

'He never returned. Only after a sliver of moon cleared the clouds did we summon up the courage to mount a search. The rats were all gone, but we found our priest kneeling on the barn floor with his hands clasped against his chest in tense supplication.

' "Quick, fetch him a drink," I said. "He looks all in."

'Philip ran for a beer but Father O'Connell would have none of it. Instead he again muttered garbled biblical passages, more in question than answer.

' "SHE is the resurrection and the life? He who believes in HER, even though he dies, shall live?"

'Philip curled his arm around the old man's neck and whispered in his ear.

' "So, please, tell us who is 'she'?"

' "I mistook her gold eyes for those of an angel…"

' "Has he gone mad?" I asked, confused.

'But Father O'Connell only renewed his plea.

' "For such fascination is commonly used by the Devil and his demons to deceive the innocent."

' "So what did 'she' do to make you feel so threatened?" asked Philip.

' "She demanded to know by what right I thought I could harm her sweetheart so cruelly?"

' "Doesn't mean you did anything to her."

' "She spoke to me plainly enough: *Sir, did you not bind yourself to me by all the obligations of nature, duty and oath and still you would hurte him which I treasure moste?"*

' "Best leave him," I said, "he's still in a state of shock."

' "Peter's right, old chap," agreed George. "He needs to rest. Those rat bites look nasty."

'It took all three of us to lift him to his feet and steer him back to the bungalow. There we sat him down at his dining room table. Still he refused to unclasp his bloody fingers.

'With great reluctance, Philip followed us back down the track to Coberley Hall.

' "What a loser! Kill a fiend is what he said, but he was just full of pathetic excuses." '

*

I looked Peter in the eye.

'The thing is, I'm still at a loss…'

My enthusiastic raconteur watched hot ash fall from his cigarette while his hand tried not to tremble. As did mine.

'Father O'Connell's undoing was his obsession with evil, Inspector, I'm damned if it wasn't. On his shelves was a 1603 edition of Henry Boguet's Discours des Sorciers. In it was his 'Examen of Witches' or instructions on how to recognise those who have renounced 'God, Baptism and Chrism.''

'Doesn't mean he saw evil where there was none.'

'You decide, Inspector. We discovered him still sitting at this very table where we had left him, dry drool sealing his lips. He sat bolt upright and was staring blankly into space as if the last thing he'd seen had appeared at that window. He was dead, of course.'

'Can you, like, remember what the medics said?'

'It was suggested that the rat bites had poisoned him in a matter of hours, but that's not the oddest part, Inspector. He sat at this very table with his pen resting on a line in his book of Common Prayer in which he had scribbled a few words: **We men are the monsters now.**'

*

I took a deep breath and the room smelt doubly awful. For a moment I thought I could detect some mephitic presence from the grave that clung to the rotten wallpaper and moth-eaten carpets, something noisome and poisonous. Of course I knew that a man had it in him to shock himself with his own savagery. Each night, did I not dream such terrors, about myself? But to scare oneself to death?

'If the rat bites didn't kill him, what did?'

'We villagers have a story we sometimes tell to frighten the kids, Inspector. Ever since Countess Lucy starved to death in Coberley Hall, she has continued to curse the house and its lands with her sorrow. She is forever doomed to grieve for the captain she would bring back from the grave until she can find a way to make him feel love again. Take care, Inspector. Through your heart-ache she would restore her lover's.'

'I very much doubt that,' I said irritably.

'No one has yet proved worthy of her. Instead, their portraits hang unwanted on her wall as poor reminders of her one true soul mate, Captain Digby, cruelly lost in the English Civil War.'

Suddenly Father O'Connell's remark held new meaning for me: *and we shall be changed.*

'Seriously? You think her curse killed the old fool?'

'What worse affliction is there than to be told that you have lost the love of your life? What sentence of excommunication, profane oath or imprecation is worse than to feel that you have been abandoned not only in this world but the next? How terrible to fear that in the afterlife there can be no love? That night in the barn, Father O'Connell hoped to glorify himself by going to meet some fallen angel, but instead he came face to face with his own demon.'

'He was heart-broken? Yeah, okay, but for whom did it break?'

'Did I not say, for the love of the God he had forsaken.'

'Doesn't mean I want to hear all about it.'

'I think you want to hear very well. Last night, Lord Hart didn't exactly believe that it was his dead brother he saw but, like O'Connell, nothing surpasses the dread and desire that come with the temptation.'

'You saying that his bruised mind won't let Philip go, no matter what the abomination that comes through the door?'

'It's that or be left alone with nothing.'

'It comes to something when a man's grief can be used against him.'

'Is it not written in scripture, "Thou scarest me with dreams and terrifiest me through visions?" '

*

I dismissed the tenet of the accusation, if not the words with which I was accused.

'Yeah. Probably never happened. But you've got to admire the local ghost busters, haven't you?'

Of my own haunting it was as yet impossible to speculate.

'You can be sure of one thing, Inspector, whatever visited Father O'Connell at his window that fateful night had nothing to do with divine intervention, I'm sure of it. He sat dead in his chair and his eyes were wide with amazement. He was not a good man, I'm damned if he wasn't. Bigotry was an in-dwelling and attendant spirit which, when freed, turned cruel and malignant. He'd gone into that barn with only one thing in mind. The ugliest bogy man is but the reification of our own worst feeling – our willingness to kill.'

'A bogy man, eh? That's a strange name for such a cruel

intention.'

'Imagine if grief, pain or guilt, could detach themselves from us to become a living, walking shadow of what we most regret ever doing? Wouldn't you feel cursed, Inspector? Wouldn't that feel like evil? To be able to see yourself pursued by something *of* yourself?'

'Sounds positively heretical. But none of this nearly suggests why the curse should bother me. Ever since Lizzie died I have done my utmost to be less and less bound by any feelings for others, have discounted what love I have left, have been that heartless.'

'What makes you think Lady Lucy doesn't feel cursed, too?'

*

All that time wasted chatting to Peter, the mist had grown thicker across the fields. I begged a ride home in his battered truck but he wouldn't hear of it. Instead he waved me a most perfunctory goodbye and drove off with only his dog for company. Somehow he seemed to take it for granted that we had done our best by each other, that from now on we must definitely work together to solve any mystery. I was not so sure. Either way, I had no further immediate use for him.

My lack of gratitude did not mean I was thankless.

Rather, I thanked him to leave my affairs alone.

27

That evening I sat in my room too troubled to write in my ledger. Instead, on my lap lay Lady Lucy's receipt book. In an entry for 1642 she had recorded how gargling infusions of hedge mustard in a mixture of scented honey might improve her voice, I noticed. Once a man stole a dead woman's secrets he had it in his power to reveal them to all and sundry. After he decided that her writing was no longer her property alone he could treasure or destroy it quite treacherously in a cold act of betrayal. He could be blind and deaf to her bequest to live again through his own sight, sound, touch, taste and smell. In order to deny life to the dead he had better refuse to respect, love and admire her mortal remains after they had lain so long under the soil. He would do best to be so cruel as to dismiss all his and her feelings, I asked myself?

Otherwise, was I no better than those superstitious villagers who told silly stories of ghosts to their children?

In the air came a faint perfume of dried flowers, either valerian or violet.

'How hunted and alone you must have been when the enemy stood at your gate ready to burn down your barns and steal your horses,' I said aloud.

Scribbled elsewhere in the receipt book's margin was a barely legible afterthought, penned in a great hurry: 'I fear the provision of corn and malt will not hold out, if this damned war continue. Poor Lady Jordan. They do saye that she hath been quite distracted since the siege of Cirencester and now only plays with dolls.'

Countess Lucy could withstand her own feelings of anxiety but not of greater tragedy.

*

A moment later I heard knocking. At first I ignored the harsh echo of each hollow rap, but not for long the urgency of the raps echoed. Someone stood at the shot-riddled front door downstairs, I realised. I jumped off my bed. There was no denying such a brutal summons at such an hour. Each blow reverberated in rooms all about me until the whole house felt at war.

I descended the staircase in a great hurry.

'Don't do it, Colin.'

I stopped dead in the gloomy entrance hall and looked round. Lord Hart sat on a stool, his face lit by a flickering sconce against the wall.

'You serious?' I asked, seeing him level his shotgun at me in the candlelight.

'It's not who you think it is.'

'So tell me, how do you know?'

'Open that door and you'll get your head blown off.'

He had set aside his dragon cane and held the gun steadily and firmly. Clothed in nautical, light-blue blazer and blue deck shoes, he wore his tinted glasses at the end of his nose. In his perpetually dark world he was a host who liked to dress to impress, but still he refused to draw the bolts on his door.

There was no sign of James or anyone else.

'Forgive me,' I said, steel entering my voice. 'I don't mean to interfere, but what harm can it do to inquire who it is?'

Despite what I knew of his volatile personality, I was surprised to see a tear roll down his cheek. Not until then did I realise what a mask of make-up he wore.

'Think of me as not being mens sana in corpore sano, Colin, but that thing out there isn't someone either of us wants to meet. It certainly isn't Lizzie. Believe me, it's your worst possible nightmare. Go ahead, consider yourself sounder in mind and body than me for the moment because you may be right, but you and I have one thing in common at least. We both know what it means to keep faith with the dead.'

I found his remark repulsive but brave. For a man to keep guard like that on such an icy winter's night he had to be positively reptilian. In order to be that reptilian he had to hold out against all warmth, ardour or affection. In a bid to stay cool, calm and collected under siege he could be no good to anyone else, he could only be his own cold comfort.

Whereupon I turned on my heels and left him to grin and bear it. For at that moment there came a profound silence, a dark stillness, a breathless expectancy. And I, Colin Walker, aware of the fix I was in, conscious of how much I did and did not yet know, but already stricken, placed my hand on my heart to steady its raging pulse, slow its vibrating beat and check its battering-ram blows.

28

'You see anything, Inspector?'

I shook my head. I could picture separate parts of the scene but not yet the sum total of what I pictured.

'Fool left the Calor gas on, did he?'

'Or maybe because he can't be sure what he did says it all?'

Susan squared her shoulders and swelled her chest. By the dark look she gave me, it was clear that she had already come to a few conclusions of her own.

'You should have called me sooner,' I said sternly.

She wiped her work-stained hands with considerable emphasis on her apron. It was half way between acknowledgement and dismissal. We were standing behind the barns at the back of the farmyard opposite Slack's Cottage.

'It was a pretty loud bang, Inspector.'

'Yeah. I mean, what happened to him?'

'He was in my kitchen eating cakes when it happened.'

'It literally resembles a war zone.'

I directed my gaze back to the sea of soot and ash at my feet. What had once been a man's home was now a pathetic, smouldering wreck. It was hardly possible to distinguish between the vehicle's sloping towing end, where its owner had sat on his sofa watching a TV, from the opposite, squarer one where he had stood doing his washing and cooking. The fire had peeled off the roof like a sardine can and exposed all those clever slots and holes into which the happy caravanner had liked to fold his tables and clothes.

'He didn't, like, think to tell me himself?'

'Too scared, Inspector.'

'Of me?'

'Not you, the other one.'

216

'Which other one?'

'Do you even care, Inspector?'

'Where is Paul Mitchell now?'

Susan shot me a surly glance.

'He has run off to live with his sister in London.'

'Because of this other person you mentioned?'

'Scare someone half out of their wits and you might forget to turn the gas off, too, Inspector.'

*

I gave the caravan a closer examination. Judging by the way the supporting jacks had sunk into the mud the chassis had not moved for years. Our retired tractor driver had holed up here in his old age, out of sight and out of mind until one big boom had blown his little world to kingdom-come.

I unearthed a jerrycan from a patch of blackened grass.

'This other person have a name, to your knowledge?'

'Does it matter, Inspector?'

'H'm, well, yeah, I very much think it might.'

'All I can say is that somebody came knocking on Paul's door very recently.'

The can of petrol had no cap and hot fuel had melted its handle like wax, I noted.

'Do you, by any chance, have the sister's address?'

Susan took hold of a pitchfork and began to poke about among the wreckage for clues.

'People say you're a top detective in London, that they do.'

'Doesn't mean I still am.'

'Now it's your job, as the new owner of Coberley Hall, to look after your tenants.'

I flipped over a fallen TV satellite disc in disgust with my toe.

'Most people don't think I'm fit to look out for anyone any more. They say I've broken God's sacred trust.'

'Doesn't mean you can't be our guardian angel?'

'Doesn't mean I should.'

Of my own tentative investigation, it was too soon to make anything at all. Instead, I followed Susan's gaze to the horizon. High on a hill, beyond the frozen fields, stood an imposing house as yet unknown to me.

'Someone has to see how one thing leads to the next, Inspector. Someone has to have the eye that discerns everything, the past and the future, the heavens and the Earth, the blessed and the damned. Knowledge is vision. Whoever has that has real power and the rest of us live in fear of him, that we do.'

'In a way, yeah, but does that make me God's detective or the Devil's?'

'You should at least do a forensic examination to rule out arson.'

'And if I no longer have faith in myself?'

'Then what will it take to make you have a change of heart?'

'If I knew that I might never have come to Coberley.'

*

A moment later, I hastened away. Other than a few tractors that passed up and down the narrow lane each day, any evidence of someone else's presence was minimal. I enjoyed the sense of solitude, if not my own solitariness. The steep little road was, at this point, strewn with freshly scattered twigs and fir cones, I noticed. A muddy slide marked the bank down which everything had been kicked by man or animal on a track worn smooth.

I hurried on, anxiously to wonder if anyone could ever haunt himself with something that was as much the present as the past. That I could sense some hideous simulacrum move with me among the trees I did not disbelieve, yet admitted the absurdity of the sensation. Of parallel progress I was doubly conscious. With my unfounded unease came a chill.

As for Susan's remarks I considered them ludicrous. I paid her no notice, nor did I necessarily plan any action in consequence of it. Instead, I gritted my teeth and gave a sly grin.

Why ask someone to be their heavenly angel when they had already fallen?

*

'For God's sake, help! Help me! Anyone?'

It was not quite a scream but I had taken one more step when the urge to scream back took hold of me. At the top of the lane a grey horse lay in the road, I observed. It had reared right up and over with someone still in the saddle. Metal shoes had sliced white moons on the tarmac.

Now the stricken animal lay in a mess of its own droppings which were quite difficult to avoid. I had to step between splodges of hot, steaming dung or else tread in some very unpleasant urine. Of course the rider was in a panic, but it was hardly my field of expertise when the apparently dying gelding rolled its blank eyes into its sockets. Pinned by her leg was a woman dressed in smart boots and Jodhpurs. It was Laura Simmons.

'You hurt, at all?' I cried, otherwise breathless and speechless.

'For God's sake, Colin, pull him off me.'

I seized hold of the bridle, shouting. The gelding heaved its head and neck away from the road but failed to stand. The willpower seemed to go out of him in my presence.

Next moment, Gemma came running out the yard behind me.

'Don't stand there dithering, Detective. Boot him in the bum before he does any more damage.'

'He's rolled on Laura already.'

'Not her, him. He might twist his gut if we don't act fast.'

219

We were all three trying to determine why the gelding had taken ill so unexpectedly, when back in its stable he began to eat his hay as if nothing had happened. That was often the way with horses, apparently.

Altogether exhausted and smelly, we retreated across the yard to Gemma's wooden bungalow.

'Should have known it wasn't colic when I put my ear to his stomach,' she said. 'Too much rumbling and gurgling.'

'Just dropped with me,' confirmed Laura, rubbing her sore knee and nose. 'There was absolutely no warning. It was like sticking a knife into his heart, it was so quick. I don't know who Pluto thought you were, Colin, but you scared him shitless.'

'Nonsense, all I did was walk up the lane.'

While it was true that I had not shaved or had my hair cut lately, I did not think that I looked too unlike my old self. My teeth might have begun to resemble unclean yellow fangs but that was because I had no toothpaste. Living in Coberley Hall was not exactly the height of luxury, it was at times more like squatting in a cave.

'He definitely panicked at something,' said Laura.

'Or smelt it,' said Gemma. 'All horses hate the smell of pigs, for instance.'

'H'm, well, yeah, I don't know,' I said. 'That rumour of an escaped wild boar hasn't turned out to be true, has it?'

'Doesn't mean a horse won't bolt when it senses something ghoulish, Detective. I've had one refuse to move at a dead deer or simply the sight of blood in the road. Are you quite sure you won't have a cup of tea?'

I ducked as she swung a kettle past my nose.

'Oh no, yeah, I'm fine, thanks. I'm good. Absolutely.'

With that, Gemma began to root about in tottering piles of unwashed cups, plates and cutlery. Elsewhere, stinking horse rugs hung like tents to dry on doors until the air was as fragrant as an old carpet bazaar. A dozen or so books on astrology sat on a shelf above an oil-fired Aga, I noted. The mess in the kitchen was literally beyond the pale, as was the inconsolable Laura's bloody sniffles.

'Actually I have some advice to give you both on account of Paul Mitchell,' I declared in my haste to change the subject.

'What about him?' asked Gemma.

'His caravan burnt out last night in the farmyard.'

'Burnt?'

'I mean it might not have been an accident.'

'Explain yourself, Detective.'

'It's not inconceivable that someone wanted to give him a fright. Meanwhile, that person could be lurking somewhere on the estate, so please lock your doors.'

'It's a dread and reverence that puts the fear of God into ignorant people, Detective.'

'That reminds me,' I said. 'Please, Laura, I need to see that photograph of Esti Dryzek and her brother Viktor, if I may?'

'The thing is, Colin, I no longer have it.'

'How's that?'

'I've looked everywhere for it but it's no longer pinned to the beam in the tack room.'

Gemma, redolent of horse dung, sat down between us.

'If you ask me, you turning up in Coberley has created a bit of a stir.'

'How come?' queried Laura, dabbing more blood off her nose.

'Some may read it in the stars but I hear it every day in the shouts of the jackdaws and crows. There's business to be finished, that I do know.'

'I really don't understand what you're talking about.'

Gemma placed her hand on my knee.

'Today is the day that his lordship goes to the woods to pay his respects every Sunday.'

'What respects might they be?'

'After someone dies some people can't ever forget or forgive themselves, Detective. But then you would know all about that. Would you?'

'Sorry, but I have to go.'

There were only so many silly, augural pronouncements that any reasonable man could absorb at one time.

'Back then they all adored Lizzie's mother,' Gemma called out before I could reach the door, 'yet none was man enough to save her from herself.'

'Save? Whatever do you mean?'

'Listen, Detective. As soon as Lizzie was born her mother was subject to terrible postnatal depression. That's how she acquired a taste for the drink. It went on for years until it turned into something chronic, but she wasn't simply depressed, she was cursed. The after-effects were like a vile malediction. Maybe, as a result, Lizzie got scared, too. That's families for you. Except her mother was genuinely happy and hopeful once. If you don't believe me, go and look in Chatcombe Wood. We shouldn't let subsequent events distort who we once were. Back then she bloomed like a beautiful flower.'

*

Never had so few words impressed me as peculiarly as Gemma's unexpected but strident challenge, yet I was reluctant to declare myself grateful. When telling me that Lord Hart went to the woods regularly she did not do so kindly, she imputed some sort of blame.

Her taunt stayed with me all the way there – I could not in any way disassociate myself from it. Once within sight of the beech trees, a brisk walk led me along an ancient, stony path shown on the map as the Cotswold Way. Clearly it had somehow gained the dubious right to grant public access to the estate. Who could say who roamed it at random these days?

Forever low in the sky, the wintry sun cast each step I took in long shadow. It fell, too, upon the wind-tanned faces of two walkers who were presuming to traverse my fields. At no small inconvenience to myself, I felt obliged to acknowledge their existence by giving them a wave.

The middle-aged women, both with neatly cropped grey hair and wearing matching yellow waterproof jackets strode brazenly straight at me.

I placed myself at the side of the track and politely smiled, as any sane person might, while I paid homage to the weather. Without a doubt a lord had never before bestowed such beatitude on a couple of perfect strangers. Speechless at first, they suddenly gasped and hugged each other. Next they backed away, but at the last minute, each egging the other on, they ran forward and dodged by me at great speed. They scuttled off, gibbering and exclaiming as if in a foreign tongue.

Yet, armed was I not and most sincerely did I not want any trouble. When two perfectly ordinary folk shied away from a man as though they had just met the Devil, it was not very civil. When people were no longer civil it bordered on the barbaric, they were being needlessly impolite, even insulting.

That was the disadvantage of allowing the hoi polloi to trespass, they were no respecters of property or person.

Frankly it was a relief to seek solitude among the trees.

Pretty much.

*

A hoarfrost had left the track very white and icy. I was teetering most precariously along frozen wheel ruts past empty pheasant pens when I heard a noise.

Rat-tat, ratatat, rat-tat-tat.

With each rhythmical blow, someone did more than make an irritating noise, they tapped a form of Morse code. Each long and short series of raps revealed the urgent need to impart some feeling, news or discovery, someone wanted to share something with somebody else if only they could summon them closer. They were striking a very dead, hollow tree like a table at a séance.

'Don't assume for one moment that the fault is all mine! Joseph Jones is the one who unleashed this evil... Him and his damned shovel!'

Once more the tree resounded like a dull knell to dry blows from his dragon cane. The caller's Panama, not the warmest of headgear in the middle of winter, slipped down one side of his brow at a rakish angle. Meanwhile he hid his eyes behind his tinted glasses like someone afraid of snow blindness. It was George, fortuitously.

Next minute I saw him walk off the beaten track and kneel among the spiky green bluebell leaves. He removed a holly wreath left over from Christmas. Then I saw him collect several dirty jam jars in a bag and throw away their withered flowers.

Whereupon, with great difficulty, he stood up and leaned on his cane again.

'Everything I did, I did for you, my love.'

Then, as much in anger as despair, he set off homeward. Something about this lonely location would have him pay homage to the afternoon of life.

Immediately I abandoned my hiding place and descended the slope to the tree that George had been tapping. Gouged out the bark were the initials **G loves E**. From there I could better follow the path to the area to which he had just tended. Beside the clearing stood the remains of a pond, I discovered, but whoever had dug this little ornamental lake had never lined it properly. Its blue clay had sprung a leak from day one. Now it was as dry as a bone.

Soon I was standing on the very spot where his lordship had wiped away the frosty, black beechmast that had glued itself to a piece of flat stone. No more than two feet square, the grey granite slab had, over many years, grown very dirty. I literally had to scuff it hard with my heel to get it to give up its secret:

In Loving Memory Of Esti Dryzek 22.9.1964-11.11.1989. Aged 25.

We Shall Not All Sleep, But We Shall Be Changed.

Every Sunday after dinner George came to Chatcombe Wood because only here, despite the sorrow of forever going unheard, was he able to stick his neck out by being so honest?

*

On returning to the stables, I met the vet on the point of leaving. He had ruled Pluto out of danger but, predictably, Laura was still being very emotional. A more chivalrous man might have stayed to walk her home but it looked like rain.

I was about to go on when I saw Gemma push an enormous wheelbarrow from the nearest stable.

'Tell me,' I said, in the middle of all the awful fuss and bustle, 'what does anyone, you know, use ketamine for?'

I watched as she upended a great pile of steamy droppings on the muck heap past my toes. Through the gap in her teeth she spat phlegm on my clothes.

'Ketamine? Why, that's a synthetic compound used as an anaesthetic and analgesic in horses, Detective. Why do you ask?'

'No reason. Except I've read in the estate's accounts that Lord Hart buys prodigious amounts of it.'

'It's not illegal. When one of his horses cracked a cannon bone a few years ago I had to box rest it for six months. It would have gone crazy if I hadn't been able to give it ketamine to keep it calm.'

'The thing is, some people use it as an illicit hallucinogen.'

'Consider Lord Hart the nightclubbing kind, do you, Detective?'

I shot her the thinnest of smiles.

'Doesn't mean a man doesn't have secret needs.'

'You see the grave, at all?'

I nodded.

'Lord Hart still loves her, you know. She was his drug, not ketamine.'

225

'And if it's the only way to stop him feeling cursed, too?'

*

By now the afternoon sun was sinking fast on the hills. Minute by minute, the sky was becoming a vast sea of yellow, red and orange flame that stretched for as far as I could see over the horizon. Not for the first time, I wondered how the heavens could burn so hot but leave the Earth so cold.

I was following a path mobbed by dozens of noisy, dark-winged jackdaws on my way home. As soon as the first birds took off they landed again a little further on, not because they feared my presence but because something else would not let them settle. Against the sky's afterglow the grey-headed scavengers marked the way ahead by flying only a few feet from the ground. Then, inexplicably, they closed ranks in the air. Like a great, all-enveloping cloak they coalesced into a black column.

My first thought was another man. In fact, my senses told me that I was in the presence of something that lived a more feral existence. But already the fields and trees were too steeped in shadow, I could not see clearly who or what plunged along behind the valley's treeline and its little singing river. Meanwhile the thievish birds cawed and shrieked most shrilly.

Perhaps because I could think of nothing except my own safety, my brain filled in the rest with the wildest of notions. Next thing I knew I was flat on my back on the ground, I was bumping and sliding downhill on my buttocks – was thrashing my arms about on the icy slope in the most undignified manner until I came to a stop with a bang on a stone.

There I lay looking at the sky like a lizard. My eyes were two dead moons in slits incapable of focus. As a shadow briefly hovered over me, I felt uncivilised, even brutalised, but that was not to say that I was not still the same human being I was a moment ago?

Clearly I had mild concussion.

Before I could smear mud off my face I had to pause because I was so winded. After one final short, high-pitched grunt of hurt and annoyance I gave a guttural growl. Dirtier, damper and altogether

226

more dishevelled, my clothes exuded the earthy smell of morbific matter. My wide nostrils snorted slimy mucus that reeked of hideous caves and rotting leaves. With my rough, asthmatic breathing I roared and snuffled blindly in semi-darkness like a bear. It was a while before the world came together to form anything more separate and substantial than my own awfulness.

I could excuse my feeling of hurt pride but not of oafish clumsiness.

Letting myself out of the field, I staggered across the lane to the gatehouse, rubbing the back of my head. Fiery icicles bled red from Coberley Hall's grim gargoyles as they glowed in the dying sun. Each monstrous, long-tongued griffin, crowned with frost, peered at me from the edges of the roof where they folded their stony wings on each gable of their ice-palace. Encrusted in crystals, the house's heart-shaped stone finials turned briefly to glittering globes. When a man's home froze both day and night he could soon feel robbed of his creaturely comforts.

With trembling fingers, I gripped the iron loop on the door in the porch but not before the obstreperous jackdaws crowded wing to wing on every ridge tile to herald my arrival. They bobbed their beaks, curled their tongues and hopped about with unbesought alarums and excursions. Far from accompanying some wild man home across the stream to his den, my garrulous friends had hard, pearly eyes for me only.

I had to hurry in at once and bolt the door on my unkempt and shaggy resemblance to a scarecrow.

29

That whole dreadful business of the woodland burial continued to unsettle me. I could discount my feeling of general disbelief but not of overall revulsion. I sought to slow my heartbeat and focus my thoughts by listening to the irregular ticking of Coberley Hall's clocks, but soon came to dread the accompaniment. So oppressively did each sharp, little tick-tack weigh upon me, so tyrannously did a sense of another time hold sway over me that I had to pinch myself not to feel in the grip of some unspecified cruelty or injustice.

Then, eerie silence.

From that dead time arose the sound of humming.

'What the devil!' I said irritably and rushed to open my door in a panic.

There was no one there.

Yet deceived was I not and absolutely did I not suffer any daydream. Even my smelly sight-hound lifted his long narrow muzzle to look and listen. Try as I might, I could not block out the irritating tune that was so toyingly playful. Had every carved wooden merman and mermaid in the house combined to serenade me with one siren voice, I could not have found it more irresistibly arresting. There carried on the air the voice of a woman quietly singing. Yet it was not wholly insidious.

If I had not known better, I would have blamed such perverse mesmerism on more of George's ancient claret. Acting on impulse, I seized my shotgun and pointed its twin barrels before me as I advanced at the red arras.

'Who's there?' I demanded to the closet.

But the three-legged greyhound, with a flip of his whip-like tail, was first in. This was not me refiguring the whole house in conjunction with my own fantasy, this was me in pursuit of the vilest ever enticement. Never mind that the singer had no business to be there, she indulged in some heinous desire to make a complete fool of me, obviously.

I held high my candle to illuminate gaudy, flame-stitch hangings whose zigzag colours dazzled me with blue, green and yellow, but no one sat at the desk or raked the room's tiny fire. Only the telescope had been angled higher at the stars through the window, I noted.

Meanwhile the greyhound ran straight to the base of some green panelling.

'What is it?' I said. 'Don't tell me – it's a rat, isn't it? No, actually, that might be better.'

Shooing the dog aside, I put my ear to the seemingly solid oak wainscot. It was not a rational thing to do exactly, yet I could not cross the room but something irrational got the better of me. I tried tapping wood with my knuckles. Mine was no full-toned rap, it was hollow. At my fingertips was a space, hole or valley. A wild foolishness drove me. It told me that if I wanted to see off my tormentor I had somehow to follow *behind the panelling*.

Seconds later I detected, or imagined I detected, that familiar protest:

'This dance I can no longer go.
Pray you good madam why say you so?
Because Colin Walker will not come, too.
He must come to, he shall come to,
And he must come whether he will or no.'

Such words should have been sufficient deterrent. Instead a post against which I was leaning suddenly yielded. It swung up and out on an iron pivot to release the panel before me. I was lucky not to drop my candle or plunge through the hole. Then, before I could so much as peer into darkness beyond, I heard the songstress repeat her refrain quite cockily.

'He must come to, he shall come to,
And he must come whether he will or no.'

She was, it seemed, within my grasp, yet quickly she retreated – she was not so near after all.

229

'I have frightened her,' I told myself happily, 'with what she considers my clumsy ignorance of her secret ways.' But still I resolved to pursue and confront her when it meant entering the innermost labyrinth of the house itself – why? Because I felt sure, as I never had before, that only good could come of ending her spiteful game.

*

I felt compelled to brave the claustrophobic darkness whose cobwebs sizzled and shrivelled at the touch of my candle. Scared myself, I tried not to scare. Soon I was gasping for breath in a narrow space streaked with drops of blood which lined the secret walls in painted, perpendicular columns. Here, at its core, the house bled from its internal haemorrhage, it was forever dying from its bleeding heart. The life-blood oozed from its walls in large red and white teardrops for the blood and water of the Passion.

At my shoulder an ancient set of vestments hung from a hook with a frontal to match on a tiny altar.

Once in this hidden, painted chapel I stood very still. I was gripped by a terrible despondency, convinced that my singer had got away from me, yet still I would hear her song in my head, a mere echo of the previous recital. A ladder stood right in front of me. I ignored it and immediately I was overcome with much deeper frustration – a total loss of heart, scarcely less than bitter disappointment in the beginning but soon even more baffling. I returned to the ladder and my confusion diminished. 'Damn it all!' I cried and placed a foot on the lowest rung.

The man was too cautious who let mere darkness come between him and the only one who could set things straight.

*

But for the candle's wretched little flame I would have been sightless. The ladder's rungs were worn very shiny which suggested someone's frequent visits. At first I had little idea of where I was going among all the false chimneys, double entrances and network of catwalks to confuse the searchers. Such a priest-hole had probably been built into the oldest part of the Hall in the 1580's

230

when anyone brave or foolhardy enough to follow the Catholic faith had been forced to do so totally clandestinely.

Whoever roamed the house could still climb down the hidden ladder to pass through false walls quite easily. I flexed my aching knees and stretched my arms out in the gloom when it became apparent that a second set of steps led higher.

Nor was my progress entirely straightforward. Twice I had to prop my candle at the mouth of a trapdoor while I retraced my steps briefly to retrieve my gun. Again, that voice! The singer would intentionally and cruelly lead me on. Now I could not seek her out unrequited. The Devil take her! While I climbed I pricked up my ears at the promise of her call, stubbornly justified my shameless pursuit with false sightings of my own.

At last I arrived in the draughty attics. I had to balance on a sagging wooden plank a few inches wide that stretched across the roof's massive framework of worm-eaten rafters. This, too, had been the path of some errant priest's desperate escape route.

I snapped shut the breach on my gun.

'Marigold, I know it's you,' I cried, while the rancid smell of something resembling birds' droppings filled my nostrils.

As I swung my candle higher I lit a rafter. There, crudely chiselled into the thick black beam were Roman letters: M, J, M, V, I. Such carvings were as old as the Hall's original construction. The initials had been put there by the builders but were not those who built it. Rather, they stood for Maria, Jesu, Mater and Virgo Virgonum, they were a very old way of keeping evil out of the house.

I started back through the ghastly gloom. The prowler of these dusty trusses knew them better than I did, the balance of advantage lay with them as they moved along beyond my view. I had no choice but to teeter blindly forwards on my toes, when once more I heard a song taunt me.

Still I was disinclined to suspend all judgement, given, as I was, to trust the truth, facts and soundness of my own inferences. That my eyes deceived me I doubted, for the figure of a woman had to be more solid image than mirage, less phosphorescent flame or ignis fatuus than actual person by the light of my candle. For, while I stood almost totally immersed in a sea of blackness, I saw bright signals and flashes enter my peripheral vision. She detached herself in order to drift across my eye's watery vitreous, wrenched free of my retina, somehow.

When a blind man discovered that he could see again he should no longer have to play blind-man's-buff, he should discern, comprehend and inquire sensibly about the one before his eyes. The white, shrouded figure that drifted towards me becoming brighter and brighter did not weigh anything, did not flex the plank beneath her feet as I did, but was driven by her own secret forces.

Long raven locks billowed in a non-existent breeze around her fair shoulders while her arms stayed pinned to her sides just like a real ghost.

I laughed. With downturned face she crossed space too instantaneously for me to anticipate. She carried no light and yet the hideous shadows around her lent her a semblance of shape. Dark was light and hot was cold. These seeming contradictions stimulated my own senses to make out her luminosity through diffused or reflected rays that remained undetected. In short, she would have me see the invisible.

She had summoned me, evidently.

No, I had summoned her.

Yes, I had. And she had come.

She raised her eyelids and through her mane of loosely folded hair I glimpsed the adorable, deep black pupils of a living creature. I saw on her lips a flash of colour. Blood flowed again through her cheeks and returned to her forehead. A slight smile showed and her burning eyes flickered momentarily in their sockets. Sternly they stared at me across an ill-defined gulf more out of pity than criticism. Which was when I realised that I was powerless to move or resist, I was defeated by my own sense of suspended mischief. Clearly she could not be dead, so what was she?

Although we were face to face the 'ghost' seemed to look at me from a great distance. With longing came doubt, I was afraid of my own 'sleepwalking'. I wanted to say sorry for what I had done to her, but if she were back from the dead then why waste time on useless excuses? Foreboding was more like it. She stood before me as someone unprepared to diminish the magnitude of my offence any longer.

At the moment the irradiant wraith raised her bony hands in grim salutation, she showed me the crimson hole where her heart should have been. Naturally, my delight at seeing her was balanced by a genuine pang of apprehension, I wanted to go down on my knees and pray for my own deliverance. When a man was so desirous of a woman's grace, he should not shrink from meeting her in the strangest of places and oddest of circumstances.

But she it was who spoke first.

'Still you do not put me somewhere safe and sound, Colin?'

'Such a place still proves elusive.'

'Would you have me lost in this cold house for ever?'

'Cannot I simply let you live on in my memory?'

'That is neither one thing nor the other.'

'Where else is there, then, to keep you?'

'Whatever you decide, it must be our secret.'

'And if I fail?'

Suddenly there came into her look a tinge of suspicion. Those same lovely eyes began to ask why I was abandoning her? Her long white fingernails closed in a claw. Her accusing gaze laid renewed claim to our agreement: why *did* I not simply do what she wanted?

No figment of fancy, it was on her lips I tried to plant some seal of atonement. With it, I attempted to squeeze her back to life. Because I aimed so hard to hold her, she had to let go of me. Because she let go of me I had to say sorry. Because I had to say sorry I broke the silence. Now there was nothing left to hold on to. Yet that tourniquet that was her bite upon my neck soon stopped the flow of blood through every artery. She was as ruthless as I had once been in the crushing of the jugular.

Kissed myself, I failed to kiss. If she mocked me with her disgust and disappointment, the golden glint in her eyes revealed a caprice, a sudden and impulsive change of mood and behaviour, just when I was the one locked in her power. If the look in her eyes was consistently unrelenting it was because she wanted me to relive all those embraces I had once given so freely. She would have me join her in one last, great passion after the event, or else. She was resolved to confront me as if I alone could solve the riddle of her dead heart's desire.

With that needle-sharp caress came the taste and smell of something bitter, like rancid toothpaste. I had smelt it before, that stench from Hades, on her deathbed.

Suddenly she reeled backwards. On my finger was the blue and gold enamelled ring that Jan had brought me from London. As soon as she saw it she let out a furious scream and tore it from me. For one moment she pondered the love token in her grasp. Then she gave a little laugh, only to appear unsure what to make of her own motives. While the ring gave her free course to give in to desire, feeling or impulse, she seemed less than satisfied with its return.

Again I approached to show her some comfort, but her blank face refused to be comforted. She distrusted my divided loyalties, evidently. Rather, I stared into features that suddenly suffered a terrible marasmus. They started to waste away to the point where bone sucked flesh until it left hardly any substance. Soon her skin lacked all its bloodiest ingredients. A visage that turned so transparent and flimsy was quickly robbed of all expression, it could no longer stretch to laugh, smile or cry. Her eyes sank deep into their sockets.

From her mouth erupted a dark brown, soupy liquid that came all the way up from her stomach. Since her bowels were blocked by so much swelling the only way out was for all that awful sewage to pour back through her throat. It belched from her lips like a filthy fountain all over my face. It entered my mouth with one great retch.

I could feel myself filling up with all the rotten, decaying sludge that smelt like dead rats from inside her festering body. Gone was the face of fond memory.

Next moment, her skin turned ash-grey, then red, black and slimy green. Even as I choked and suffocated on her putrid entrails I was face to face with my own grief, guilt, cowardice, betrayal and lies.

*

Released from paralysis, I fell to my knees and groped about for my fallen gun which had somehow bridged the rafters. Incumbent on the catwalk, I felt my neck where teeth had held me rigid. That harsh, bloody bite had been brutal but not lethal. Instead, the brief, crude stoppage of my throat had meant that I could not cry out, but it was the uncertainty, not the trickle of blood, that had been such torture. It was not knowing whether each wheezing intake of breath was temporary or final that was so dreadful – it must have been how Lizzie had felt when I throttled her.

With my gun in my grasp, I felt back in charge, fired both barrels.

The recoil blew me sideways, even as the blast lit up the roof in a deafening double explosion. When a man chased the living but met the dead he did not expect them to respond to anything moral or emotional, he expected them to be repugnant. When they were repugnant they were incompatible with everything he had ever loved, they were of a world not his own. Since she was of another world there should not have been in her the slightest glimpse of anything human. Was she really all horror book vampire? Either way, she had a voice quite defiant:

'Heare my crie. Anyone canne stoppe a woman's life, but few her deathe, a thousande doors opene on to it.'

*

However much the prankster had got the better of me, they did not challenge my retreat along the narrow catwalk. Nor was I one to lose my reason. Any rotten, decaying smell stayed in my nostrils, not

235

least because vomit stained my jacket where I had spewed up the contents of my own foul stomach. When a man was so bilious but had no illness he had to be suffering from the effects of himself only.

My bare, ringless finger burned.

In order to entice me closer someone needed the best bait they had. The easiest way to bait a man like me was to put a familiar face to his greatest moral and emotional dilemma. Just because I had set out to kill my wife didn't mean that there couldn't be love after death – someone fully intended to declare that, for me, it was not over.

30

'Never seen you look so drained,' said Jan, dusting the pew before she sat down in her impossibly smart, grey cut twill trousers. 'Never seen a man eat his heart out so. You look as white as a sheet.'

Beyond the Lady Chapel's pointed arches, the Parish Church of St John Baptist in Cirencester echoed to the noisy sound of a service being conducted in the nave, but I did my best to endure the distraction.

'Never mind me,' I snapped. 'What about London? Did you, like, find our man?'

'First, what's all this about your latest fright? You really meet a prowler, Colin?'

'It's okay. I have a gun.'

'Doesn't mean you're not irritated or distressed by something. You look on tenterhooks.'

From the south wall the Devil smirked at me while he shovelled screaming men and women into fire.

'Honestly, I'm quite all right. I still can't sleep for nightmares, that's all.'

Jan unfastened the mother-of-pearl buttons on her black, fingerless cashmere gloves. Then she rucked down each long cuff for extra warmth one by one. She did it in a way that truly meant business.

'Maria has thought long and hard about your visions. Any doctor will tell you that such terrors only live in the unconscious, Colin. They might affect our behaviour and emotions when we dream but otherwise they remain as inaccessible as our own souls.'

'I've begun to see this world afresh. Believe me, it's full of ghosts and monsters.'

Jan patted my hand reassuringly.

'Maria says that none of it exists beyond the mind's eye.'

'Yeah, yeah, yeah. I don't doubt it. But that was before.'

'Before what, Colin?'

'Not everything stays in the head, some things get to break free. I've felt it ever since coming to Coberley Hall. Something *unrestrainable*, from within me.'

'Must I say it again? You need to come back to London.'

There arose a bitter impatience. I acknowledged the common sense of her advice, but not the sense advised.

'Don't you see? In Countess Lucy's time the Civil War changed everything. Everyone was deemed to be on one side or the other: God's or the Devil's. There was no military or spiritual middle ground, especially for women. If you spoke your mind or did as you pleased you could just as easily be cast as a witch or an angel. Imagine what it felt like to lose a battle as well as your fortune. All over England, grief-stricken families were subjected to heavy fines and confiscation of their houses and land.'

'You mean Coberley Hall became a microcosm of a national tragedy?'

'When 250,000 men, women and children died of wounds, hunger and disease, each death had to be a personal tragedy but, yes, you could see a house like hers as the epitome of loss at a time when looters, rapists and killers roamed England for years.'

Jan raised her eyebrows.

'Er, how is it that this countess seems so alive to you suddenly, Colin?'

'Do you good to listen.'

I should have told her about what happened in the attics, but I didn't.

'Listen to me, Colin. There are no ghosts beyond the ones you create yourself. That goes for any other creatures, too.'

'Have I not described him to you in every hideous detail?'

'Doesn't mean you met a dead soldier.'

'That's just one of his manifestations.'

'You talking about something from folklore, Colin? Because I did some research. And, yeah, the word 'bogle' is very old. See here, it says it can mean a phantom, scarecrow or simply devil.'

Leaning one hand heavily on the pew, I peered over Jan's shoulder and saw words appear on her phone that were so small and alien as to be almost unintelligible.

My eyes had not been too good lately.

''Bogle' is just one word for it.'

'Actually it says here that the word goes right back to 1500 and beyond. There was a Middle English word 'bugge' which meant bugbear, but origins are obscure.'

'Stop right there. Please. Yeah, please do.'

'Sit still, Colin. It seems to me that you have literally been made to conjure some shape-shifter from the oldest, most primitive parts of your subconscious brain, a part we all still have buried under layers and layers of apparent sophistication. You've drawn something out of the darkness and given it life through your own fancy or conscience.'

'What's wrong? Are you about to call me a liar?'

I distrusted her objectionable sensibleness.

Jan's jaw dropped. Then curiosity again got the better of her. She rested her phone in a fold of her cape where she dabbed her finger frantically on the touchscreen. Looking sideways over her fake fur collar, she shot me a look of totally uncomplimentary pity.

'Since Lizzie's death, have you not come to see *yourself* as a bit of a bogy man, is that what you're saying?'

'I feel like Lady Lucy does.'

'How's that?'

'Rejected by my fellow men? Abandoned by God? Driven by demons? Nowadays we hardly have the vocabulary to express such things, but in her time everyone knew perfectly well what it is to be damned. She, alone, understands my predicament. She lived in an age when men behaved like beasts, too. I am…as one with her.'

I jumped up to walk about with such decisiveness as was still available to me.

Jan tried to take my hand.

'I don't know what else I can do to get you to calm down. Please lower your voice, Colin. You're acting quite wildly. Will you not admit that you haven't been right since you banged your head in that car accident? Doesn't mean you're haunted. Forget this Lady Lucy. Forget the Wild Man. They don't belong in our world.'

I clasped my head and my eyes were hardly able to focus.

'And if he haunts her, too?'

'Or there's something of a civil war going on in us all?'

'Really? That's what you think?'

'Yes, Colin, I do. Quite simply, there lurks in our psyche a prehistoric memory. Stuff of myth and legend, no less. Migrating tribes probably met real monsters millions of years ago during the Ice Age when they roamed Europe. Even today some people in remote places purport to see what you do in Coberley. In America they call it Big Foot but in Bhutan it is called Migou, in Tibet it is called Chemo. In Nepal they call it the Yeti.'

'That is just people putting flesh on their fears.'

'Sherpas call theirs an animal of God.'

'Okay, yeah, I don't think so. This bogle spoke to me.'

'It says here that the Neanderthal genome was only sequenced in 2010. Many of us contain Neanderthal DNA – up to two or even four per cent. Even today we do battle with a very old part of ourselves.'

I folded my arms, said nothing. Meanwhile Jan regaled me with some more of her ridiculous theories.

'Another possibility is that the word 'bogle' is a corruption of the old word 'bog'.'

'So?'

''Bog' means 'from the north'.'

240

I wrung my hands. Next thing, Jan would have had the Abominable Snowman sit down between us. But she was not all wrong. If, over thousands of years we had forgotten the real monster we had not forgotten the fear. If we still had the fear we still had the instinct. If we all had the instinct we had the unconscious skill to see irrational things without conscious design. If we could still see things without being conscious we might be able to recall what our forbears saw in the darkest corners of our eyes.

'What if I told you that Countess Lucy can bring back Lizzie?'

'You convinced? It isn't a fact. Is it? It's you picturing her to yourself, just like your monster.'

'Nonsense!' I replied angrily. 'I am not such a dreamer as to desire to give things a life they can never have.'

'So why try?'

'Fuck you, Jan.'

'That it? You think you can simply ignore what you have already resurrected? And this… this countess, how can you be sure she will do what you ask?'

'Because I have something she doesn't.'

*

Singing erupted again in the nave. That is, people's voices rose in a song of praise in a harmonious union of body and soul.

Seconds later I felt able to focus again.

'So tell me, did you have any luck in London?'

By way of reply Jan felt in her bag and brought out her camera.

'Okay, his sister does live at 33 Jessica Road as you said, but he is hiding out in a derelict coach-house at the end of the garden. You're right, though, he's shit-scared of someone.'

'If you won't believe in my bogy man then at least tell me about his.'

Jan narrowed her eyes. It was as though my friend, sensing I was at the limits of reason, surrendered temporarily to the demands of my strange obsession. So saying, Paul Mitchell's wizened features sprang to life on the bright, colourful screen as she pressed play on her phone. Frightened little eyes stared straight ahead while his lips struggled to work against a spasmodic tic of his facial muscles.

Yet deranged was he not and most definitely did he not refuse to speak on camera.

*

'It all dates back to Gerald Turner, Miss Shriver. He had been spraying fields with DDT when his wife Louise arrived with some sandwiches. The wind must have changed course because she was soaked with insecticide. When she died from cancer some years later he couldn't cope. He blamed himself. Which was why Esti and Viktor Dryzek's arrival in 1979 seemed like a gift from heaven. That's how it started, Miss Shriver, he paid them in cash out of his own pocket to help him run Upper Coberley Farm.'

'For cash, you say?'

'On account of the fact that they were illegal immigrants. There wasn't a thing that the youngsters wouldn't tackle, all except the Tamworths in the piggery down the lane which were deemed too unpredictable. Mr Turner never fed his animals well enough and hunger made them very bad tempered. Regularly he would beat them with a rod of iron. Not that it matters now.

'In Gerald Turner's eyes, he was doing the destitute teenagers a big favour by letting them live in a stable. They washed in the yard and ate scraps off his table.

'Then, one day, I was loading hay in a barn when I heard a shout. Leaving my tractor's engine idling, I ran up the side of the stables to the backyard of the farmhouse to find Esti with her back pressed hard up against the wall. She was stark naked. Mr Turner stood over her with perspiration pouring hot beads down his cheeks. In his hand was a towel.

' "Best let her alone, Mr Turner," I said.

' "Stay out of this, Mitchell. It's simply a misunderstanding."

'He might have said that, Miss Shriver, but Esti shivered and wriggled between the old man's hands. He was pressing with all his weight against the wall either side of her head – I could see the whites of his knuckles.

'That afternoon I overheard him and Viktor argue.

' "Touch my little sister again and I will kill you."

'Suddenly Mr Turner stormed off.

' "Esti's no fool, she'll soon see that a farmer's wife might suit her very well."

'As things turned out, his words proved prophetic. But not for him, Miss Shriver, not for him.'

'Then what happened?'

'For that year and the next Viktor guarded his sister like a child. No longer would she cook their meals in the big house by herself, he would always accompany her. Nor were there any more hot baths. But Esti grew restless. No girl likes living in squalor for ever. Several times I came across them deep in conversation and it was always the same: she it was who was prepared to be more pragmatic.

' "Don't you see, Viktor, if we're a bit nicer to him, he might let us live with him in the big house."

' "If you're nice to him, you mean."

' "How many times must I say it, Viktor? Nothing happened, he was just trying to give me a towel."

' "We can't trust him."

' "A smile now and then wouldn't hurt."

' "It's a smile that got you into trouble."

' "Spoken like a man."

'Once Viktor came up to me in the yard, fretting and fuming. He made me his unwilling confidant.

' "Has he told you? He's promised her a car."

'It was true, Mr Turner was teaching Esti to drive a tractor, but then both she and Viktor had been raised on a farm. She had great plans. I think, on a good day, if the old man wasn't being too overbearing, she could imagine herself back home with her father in Poland. Every other day I saw Viktor berating her about something in the corner of a field or alongside the stables and always Esti shook her head as if to deny any wrongdoing. Always it was because she had chatted to Mr Turner or accepted some minor gift from him. Several times he drove her into town and bought her new clothes. He was trying to say sorry, I suppose. Not that it matters now.'

'Doesn't mean he succeeded?'

'The odd thing is, Miss Shriver, the day it happened I'd only just stopped at the piggery to unload a bale of straw from a trailer. It wasn't feeding time, but as I said, sometimes Esti would stop by in secret to give the Tamworths a carrot or two and they'd get very excited. Then again I would hear them squealing when Mr Turner beat them. But this wasn't that either, this was like nothing I had ever heard before. It never occurred to me that they were doing something so extraordinary. A moment later I looked round and saw Viktor and Esti emerge from a shed furiously bickering.

' "Don't you see, Esti, the police will come and will want to question everybody. They'll discover that we have no papers."

' "But, Viktor, if we run away now they'll blame us anyway."

' "I'm going, even if you're not."

' "Where will you go?"

' "Anywhere but here. Maybe I'll return to Europe. Please, Esti, this is your last chance."

' "No."

' "Then what will you do?"

' "I'll hide in the woods, or somewhere."

' "Are you crazy?"

' "Not as crazy as you. Why the hell did you have to push him so hard?"

'How exactly the old man had come to collapse, Miss Shriver, I didn't know. He might have had a stroke or heart attack because his

244

father had died that way in his fifties. Glancing down, I noticed that a man's cap lay in the mud at my feet. That's when a terrible fear gripped me. My heart still pounds when I think of it. Of course, I knew then. As I said, Tamworths can be very aggressive. Seizing a broom, I climbed into the sty to drive them back but they threatened to turn on me in a frenzy. Cartilage tore off in great strips of gristle and one of Mr Turner's eyes popped right out of its socket. Almost before I knew it, the pig at his neck opened his throat in a great fountain of blood. I heard him choke and bubble as the life poured out of him. Each rosy snout snuffled and gobbled. They say a cat will always eat the head off a rabbit first. It might have been my imagination, Miss Shriver, but I thought those pigs took their revenge on their mean master. Seconds later he was dead.

'Viktor cornered me in the yard. He made me promise not to ruin Esti's life for the sake of a bully. Naturally I went ahead and called the police straightaway, but by the time they arrived Gerald Turner was as good as eaten. I kept quiet about Viktor and Esti, decided not to point the finger now that there was no incriminating wound left to display any evidence. I didn't want her to suffer for the sake of a stupid quarrel I might have misheard. I've stayed silent all this time but now I feel implicated all over again. What if Viktor's blow did precipitate Mr Turner's fall into the sty? The uncertainty of it has turned into a curse. Now I'm haunted by my own cowardice, by a truth about to resurface long afterwards.

'In the event, Joseph Jones made other arrangements to farm the land and Upper Coberley farmhouse was let out as a private dwelling. A couple of years ago it was sold to Laura Simmons.'

'Which should have been the end to it.'

'Except Viktor decided to return. He didn't leave England after all, he took to roaming the countryside as a tramp. For weeks he had been back on the Coberley Estate and living like a wild man in sheds and caves. Several times I caught him poaching game, setting traps or stealing things from the crewyard. He had always been a bit of a thief anyway. He told me that he was going to take Esti away with him and I had to help him, but I told him that he was too late. Esti was living with Joseph Jones in his new house called 'The Firs' on Wistley Hill…'

245

'That it?' I said. 'Did Paul Mitchell have nothing else to say? What about the bogy man?'

Jan rose to her feet.

'Sorry, my camera battery went dead. But he and I did talk some more. He explained that, while living rough, Viktor had sold things he had stolen from Coberley Hall to acquire forged passports. He wanted Esti to start a new life with him in London. Either that, or he was going to join the army.'

With no great thanks I paced the chapel, harboured too many questions to explain exactly the quandary that gripped me. It was a feeling of ineffable frustration – I thought myself incapable of rationalizing the irrational.

'So what happened next?'

'That's just it, Colin, Paul Mitchell never saw Viktor Dryzek again, not until a few days ago. He simply turned up, in search of news, at his caravan. Years ago the army had discharged him after some sort of accident.'

I swore.

'Viktor was here?'

'He'd heard that you, too, were asking questions about Esti.'

I swore again. Of my own folly I was in no doubt. Yet, convinced was I not and most determinedly did I not believe everything.

*

Having given Jan a curt goodbye I was in time to endure the bumpy bus ride back to Coberley. I stepped down at the bus stop in some discomfort, dusting dirt off my coat, when I looked across the road. How reassuring it was to see that, in my absence, the ever industrious Adrian was choosing to drive his tractor in tedious lines up and down the field. Without thinking to consult me, my stalwart friend was taking it upon himself to make all those boring measurements necessary to calculate how much nutrient we would need to add to the soil hectare by hectare, in the spring.

'When a man feels part of the natural cycle of planting and growing things, he can be at one with Nature,' I told myself confidently. 'By binding himself to life and death in a larger world he need never feel like a bough wrenched from a tree again, he need never be all on his own. A man not alone need not suffer a broken heart, need not break down like a hollow trunk that has rotted irrevocably from the inside.'

I let myself into Coberley Hall's gatehouse and moodily kicked stones down the path that led to the church. As I unhooked the creaking metal gate, a jackdaw patrolled the stone wall that once led to a dovecote at the corner of the graveyard. At first I did my best to ignore the gentlemanly creature as it folded and refolded its wings like a cloak.

Suddenly my watchful guide dropped down to a pile of pointed slabs which stood propped like blank Gothic windows against the base of the wall, not far from the closest burials. It was not exactly a communicative bird, yet I could not heed its look but a certain communicativeness directed my attention. At my approach, it squawked and took wing again.

I was seized by a definite desire to discover something and turned the first slab over. There was writing on it. Already I could see and move the second stone underneath. It was similar. If the slabs had been abandoned, they had not been defaced or destroyed except by wind and rain. I came to a third, traced its faded lettering with my hand and started to read:

HERE LYETH LUCY POPE DAVGHTER VNTO JOHN DUTTON OF SHERBOURNE IN Y COTIE OF GLOSTER ESQVIRE.

MARYED VNTO THOMAS POPE ONE OF THE SONNES OF WILLIAM POPE AND HAD ISSVE BY THE SAIDE LUCY ONE DAVGHTER ELIZABETH.

LUCY POPE BURIED THE VIII APRIL ANNO DN 1656.

Like the other headstones, Lady Lucy's had long been set aside to be forgotten.

'You lost something, old chap?'

I snapped out of my dream. Advancing towards me in his wheelchair, Lord Hart bade his nurse do a detour across the grassy graves.

'So, please, can you tell me who discarded these slabs like so much rubble?' I demanded.

He leaned forward from his blanket and peered at me from under his Panama. Suddenly he raised his dragon cane. In response, Rebecca shot me a sour smile and narrowed her sea-green eyes beneath her fringe of auburn hair. Still she uttered not a word to me or master. Instead she manoeuvred his wheelchair to a halt at my toes.

'Headstones come and go in every graveyard, Colin, the devil they do,' declared Lord Hart. 'There's only so much room in the ground for us all.'

'You mean after centuries we must pick and choose whom to remember?'

'The old dead must make way for the new.'

From a gargoyle at the top of the church tower came an angry shriek. It was our presiding jackdaw once more. His lordship's face paled. So did Rebecca's, but she was first to recover. When a woman felt ignored she could feel contemptible. When she was contemptible she had to stand up for herself, she had to remind everyone of her presence occasionally.

'Come along, George, it's too cold out here. You mustn't linger any longer.'

'Answer my question,' I said. 'How did Lady Lucy's headstone come to be taken from her grave?'

'My stepfather excavated every inch of the grounds of Coberley Hall. He wanted to unearth artefacts left behind by the English Civil War. Musket balls and an officer's rusty carbine still reside in a drawer. His obsession knew no bounds, the devil it didn't. He exhumed the countess with a shovel to see what he could salvage.'

My heart skipped a beat.

'So did he, like, discover anything very much, to your knowledge?'

'A blue enamelled ring still rested on her bony finger.'

Again Rebecca went to hurry Lord Hart's wheelchair towards the house.

'Wait,' I cried and stayed her hand. 'Who took Lady Lucy's place in her grave?'

Lord Hart held his hand high and rigid, not blinking except with cruel intent.

'My stepfather left strict instructions in his will – he wanted to lie with her for all eternity.'

'Honestly? Like man and wife? Why?'

'To make amends.'

'How come?'

'Never you mind, Colin.'

'Why not?'

'Because I know what a man's obsession with the countess does to him, the devil I do. I've seen how mad that man can suddenly become until he's driven wild. Joseph Jones came to rue the day that he dug her up, the devil he did, but not before my brother and I had to scrape his blood and brains off his bedroom wall.'

'So what did become of her remains?' I asked.

He shook his cane at me quite violently.

'Relax, old chap, they're just bones.'

'And the ring? What of that?'

'Esti Dryzek took it for her own.'

*

That night Countess Lucy's receipt book lay open for me at a new page on my bed. Tucked inside was a folded frontispiece torn from

Henry Lyte's 'Niewe Herball or Historie of Plantes' on the back of which was the draft of a letter:

'Honoured sir, my comfort is that you are gone from here, lest my husbande should take you too, but I do sorely miss you. Deare Captaine Digby, come to me, though you be turned highwayman or pirate or otherwise long gone to the Americas, as I desire to do. The thought of you doth, like seede of basil thyme, cureth my infirmities of the hart, taketh away sorrowfulness, from which cometh malancholie, and maketh me merry and glad. Yet with all malice doth my husbande use my own cures in mighty violence against me. He would revenge all that I have done upon him, soe that I shall feare to live lest he call me witch in publick. To them I saye:

'*Come feareful bogle in forme of divel. Pore grete greife on this damnable house daie and night ever afterwards.*'

In short, I am poorly used and not yet set at liberty since I am still suspect, for is not Love our greatest Loss? *I am with childe.* And soe I hereby with longing am enforced to lye in my bed without you, which is no small greife to me. I do eat potage of goosegrass which when drunken doth cause lankness and kepe me from fatnesse, since in my stomach all food with great inconvenience makes hard shift to dwell in. I feare I am forgot of you, but by my bodily labour and endevours when I am able and in health do yearne to meet you again very soone. Whether this or som othere letter reach you or no this month or next, I will have you send word to me from whatever place ye be or elce to come before me to the gatehouse at Coberley som night by 12 of the Clocke to answere my call.'

*

I took heed. I also took hope from it. Forsaken myself, I refused to forsake. For while my very own Lady Lucy wept for her dead dragoon, we both knew that she could do better than to settle for the phantasm of a living person when I was flesh and blood and the other heartless.

250

31

The following day I kept indoors, watching a remarkable and unsettling haze descend upon Coberley Hall. The next day I did the same. Everywhere the miasmal vapours smeared the leaded panes of its darkened windows with sticky, crimson fingerprints. Never before had it occurred to me that I inhabited so dismal a world. Something inauspicious seemed to come with the bloody veil.

I was soon asthmatic, sore-throated, hoarse. For a while I paced up and down the long gallery, as did Countess Lucy when she took her winter strolls.

'Did you ever see such gloom?' I declared, upon meeting James downstairs in the entrance hall. 'Will it ever be safe to leave?'

'It's only a few dust devils, sir.'

'That it? Really? That's your explanation?'

James rolled his head at me in sad, perpetual motion.

'They are whipping up exceptional storms in the Sahara, sir. They're mixing sand with power station emissions and it's all drifting our way very high in the atmosphere.'

'Blind forces, more likely.'

'Excuse me, sir?'

Even to put my hand to the front door was to feel the life-blood begin to drain from it.

'Heaven knows, it can't do a man much good to go out in such a pea-souper, can it?'

'You feeling quite well, sir?'

'What do you expect when someone flings sand in the face of God?'

James held up my coat for me to enter my arms.

'So what are you going to do, sir?'

'There's a house I must see on Wistley Hill.'

'Do you good not to spend overlong indoors.'

'Whoever said I did?'

James fixed me with his slate-grey eyes as he helped fasten the top button of my coat quite vigorously.

'Excuse me, sir, if I spoke out of turn.'

That was the trouble with servants, they were far too fond of taking exception, they were always trying to catch their betters out with their own weasel words as if everything I said was bothersome excuses. He would imply that I was somehow in hiding when he had to know that I could have left days ago if that was what I'd intended.

*

The smog was more clinging than I anticipated. In no way was it a trap, exactly, yet I could not walk far but a sense of being trapped came over me. Then, darting across the busy main road, I began to feel my way along the kerbside until at last I came to a junction at the source of the Thames called Seven Springs.

Scratchy wipers worked ceaselessly to wash away the red desert sand from the windscreens of cars, buses and lorries that crawled in maggoty momentum up the hill. Twice I nearly fell off the totally inadequate grass verge into the path of blinded drivers.

Not that I cared.

'What the devil!' I cried.

The red-tinged mist coalesced into a figure right in front of me. More specifically I became aware of a shadowy silhouette that blocked my way, something that appeared seven feet tall in my otherwise shrunken, myopic world and which fast assumed all the presence of a Wild Man. With it came much growling and slavering. Even someone who already had all the creatures of hell in his head hoped never to meet the very thing he was thinking.

I knew him at once. The putrescent odour of rotting beech leaves and wood smoke on his filthy rat-coloured cloak filled my nostrils. On his head was a green hat trimmed with a buzzard's feather. He was of indeterminate age, powerfully built, disfigured and recently wounded in the arm. Spurs jingled on his boots and the silver handle of a dagger protruded from his belt. His long grey hair fell to his shoulders and his look was guarded and devious.

'You!' I cried, raising both fists. 'It's hell not knowing what you want.'

He shambled past me like some sort of sandman. I could believe my eyes but none of my other senses. He was distinctly anthropomorphous. While somebody could go mad for dreams alone, they could not deny the proof of their deepest fear – if ghosts literally existed, so could monsters.

I launched myself after him in a fury, when a voice called.

'Drenka! Inside!'

*

Suddenly one thing interrupted another. A dog began to bark furiously. I had strayed into a long layby for lorries at the side of the road, I realised. Growling and whining, an Alsatian sat at the top of six wooden steps of its horse-drawn home and blocked its entrance.

I looked down. At my feet lay the bear that I had just fought to a standstill.

Yet insane was I not and most surely did I have a witness. A small woman dressed in a multi-coloured quilted coat descended the steps of the red caravan.

'What's this?' she asked severely. 'Would you fight my best work with your fists?'

As large as myself but completely inert, the bear's chiselled jaws now gaped very wide in a grin. An amber bead filled one startled eye while enormous black claws at the tip of each paw were poised in mid-air very convincingly. Only a hopeless fantast would have felt his heart stop beating when he touched it, only a dreamer in love with his own crazed vision would have still grasped at something so obviously wooden and lifeless.

I gave my fraudulent opponent a kick in the groin. Santa's tiny bells jingled on its ankles while every aspect of its hideous smile was a mocking reflection of my unnatural state. Painted in large gold letters across a nearby board was an advertisement: FOR SALE. BEATA'S GARDEN STATUES.

'Whoever knew of anyone selling such grotesque carvings at the roadside?' I protested.

Beata laughed.

'It's a delight, in a way, to see you so credulous.'

My wood-chiselling friend laid her crabby fingers on my arm and felt all the way up to my face.

'I sense someone very important.'

Which was when I realised she was not nearly as blind as I wanted to believe.

'All I sense is you in my way.'

'Really, Inspector, is that all you have to say?'

It was too late to duck by or ignore her.

'How do know who I am?'

'We travel this way every New Year.'

'We?'

'My son and I.'

'From where?'

She blinked her damaged eyes at space.

'We come from Eastern Europe.'

'Honestly? How long have you been parked here?' I asked charily.

'The same as you, give a day or two.'

'You seem to know all about me.'

She waved at the lit windows of a converted single-decker bus at the end of the layby.

'There's much talk of you in the diner, Inspector.'

Again the Alsatian bristled. He would not stop snarling from his shack on wheels for a single second, lest I stray any closer. Swinging from the caravan's ceiling, a brass oil lamp flashed in the light from a stove, I noted. Someone was placing a log in its furnace. Whatever hunched and lumbering passenger caused the whole vehicle to rock, they struggled to move about the untidy assemblage of rugs, stools and cushions without banging their head every time.

I felt the woodcarver squirm in my grip on her arm.

'See here, madam, I don't wish to find you or anyone else anywhere on my estate stealing wood for your wares.'

Beata picked up her chisel, ready to finish carving her latest clever simulacrum.

'Shame on you, Inspector, for not buying it.'

'Another day, perhaps.'

'How many more will there be, do you think?'

'I beg your pardon?'

'Can't you smell it?'

'Smell what, exactly?'

'That's the smell of The day of Judgement.'

I gave a snort and wiped my runny eyes.

'I smell carbon monoxide, nitrogen dioxide and ozone. If that's, like, God's angry breath, so be it.'

From inside the caravan came the sound of more wheezing. It could have been asthma or chronic bronchitis.

My inquisitive sculptress sent wood chips flying at me as she resumed work on the toppled idol.

'Is it true what they say, Inspector, did you refuse your wife a Christian burial?'

'Doesn't mean I don't hold her very close to my heart.'

'No, but do you?'

'Every day and every night.'

I resumed my hurried climb up the hill but had only the vaguest idea of where I was heading when I chanced upon a rough stone track that left the road just short of its summit. Along one side of the pot-holed driveway someone had taken the trouble to plant thousands of snowdrops, I observed. Since the labour had been so great, so was the extravagance. When something was that excessive it exceeded the bounds of common sense. Since it was so profuse it had to have been either an obsession or the expression of a very real, heartfelt love of all things living.

So far did the ghostly white border stretch into the distance that it was logical to assume that somebody resided at the other end.

I wiped my sore eyes and smiled.

When Joseph Jones had given up his ambition to reside in a romantic Gothic pile in order to escape the unbearable mists of Coberley, he had clearly chosen a place with a view high over the valley. Two wooden seats sat side by side looking out from the path I was following. Because they were so small against a vista so vast, they had an air of defiance about them. They looked like the last two chairs left on the planet.

It was a similar story when I did a detour off the driveway to inspect a few empty stables. Dumped at the entrance to the yard, a large yellow tipper truck's rusty metal bucket spilled over with rotting fir cones in rank rainwater. Close by, a bulldozer leaned precariously on its side because one set of seized caterpillar tracks had sunk into the bank's soft soil. I climbed into the cabless driver's seat and reached for its jammed controls. I could have been back in the 1950's, could have been on my trusty tractor ready to carve out roads and reshape fields to build the future that one man had planned for himself and his family. This graveyard of machinery had once been marshalled to advance the greatest dream.

*

Shortly afterwards I was deafened by the most blood-curdling cries. With their tails aloft, a pair of pernickety peacocks flew out the fir trees and strutted across the house's gravel courtyard. They paraded about in their own special pageant just for my benefit. 'So this is where you little devils prefer to hang out rather than Coberley Hall's own lawns,' I said aloud. By them this semi-derelict place was still regarded as home. How could I deny it? There was enough left behind to render the illusion stronger than the reality.

I shooed the traitors away and descended the path through a high laurel hedge into a small garden. A less curious man might have passed right by, only a shed door stood ajar to the elements, I discovered. Rusty metal plate-work peeled off its wooden doors like ragged brown paper. Actually a former British Railways fish van, it had lost its steel wheels and now looked sadly earthbound so far from its rails. Inside shiny white, insulated walls, dozens of dull-eyed corpses hung by their necks. Just to touch a bloody beak or two was to spin each pheasant or partridge in one last twist on its skewer.

I left the meat store how I found it. There were so many interactive levers and bolts on a second van that it looked locked for ever.

For a moment I stopped to listen.

But that was just another peacock uttering its awful shriek somewhere, I decided.

If 'The Firs' had been Joseph Jones's fresh start, it had also been nothing like Coberley Hall. No seventeenth century girandoles twisted in agonised turns on the walls to light the rooms, no elaborately, black-painted Jacobean chairs stood round its dining table when I peeped in through a window.

The front door of this plainest of Cotswold stone houses stood wide open, so without so much as a knock I went in. It was as though the great man himself had completely changed his mind about his former home and all its history which he had once held in such rapture. His whole soul had revolted from it, apparently.

'Anyone there?' I cried, pausing in the presence of a few stuffy prints of hounds and huntsmen that hung on the living room's wall.

Peter Slater rented this house now, but he wasn't here.

I pulled out a bottle and two glasses from a tasteless 1980's chromium plated drinks cabinet. If somebody couldn't do the decent thing and show up on time, he had to expect his whiskey to suffer.

Pretty much.

But absolutely was I expected because someone had lit a fire in the grate with a lot of old correspondence. A smouldering collection of letters and notebooks slowly curled into black, wrinkly ash and then crumbled to pieces.

I took hold of some brass tongs in order to stir the hot embers. Even as black-edged paper resurfaced and with Peter nowhere to be seen, I began to retrieve some smoking remains in no particular order. The initials JJ, embossed in gold on a slowly burning, brown leather cover, brought to my attention some torn up pages from a diary:

May 12, 1981: Beat the shit out of George with an iron bar. This conflict with my stepsons is like a war.

Fragment: …since Sally bled out at the roadside I hardly feel safe in my own home.

Fragment: It's always the same! If I don't want to be with HER why on earth did I dig up her bones?

Fragment: As soon as I try to sleep I see Sally's car hit the tree and glass slash her throat. If she did swerve to avoid someone she didn't stand a chance…

May 10, 1982: Thirteen Herefords with their calves left their winter sheds for the spring grass today. After all my hard work in the winter it was wonderful to see them kick up their heels and buck like broncos. I'll miss rearing stock. The bull has been sold to France. The rest will go soon. I'll miss the four-week-old calves the most…

Undated: It's Sally's fault both boys just laugh in my face when I tell them to call me lord. She never taught them any discipline.

August 1, 1981: Had just popped into the Hall last night to fetch my toolbox at ten o'clock when I saw her dart across the flagstones in the courtyard. She knocked on the window. Rat-tat, ratatat, rat-tat-tat. To my utter astonishment Philip and George let her in. Imagine the surprise on their silly faces when I walked in on them in the kitchen: they were about to feed her like a stray animal!

August 21, 1981: Her name is Esti Dryzek. I catch sight of her big blue eyes momentarily but her gaze simply floats past me. At seventeen she's the same age as the twins and already treats them like brothers. No wonder Gerald Turner kept so quiet about her. The old fox! She hardly ever says a thing in my presence, but drifts from one room to another in an eerie, rather beautiful silence. Hard to believe she's only a girl from Poland and not some angel come to tempt and torment me.

Undated: I sleep better up at 'The Firs'.

Undated: Is Esti the future that Sally failed to provide? That barren bitch gave me nothing.

Fragment: Now SHE has her house to herself SHE can leave me alone?

August 2, 1982: Every night I'm dreaming of Sally's blood-soaked face when I wake up at the sound of someone trying to get in. I sleep with my gun on my chest in bed nowadays. IT will not take me with it, not in this life… I'll blow its brains out before I let any bogy man walk through my door.

Fragment: The rudimentary stove was still warm when I kicked it over, there was still a piece of skinned rabbit sizzling on its rusty lid… Whoever's living wild in Chatcombe Wood knows how to survive, like a soldier.

Undated: …won't say where she went. Her knotted hair smelt strongly of wood smoke and her toenails were filthy black. Caught her creeping back into 'The Firs' with her shoes off. She met someone, I'm sure.

Fragment: SHE must take no for an answer. I love Esti, not her. Damn the consequences, in this life at least.

Undated: Just because I'm sixty-five doesn't mean I'm too old to have a love of my own. Esti spent all today again planting snowdrops…

August 12, 1982: No one knows that the baby will be a girl – it's Esti's and my secret.

May 30, 1982: …those boys are like a millstone round my neck. If they want me to act like a father to them they should obey me, they should know their place. Fact is, their real father died at sea and can do nothing for them.

Undated: Drafted a new will at my solicitors today. The boys won't like it, but it is my only chance to put things right. No *man* is safe in Coberley Hall, no *man* should even try to call himself HER master… Believe me, I'm doing them a favour.

Undated: …George and Philip blame me for the death of their mother. If I hadn't been so vile Sally would never have been on that road so late at night to see her lover. Fuck them. They expect me to give them everything but they won't get a penny.

*

Still no call from Peter. No answer when I ring.

Retracing my steps past the long line of dazzling snowdrops, I hastened by the two wooden garden chairs that looked out over the valley. Whoever chose to sit there now had only the flowers for company.

*

Many a man might have counted their blessings and gone home, but not me. Not yet. Not ever. I refused to bury my head in the sand.

Instead I marched left over the hill and turned right into the long tree-lined road that led to the Shooting School. Skid marks covered the frosty forecourt. Otherwise there was absolutely no sign of any living soul. The neat brick house stood silent amid the immaculately mown lawns. I pressed my nose flat to a window.

'Peter? It's me, DI Colin Walker. You're right, we should tackle this thing together. You say we're cursed. Or maybe the fact that we both know who he really is means something. Bogle, bogy man, bugbear, how expedient it might be for others to blame everything on the supernatural when it lets them off the hook?'

But something wasn't right. Inside the workshop I could make out the workbench on which Peter usually repaired his guns. For an unbearably fussy man who liked to keep all his accessories in a smart, baize-lined wooden case, he had left his armoury in some disarray. At best, I would have said that he had quit the place in a great hurry. A brand new, white bore snake lay gathering dirt on the floor where someone had ground its fluffy white cloth into the carpet with his heel.

I strode about trying more windows and doors and then walked out to the range. But literally there was no one about to blast clay pigeons from their traps that day. He could have been plucked from the face of the Earth.

*

Back at Coberley Hall's gatehouse, I found the one-eyed greyhound digging at its door. The fretful animal was sniffing and whining at the base of the thick steel plate that completely blocked access to rooms over the archway.

Yet, stupid it was not and very determinedly did it attempt to tunnel.

'Please don't concern yourself, sir,' said James, clutching a hammer and a plastic bag of blue grain in his hands. 'It's only rats. They're moving in now that the pheasant shooting has ended.'

'H'm, yeah, I know. I keep hearing them behind the walls of my bedroom.'

If the rats had dug a hole in the cement it had to be because they had discovered something to interest them upstairs. But not long enough was I permitted to linger.

'Leave it to me, sir, I have enough poison here to kill them all.'

*

That night I sat in my coat and boots and glanced restlessly at the ever attentive cherubs that grinned at me from the ceiling while I wrote up my journal. Twice I heard the solid thud of something metal and with it a squeal, but it was all right, it was just James patrolling the landings with his hammer and poison.

Afterwards I could not help but doze off to dream the most vivid dreams of Lizzie. When a man's wife died he ought to have been able to mourn. When he mourned there ought to have been memories to cherish. With cherished memories there should have come some sort of consolation. With consolation there should have been some happiness. Once he felt happy he could be truly glad she was dead and gone forever.

*

I woke with a start and rushed to relight my candle. Whispering in the ear of my snoring sight-hound, I whistled him to go with me but the stubborn animal lay on the bed and refused to move. Not that the creaky old floor unnerved me in the slightest. As for the unsettling portraits that hung along the gallery wall, I shut my ears to their sad sighs entirely.

Outside, the smog clothed the courtyard in its gritty mantle. I had to find my way almost by touch alone, had to use my fingertips to follow walls and duck through the porte-cochere in the quiet hope that the fog would hide my nefarious progress. The frozen ground proved quite treacherous but even so I broke into a run.

Thanks to Lord Hart, I knew precisely where to go with my spade in the graveyard.

32

'You dug her up?' cried Lord Hart, slicing his mallet hard into the crisp white lawn. 'Are you insane? What the devil did you do that for?'

Thanks to me he failed to croquet his opponent's ball. I had to hop like a rabbit to save my toes.

'Not her, him.'

Naturally, I acknowledged that I had done something wrong, but he looked at me in order to reproach me from what moral high ground I could not know, would not tolerate. Besides his thick grey woollen scarf, he wore his familiar combination of blue blazer and ridiculously inadequate shoes in the morning's bitter cold.

He behaved with alarm but quickly rallied.

'That's even worse, in a way, to know.'

'The thing is, somebody didn't follow Joseph Jones's instructions left in his will, did they? Someone didn't bury him with Countess Lucy after all. Am I right, George?'

Straightening his back, he pushed his tinted glasses higher up his nose. He looked incredulous. If ever there was a cheap trick, this was it, given that he it was who had first implored me to believe that the dead could return.

'I never took you for a fool, Colin.'

'So, please, will you tell me what you have done with her?'

'We did what we thought best. We did what she wanted.'

'We?'

'Philip and I.'

'So what did she, like, *want*, in your judgement?'

'I'd tell you but it won't make any difference.'

*

All about us, sculpted birds and monsters eyed us from their vantage

263

points high up on top of the yew hedges. Somebody had been clipping beaks, claws and wings back into regular shape in the garden, he or she had begun recreating the original seventeenth century topiarian 'fancies'. Half bird and half dragon, their sun-lit heads all peered one way as if at any moment they expected another person to walk through a gap at the end of the vine-covered arbour.

I picked up a mallet. Challenged myself, I resolved to challenge.

'What is it you won't tell me, George?'

A stone bench stood at the side of the garden and on it sat a solid silver tray. A pot of hot chocolate steamed in the chilly air and an extra cup lay at his disposal. It wasn't for me.

'Stand back, old chap, or I won't have the ghost of a chance.'

'Who cares, if it's only ghosts you're playing?'

His next shot went wide, too.

I tapped a heavy wooden ball of my own, sent it trundling. Lord Hart's blue eyes darted to and fro behind his tinted glasses, as much out of hope as nervousness, while gleams of winter sun lit bristling beads of perspiration on his knitted brow. Whereupon he produced from his pocket several scorecards and a pencil.

He smiled.

'Come, finish the game with us.'

'You need to work on your swing first.'

'You prepared to do a deal with the Devil, after all, Colin?'

'Sounds extreme. I haven't exactly been in contact.'

'Doesn't mean you haven't disturbed the dead for no good reason?'

From my coat I held out the thing that I had exhumed last night. I opened it for him in the palm of my trembling hand.

'Look here. This ivory box lay among your stepfather's remains. You spoke as though Esti Dryzek made off with the countess's ring, but I think that you and Philip robbed it from the old man's corpse after he asked you to bury it with him in the grave. One of you made a present of it to Esti. It was you, wasn't it? Should there be something on the broken bones inside this box? I think so. This is Lady Lucy's finger, isn't it?'

The four separate but interlocking pieces of bone were so ancient that they had turned a disgusting, reddish brown colour against some very old cerecloth. Each segment of finger left a dirty red smear on my own.

Upon sight of the box's contents Lord Hart lurched forward. Because I caught him off guard he momentarily looked cornered. Then he lifted his eyes again in horror. Next minute he gave a wobble. Rigidity took hold of his arms and legs. Even as he toppled over I saw him stare wildly at something beyond me. Such tomfoolery was too like catalepsy for me to approach too close, followed by violent, successive muscular contractions and relaxations. Each clonic fit made him double up like a foetus on the ground.

With his hand he gripped his heart to his soul.

'George,' I cried, too late to catch him. 'Don't be such a prima donna. I'm not deceived any more, I want answers.'

*

Almost at once Rebecca arrived in the garden to take charge of our little drama. I had to suffer the disgusting drivel from his lordship's lips as I helped her haul him safely into his wheelchair. Avoiding our patient's proclivity to vomit, I stood well back while she slipped a fresh hot water bottle beneath his blanket.

'What nonsense is this, Mr Walker?'

'He lied to me about Countess Lucy.'

'Why mention that name when you can see how ill it makes him?'

'H'm, well, yeah, I don't know. I think he puts some of it on.'

Rebecca's sea-green eyes glared at mine as she drove her charge fast at my shins. She threatened to push and batter me with the chair's front step. With a toss of her wild auburn fringe she would have driven right over me simply because I wished to wring the truth out of someone for whom illness was a weapon.

'He doesn't have to listen to your stupid questions, Inspector. Are you even a bona fide policeman, any more? Could it be that it's all over for you in the Met from now on?'

'How long was I out?' asked Lord Hart, suddenly sitting straight in his wheelchair.

'Er, no more than two minutes I'd say,' I growled and set his Panama back on his head.

He gaped like a man coming up for air.

'What are you doing here, Colin?'

No sooner had he spoken than Rebecca interrupted us. His forgetfulness seemed genuine this time.

'Did you take all your pills this morning?'

He nodded absolutely taciturnly and calmly.

'Then we mustn't let Mr Walker frighten you any more, must we?'

'Frighten? What do you mean?'

'Come, George, you know how stress exacerbates the symptoms. You know the hallucinations can be triggered at any moment.'

'The visions are the least of the problem...'

Ignoring him, Rebecca concentrated on getting him to focus. While she did so she rubbed frantically at his left side in order to reduce its lingering muscle rigidity.

'Remember what we said about relaxing the diaphragm,' she said urgently.

'Did I really scare you, George?' I interrupted. 'Or did you see someone pass by the gap in the yew hedge in the garden?'

Again Rebecca's eyes met mine. In order to serve someone so imperious she had to act very calm. In order to act very calmly she had to be two different people. Since she knew how to dissemble to

266

keep her master's confidence, she could be as close and reticent as his secret agent.

'You should leave us alone now, Mr Walker. I have to give his lordship his injection.'

Lord Hart frowned. He could admit the truth of what had just happened but none of the truth admissible. Instead his gaze fastened on the hideous frieze that ran round the top of the wall of the gloomy passage we had just entered. Naked Bacchanals danced in very bad taste in honour of their riotous gods in lavish Italian-style grotesques that were more at home in Roman catacombs and grottoes than the Cotswolds. However primitively painted they were, the sylvan nudes, tigers, lynxes and spotted panthers were definitely not Elizabethan. No, really, they were.

'What's wrong?' I asked.

'See what I see, Colin? Do you see the monster?'

My eyes came to rest on a naked, bearded figure with goat's horns and hooved feet.

'I see one hell of a party.'

'For years I told myself that he was a Herm of Pan, the devil I did. I took it to be a personification of Nature, of the pre-Christian or non-moral world who would frighten travellers as they passed through the woods. The name signifies 'all'. He's representative of the ancient gods and heathenism itself, but now I'm not so sure what to call him.'

'Who else, if not Pan?'

I had to peer into the corridor's darkest, cobwebby corner, had to stand in the shadows where I came nose to nose with the man-beast with a shudder.

'Whenever I consider his presence in this house I wonder who put him there, Colin. Is he a celebration of desire or a warning?'

'Okay, yeah, I don't know. Doesn't mean one of us is going to drop dead right now, does it?'

'If only we could be sure what he wants to tell us, old chap?

What hope do you and I have if we can't speak his language?'

'Us?'

'Vae victis. Woe to the vanquished, what? Don't say you don't feel him looking at you, too, Colin? You and I are fighting the same battle. So please, take my advice. Forget Lady Lucy's grave or any other, unless you want to pay the same price I have for the sake of my brother.'

'What good is life without those for whom we lived, anyway? If you literally won't tell me about Countess Lucy's grave, then tell me something else. Was it you who had Esti Dryzek buried in Chatcombe Wood? It was, wasn't it?'

'Haven't I said, Colin? Why damn yourself for someone long after they are dead?'

'Perhaps it is the dead who want to know.'

*

I was impressed. For Lord Hart to put a name to Coberley Hall's curse required a great theatrical belief in the enigmatic and mysterious. Why should I *not* place my trust in his farcical performances?

I appealed to Rebecca who at first parted her lips sweetly and seemed sympathetic. It lasted but a second, this delightful smile of understanding and empathy before it reverted to a mask. Already she had taken hold of her patient's silky blue blanket and was drawing it higher up his legs to make him comfortable. She was his guardian angel, not mine.

But I was not one to be hoodwinked that easily.

'At least tell me what happened to your brother – at the end?'

'Exeunt omnes, Colin. We must all leave the stage eventually. It's the ones who choose to return that should concern us. We must be fully prepared when they remind, blame or worst of all demand the show must go on.'

'That it? Honestly? You won't tell me about him, either?'

'Philip slit his wrists, old chap. What else can I say?'

*

Alone in my bedchamber I frantically studied my face in the mirror. My hair was almost as long as that Wild Man in the grotesques. Seconds later, I set to work with my scissors and razor. I poured cold water from my ewer into my basin in order to wash off surplus bristles. Soon I ran my hand round my new goatee and along the line of my neatly trimmed moustache. No amount of beard shaping could return me to the once virtuous man of law to which I had aspired. At least now, though, I aimed to be more Cavalier than pagan.

*

After dinner, I took refuge in the smelly library where I set to work all afternoon on Coberley Hall's fusty accounts. I sat at the table that was strewn with old invoices and receipts and combed through details of such awful things as tangible fixed assets. Screwed up letters had gone unanswered and bills remained unpaid which was, frankly, perverse because Lord Hart was not a poor man. For hours I sat making sense of unexciting facts and figures.

It was a poor soul who failed to find much consolation in his own newfound wealth. Clearly Lord Hart would have me believe that the dead were not to be trusted, but it was not always the dead who were the monsters. I saw through his little masquerade. After all, I was not the one who was mad or ill.

With that, I marched down to the kitchen in the futile hope that Sara might have done my washing.

*

It was tempting to feel that, in such an irredeemably dismal part of the house that I might meet its ghostly chatelaine. Certainly the kitchen held many an old porringer, flagon and copper kettle that dated from her day. Soot and smoke coated the gloomy cavern's vaulted ceiling whose vast weight of stone bore down like a sepulchral monument placed squarely on top of me.

For the future state of my stomach, I felt obliged to investigate how anyone could cook any food in a place so frightfully antediluvian.

Like a slightly drunken celebrity chef, I began to issue imaginary orders to gentlemen waiters, slaughter-men and kitchen boys. I instructed girls to pluck the peewits, partridges and larks on the blood-soaked wooden tables. My eyes wept at the onion sauce that was to go with the rich aroma of a stew and I sniffed the March-pane and ginger for sweetmeats after dinner.

Already I could touch the cold flesh of a carp fresh from the fishpond as my knife slit open its stomach and I could hear the dull thud of my blade as I tore open the belly of a deer recently killed in the woods. I sniffed the herbal sauce I was making from the fragrant yellow-flowered fennel and tasted the salt in the veal. Most of all I could see the sudden light of the fires as the oven doors burst open and gave the copper pans and tureens on the walls back their brightly burnished glow.

Here I had the trappings of a lost world at my fingertips, had all the props necessary to stage its revival in my head. The past's best role was to be its future?

'You want something, Mr Walker?'

The belligerent, red-haired Sara sat by a barred metal gridiron on which a chicken slowly roasted. On her lap she gave a pewter candelabrum a few desultory rubs with her cloth soaked in vinegar.

'Why has his lordship sealed the door to the rooms over the gatehouse?' I asked, looking straight into her hostile emerald eyes.

Sara let go her cloth and began to scratch the bad skin on her forehead. She poked spots and pimples with a broken fingernail.

'I'm sure I don't know what you mean, Mr Walker.'

'Somebody burns a candle in the gatehouse window every night.'

Had I thought to surprise her by my directness, I was mistaken. Her eyes simply narrowed very severely.

'Nobody but you could think anyone lives there, Mr Walker.'

'Really? Not at all?'

'Not since his lordship's poor brother Philip.'

As it happened, I forgot to ask her for one of the dead man's shirts to take back with me to my bedchamber.

*

That night Lizzie appeared to me in a series of pictures and events so vivid that they were more real than I had ever before dared dream them. In fact, the difference between what had gone before and what came afterwards was sufficiently blurred to be utterly irrelevant. How else could anyone share past words in a wordless future?

Day 2. April 7. 2014.

Very sore throat – can't drink a lot – vomits and brings up acid which burns her from the inside out. The visiting nurse agrees that there is some thrush which can't be helped.

I give her sips of water from syringe and beaker.

Even throat spray hurts her now. Can't swallow.

Day 1. April 8. 2014.

Cold again. I have to pull her thin sheet right up to her chin and close the window.

'Don't forget to pay for the newspaper, Colin.'

Old routine from home?

Her top lip is wasted away. Pared back. Her face has altered so much in the past few days. Skin baggy and wrinkled.

The semi-silence is almost unbearable – death is a reality just when we've settled into this new routine.

'I must make the effort to stay awake, Colin.'

Extraordinary attempt to be sociable in the face of onslaught of so many pills and potions. In constant pain – rubbing her stomach. Same when she becomes lucid for a few sentences to explain.

'It's time, Colin. I'm sorry, I shouldn't ask you to do such a godless thing. I'm sending you to hell, for sure, I know.'

'We've talked about that already.'

This cancer of the ovaries is not about to let go.

33

I sat up in bed wheezing and choking. I fought to suck in sufficient oxygen to restart my lungs. Yet dying was I not and most definitely did I not delude myself. From outside my window came the sound of my name.

I had already made it my business to observe the garden in which I knew Lizzie had once walked and run. I did as any griever might do when a place survived but the person didn't. Speculatively, I made a point of imagining her playing games of hide-and-seek or gave conjectural expression to her childhood thrills and spills.

It was not a hopeful scenario, particularly, yet I could not watch but a wave of hope swept over me.

This night, I pressed my face to the leaded glass as usual to see frost bedeck the paths below with silver crystals. Something was all glitter and glimmer. What began as a bright and fluid cascade of water soon assumed the solid shape of an actual person, next to the figure of Venus. Neither nostrils nor lips condensed steamy oxygen but somehow she breathed in the gaseous night. Someone so aeriform had to be too insubstantial to be alive. Still she was every bit the projection of my own longings and dreams, a figure that was both opaque and transparent, close and far. She had a mind to dance while the fountain flashed and flickered.

Without moving her lips, she projected her voice with a commanding cadence.

'Col – in. Col – in.'

She wore the same drab gown in which she had last lain at my mercy on the police mortuary's dissecting table in London.

But this was more than me restaging bad memories. I found the will to mouth words back.

'Thank God,' I said. 'You're real.'

She knit her brow in great determination.

'I'm as real as you would have me…'

'Lizzie. My love. My darling.'

But she shook her head very firmly.

'The thing is,' I said, 'I haven't yet found the perfect place you'd have me put you.'

'If you don't do it now the countess will take me.'

'But like me, is she not simply grieving?'

'Have you never considered if the dead mourn, too? I'm to be her new lost daughter Elizabeth, for eternity.'

'All she wants is her family back.'

'Then you'll have to be her dead dragoon.'

'Wait, Lizzie, please. I can't live without you.'

'Don't you see, Colin, that's how she wants it.'

It was my turn to shake my head. If at last a man found the key to life and death, he was no longer his own gaoler. If he was no longer his own gaoler, he was free to cross from this world to the next. Pulling on shoes and coat, I ran at full pelt downstairs to the garden. There, the chilling air stung my face like needles.

With little moonlight there was no way to see far ahead. Since there was no way to see far ahead I could barely follow the path through the remains of the knot garden in the 'hortus conclusus'. Such intricate lines of evergreen rosemary and hyssop suggested something unending and infinite. If the air was as cold as the grave, there was also ice on the ground and all over the fountain. What I had taken to be spouting water turned out to be solid crystals.

Closing my arms on my dearly departed I would press my mouth to her clay-cold lips, I fancied, would let her breathe my warm breath for my own salvation. But I was left with the stone statue of Venus.

'Lizzie?' I cried. 'Where are you?'

Only the goddess raised her warning finger to win my scant attention.

Of my dead wife there was no other sign.

Yet Venus's eyes were not simply blank but stared straight ahead with all the passionate gaze of an interested adjudicator. I followed it. Poised in the gap in the yew hedge was another figure, slowly passing. I hurried closer and looked through the entrance to the pure white lawn beyond. There, someone picked up Lord Hart's mallet and mockingly began a game of croquet, whereupon the expression on her face came across as more immediate and tangible. The nearer I approached her the more defiant she appeared. When the dead played the living they needed little rehearsal.

Defiance like that came with a challenge. The first, hollow strike of the ball amounted to absolute disdain since she let my presence count for so little. That hit was also the last. The roving ball passed all hoops and pegged out at the final stroke of a game that finished itself.

Resplendent in her scarlet gown and pearls, she trailed brilliant snowflakes behind her in a long glacial train. The point of her richly embroidered stomacher reached down from her breast to overlap her skirt with more gems. She was dressed in another dress taken from the chest in the cellars. She rested the mallet in her crooked finger for moment.

In her blazing eyes cried the wild screams of men and horses and the roar of cannon. They reflected the terrors of a civil war whose hell would never be forgotten or forgiven. Immediately she curled her sharp fingernails my way and her voice boomed in my ears to bring me back from the brink of distraction.

This was her garden and any denials from me, no matter how passionate, would be found wanting.

'Come sir, it is the very Divel's Delusion, for they would starve me from my own house, take away my rents and burn my crops and then WE shall have nothing to live upon...'

'Wait, Countess, tell me what you just did with Lizzie?'

'Don't be silly, Inspector. It's me, Marigold.'

I wrenched the mallet from her hands.

'If that's true, let me see your fingers.'

34

For the next few days I greeted Lord Hart most effusively, whereas he turned his face to the wall or stared hard at the floor. Although I gave him no good cause to start or spring back, he appeared to shrink from me both physically and mentally. I definitely could not explain his abrupt change in attitude, unless he took exception to my newly trimmed bristles and moustaches. In actual fact, my pointed and waxed chin-tuft, like a goat's beard, was as novel to me as it was to him.

Also, my skin had become a peculiar whitish or ashen colour, but not at all unsightly.

If I said that I thought him a little in awe of me I would not have been too far wrong.

As usual I dined by myself in the great hall where in fact I ate very little. It was as though suddenly George and I could only live in Coberley Hall at each other's discretion, we had to be silent partners in the non-betrayal of its secret.

Pretty much.

Those few times when he did choose to interfere in the daily management of my estate I was deeply enraged and soon flew into a temper. Forced to conciliate, I did my best to defy his defiance, but noted in his eyes a flicker of anxiety at the forthrightness and urgency of my demands. In truth, I was not unaware of my own growing restlessness and unsociableness.

I decided to defuse the situation by shutting myself up with great bundles of estate documents in the disordered library. Perhaps its contents would make more sense than its owner.

*

At a twist in the steps of the great oak staircase I met James about to descend from the next landing. He was creeping about like a mouse to check doors which he did every morning and evening.

'You still speaking to his lordship, at all?' I asked.

'Excuse me, sir?'

'Is he sulking about something? I must say that I find his sullen attitude towards me very disconcerting.'

He rattled his keys very loudly.

'What attitude would that be, sir?'

'H'm, well, yeah, George is quite unwilling to discuss my management of his affairs, but I literally do feel that certain things need to be settled in a hurry. For instance, I've almost completed my tour of the estate's boundaries but need to settle any queries with the Land Registry now that I've decided to earmark certain fields and property for sale. The thing is, I do not understand the maps in their entirety.'

'What in particular is the problem, sir?'

'Someone has drawn a thick red ring round an area called Hilcot Wood.'

James fixed his grey eyes on mine with great firmness.

'Consider it a warning, sir. Hilcot Wood is a very old place full of little grassy glades that are really marshes. One wrong step and you can be in over your head in a bog in seconds.'

'But Peter Slater must go there regularly to feed the pheasants?'

'Naturally he knows its secret ways.'

'Okay, of course, I should hope so. Has anyone seen Mr Slater, at all? He's not at 'The Firs' or the Shooting School. And he won't answer his phone.'

At which point James started downstairs past the nearest newel post's grinning monkey.

'Excuse me, sir, I think I hear his lordship calling.'

*

Everywhere I went I met fresh grounds of suspicion. This was not expressible in so many words, but that was the gist of it. I could not but help feel prone to the partial or unconfirmed belief that although naturally I regarded myself beyond reproach, other people suddenly held me in suspicion. They said very little to my face, but such hostility as they could muster in a glance or grimace I felt obliged to avoid by doing without them. With map in hand, I chose to walk round the estate in the manner of a soldier or sentry. Of my patrols I gave no advance notice.

One afternoon found me in the vicinity of Father O'Connell's derelict bungalow. The white winter sun pierced the black thorny hedges along the lane, exposing old birds' nests and discarded beer cans. Coming to what was in fact a muddy public footpath into a field, I saw hard at work the unmistakeable figure of Adrian. Now I was myself buoyed by my latest ambition, so I advanced with an emphatic wave in order to spur him on.

Ever since a thrilling new confidence stiffened my resolve, I felt driven to issue orders which in no way could be construed as impudent, only bold.

'Do hurry up and get this field cleared.'

Adrian hitched his baggy jeans up his skinny buttocks and climbed in the driver's cab of his tractor.

'That's all very well, Mr Walker, but you can't simply spray couch grass with insecticide, it's too resistant. Absolutely it is. The only way to kill it is to dig it up and then spray it. You'll see, soon nothing will grow in this field until you want it to. That's the wonder of weed killers these days, they're the farming equivalent to mass murder.'

'I simply meant to say that first you must finish fencing the new boundary. That way I'm not just selling an abandoned building but an attractive land package. The money I will use to restore Coberley Hall to its past glory.'

'It's about time someone took a proper interest,' said Adrian, scratching his closely cropped grey hair.

'You and I know how difficult it is to persuade George to do anything?'

'All that will change now you've decided to stay on, your lordship. Coberley Hall needs a man with fresh blood. Absolutely it does.'

278

'What did you just call me?'

But Adrian slammed shut his cab door. His deadpan voice faded with the first rev of the engine.

I tried shouting at him, to no avail. Deafened myself, there was no point trying to deafen. Instead I folded my shotgun over my arm and resumed my march up the lane, feeling proud.

*

Once a man decided to put down roots in a place he could feel bigger and better about himself, he could take considerable satisfaction from being king in his own little kingdom. I drew my map from my pocket and the lonely red ring that had been drawn around a square mile or so of woodland drew my attention. The disfiguring delineation was more smear than carefully penned line, more blood than ink.

A crimson thumb mark denoted Hilcot's hidden entrance which, in reality, proved to be a mere gate like any other. An uninviting and much overgrown track led into a gloomy plantation of beech and red cedars past a sign which said PRIVATE.

I had taken but a few steps when a piercing cry filled my ears. So shrill was the sound that I looked up – a large, companionless silhouette circled the sky high over my head. I thrilled to the call of the wild, if not to the wilderness called. Only a bird of prey had a scream that ghoulish. Any man's heart had to expand just to see it. Then it was gone with its ominous significance. It shot over the next horizon as fast as an arrow, took with it its promise of good or ill fortune. It was a red kite.

As it happened, I chose not to venture any further into a place so unfrequented until I found Peter.

*

Physical exercise did little to alleviate my feverish state, yet inwardly I was more serene. Fewer were the loud and irregular beats of my racing heart which had threatened to throw me so off balance. It occurred to me that my pulse tick-tacked now with the slow steady rhythm of some increasingly deadly purpose.

The growing awareness of a change in my mental character lessened the fright at the visible ravages to my body. I felt elated by my own emaciation. Ill was I not and quite obviously was I not dying.

*

My first action upon my return to Coberley Hall was to revisit the churchyard. Only someone who did not feel proud of the dead that he inherited could refuse to show some humanity towards the sadly departed. I glanced at all the pretty slabs and impressive inscriptions that marked each plot as I took time to imagine my own name chiselled here in large, elegant capitals.

Turning alongside the church's weather-stained south chapel, I was dismayed to have a man's voice spoil the dead's solemn solitude.

'Can love ever outlive the tomb? Or am I wrong as well as wronged?'

No sooner had he spoken than Rebecca parked his wheelchair at his side.

'What's going on?' she snapped. 'Who's that with you?'

Lord Hart ran his overgrown fingernails through his long hair.

'I was simply confiding in Philip, my dear.'

By now I was in deep shadow at the south side of the church tower where I halted, eager to overhear whatever new conspiracy the two of them were hatching against me.

'So, please, tell me what is there, honestly, left to say to your brother?' asked Rebecca, flicking her untidy fringe from her eyes.

'I came to tell him that dies irae is here. Our day of Judgement. He never could stomach my use of Latin phrases, never could see how a dead language could be of any use to the living, but would he not agree when I say the Coberley Estate is damnosa hereditas – it's an inheritance that brings more burden than profit?'

That I was furious could not be doubted. The key to my whole future happiness was my stake in Coberley Hall and its land, which

I now regarded as part of my very being. How should I react? I could see nothing sane in his assessment.

'Come away at once,' said Rebecca sharply and led him to his wheelchair. 'Didn't we agree how much better you can cope by following a strict daily routine?'

In response, he tapped the metal ferrule of his dragon cane against the headstone and repeated aloud its inscription:

Let Fate Do Her Worst. There Are Moments Of Joy, Bright Dreams Of
The Past, Which SHE Cannot Destroy.

'Really. You done?' declared Rebecca and unscrewed a silver Thermos flask which she had in her pocket. 'Please, no more 'SHE' today.'

Lord Hart's eyes flashed blue. Then he nodded.

'It seems that Marigold might have been playing with me all along.'

'Does that make you more sanguine?'

'Not sanguine, suspicious. It is all part of her plan.'

'I wonder if you really are making as much progress as I thought.'

'There's no trusting her. But then to Marigold, the countess *is* the answer. Fraud or not, she believes in ghosts. She refuses to accept that some genetic link with the fatal disease that afflicted my brother might explain things better. I think I agree with her.'

'Just because Philip said he saw the countess, too, doesn't mean you can't move on.'

'If I do, won't I lose him forever?'

'You don't have him now, you only have a few grievous feelings.'

'If Philip were here he'd know what to do.'

'So, please, tell me. What would he do, in your estimation?'

281

From my hiding place I could not read the exact expression in Rebecca's fractious face, but I could tell that she was fighting what she considered a cruel fantasy and product of his condition.

'He'd say we have to kill the bogy man. He'd say we should settle the unfinished business that death leaves behind.'

'Ah, yes, your childhood hero. You don't still doubt Philip's demise, do you, George? You have his death certificate in a drawer. It's down in black and white. So why let him live on in your head?'

'You can't kill the dead with a piece of paper.'

When I sneaked another look I saw Rebecca take her patient's Panama and set it straight on his head. She treated trifles as ridiculously important.

'No one can bring your twin back to you, George, not even with Marigold as medium.'

'You say that. You tell me to stop wishing for the impossible, but who are we without each other except ghosts anyway?'

'None of us should assume that the dead speak our language.'

He let slip his stick.

'Marigold thinks I'll take her back if she gives me Philip.'

'Yet so far she has brought you nothing but false hope. Does she even know what she can and can't do?'

'We say the heart is the seat of our emotions. We say a man has no heart or a heart of oak. We learn lines by heart or speak from our hearts, we try to win the heart of someone. A man in low spirits is out of heart and he who overwhelms him with sorrow breaks his heart. All this for a hollow organ of flesh and blood that circulates our blood simply by contracting and dilating. That is the riddle.'

Rebecca unscrewed the little cup from the end of the flask.

'We've been over this a thousand times. Marigold has indulged you to manipulate you ever since you threw her out of Coberley Hall. How can anyone guarantee that you and Philip can be together? Would he know who you are?'

I could not rightly explain how I felt. But my blood was up and I believed I detected in Rebecca a dangerous intent to malign all attempts to revive the dead. In my fury I scratched and clawed at the stone tower beside me with my fingernails until they broke. From there, however, I took not a step. Not yet. I growled.

Lord Hart did the same.

'You know what I'm thinking? I should never have told her that I believed in her. Oh, why the devil did I do it? Of what treachery have I been guilty? At Coberley Hall she only wants to be chatelaine again. What good did she ever do me?'

'Consider it a warning. The dead can't love the dead or the living.'

'It's not me she's rash enough to turn to now, it's someone else.'

'Who else is there?'

'Colin Walker.'

My forceful host dismissed Rebecca's look of concern, but left her to fill the awful silence.

'So, please, tell me, where does that leave Marigold, in your mind?'

'Since it seems that neither of us can have what we want she can go to hell for all I care.'

*

I had uttered but two or three silent profanities when a sudden clarity of intention gripped me. I almost shouted out with rage. I walked up to Lord Hart. It made me sick to hear of his lying scheming.

'What hell is that, exactly?' I cried and clenched my fingers upon his shoulder.

My astonished host wriggled beneath the weight of my hand. I gazed down at him with the same vehement hope with which he had first welcomed me into his home. Only the truly cursed had that stare.

'It is what the living are sometimes pleased to dismiss as

283

loneliness, the devil it is,' he declared with a single, damning smile.

There came a sudden weakness in my legs as if my blood felt somehow deficient. Sensing my hold on him lessen, Lord Hart had Rebecca push him back to the house. He fled before I could ask what he meant by his obscene duplicity.

*

Later, I unfolded the letter that George had sent me six weeks ago – it could have been a lifetime – before I could guess what truly lay in store *afterwards*. If not a warning, it was definitely an admonishment. It was totally uncalled for, absurd, intrusive. The advice ill-suited the advisor. Likewise, only a complete fool could accept that the mere mention of his name was so pertinent and relevant to recent events that something other than his wife's death could draw him against his will to such a place as Coberley Hall.

The missive was a mass of black, serpentine squiggles. They writhed like snakes from a quill at my fingertips, but it was the postscript that really aroused my disgust with its hateful, bitter spitefulness:

'We can never live in peace *with* those we've loved and lost, Colin, we shouldn't even try.'

35

Not even the most consummate liar would try to fool someone like me with his show of penance and passion, yet daily George began to behave in a way which was beyond my comprehension. This was frequent visits to Coberley Church. The more he brooded and plotted against me, the harder it became to predict his malevolent intentions. The wilder the desperate petitions that he made to the dead, the more unpredictable grew the outcome of his actions.

I literally could not bear to linger any longer out of sight among the graves. Suddenly I heard the squeal of his wheelchair's wheels roll down the path towards me. His face paled until his features were bloodless, ashen and drawn. Frustration and disappointment showed in his staring eyes and slack jaw. Despair was still more evident. His lips leaked drool which suggested someone at the end of his tether.

Had he been an animal I would have chained him like a dog – a rabid one.

At once I left the cover of my tomb and undertook to follow him quietly into the church, with every intention of overtaking him down the aisle. The moment both doors swung shut on their elaborate wrought iron hinges, a chill wind blew in a few dead leaves behind me. Worse, on the shelf of the nearest pew hymn books flipped their pages in frantic applause as if an invisible hand flicked through them in passing.

He did not once look back to observe the disturbance, appeared oblivious to my intrusion upon his ridiculous devotions. Stopped at the carved Jacobean pulpit, he tapped his dragon cane on the little diamond-shaped graves that were set into the floor of the chancel. I had heard his pathetic cries before but not what he cried exactly. Today would be different.

> 'Search us out, O God, and know our hearts;
> try us and examine our thoughts.

> See if there is any way of wickedness in us
> And lead us in the way everlasting.'

That he was almost at the point when I could call him deranged, I did not doubt. He was terrified and had only God to turn to. Inside that creaseless, bone-white suit, his upright body suddenly sat very still. Clearly, on detecting his hypocrisy detected, he could no longer suspend his wily dissembling in my presence.

'You ready to pray with me yet, Colin? You've been trailing me here for days.'

'Oh no, I'm okay, yeah. I'm fine. Definitely. Lizzie was the religious one, not me.'

'Doesn't mean you can't trust in the afterlife?'

'Are we talking heaven or hell?'

'You know what I mean, old chap. This is the place where it should have all ended. This is where Lady Lucy was buried after eighteen years of marriage to the 2nd Earl of Downe when there was 'no liking' between them. Did she not lose her heart to Captain Digby only to be left broken-hearted? She ate her heart out to die of heart-ache. In an age when scientific reason had only just established how the heart pumped blood round the body, she can be forgiven for thinking that a loving heart is responsible for our very existence.'

I fixed my eyes on the brown tiles at my toes and I was standing on an inscription to the Reverend Robert Rowden, Rector of Coberley from 1651-1672. I could grind my heel on the remains of the man who had first tried to commit my countess to the ground for ever.

Already I was trembling with anger, but tried to stay rational. It was obvious, for all his apparent obligingness that, in resisting this devil, mere contempt gained me no advantage.

'I've seen the Ouija-board, George. Damn it, man! Are you not afraid to lose the dead to a few cheap tricks? Would you have me fooled, too? Only, I've proved too strong for you, I've turned the tables.'

Lord Hart rose stiffly from his wheelchair and struck matches to light various candles.

'Since your arrival, Colin, I've come to realise that you have the same excessive belief or superstition that I have. The Germans have a wonderful word for it – aberglaube. At first Marigold and I feared that we had done the wrong thing, that your credulity regarding the supernatural might drive you wild before you chose to leave. Our fear of the unknown and mysterious is not irrational, old chap, and neither is our reverence misdirected. We can learn to live in peace with those we've lost, if never with them. Did I not say so in my letter?'

'Not too disbelieving, then?'

'Should not you and I help each other to give grief a purpose? I speak as a friend.'

The fickle wicks of candles burst into flame. They lit not only a depiction of the Crucifixion near the altar but the knight in armour whose freestone effigy lay next to his wife in the South Chapel. For a moment it was possible to feel that I was the victim of some terrible fraud, that it was I who would soon lie over there on the slab for centuries.

A moment later, Lord Hart seized my arm like a brother.

'As one bereaved man to another, let us learn how to profit from our sorrow, Colin. Has not Marigold shown us that the dead cannot love us back, but will resist all our ferocious exacting and bargaining? Has she not given physical forms to our own doubts and longings only in so far that we might *invent* them? We see the dead as still living, we think we pass them in the street or expect the next text or phone call to be theirs long after they've been buried. Yet these are the sad tricks we play on ourselves, which prove quite fake in the end?'

The logic of his weasel words made me shake and perspire. I did my best to free myself and focus my mind by summoning fresh thoughts of my lost wife, but I was filled with a chilling sensation of someone else's presence, a presence I both feared yet craved to acknowledge.

I shook and wavered the same way the candle-light did.

Lord Hart noticed it, too.

'Is someone here now, Colin?'

'I believe so.'

'But she can't see or hear us?'

'Both.'

'Where is she?'

'Over there by the tomb.'

'How is it you can see her and I can't?'

'Maybe it's her way of saying that I now mean more to her than you do?'

In that instant, the chapel appeared very different. Its beauty grew, enhanced by the candles whose flames lit up knight and lady as though they were lying in state in their very own chapell ardente.

Lord Hart retreated in horror from the glow.

'You're not real,' he shouted at the flicker of torches. 'You're only a figment of some spirit-rapper's conjuring and trickery.'

'Careful, George, she will hear you.'

My fractious host swung his cane across the aisle to bar the way. With mischievous intentions he stood guard and looked all round him. I could not say that the ghastly twist that took hold of his lips was not a smile, but it was also a gasp of indefinable dread and malice.

'The countess comes to mock the monuments to Coberley Hall's previous owners,' he said quickly.

I watched the candles light up the walls and did think for a moment that I saw a woman standing between light and darkness. It wasn't Marigold. Today she was clothed in a brown dress and stood with arms held down her sides as if aping someone forever robbed of her coffin. She kept vigil silently and attentively and would brook no distraction, only remind herself of what the living did with the dead.

'Why haunt a place where no ghost can belong?' I asked.

After which George's gaze drew my attention not to the effigy of the knight on top of his tomb but to someone else's oval portrait that was carved on the wall of the sanctuary. A chevalier in armour filled a pillared recess, I noted. It was not an image of peace exactly, yet I could not peer at him but a peacefulness settled on me. All paint had long since faded from his arms and legs and his face was an unappealing, almost featureless mask of white limestone as he clasped a casket firmly to his chest.

'She would lay claim to all those who have gone before and come after her,' explained Lord Hart, nervously.

'Lay claim?'

'To all but Sir Giles de Berkeley. When he died in 1295 he had his heart laid to rest in this chancel wall while his bones were buried miles away in Little Malvern.'

'Honestly, this is a grave?'

'By placing his heart in a box in the wall it is neither inside nor outside the church to foil the Devil. That's the miracle. That's why it eludes her.'

Whereupon, the brass oil lamps that dangled from the rafters began to sway slightly on their long black chains. Their ugly metal brackets grew restless, twisted and groaned above the pews, while a shadow darkened each white ceramic shade in the grip of someone's agitated fingers. Had I not shut the church door properly?

'Take care, Colin. Marigold is jealous of the dead and will use them against us.'

'It's thanks to her that I can still see Lizzie.'

*

Back in his wheelchair, George clutched his blanket high up his chest and began to shiver. Then he wheeled himself away down the aisle at some speed. I had to chase after him to catch up.

'The thing is, George, Coberley Hall was where Lizzie was born. The end is indeed in the beginning. I promised her on her deathbed that I'd keep her safe in the grave.'

'How so?'

'She was particularly insistent that I didn't bury her anywhere where she could be exhumed afterwards.'

'Did she really think that disposing of her remains so would save her soul?' asked Lord Hart over his shoulder.

'Not hers. Mine.'

I alarmed and surprised him not simply by what I said but by the context in which I said it.

He spun his wheelchair to a stop at the font.

'You wouldn't set so much store by this place if you knew the whole truth, Colin.'

'How is that in any way relevant?'

He rapped the stone floor with his cane again and listened. Detecting no objection, he went on.

'My stepfather was a very selfish man, the devil he was. Joseph Jones lured Lizzie's mother to his new house on Wistley Hill. He intended to start over at 'The Firs' with his mistress. When Philip found out that JJ had all but persuaded Esti to move in with him, he decided to confront him. We all did.'

'All?'

'Me, Philip and Peter Slater. One night in 1982 we crept up to 'The Firs' where we found JJ in bed with his loaded shotgun clutched to his chest. No one had reckoned on finding Esti soundly asleep beside him. Both must have dozed off just before our arrival. JJ had his finger on the gun's trigger as if he were expecting the Devil himself to visit, so my brother went to pick it up to avert any trouble. Too late, Esti woke with a scream. That's when it happened.'

I placed my hand on his shoulder to steady him, but still felt him tremble.

'What happened, George? Tell me what you won't tell God.'

'Esti's shout woke JJ who refused to let go of his gun. Next minute he had his brains blown out. He died in an instant.'

'Honestly? Philip killed Joseph Jones?'

'Except he didn't pull the trigger, Colin.'

'If he didn't pull the trigger he can't have done any harm.'

'It was me. I did it. I rushed to help Philip wrest the shotgun from the old man's grasp. In so doing I put my finger on his and squeezed it for him. After that we hurried Esti back to Coberley Hall before the police could find out that she had been anywhere near that awful room. As far as the world was concerned Joseph Jones blew his brains out because he could no longer live with his bad lungs. Two days later his cancer test results came back positive.'

'Go on.'

'Esti wanted to know why the three of us had been in JJ's room that night. She knew in her heart of hearts that we had gone there to do him great harm. As years went by, she found it harder and harder to live with the probability that her scream had caused the gun to go off, she had to drink heavily to keep the secret. A sense of her own guilt grew like a choking weed inside her. Because she had been prepared to sleep with JJ to gain her own ends she somehow thought of herself as complicit in our crime.'

'What you're really saying is that she became dangerously depressed with some sort of post traumatic shock?'

He assented.

'When Peter showed me Joseph Jones's diaries a few days ago, I realised that Lizzie was my stepsister after all. Why else do you think I burnt them? She was the child that should never have happened. Now, since prayers don't appeal to you, old chap, please push me back to the house where I belong. I feel very tired.'

Once in the churchyard I glared at the grave of the man who had died so violently, wondered if prayers alone could ever intercede with one for another as I plucked up the courage to do as George asked. If he expected me to hate his murderous ways he could have done no better than to offer me such risible explanations and excuses.

Not an hour passed that I did not feel observed more closely.

Next day, I was acutely aware that it was my turn to be pursued with malice aforethought. After all, had not George told me his secret? 'His curse is now mine. He might murder me, too, at any moment?' I said aloud to the house. This was intolerable and dangerous. I would not be the victim of a madman.

But the best method of defence was not to show offence, nor to let him know that I knew what he intended.

'The devil!' I said, trying not to feel trapped within my own walls. 'Must I, who until recently was the representative of the rule of law, live in fear of someone who has no sense of moral order, I, who also was not afraid to kill – must I, then, accept another man's fervent fear that the dead might never walk again in daylight?'

Such lies were unworthy of the liar.

*

The first chance I had, I sought out Rebecca by the frozen lake. She saw me coming but said nothing, only let fly with a stone at a swan. She sent her missile bouncing across the icy surface all the way to the medieval fishpond's pretty little man-made island edged with dead bulrushes.

My heart skipped with it.

'So, please, tell me this. What kind of person lies about his stepfather's death for over thirty years?'

Dressed in her drab blue uniform Rebecca exuded the authority of one paid to take care of the sick and yet she struck me as more advocate than nurse. She behaved like someone who had power of attorney over person or property, or both. She could be less guardian angel than custodian.

'Someone who finds it impossible to live with the truth, Colin.'

'Really? You knew?'

Rebecca juggled another stone from hand to hand like some obstinate, unfeeling body. Then she hurled that too, far away into the distance.

'I take it we are talking about George?'

'He's as good as told me he murdered him.'

'I hardly think now is the time to resurrect that particular confusion, do you?'

'Don't you?'

'Joseph Jones shot himself, Inspector. No one in Coberley will tell you anything else.'

'H'm, well, yeah, I know different. George should be certified, at least.'

'As time goes by and more symptoms manifest themselves it becomes less and less productive to confront him about the difference between what really did happen and what didn't.'

I felt my feet freeze in my boots on the frosty ground. When someone felt that he was in pursuit of something he could leave no stone unturned. When he left no stone unturned he tried every possible means to persuade others to listen to his concerns. When they refused to listen to him he had no choice but to make accusations, he had to be prepared to cast aspersions on a man's honesty or loyalty, he had to be prepared to throw a stone or two of his own.

'All this business about bringing his brother back from the dead is guilt at what he did that night in 1982?'

'Please stand aside. I must get back to my patient.'

'What nurse treats a man who can't live with himself, anyway?'

'Best ask yourself that question, Colin.'

'That it? You won't give me an answer?'

'One thing I have always been very clear about is that George can't control his shifts in personality by himself. He has always made it plain that he needs me to act as his anchor as soon as he begins to drift from one hallucination to the other. I'm his lodestone that gives him direction. Unlike Marigold, I place the blame squarely on disease, not the dead.'

'Really? What disease is that?'

Rebecca took aim at a swan.

'Doctors call it Lewy Body.'

'I've never heard of it.'

She pitied my ignorance.

'Rare it may be, Colin, but in America, for instance, it affects two million people. There's no cure. A victim suffers hallucinations, trembling and fits until they lose all control of both mind and body. It can kill very slowly. In Philip's case, it drove him to distraction.'

'You'd dismiss a man's belief in ghosts by reassuring him that he is dying the same way his brother did? What sophistry is this?'

'Because most of the symptoms fit. His lordship has the same visions, too.'

'Only, he thinks he's cursed?'

Rebecca turned her face away and into her eyes came tears.

'I try to reassure him that what he sees is just another part of the disease he doesn't want to admit having. That's not to say that in his mind's eye Marigold isn't sometimes too strong for me. Each day, here we are, fighting her for his sanity all over again… It's why I had him banish her to the woods six months ago.'

Our hot breaths condensed into one spectral cloud in front of our faces.

'Why fight her offer of help so cruelly?' I asked.

'Because the alternative is too awful to contemplate.'

'I don't understand.'

'Oh yes you do, Colin. You understand only too well. Better a disease that drives you insane than hell itself.'

'What makes you the arbiter of mind and soul?'

'Because I have medicine for one but not the other.'

*

Suddenly the swan glided boldly by on the icy water and its awful amber eye challenged us with its defiant confidence.

Or it knew how much I hated birds. In my hand I weighed my black, fire-tempered nail from the lost tithe barn, which made the perfect missile.

'Wait,' I said, rushing to keep pace with Rebecca over the bridge on our way back to the house.

'I really don't have time for any more of your questions, Mr Walker.'

'If a man is sick to his soul from guilt or grief, will he not see ghosts without any illness?'

'I don't say ghosts don't exist, I say they have no separate entity or being outside a person's own mind.'

'And if our mind's eye should suffer its own form of vitreous detachment?'

'I won't stand by and let poor George's ex-mistress or you scare him half to death because you've put it into his head that the dead can still survive.'

'Consider yourself an expert on the afterlife, do you?'

'The truth lies in your hands, Inspector. That nail comes from the barn that George pulled down to be rid of his demons.'

'It's where Esti Dryzek died of liver failure, I know that.'

'Because of her, one man lost faith in the other.'

'What do you mean?'

'I mean Philip stole her from under George's nose even before Joseph Jones was cold in his grave.'

'And I thought George might have betrayed Philip.'

'Eventually Philip couldn't live independently. Thanks to the disease, he became too delusional. Keeping him a virtual prisoner in the gatehouse was in his own best interests but it was also a punishment. George wanted to get his own back, which is another reason why he can't forgive himself for his brother's suicide. But it's not the chief reason. He still *loves* his twin.'

I felt my lungs work hard, the air being so thin and empty suddenly.

'According to George, Lizzie never knew any of it.'

'Oh, but she suspected all right, Colin.'

'Did George never explain to her why he and Philip decided to send her away to be raised by some other family?'

'You have to admit that Coberley Hall was no place for a child.'

'So all this time there was this unspoken misunderstanding between them?'

'Lizzie felt certain that her uncle harboured some dreadful secret which soured the Hall in her eyes forever. She was right. But no one told her exactly who her real father was or how he had come to blow out his brains. Not even her own mother. Esti couldn't. She was in love with Philip. As far as he was concerned the child was his. It's why George was so jealous.'

I had to admit that my motive in being so inquisitorial went beyond my help or health. If I were to counter the plot against me I had to rebel against the very man who would have me doubt my own reason. I had to resist his nurse, too. But a vital ingredient in undermining me lay in Rebecca's shameless and unhesitating appeal to common sense. She would have me believe that she knew the difference between physical and spiritual symptoms!

*

I caught up with her again at the end of the avenue of pleached lime trees. I tried to take her arm next to a trellis of tangled roses.

'Are not you and he simply working together to drive *me* crazy?' I said. 'Have you not drugged me the same way you did Philip?'

My belligerent carer stopped.

'We only ever gave him what he needed.'

'But you knew all your nursing was doomed to failure, so why do it?'

Rebecca gave a toss of her head.

296

'It was George's decision to 'manage' Philip's dreadful deterioration in his last few years. That's why he hired me. The outer gates of Coberley Hall were kept bolted as well as the doors to the house, but only because he would escape to wander about stark naked like the Wild Man he said he met in the woods. He would bang on windows and claim to see the dead come alive on the lawn, until the only thing that would calm him was ketamine.'

All of which was highly relevant to my mind in view of what else she had done to me.

'Damn you, I see what you are. You're Death incarnate. The only reason you want to consign all ghosts to their graves with your false hope of a cure is because *you*, and *you* alone, want to be Coberley Hall's next chatelaine?'

'If you think you're so much better than me, why haven't you left?'

'Meaning?'

'When loved ones die we must give them space to forget and deny our presence. It's for the best, don't you think? How else can they ever rest afterwards?'

'How can you be so sure?'

Rebecca ran her hand through her hair and her cold, hard eyes fixed mine through her fringe.

'Because I'm not like you, Colin, I can let go.'

36

They say an Englishman's house is his castle. So it was that Coberley Hall infused into me not only a rightful regard for my surroundings but the novel state of mind with which I regarded them. When sitting at the high table in the great hall, I increasingly found myself in tune with its sepulchral walls. To eat within them was to enjoy magical effects by strange means, to drink was to perform similar marvels.

I had a fancy to call myself its castellan, though had still to learn how to live like one.

Of the dust-covered, cobwebby furniture and rusty Civil War armour I was less forgiving.

I had the dream of happiness, if not yet the happiness dreamed.

From high up in his portrait on the chimney piece, Joseph Jones stared down at me doubly hard. Seizing a pewter candelabrum from the table, I raised three lit candles to his grinning features. In them I now detected a crafty curiosity. At first, I could not see how I deserved his fresh attention, though clearly I did. Ever resplendent in his Cavalier's silver lace, buttons and galloon, he did, I was sure, honour me with a peculiar and ugly triumph of his lip.

Touching cracked oils, my fingers followed the leathery lines of his saddle while, on his horse's shiny neck, serpentine veins boiled beneath the skin of glistening black paint. I pressed my palm flat to the canvas, absorbed hot, fire-lit skin of man and animal. Voluntarily, I heard myself hiss some voluble, clear and intelligible whisper, part thrill and part wonder. It was a guttural, growling, savage cry, the snort of a dragoon and his mount in the heat of battle.

Not only did a knowing wiliness and corresponding cunning transform an old man's worn-out features into this soldierly and more vigorous double-ganger, it hinted at something akin to eternal youth. His eyes contained some malevolent promise. Soon, he appeared to say – like the medieval saying on the plaque below him – that I would soon be like him:

As we are so shall ye be.

From where I was standing, that same translucency of flesh left him doll-like and pretty. While he impersonated so well a seventeenth century Royalist captain, he was distinctly wax-like. Although in the style of the Old Masters, his face was less masterpiece than death-mask.

*

Not long could I bear to stand amazed at the significance of the portrait's reincarnation, but hurried away from hall to grand stairs. There I unlatched the spiky dog-gate and with the one-eyed greyhound hard on my heels, climbed the dusty oak treads. Above me, an impossibly youthful Adonis clutched Venus's plump breast on the magnificent ceiling. Before, I might have had eyes only for the jealous, covetous goddess who stared at all who lingered. This time my heart reached out to her lover, too. Suddenly I sympathised as he fought to be free of his mistress to go hunting wild boar, yet so needed her embrace to stop him falling.

As it was, I rushed up the last few steps to the candlelit gallery, felt myself pushed along by my own figure fashioned from darkness. I marched past the row of open-mouthed, gasping Cavaliers imprisoned in paint when, unexpectedly, the door ahead of me opened and closed. It was James.

He was responding to some hullabaloo faraway in the kitchens.

If I had not been so busy I might have investigated further.

Instead I arrived with my heart pounding at the end of the landing. There I stared at Countess Lucy's portrait. She half turned towards me in her low-cut, green and white dress in which she looked so magisterial and queenly. As a woman who had been wed first and foremost for her dowry, she was required to pose against the contrived background of classical ruins and leafy landscape. In much the same way, her husband had posed his pictures of dogs and horses. For an artist to capture her so casually in oils required some willing participation in the necessary device and artifice, she had to deceive to be both humble and haughty. So it was, she crooked a finger at me in a simple gesture which was both steely and inviting. Yet deceived was I not and absolutely did I not imagine it.

Sure enough, her blood-red lips visibly acquired a vivid hue as of a living person. They not only embodied an air of self-possession but stood proud of the canvas where she would have me step up and kiss her.

With new understanding I clamped my hands to each side of the picture's bulky frame. Instantly, her dark eyes turned liquid and silvery. Where her thick, curving eyebrows almost touched mine head to head, she frowned in great concentration. Meanwhile the pearls at her freckled throat gleamed and glistened.

'Trust me,' I whispered. 'I know what I'm doing.'

*

The almost life-size picture tipped so awkwardly in my grasp that I was obliged to negotiate every step virtually blindly.

On the worn, smooth stairs it was hard not to dip to the right very dangerously.

Back in the great hall, the twelve sons of Jacob scowled at me from atop their screen, to observe what I was doing somewhat contentiously. Next minute, I offered up the painting to the recessed hole in the chimney breast with some trepidation.

But not long did I hesitate to trust my own instinct. At once, the pairing of pictures restored a pleasing symmetry to the chimney piece's elaborate stonework. No blank, recessed space rendered the Cavalier's portrait unbalanced, even wistful. No more was he the odd survivor of a set of two, he was no misplaced complement to a couple whose corresponding parts were never meant to be displayed separately. No more did a pale, ghostly suggestion of the missing person cry out for redress or forever prompt the prospect of some as yet undisclosed purpose.

For a chatelaine to lose her place at the head of the great hall was to lose her identity. If she lost her identity she could lose not only her title or home but also her place in history. As though the dead should ever be supplanted by the living!

I shuddered. The logs in the fire basket cooled in a cruel draught that threatened to blow out my candles. Then it was I realised that I was making a terrible mistake. Yes, with his long, flowing curls, goatee and thin waxed moustache, the Joseph Jones I knew had successfully recreated himself as a fine dragoon. Yes, he held his plumed hat dextrously in one hand as he sat astride his gallant black Barbary horse. But he was no living, breathing portrait of any soldier, he was only ever a pathetic old man mummified in oils and varnish.

Surely a much truer likeness of Captain Digby was what Lady Lucy really required to have mounted beside her?

JJ had never truly caught her fancy. What a crazy fool to think *he* was the one! I could acknowledge the harmony of the pairing, but not of the two people paired.

Instead, I felt driven to consign him to the gallery wall at the top of the stairs with all the other discarded, so-called suitors. He could hang with the other eight, heartless rejects to make nine bleeding hearts, as on the family shield. Anyone else who tried to pass himself off as Lady Lucy's lover was unworthy.

So long had her presence graced the house that she would always be its possessor, not possession.

About an hour passed – it could have been an eternity – before the one-eyed sight-hound began to bark and growl most aggressively, not at all like an ordinary greyhound. No one was at my door. In the interests of sanity, I opened it with annoying regularity in order to surprise some invisible attendance.

I had read not a few stories of haunted houses but had never thought to join in the haunting.

*

With fresh eyes, I was drawn to the domestic scene that hung over the desk in the closet. Within its black and gold frame her ladyship sat on her chair's silky red cushion and rested one hand beside her pot of frangipane on its green velvet cloth. Only, this evening, she was considering what travel clothes to wear with the help of her gentlewoman, I decided? Tonight, did she not hasten to ready herself for some secret rendezvous at last? The light from real candles caused her long black hair and lovelocks to shine. Each glowing flame heated the oils in the picture and gave her gown its silky gleam even as she peered earnestly into her mirror set into the lid of her exquisitely carved jewellery box. Far from being immobilised in stiff paint hundreds of years old, this private moment in her existence was now forever ready to take on a life of its own. That it was Lady Lucy, I'd never doubted.

Quickly she dabbed a blush of Spanish red on her bloodless cheeks, then powdered her lifeless hair to give it back its colour. From among her pots of musk and amber grease she chose to rub oily balsam into her withered fingers and perfume the insides of her shrunken wrists with the smell of red jasmine. Meanwhile, her astrological globe by the fireside stopped at Pluto, ruler of the underworld. The way her hands trembled, she was looking forward to something that would at last put an end to all her waiting?

On her middle finger her blue and gold enamelled ring shone bright behind her bony knuckle. Aware, perhaps, of my reflection at the periphery of her mirror, she jerked her head my way. With hard, golden eyes she not only glared, she dazzled.

*

Restive clocks stayed their beat for a second.

Suddenly a girl's voice joined a man's in the host of gathering shadows. Then, more frantic footsteps. I chose to hurry downstairs when I saw a light flash on the landing below me. My sensitised eyes were equally responsive to the gloom by night or day, such was the house's effect on my world since it had suffered its strange reversal.

I suppressed my shiver of slight alarm but not of bewilderment. The greyhound at my side followed suit.

James waved a sconce about in wide circles. By his side hovered a fretful Sara.

'What's going on?' I demanded.

'Search everywhere,' said James, ignoring me. 'He has to be in the west wing.'

The sullen kitchen maid shook her head.

'Too late. I saw him run across the courtyard.'

James rolled his head in perpetual, agitated motion.

'Where is his lordship now?'

'Gone after him. To the woods, I suspect.'

'But it's pitch black out there.'

I descended a few steps to interrupt the confused discussion on the landing.

'Can you please tell me what's going on?' I demanded.

'Didn't you hear, sir?' said James. 'Peter Slater is dead.'

*

I seized James by the arm. He was shaking more than usual.

'Please, in your own time, tell me again what's happened.'

'Mr Slater's dog came whimpering and whining to the farmyard at Slack's Cottage. If Adrian hadn't followed him all the way back to 'The Firs'…'

Confused myself, I tried not to confuse.

'Spit it out, man.'

'He found him locked in one of his insulated meat vans.'

'I doubt that very much.'

'Mr Slater had scratched off all his fingernails before he suffocated, sir. There was blood down both doors.'

Sara butted in.

'His lordship said he knows who did it…'

James cut her short.

'She means that we've just had a fright of our own, sir.'

'And Lord Hart has given chase,' said Sara, breathlessly. 'He thinks he can catch him, as we speak.'

Of my own thoughts, it was hard to make sense.

'You see his face, at all?'

'I'm thankful, in a way, I didn't.'

James rattled more keys. He tried in a vain attempt to come up with a plan of action.

But the interfering Sara had not finished yet. Fear and loathing lit her face.

'What are the odds one of them will get hurt?'

'Fetch a lamp,' I said immediately.

'What good will that do, sir?' asked James.

'Doesn't mean one of us shouldn't try to stop him.'

'Take my advice. Don't go without your gun.'

'Honestly? How come?'

'Because what I saw was a beast of a man,' added Sara, recklessly. 'You ought to be careful, Mr Walker. Some things are best left to others.'

'Okay, it's just that I'm in charge now.'

That's when she gave me a fatalistic look I couldn't quite fathom. Her wide emerald irises filled with dismay at my woeful predicament as though I deserved as much pity as his lordship. If the wretched girl could not understand that I had to go on the hunt of a lifetime, it was because she had no idea what it meant to get the chance to lay to rest a bogy man, bugbear or bogle.

'Do either of you, like, know exactly where George is headed?' I asked.

James brought me my boots from the kitchen.

'It could be Chatcombe, Mercombe or Hilcot Wood, sir.'

'Where would you run to if you really wanted to hide?'

But I'd guessed that already.

*

My biggest regret was that I had entirely the wrong sort of weapon.

Whereas a hunting rifle could have brought down a man at considerable range, my 12-gauge, double-barrelled shotgun was a blunt instrument more suited to blasting rooks or rabbits. To be effective I was going to have to go in close, I was going to have to see the whites of his eyes, not just be within eyeshot.

I counted spare cartridges into my trouser pocket. Then, briefly, I stopped by the door to the inner courtyard in order to don my cap and coat. At that moment, the reluctant Sara came marching up to me dressed in a dreadfully fluorescent, yellow anorak and Wellingtons. In her hand was the oldest oil lamp I had ever seen in my life.

'James says I have to go with you.'

I shot her a smile.

'The dumbest animal will see you for miles.'

She flicked a curl of red hair.

'It's not an animal we're after.'

'Whatever he is, we have to hunt him down.'

'Even if he is a freak of nature you shouldn't talk of hurting him quite so casually.'

'Sorry to disappoint you, Sara, but your sympathy won't save him from my gun.'

'Some things are not what we imagine, Mr Walker.'

'Do I look like a man who doesn't know how to hunt his own monster?'

*

It was agreed that Lord Hart could not have gone very far with his limp and cane.

'Why chase after someone all by yourself on the spur of the moment?' I asked, studying footprints left in the hoar frost. 'What is the fool thinking?'

'I didn't say he went willingly,' replied Sara.

'You mean he was taken?'

'I mean he wasn't himself, he was incredibly elated. Never seen a man so animated.'

I smiled again. When something happened that coincided with someone's most fervent wishes he had to think of it as a God-given opportunity. When something was that opportune, he did not stop to consider whether it occurred by accident or design, he simply rejoiced at the favourable timing. He didn't always show the caution he should.

Crossing the bridge by the lake, we followed the grassy carriage drive diagonally across the field. We passed the overgrown entrance with its two loury griffins, then crossed the main road to climb the hill to Upper Coberley.

The wretched Sara stumped along behind me with her arms folded. I had to chivvy and chide her every step of the way as she kicked stones idly along the pot-holed road.

'Do try to keep up,' I said.

'It's these stupid boots, they're rubbing my ankle.'

'Just tell me where to go and I'll go on without you. What else did George say, to your knowledge?'

'He said something about we each have our own cross to bear which has to be answered.'

'Doesn't mean I can't give him a helping hand.'

'What if you find yourself answerable, too?'

'I'm still going.'

'Are you mad? What if you meet your death?'

I felt too enlivened to listen.

'Honestly. Do I look out of my mind?'

'I don't know. All I see is you.'

37

If not openable, Hilcot's newly padlocked gate was at least surmountable, I discovered. A shiny red and white police sign, displaying the web-like cross-hairs of a gun, proclaimed 'POACHERS! WE HAVE YOU IN OUR SIGHTS.' A second bull's eye had been nailed to a tree beside the road, which struck me as somewhat melodramatic. The threat was deadlier than the warning. Even as Sara and I set foot in the maze of trees it was odd how eerily bound on all sides we felt, so completely did two ominous features at once unite against us. They were the stillness and the silence.

I had not the nerve to step off the path, which was why I chose not to reveal any of my ridiculous apprehension, only follow. For Sara's sake, it would do no good to panic in all that crepuscular gloom which was otherwise so utterly black as to have no other distinguishable tint or hue. Frankly, we might have been the first people on the planet. Or the last. I favoured the last.

Seconds later, she gave me a whistle and I came running.

'What is it?' I asked, gasping.

'We have to take that track over there.'

'How can you tell?'

'My father and I came here poaching.'

*

Not only did every bush or bramble against which I brushed sprout spiky pelts of tinkling ice, the very air I inhaled felt full of cold barbs. Soon I was struggling to breathe in a place bleached by age, not frost, it seemed. My rough, husky voice was suddenly that of a very old man in some afterworld.

When at last Sara lowered her smelly spirit-lamp close to a frozen puddle, we saw by its yellow glow how someone had recently sliced through the brittle grass. I drew attention to one deep, cloven print in particular and then pointed ahead towards our quarry.

'It'll be the devil to pay tonight.'

Sara marched off in a most cursory manner.

'I know a stag's print when I see it, Mr Walker.'

She meant well, but hunting a demoniac required a more refined set of tracking abilities. One had to have great skill in detecting things ordinarily hidden from the human eye, one had to hone an almost supernatural sense of touch, smell and hearing to pick up the slightest signs of a trail. You had to see what the moon did.

I glanced anxiously over my shoulder. Already we had left the gate marked PRIVATE far behind us. A decent flashlight would have been nice. Honestly, it was too late now to change my mind.

*

Sara assumed pole position at the head of our expedition. Anyone else might have thought she could do without me.

We stumbled downhill past some enormous cedars which, like Solomon's Temple, towered all the way up to the night sky. Each mighty red pillar joined the earth to the heavens.

We spoke not a word to each other until, half way down the slope, Sara sat on her haunches. Next, she ran her hand quickly across some soggy brown pinecones. In a display of ungainly dexterity, she moved sideways and backwards like a crab, while exploratory fingertips considered different surfaces.

'See these holes, Mr Walker? Note how they're all dot one and go.'

'H'm, yeah, well, I see that now.'

Even the cleverest, most devious soul had to leave a few obvious clues behind them.

'Notice how each jab of his stick sinks deep into the ground. Lord Hart is really tired. From hereon he'll be going slower and slower, that's for sure.'

So apt was she to make such bold assertions that fewer and fewer did I trust to satisfy my feverish impatience. It was like going prospecting for gold. At the slightest clue she uttered a short 'h'm', then more than before, blundered on. Eventually she slunk along much more sure-footed, much like she had with her poacher-dad, no doubt. Her skills had to be of more use to me than her morals.

Next minute, the sky sizzled. We were in a clearing around which storm-tossed trees had been felled by unnatural forces, the exact circumstances or battles of which had been lost in time. White with ice, piles of fractured branches lay all about us in shipwrecks of broken bones. Here, though, was the real reason why Hilcot Wood had been largely left alone for half a century. I looked up to see crackling, high voltage cables divide the trees from east to west. It was pylons.

To cross under such high metal towers in such a hidden place was a surprise, but not even the showers of hot snow that rained from the buzzing lines could quite account for the air of disconcerting hostility they showed. Each pylon hissed at us venomously.

I could just about tolerate my tremors of cold but not of trepidation. Sure enough, we passed old guelder roses which had over the centuries grown into impressive snowball trees. We were in an ancient domain where every now and then a twig shed a sliver of ice down our necks or spat us cold kisses. Then it was that I was overtaken by a withering impression of decay and disaster – a sensation which was more fact than fanciful. Carpets of stinking dog's mercury released their morbific, fetid smell as I waded poisonous green leaves crushed flat by man or beast.

At the edge of the clearing, we arrived at a precipitous slope down which I hesitated to slither.

But Sara was not interested in my premonitory diversions, she was holding her lamp to a handkerchief on which I was treading.

'His lordship passed this way a moment ago.'

I snatched the blue-edged cloth from her fingers. I could barely distinguish it from any other awful rag, but then, unlike mine, she did his washing.

The deeper into the wood we penetrated the more I found myself beginning to people the trees with grotesque and capricious fancies. These I could not wholly rule out as unreal. Mind and trees merged in one dreadful tangle of veins and branches, they writhed and wriggled round me in living projections of my innermost fears. My shotgun weighed more heavily in my hands as I prepared to shoot devilish things.

A moment later we heard an awful scream.

'Quick, Sara. Go and see who it is.'

'What about you, Mr Walker? What will you do?'

'I'll climb the ladder of this deer hide while you scout ahead to confirm our line of attack.'

'But…'

'No buts, that's Lord Hart shouting.'

'Since when do you give all the orders?'

'H'm, well, yeah, I don't know. We can't both get lost in the night, can we?'

I listened again to the high-pitched scolding and it did sound to me like man and fiend fighting.

*

Not that Sara was gone long.

Thankfully.

She lifted her hot lamp half way up my ladder.

'It was only two foxes courting, Mr Walker. You've not seen them go nose to nose to scream in each other's faces before?'

Clearly this wilderness could be more misleading and deceptive than I imagined. Meanwhile the shapes that I tried to see dissolved into nothing. I resolved to descend at once and rescind our attack when suddenly a grotesque shadow bridged the narrow gap in the trees at the top of the bank. It shot off sideways.

With my gun held high in my hands, I peered all about me with deadly intent at whatever or whomever it was I was supposed to be aiming.

'Pay no attention,' I said. 'It's that stupid dog fox and vixen again.'

But Sara stared ahead in absolute silence. With a finger pressed to the tip of my gun she slowly lowered its barrels.

Next moment, she motioned me to follow, but not make a sound.

Of my own astonishment it was impossible to speak.

Ahead of us, two shadowy figures stood ready to wrestle. Snow peppered their hats like loose diamonds. At once I recognised Lord Hart, but Sara poked her finger in urgent mime at the other, she had me note the bloody bandage round his upper arm where he had been wounded? I shuddered. If so, Patrick McGuinness had indeed nearly done for him on beaters' day, as I'd thought.

Framed by the weak glow of the moon stood a creaturely man with strong hands and a long nose. A thick, white fell of untidy hair curled in rat's tails down each side of his massive head where it trailed past his stout neck.

Valorously, I ducked lower. Next, I gestured frantically to Sara to dim the wick in her lamp just as the voice of Lord Hart drifted from over the lip of the slope. We had circled round and were close to the line of pylons again.

'It's been so long. Are you really dead or alive?'

There came a gruff, bear-like snarl.

'Isn't it enough that I'm here?'

'How long will you stay? How long were you gone?'

'Does it much matter?'

'Because I know what you're capable of,' said Lord Hart. 'I know how murderous a man can become when he's allowed to stray or run wild.'

'You more than most.'

'What greater hell is there than grief?'

'Then why didn't you save her?'

'How do you stop someone drinking herself to death?'

'You did nothing to help her. You didn't even try.'

*

Peering from the tree-line, I peeped again at the misshapen figure that was so quick to accuse. With the moon's bitter look reflected in a dull lake behind him, the barrel-chested scarecrow stood seven feet high while his face remained a mass of conflicting shade. His wretched clothes hung off his shaggy body where his bulky torso bulged inside his rat-coloured cape. With his long leather gauntlets and green floppy hat trimmed with a brown and cream buzzard's feather, he was the kind of outlaw everyone instinctively wanted gone.

I did not have to wait long for more vociferous exchanges.

'You forget how much I loved her,' said Lord Hart. 'I wanted to marry her, for God's sake.'

'And you forget that she couldn't live with what you did in her name.'

'But I lost my brother, too.'

'Doesn't mean he was any better than you.'

*

Sara leaned closer to me on a carpet of dead beech leaves.

'This isn't any good,' she whispered, 'his lordship doesn't have a gun.'

'You see that?' I said. 'The other has a knife.'

'So it will be a fight to the finish.'

'You've changed your tune.'

'You want to settle it, Mr Walker? You want to play the hero?'

'Let's hear what else they have to say first.'

312

'Do you even know how to shoot?'

'Shut up and listen.'

*

With raised voice, Lord Hart was becoming angrier and angrier.

'Are you quite sure it isn't more money you're after?'

'We've been over that already.'

'Cash suited you well enough before.'

The gorilla of a man gave a grunt and shifted one foot in the mud. He rolled a massive shoulder, then bowed low with his hat in his hand like a Cavalier. It was pure buffoonery.

'Your blood money was never enough for me, you know that, George.'

'How else have you managed?'

'Since the army wouldn't have me I've carved wooden bears.'

'So what else has changed?'

'You have.'

'We agreed you'd never come back.'

There was another growl. A fiercer one.

'A few weeks ago you set a trap for me, tried to spear me like a wild animal.'

'Isn't that what you deserve?'

'It's no way to treat any man.'

'Not a man, a bogy.'

'I'm finished with you all anyhow. You're the last.'

'Is that why you killed Peter?'

There followed a bitter laugh. It chilled me to the bone. I could choose to run away but could not stomach the choosing.

That appeared to go for the beast, too.

'You think you are superhuman and judgement is yours to give as you see fit, don't you George, but you're no different from me? At heart, we're both killers.'

'I never set out to hurt anyone who didn't deserve it,' replied Lord Hart defiantly.

'Consider one death very much like another, do you?'

'What do *you* know?'

'I've let Esti's fate go unpunished far too long.'

Lord Hart brandished his cane higher.

'If you hadn't been on the run in the woods after you fed Gerald Turner to the pigs you never would have seen us leave 'The Firs'. You would never have had the means to blackmail me.'

'Gerald Turner was no different from the rest of you. You all did your damnedest to ruin my sister with your lust and ambition.'

'Whatever I did, I did it to spare Esti, too. That at least should put us on the same side?'

'You have to answer for your sins like all the others.'

'You don't know what it was like back then. Joseph Jones was a vicious bully. Many a day saw my brother and me hide in fear of our lives. When our mother died Philip changed irrevocably. Even *before that* you can't imagine what it meant to live in the shadow of his growing delusions. To this day, I still don't know for definite if he skinned that tramp alive or what he did to Father O'Connell. I had no choice but to protect him from himself.'

The bear of a man stirred while the primeval mud sighed and sucked at his heels.

'Doesn't mean you can escape me by pretending to be cursed already.'

'My brother blamed everything on his 'monster'. Now I see how prescient that was.'

'Doesn't mean any lord of Coberley Hall is above retribution.'

'You talk as if someone else has sent you.'

'You know that very well.'

Lord Hart raised his arm more threateningly. Then he hacked at the air with his cane.

'You'll get nothing more from me. I'll be my own master from now on.'

I clamped my hands to my ears, tried to shut out the penetrating cry of outrage which followed. It was part hurt animal, part caveman.

Its roar was so soulless yet human, so cruel yet vulnerable, that I doubted if any gun could ever silence something that full of love and sorrow.

'My sister died the moment you blew a man's brains out all over her face. Thanks to you she was cursed ever afterwards.'

'Damn it, Viktor, you're insane.'

'No, I still love my sister.'

*

The wanderer slavered and for a moment I saw the whites of his eyes as I raised my gun on the point of firing. Instead I turned my head briefly to Sara.

'You knew he was back, didn't you? Esti Dryzek's brother has always been our prowler ever since I arrived in Coberley. Why didn't you say?'

Sara shook red hair from her face.

'You heard what he said, Lord Hart paid my father to set a trap for him in the woods. It was unfinished business, he said.'

'Since then you've felt obliged to let him into Coberley Hall? He's been roaming about ready to steal God knows what?'

'Please, Mr Walker, I tried to stop him.'

'Hence your cuts and bruises?'

'I should never have left the gatehouse unlocked, I know that now.'

'It explains why James is so keen to check all the rooms in the house every night and morning. I was right. He does want to keep out a real bogy man, after all.'

'There are no bogy men, Mr Walker, only life.'

*

Too late Viktor saw bright steel. Pain and shock brought him to a stop but did not bring him down. Instead he turned and with his bare hand drew out the bloody point of a rapier from the slashed fold in his coat. Wading straight at Lord Hart, he scooped him up like another beast. Holding him close, he twisted and staggered on the sea of dead horse-tails that carpeted the lake with their miniature and primitive trees. The flowerless, black stems snapped underfoot so low and close together like a carpet that it was impossible to see where land and water merged.

Sara and I ran forward, only we, too, sank into the boggy ground.

I was not trapped exactly. Still I could not move my feet but a sensation of imminent entrapment gripped my ankles.

The swamp began to give off a foul, rank smell of things subterranean. Lord Hart fought to seize the Wild Man by the throat and break his grip while the other crushed him deeper and deeper into black slime. The sword-cane had gone flying. Now both were covered in splashes from the treacherous mire. They looked and smelt putrescent, appeared like two corpses in the process of rotting. Each blow, bite and punch threw up something offensive and rancid in this indecent, virulent and gross place that could suck flesh off bones.

Sara prodded and pushed me forwards.

'Get between them, Mr Walker. Seize your chance.'

I had my gun ready to shoot but not a clear shot to fire it. The sly eye of the moon cast its livid sheen across the water. From the gleaming pool came a deeply inarticulate sound that was both grief and disbelief all in one groan. If it was a cry of agony, it was also a sobbing mewl. It rose to the tops of the trees in a terrified shriek as Lord Hart swept his fist at his adversary in a savage blow. Such yelling quickly turned to a cry of downright alarm. It was too awfully apparent to me that he was already up to his groin in the bog, which was rising round him even as he was powerless to resist it. He lifted his mud-streaked face and it looked bedraggled and disheartened.

'For God's sake, Viktor, give me your hand!'

But Viktor had already waded mud and water at the far end of the lake, he was using his superior height and strength to stride through the slime and mount the slippery edge ready to slide down into the valley beyond.

I fired a shot after him but it did nothing.

Instead I threw down my gun and called to Sara.

'Shine the lamp over here! Now!'

Pulling off my coat and boots, I risked another few steps forwards. This part of the mere was no surface-silvered mirror but a sheet of smoky grey ice much clouded with rime. In its crazed glass I could just see my mocking shadow. Spiky clumps of sedge protruded from their icy prison, otherwise the shore was all treacherous deception.

This frigid crater was so torpid and chilling that it numbed and dulled my senses, it would defer and annul any possibility of life itself. At the same time, it was a place so old as to hold many secrets.

*

I made some freezing progress and saw Lord Hart's face emerge from the mud. It oozed treacly liquid that gushed from his nostrils. He called something to me, after which he vomited until his head fell back and gazed wildly at the fireflies of snow that floated from the pylons.

Already considerably vexed by my strenuous exertions, I, too, paused for breath. Within a few seconds I had sunk to my knees until I was held in a vice-like grip by the welter of rotten matter. The ice around me offered a tantalisingly firm grip that was all enticement and lure.

'Sara, go back to that deer hide we passed and fetch its ladder,' I shouted. 'Hurry.'

I looked round for Viktor but he was gone. The abominable man had let out a loud cry before bounding away into the valley in great strides. His high, wild peal of laughter sounded through the frosted trees but, growing ever fainter, soon disappeared into the lost byways of the wood's prehistoric paths where our forbears had once roamed. And yet it was not altogether so – such a cry was also forever mine, since it revealed to me the very depths of my nature. When Viktor looked back from the brink of the void, that face was my own.

*

Lord Hart gasped and gurgled.

'Damn it, Colin, I'm done for. The devil I am.'

His voice trailed away but not before he shot me a last look of hope.

'I'm coming, don't worry.'

I wriggled, felt myself subside even more. Now I was in the hellish pit up to my shoulders. Inch by inch I trod the clammy, sticky swamp until I could stretch out and touch the other's head with my fingertips. Sara was taking forever to come back with our lifeline. As a result, I could feel myself sink every time I moved a muscle. She was our last, best bet.

Up to our chins in slime, George and I were powerless to move when, at last, I placed my hands squarely on his scalp and pushed him down. With one last, suppurating bubble, he went alone to the bottom.

*

The dilatory Sara at last arrived back at the bog, dragging the sniper's ladder. Thanks to the moon's bloodless witness, I could see well enough to place one fist over the other to elbow myself shoreward along the wooden rails.

Lord Hart's Panama lay on the surface of the swampy pool, but not necessarily at the place where he had gone down. In any case the blood froze in my veins. For a whole five minutes I had to lie on my side spewing awful mud while Sara covered me as best she could with my coat.

'Couldn't save him…,' I gasped. 'I did try.'

She scooped black sludge out my hair.

'What's the odds? He shouldn't have gone in there, he made a wrong move.'

'Without you I would have gone down with him.'

'In the end you had the advantage.'

'But he's dead.'

'Too bad, he lost.'

*

I huddled inside my coat while Sara pulled on my boots. I stank of the swamp and its slimy decomposition of mud and vegetation tasted foul in my throat. It left me feeling corrupted. I could have been coughing up my soul.

When one man survived at the expense of another, he could not predict that some kind person would dismiss the dead quite so casually. In actual fact, Sara set my cap on my head and put my gun in my hands most properly.

'This way, your lordship.'

*

Only the most ungrateful man would have distrusted what had just happened, only a fool would not have thanked God for his deliverance.

Sara shone the way ahead with her spirit lamp. I did not question the deferential look on her face when she called me 'lord' because I detected no wry cynicism on her part in her changed attitude towards me. I saw no pretence in her acknowledgement of my rightful title, no attempt at ridicule. Clearly she, too, chose to accept that the ill-timed and perverse chain of events was in itself accidental and not

319

due to the dead hand of fate or some other malignant control?

When one man tried to save another only to nearly die himself, he could be forgiven for not doing things by the book. Because death had no rules one could not always behave within specific boundaries, one had to stake everything on simply staying in the land of the living. Lord Hart was gone forever. I had had to finish him off to give myself a chance, but as Sara so elegantly put it, he had overreached himself and his foul game was up.

Even if I was a bit player in someone else's sinister gamble, it no longer mattered. I'd won.

Actually, matter it did. It mattered a lot.

It mattered more to me than I could ever have predicted.

Incredibly, wonderfully, I was still alive!

38

My trying experience in Hilcot Wood left me excitable and restless. Ignoring James's tedious protests, I took the keys to every room in Coberley Hall, responded to the pressing call for immediate action. Because I felt such an importunate and insistent demand take possession of me, I began to search the house from top to bottom as soon as it was morning. There were no feelings to express the frightful emptiness that met me everywhere, it was an atmosphere of meaningless joy – it was like looking for something which was unattainable.

I had the house to myself but could not, by myself, bear to have it.

*

Quickly I proceeded to the gatehouse whose side door, being sealed, presented a challenge. But I went prepared. While the sun struggled to rise over the treetops and shine into the outer courtyard, I unscrewed the metal plate that blocked the entrance to the living quarters above the archway. It was an unlucky owner who had to break into his own property.

My cigarette lighter was out of fuel, so I was obliged to feel my way through the darkness by touch and good luck only. Ascending some narrow, twisting wooden steps, I saw a chink of light show up round a door just above me. Each stab of my heart's resurgent beats left me breathless. My actions were those of someone who was suffering from a sudden but terrible suspicion. On trying to explain it to myself, I could only say that something about Coberley Hall and its environs had begun to castigate me for my vacillatingly, even perverse behaviour. Sometimes the mistake was the man. I heard walls whisper: *Why are you not satisfied? Why have you changed? Why can you not simply let love live on forever?*

*

At first the door jammed against some invisible body or object. I had to put my shoulder to it, had to try very hard not to double up with a fit of coughing in all that dust I disturbed in a small room that might have once been a sentry post.

None of the windows had been opened for a very long time and the air tasted unbearably stale. Somewhere that worse for wear did not simply smell musty but reeked of the shelved, dirty and forgotten. I was standing in a guardroom that had not been altered in any substantial way since the seventeenth century. Like a soldier defending Coberley Hall long ago, I could soon imagine myself helping my fellow Cavaliers fight off the enemy. My head was all set to explode with heavy, continuous artillery bangs like drum-fire. The clash of razor-sharp halberds and the blast of hand grenades rang in my ears although in reality the room itself remained absolutely still and quiet. Turning dizzily, I could have been standing on some pivotal spot where past and present still did battle.

From this dreadful place the terribly wounded Captain Digby had been dragged off to prison.

*

I tried to quell all the rhythm and racket and clear my head by focusing on my physical surroundings. That peace of mind should still elude me was too grotesque to contemplate. Why should anything prevent the absolute pleasure of being master in my own house, which in every other respect seemed so peaceful and perfect?

Yet dazed though I was, most definitely did I not beat a hasty retreat.

Part shrine and part museum, boys' home-made swords, cuirasses, pikes and axes lay beside an orange, rust-encrusted carbine left behind from a real battle.

I advanced to a very old table on whose green baize lay pens, rulers and papers. I recognised maps of the Coberley Estate next to a great number of diagrammatic figures and sketches. At hand was a book on tracking and hunting, I noted. Where most sketches degenerated into mindless doodles, one animal trap struck me as more than work in progress. Whoever had sat here had reworked the plane of the weapon, both horizontally and vertically. They had established the exact killing range of its spears.

It was all strangely precursive of everything I had seen or done since coming to Coberley, as begun years ago but for my own imminent arrival. Struck dumb with dread and in fear for my soul – I had no other word for it – I felt caught in the deadly aftermath of an ongoing conflict.

I could reject my sudden shiver of revulsion, but not its relevance. New shotgun cartridges, ropes and knives rested in boxes on the floor at my feet. I was not simply standing in a shrine to a dead sibling, I was in a current centre of command. In a footnote to the drawing of the trap big enough to spear a bear was an amendment made in biro: KILL WALKER. George never intended that I should take his place in Coberley Hall, he never even wanted me to be alive.

*

I stopped dead at a photograph on the wall, next to a cabinet of preserved butterflies. The print showed two boys dressed in the brand new blazers and black and white ties of the local grammar-school. Neither child looked any older than eleven. In the background of the photograph stood the entrance to Coberley Hall with its bullet-riddled door and its inscription to TP and LP 1638.

The twins looked very stiff and unsmiling. Thanks to their mother's marriage to Joseph Jones, Philip and George had been brought up in a world of someone else's making. Nor had I yet learnt their real surnames, only that their stepfather had tried, then refused, to make them his own. In their black frames they were as trapped as the Cavaliers in their portraits. Surely they had never wished to be called Jones.

A moment later, my gaze came to rest on the high-backed Jacobean chair that had been placed at one side of the window. The nauseating smell of recently burnt wax emanated from the candle placed on the stone sill, though with it came a much older, earthier odour that immediately I resented.

But not much longer was I left wondering. Trailing from one side of the oak chair was a human arm. I let out a cry. In taking a step back, I saw seated upright before me a woman draped in a long green and white dress. Her bones were less like human remains than pieces of glossy ivory. Her skeletal head, shoulders and fingers had a shine worthy of something elemental and precious, much the same way that impurities were scarified like dross thrown off from metal in melting. Such an assemblage could have walked through all the fires of hell itself and emerged unscathed.

The polishing of the skull in particular helped mellow the slender black and irregular cracks that ran across the cranium both vertically and laterally. Clearly such defects had been acquired during the long time spent lying underground. The edges of each disconcerting eye socket were peppered with hundreds of tiny holes where bone had turned very slightly porous but had not actually disintegrated, I noticed. Slightly irregular teeth were still firmly in place, even if one jaw did no longer align with another.

Technically.

That's to say, the bottom row of teeth hinged low on the movable joint of the jaw where the skull would forever utter its agonising cry of anguish. The eyes were the same. Of course, no aqueous or vitreous humours lent transparent fluidity to either bony socket and yet so highly buffed were both black holes that a living glint did appear to linger. Likewise, there was no tongue to taste or ears to hear, yet it was noticeable how the breast bone ran robustly from neck to stomach and the ribs articulated with it so freely that some sensation or movement was not to be entirely discounted. The nose was an ugly, rat-gnawed cavity, but it did not take much imagination to see how once it had been able to smell wild flowers.

With rash intent I knelt before her and caressed her hand. She dipped her chin and stared straight at me. There was no way to express the awful compulsion that passed through my lips, it was a feeling of loathsome desire – I had thought myself in love with the dead! But that was the other Colin Walker.

'Damn you,' I cried and, raising myself up, went to kick the skeleton to smithereens.

Instead I vomited. Jumbled bones could be swept away like so much rubbish. No one could ever find her again, or know she was here. To remember of this woman that she had existed at all was sufficient torment.

But strike her I did not, nor could I. Rather, a din of battle, this time swelling and grinding round me with its dreadful auricular percussions, began to thunder in my ears fit to burst their drums. Here, a gallant colonel was shot in the throat while over there a soldier's skull was beaten to a pulp by a musket-stock. Horse flesh smoked and sizzled on the end of fire-pikes and cannon blew off men's faces with iron-slugs and pike-shot.

The more I raised my fists to the skeleton the louder and harsher grew the screams of lice-ridden combatants, like wild animals, amid the smell of burnt gunpowder. No longer the surfy roar of some distant scene, I could make out the pain of individual soldiers. The brutal chipping of blades on armour and the boom of pistols put me in the presence of rival armies besieging and defending. These maddened, monstrous creatures choked on the smoke from their own muskets and the blasts of culverins. To the roar of their captains, they trampled the dead and dying to do something glorious as parched, riderless horses refused to drink from blood-filled puddles. A tongueless man put a finger to his jawless chin as his blind enemy felt for his eyes which slimed his cheeks. Now, on the cluttered ground, a helmetless Roundhead waved the stump of his severed arm, its veins pouring red in fountains each time he let out a howl. While the barely human laments reached a crescendo, I saw how the occupant of the chair clutched her fingers to the point of breaking, not at the shrieks of unlucky men shot in the thigh and bladder, but at me.

'Hold, sir, would you behave worse than the beasts on the battlefield? Would you hurt even the dead?'

I fell back chastened and for a minute found not the strength to resist.

Whereupon her foul fragrance that hung about the room seemed less decomposition than arrested putrefaction, not least because two Spanish pockets of sweet-smelling violets hung from her waist to disguise her decay. Not only had someone rescued her from the grave, they had sought to give her back her name, appearance and history. In order to revive her life through bones alone they had gone out of their way to maintain their quality and condition, they had dressed her skeleton in her own dress and placed her away from direct sunshine.

But if the steel plate over the public doorway downstairs had been designed to keep unsympathetic detractors out, it had not kept her in? Without any skin to touch there was still sense to stimulate, despite no cuticle or cutis. Being nerveless, she was not inert. Any sinewy flicker or muscular tremor was not purely mine, any agitated or timid flinching did not just originate in my own highly strung and agitated reaction?

Where connection between bones had once been made by intervening muscle, these were all now wired together in the same relative positions as in life. The framework of bones was threaded in such a way as to re-unite every joint long after all animation or usefulness had elapsed. One drop-pearl earring, resplendent with its tassel of men's hair, dangled from her ear cavity while a pearl necklace had been draped round the bare joints of her throat. Only the missing finger on her left hand detracted a little from everything she once was.

From the angle of the skull, her eye-holes could see down the lane and keep a look-out for the one man she hoped might be approaching. Had not George told me that he and Philip had done what she wanted?

Whereupon I felt in my pocket and drew out the little ivory box in which resided the bony segments of finger. As I pushed the pieces close to her fleshless grip, the fourth digit came together perfectly.

'Forgive me Countess, for what I'm about to do.'

*

That's when I noticed in her lap the swan's quill. Ink sparkled across the surface of a letter.

'Dear husbande, you are very fond of argument when you think I am a moste unfeminine and unnatural she-wolf. You suppose me repugnant to nature, cotumelie to God, a thing

most contrarious to his revelled will and approved ordinace, and finallie I am the subversion of good order, of all equitie and iustice. You would not have me be your good Catholik wife since I cannot seat mysealfe at Coberley Hall without I bring gret greife upon you. You say that I must recant my heart's one true love or damne my pittifull soule before the eyes of God, but I will not be more slave than creature evere was. To what sort shall you rank that Woman that tells Men of things stolen and lost, and that shew Men the Face of the Thief in a Glass and cause the dead to be brought back; who are commonly called ghosts? You and all who come to my house will have so many credible reports of such, as will allow not reason to doubt of it. For I cannot tell what more unkindness one of us might shewe another, or wherein we might work more wickedly than to bring ourselves into so miserable a state not to choose love by our own likinge. For let this cruell house beare witness that whosoever doth not let me love shall ever more have a window shew him his soul and make him sorry.'

*

I was standing in an awful feretory for saint-like relics, I realised, but it was in no way a tomb, it was a protest. So fanatical had been Joseph Jones's love of recreating scenes from the English Civil War, yet so in awe of them had he become, so afraid of what he'd done, that he had vowed to continue his passion in death to make amends. Only, he had reckoned without his stepsons' own obsession which was to subvert his greatest wish. Whatever little love they might once have felt for him had changed to hatred, they would not let him lie with the one he had exhumed according to the dictates of his last will and testament – they would have revenge in the afterlife.

*

That afternoon I carried my tools and black leather bag unseen into Coberley church. There I chiselled a hole in white limestone behind the broken, top right hand corner of a panel that depicted the Crucifixion of Christ in the north side of the chancel. Having created a gap no bigger than my fist, I opened my bag and took out its screw-top glass jar full of formalin in which floated its precious contents.

I opened the jar and removed the slippery mass of hollow organ. It beat in my hand at each contraction and dilation of my fingers. If this were the seat of every emotion, it did not feel dead despite any loss of sensibility.

Or, I was shivering because the church was so cold.

I placed in the hole the heart that the police pathologist had, at my request, incised from Lizzie's body while she had lain on the mortuary table – I deposited it in the one place where no ghost could ever reach it. Then I cemented shut the orifice again for evermore.

I did what I promised.

39

Try as I might, I could not bear to stand before Countess Lucy's portrait in the great hall while no matching frame filled the empty recess beside her. On the enormous, ornately carved chimney piece, her picture looked so unbalanced and wishful. Once more the ghostly, pale outline of the missing person cried out for redress and forever prompted the prospect of some secret purpose. No chatelaine should hang in such asymmetrical misalignment.

Consequently, I have decided to affix my own image beside hers to restore the balance. I am dressed rather flatteringly in rat-coloured cloak, silver lace collar and close-fitting breeches. Sitting astride my black horse, I am elegantly clad in a doublet of scarlet serge lined with tabby silk and trimmed with close-woven galloon in best Cavalier fashion.

I wanted the brushstrokes to be quite realistic, if not exactly as I appear in real life. Therefore, there is neither too much colour nor over-mixed oils in my long, flowing curls. At the very least the picture strives to capture my blue eyes and slightly crooked nose in some heroic pose.

Meanwhile, Lady Lucy grows more resplendent by the day. Posed in her low-cut, flowing green dress with its white under-robe worked with wild flowers, she can be seen in her true colours now that I have removed more grime from her varnish. Together, we look as if we have hung in the hall for hundreds of years. Her black, gold-tinted eyes shine with wakeful vigilance. At her waist dangle so many chains from her chatelaine that by now she must have a key to every room in the house. My overbearing presumption of ownership might sit awkwardly with hers, but who can deny that she makes us both appear the perfect couple, not least because something about her reminds me so much of Lizzie.

In some lights, the resemblance to my lost love is less a likeness than a leer, but generally I see nothing sly, lascivious or vampiric in her expression. True, an unusual translucency of flesh does sometimes show through by the firelight, but I do not agree that a wraith would better suit the description, I think that the lean, almost emaciated semblance simply has the sophistication, elegance and grace that come with good bones. Her sharp, pearl-white incisors press lightly against her lip.

*

Once George's body was dragged from the bog we buried him in the ordinary way in the churchyard at Coberley. As the new lord of the estate, I implored all the villagers to attend. No man should go unmourned after such a tragic incident.

Not for nothing did I give a fulsome eulogy.

Some while afterwards – I remember very little about it – I was doing a tour of the house when suddenly I felt drawn to re-examine with pride the plates and glassware on their long oak shelves. I had begun my impromptu inventory of my inheritance and felt quite beside myself with joy when I sensed someone else's presence. There I was, the covetous owner of ink bottles, bedpans, paintings, swords, china, tapestries, clothes, clocks and all sorts of other quite bizarre objects that had been accumulated over time, when someone else's hand seemed to guide me. It was the strangest thing in the world. It was as though they would have me fill their shoes, see with their eyes all the attributes of my forbears. A man could feel so much better when he had a genealogical tree from which to hang himself.

In fact, it was Marigold, come to collect her Ouija-board.

Next minute I had a need to sit down. My left side seized at some flash in my head. At a stroke, I felt my knees go weak and fail beneath me.

I could resist the sudden feeling of falling, but not of the void into which I fell. Since then, I have come to expect bouts of almost total greyness or blackness. The gatehouse and its Court of covered barns and Riding House are where I must now reside, I've accepted, which is just as well because Jan and Maria are coming to visit. Sara has found them a room in her cottage, which is better than anything James had to offer.

*

Fortunately, Rebecca is constantly present with pen and paper.

When a man chooses to trade one life for another he needs someone on whom he can rely. A vision is a blow when it blinds the seer. Since I have someone on whom I can rely, I can trust her to record those things for which there are no real answers. When a man has such a kindred spirit he can share with her the secret of his guilt, grief and damnation in order to leave this world and try again in the next.

'How are you feeling now, your lordship?'

'Not bad, all things considered.'

'What about muscle movement?'

'Weak in my left side but it's getting better. I think you could call it a timely warning.'

Rebecca pulls my blanket over my knees in my wheelchair.

'Perhaps you should go back to the doctor?'

Despite the fire in the room I feel a chill creep through the window. This particular fog wasn't forecast.

'What doctor will accept an explanation that isn't in any medical book?'

'And you? What do you believe in?'

'Visions. A vision. Here in broad daylight.'

'Is it Lizzie?'

'Not always, no.'

'Hostile or friendly?'

'Either. Like a waking dream.'

Rebecca unscrews the cup from my thermos flask as I keep watch on the lawn.

'Does she talk to you?'

'No.'

'Does that make you afraid?'

'Not afraid, broken-hearted.'

'You never told me what happened to her, exactly.'

I sit forward in my chair in order to overcome my repugnance at so many pills. Then I toss back my head to swallow the inexplicable.

Of my own pain there can be no mitigation.

'By the end, Lizzie couldn't even ingest sips of ice-cream or speak clearly. All I could do was dab her lips with cotton tipped swab-sticks dipped in a 5ml artificial saliva solution. I had to moisten her palette, teeth and mouth floor while she took a cocktail of drugs to dampen the agony by way of a single syringe driver. She begged me to make up a lethal potion of painkillers for her to drink unaided through a straw, but she could no longer swallow any liquid because her stomach was regurgitating so much acid, it was burning her alive from inside. It was like being roasted in hell by the Devil, she said.

'At the same time, she was so afraid that if I helped her commit suicide I would serve up to fourteen years in prison, was so fearful of how her last days on this earth would end, since she could barely see or talk to convey a decision. In fact, we both hesitated to take the gamble. Each of us was in a very dark place – couldn't see the wood for the trees. Yet she was correct. By then her breathing was noisy and shallow, then slow and quiet. But as I took hold of a pillow and pressed it hard on her face and throat, a nurse walked in and caught me red-handed, just as the sun came up and the birds sang at 6.20 in the morning.

'Lizzie died from her disease shortly afterwards. All charges against me were dropped but not before I went public to argue my case. That's to say, Lizzie's.'

Rebecca studies me with her sea-green eyes and then screws the cup back on my flask.

'Truth is, you didn't kill her, Colin.'

'But I had it in me to do it, I released the bogy man.'

'If you don't let go you'll never get out of this house.'

'Every day offers some hope.'

'You won't change anything by trying to bring her back, Colin.'

'What else is there?'

'How often do you see her?'

'Day or night. She never sleeps. Neither do I.'

'Because she's always in your thoughts and dreams?'

'As I said, it's not always Lizzie.'

'But Lizzie is the one you long for?'

'I live for each new appearance.'

Rebecca begins to push me along.

'You do accept she's safely interred now in the church, don't you, Colin?'

'I can't think like that any more. If I can see her, she must still need me.'

'When someone we love dies, they change us. We love them in a different way. We become them and they become us because we are the only living, breathing receptacle of their past life. They live through us for as long as we let them. Could it be that, far from cursing you, Lizzie is trying to lift the curse you've put on yourself? She's gone but it was your life, too.'

'You mean I'm grieving for a ghost only.'

'*She* means that you should not give up on this life too soon?'

*

Since the sun is trying to shine, Rebecca has steered me along the walled path at the back of St. Giles. We have gone to the Gothic doorway in the crenelated defences next to the church in order to look through the gap into Coberley Hall's inner courtyard.

'Are you ready now, Colin?'

'Yes.'

With that, my solicitous nurse opens her little black bag and takes out a syringe.

'Ketamine can have a dramatic but often short-term effect in some patients whose lives are blighted by chronic severe depression.'

I watch her prepare the needle quite expertly.

'It's worth the risk.'

Rebecca works quietly and remains intentionally uncommunicative. By exchanging unspoken and unwritten confidences for a moment we are able to maintain the fiction that I am simply ill, I can charge her with special duties in the same way someone else might a spy or special agent.

'If your lordship thinks what I am doing will work this time?'

I clutch my dragon-tipped cane and command the air. Rebecca manoeuvres my chair so that I can see clearly through the gap in the wall to the void beyond.

'I do.'

'Then I'll go ahead and give you six infusions of up to 80mg during your three-week course of treatment.'

Slowly begins the series of pictures and visions, when in reality I'm still awake. I'm back in a dream world outside the laws of nature, I'm briefly inside Coberley Hall where lords and ladies walk the floors and Pan is back in place on his frieze on the wall of the screens passage. Once I fancy that someone tries the door to my bedchamber but it is probably only James doing his rounds. Hopefully it is not the wretched, thievish Viktor, though he may have seen what I did to George. After that, a restless silence hangs over everything, broken only by the ticking of the many clocks that mark time so ceaselessly even though I never see anyone wind their keys, not once. I feel as if I'm on the other side of all the hours and minutes that ever were. But I'm not mortified, I'm back in.

*

On the far side of the courtyard and behind the church, there stretches a wide, open meadow under whose surface resides the foundations of an old manor house. From about 1720 its estate, village and church were gradually left deserted for a hundred years. Tombs were smashed and brasses stolen from their slabs. Whole cottages fell into ruin, as did Coberley Hall. Soon the house was uninhabitable and the owners moved into the rooms over the old entrance gateway. Eventually the Hall was pulled down and most of its stone used to build a road, but sometimes in the twilight I see a woman cross the grass wherein lies the last of the rubble. At her side runs a white, three-legged greyhound. That's when, for a moment, I'm drawn closer to a simulacrum of someone as she once was, only she picks wild flowers with such elegance in her green and white robe that she seems to glide along. Her self-absorption and distance suggest somebody beautiful and proud, who will forever point the way around her beloved gardens. As she lifts her face to glare at me with her empty eyes, her pearl earring and its keepsake give off a glimmer while on her hand shines her blue enamelled ring.

I now know what happens when you fall in love with the hereafter – the dead won't rest without you. You have to let them go or they'll take you with them, they'll have you give up on this life far too easily. They'd have you care about no one but them, least of all yourself. At such times as I can't bear to be alone, she strikes me as thoughtful and sorrowful, too. Those days, I dread that she'll have done with me totally, that I might never be the one she'll adore, only another of her pictures on the wall. Suddenly, though, she surprises me with her radiant smile at my return.

Printed in Great Britain
by Amazon